Blossom Tree

by
Sharon Fevrier

Copyright © 2017 by Sharon Fevrier

Chief Editor: Rhoda Molife

Editor: Daniella Blechner

Printed in the United Kingdom

First Printing 2018

Published by Conscious Dreams Publishing
www.consciousdreamspublishing.com

ISBN 978-1-912551-05-7

Dedication

To my beautiful angel Janaii —

I pray that your light forever shines bright and that you continue growing into the beautiful life that has been promised to you. Your heart and soul inspires and motivates me to be the best mother that I can be. I will teach you many of life's wonders. Let's continue to learn, love, laugh, sing and dance.

Acknowledgements

Thank you to each and every one of you that has supported, motivated and inspired me. I appreciate your mentorship, your patience, your love and your encouragement to become the woman that writes these words.

Dad — you've raised me to be resilient. Your words of wisdom have enabled me to manoeuvre around the challenges of life.

Mum — sometimes I laugh uncontrollably at the silliest things, no doubt a trait inherited from you! You taught me to wear that smile unapologetically.

Lorraine — my beautiful, trusted friend. You kept me sane then, you keep me sane now and no doubt, you will keep me sane in the future.

'Write it down,' Fiona always said. So, I did. You are strong, powerful and inspirational! Thank you for always remembering and caring.

Ruth — keep speaking those positive affirmations! You make me believe that everything is possible.

Nadia Vitushynska — you have beautifully transformed my book with your typesetting and design skills. Thank you.

Wendy Yorke — your advice and guidance was invaluable. Your book assessment helped to shape the dream. Thank you.

Danni Blechner at Conscious Dreams Publishing — what a lady! Thank you for confirming that my message to the world is valuable.

Rhoda Molife, my editor — thank you for bringing sparkle to *Blossom Tree*.

Contents Page

Love

Chapter One:
Unexpected Encounter

A relationship was the last thing on my mind. I was actually quite content with my life. They say that a man comes into your world when you least expect him to. Sometimes you can instantly recognise time wasters. Other times, you don't because the charm and looks just blow you away. Well, that's what happened to me.

I was a single, working woman with an active social life. One evening, Julie, a friend from work, had invited me to a dance. It was a Saturday night but I wasn't fussed about going. I felt like a free spirit. This was the most relaxed I had been for years. I had just returned from Dominica where my parents had resettled after living in England for over forty years. They were happy and comfortable in their new home on a hill, near the capital of the island. Dominica was lush and green with plentiful streams and rivers, and their house had a stunning view of the ocean. They had transferred all their belongings in a forty-foot container from sleepy Bedfordshire. It hadn't taken too long to unpack the boxes. My holiday wasn't all about unpacking and chasing energy providers though — it was pleasurable too. I loved the island and had been there several times. Going there was certainly a break as it gave me an opportunity to move at a pace that the natives did so effortlessly: slow and steady. London was always a rush. Rush to work, rush home and rush to meet friends. I guess I was not always the most punctual person and maybe I could cheekily blame that trait on the nature of my people. Well, that was always my excuse! Maybe I was also relaxed knowing that my parents had finally achieved their goal of going back home. I always found saying 'back home' quite funny, considering that they'd spent most of their lives in a country so far away from their home. They had adjusted to the culture of Britain and now that they had returned, what would their lives be like as 'British-Dominicans' living on the island again? I felt reassured that they would be comfortable though. On top of that, they had plenty to occupy themselves with as they turned their newly built house into a home.

Though it had been a few days since my return, I still wished I was there. Ok, the mosquitoes were a nuisance and the hot weather was dehydrating, but I was at home with my parents. I was protective of them, and as their only daughter and last born, they were also protective of me. I felt blessed to have such supportive parents. We didn't have that much growing up but what we did have was all that my brothers and I needed. Even though I had bought my own flat in London and hadn't lived with my parents for a few years, I knew I would miss them. In fact, I'd bought my flat because my parents had encouraged me.

"You've finished university now. Save your money. Get a deposit together and buy yourself a property. Me and your mother are going back home," my father revealed one day after work.

"Oh!" I replied, realising that this time they probably meant it.

My parents gave me enough time to raise a deposit for the flat. With £5,000 in the bank, I was ready. They and some friends bought me house gifts so I was prepared to fly the nest, or rather to be pushed out of the nest. I had thrived on the relationship that my parents had and the love they had shown me. I had observed good examples of how a couple can work hard to maintain a relationship and build assets together. They were all I knew and I was happy that I didn't have to deal with the family issues some of my friends had gone through. Truth be told, I went to university at eighteen years old to postpone my entrance into the world of nine-to-five; as far as I was concerned I was too young for that. I realised that having a degree gave me a few more years of freedom from responsibility, having fun and of course, the potential for a wider option of employment opportunities.

My spacious flat had two bedrooms. The exterior was an embarrassingly dated 1970's style. However, it had a large living room, bathroom and kitchen. I quickly personalised the flat to make it my beautiful humble abode. My parents would regularly stay over until they retired to Dominica.

It was 7 o'clock and I started getting ready for my night out. My skin was glowing and sun-kissed from my Caribbean holiday. My hair was thick and black; I rarely felt the need to straighten my locks. Today, I decided to embrace my relaxed state of mind and not go over the top for the dance. I was happy to listen to good music and enjoy the company of my friends. I threw on a short, brown, sparkly, boob tube dress with slits down each side. It was a sexy number which didn't need much in the way of accessories as it had a beautiful diamanté pattern on the front. I wore my sparkly shoes, diamanté earrings and bracelet with a bag to match. A touch of rose-pink lip gloss and I was finally ready to go. I hopped into my car and arrived at Julie's house around 9. She was ready and waiting, wearing a long elegant green dress. She was a beautiful woman who apparently used to be a model, though I had never seen any photos or a portfolio. She called her friend Darren to let him know that we were ready, and within minutes, he and his cousin were downstairs waiting in the car park in his shiny new BMW.

The traffic was horrendous in London that evening. However, the drive from Ilford to Streatham, though long, was comfortable. Darren manoeuvred through the streets with ease while the music played loudly. We arrived at the club for 10:30. It was a little later than planned so the comedy show was already thirty minutes in and in full swing. After the show, there were live vocal and instrumental jazz performances as well as poetry readings. It was a perfect start to the evening and the club was now packed. Darren and his cousin took off, scouting the venue for their next victims. Julie and I decided to position ourselves by the bar. Not only was it the only place in the lively club where we could have some space, it was also well lit and cooler than the front of the club. I asked for a Long Island Iced Tea and Julie ordered a brandy and coke. I was already feeling very mellow as my cocktail began to take effect. Or was I still jet lagged? Julie spotted some colleagues from her office.

"Come over with me Shantel. I want to say hello to some people I know," she said.

We walked over to her friends. Julie started chatting with them, but strangely she didn't introduce me. I thought that she was being deliberately rude but I wasn't fazed by her excluding me from the conversation which lasted all of five minutes. The music was more than enough to keep me entertained. Julie wanted the limelight so I let her have it. She embraced it but somehow it didn't have the effect she had hoped for.

"Your friend hasn't got a patch on you," boomed a deep voice behind my right ear.

I turned around and was greeted by a friendly face. I smiled.

"Do I have the pleasure of this dance?" he asked politely.

"Knock yourself out...by yourself!" I declared with a cheeky smile. We both laughed and it occurred to me that he was harmless. He held out his hand for me and led me to the dance floor. The music was upbeat so there was absolutely no need for up close and personal contact. The handsome stranger spun me around and I noticed that Julie was standing with her back against the wall watching her friends from work dancing and talking to each other. Guess that's what happens when you don't make introductions. The song ended and I thanked the gentleman for the dance and went to join Julie.

"Hey, what are you doing over here Julie? Thought you were chatting with your friends?"

"Let's get a drink." She looked a little distracted but I wasn't responsible for her frustrations.

Julie was quite competitive and I was just the opposite. She had her eye on someone who wasn't looking back at her. I realised she had a jealous streak. We got ourselves more drinks. I had another lethal Long Island Iced Tea. We walked away from the bar and I noticed one of Julie's colleagues staring at me. He was tall with beautifully glistening skin and a goatee beard. His face was warm with a nice smile. Although he was of medium build, he carried his weight comfortably and was well-groomed with a sharp brown shirt and tailored trousers. I thought he was attractive but thought nothing of the eye contact, though he did appear uninterested in the young woman that was talking to him. Just another man making eyes at me but lacking the courage to say hello. Maybe he thought he had missed his chance when Julie decided not to introduce us. Anyway, I really was not focused on meeting a man that night. I wanted to mingle and have a fun time. I still had the spirit of Dominica in me, laid back and relaxed. Then all of a sudden, this six-foot-two man was coming towards me.

"Hello. I'm Andre. I see you're a friend of Julie's. Fancy a drink?" he asked as he was making his way to the bar.

"Err, yes please. Red Bull please."

I felt a little bit tired which I guessed was a combination of the alcohol and jet lag. My body clock had still not adjusted to being back in England. The queue at the bar was now really long, but he was back within five minutes. I watched him as he skilfully manoeuvred his way through the crowd. He smiled. I smiled. He handed me the drink. I knew it was safe as I literally watched the glass from the moment he took it from the barman to him bringing it straight over to me. I was always particular about accepting drinks from strangers but this night felt different. The whole vibe in the club was friendly with positive energy. There was a feeling of peace and love, probably because it was also a charity event raising money for sickle cell disease, a condition I had lived with all my life. It was unusual for a club to create such an atmosphere — maybe it was my own state of mind.

"Thank you I said. I'm Shantel."

We smiled at each other and we sipped our drinks. Julie had returned from the ladies' room and headed straight for the bar when she saw that I had company. Her nose looked a little put out of joint but I didn't pay any notice. Julie and I were just party friends, not necessarily confidantes. She was someone I could go out with occasionally to shake a leg. Andre and I chatted for a short while. The music was loud and I could hardly hear him but it was nice to drink with a man who simply wanted to chat and stand with me for a while. Moments later, Julie joined us, but Andre said he had another party to go to. It was a family event so he couldn't miss it. He thanked me for my company, gave me a kiss on the cheek and said goodnight. He turned and said goodnight to Julie and walked away.

That night I was quite lucky. I got three telephone numbers but unfortunately none of them belonged to Andre. Nevertheless, it was a great night. Julie and I danced the night away until our feet were sore and our heels were ready to be dumped in a bin. Darren and his cousin found us just as we were ready to leave. Bed was calling and I was relieved that we could head back to Julie's flat in a prestigious and comfortable car. Once we arrived, I thanked everyone for a great night and with my crippled feet limped all the way to Julie's spare room where I fell into bed. I would head back home in the morning.

The following Monday afternoon I received my usual call from Julie at work. We always spoke during the week. I guess it was a distraction from the monotony of working life. The conversations were usually short but this one was different.

"What's up girl?" Julie asked.

"Ahh nothing. Just got these cases coming out of my eyeballs," I replied jokingly.

Julie had worked in the same department as I until she went for a role in a different borough. So she knew the stress I was under.

"Did you enjoy Saturday night?" She quizzed me about the telephone numbers I had received that evening.

I told her that I wasn't really interested in any of them though dating allowed me to socialise. We chatted for ten minutes until she suddenly told me that there was someone in her office that wanted to speak to me. Of course I was curious and a little flattered.

"Hold on," she said. "Let me put him on."

"Who are you talking about Julie?" I asked but she had already gone.

"Hello Shantel," a deep voice greeted. "Do you know who you're speaking to?"

"No actually. I met a few of Julie's colleagues on Saturday and you were all pretty friendly," I responded. Nevertheless, I had a feeling I already knew who it was.

"Did you accept a drink from all of Julie's colleagues?" he asked.

Instantly, I remembered who it was and wondered how long I should prolong his line of questioning. As we were both at work, I decided better be straight with him and answer his questions.

"Hi Andre. How are you?" My voice softened as I didn't want to deflate his ego. I was always jovial but he didn't know this about me so I went into my neutral mode.

"I'm good Shantel. It was nice to chat with you on Saturday night. I didn't tell you then, but you were the most attractive lady in the whole club. Absolutely no one compared to you. I hope you had a good time after I left."

This man was expressive and the compliments were lovely. I never compared myself to other girls on a night out but I did notice that I was perhaps one of the few natural-looking girls. Real hair, no fake nails, not plastered in make-up either. That wasn't my style and besides it was far too expensive to 'fake it up.' At twenty-nine years old, I still felt young and was aware that others my age hadn't fared as well. I wasn't over-confident or full of myself though. I was just happy that I still had it!

"Thank you Andre. I didn't really check out the other girls, but I know there were some pretty ladies in the club. Both the ladies and men were looking good."

We chatted for a few more minutes until we exchanged numbers and agreed to speak later. I asked him to tell Julie that I would catch up with her later too and continued with my stressful workload.

I got home from work at 5:45. It was only a fifteen-minute drive from the office to my flat along the A13 towards Essex. I was happy to have a job so close to home. As soon as I was in, I changed into a comfortable track suit, poured a glass of wine and made a seafood salad for my dinner. The wine was already working on me. About a quarter past 6, I had almost finished eating when my mobile rang. It was Andre.

"Hi Andre. How are you?" I asked.

"Hi Shantel," he replied, "How was the rest of your day?"

"Good thanks. Glad I'm home now."

I told him I was just finishing my dinner. He said he didn't mind me eating while we talked and he encouraged me to continue. So I did. I could never let seafood go to waste. We talked and talked. We discussed so many different topics. The conversation flowed from work to play, from God and religion to aspirations and family. We thrashed out so many different topics but we didn't seem to get tired of speaking to each other. Hours had passed. The sun had gone down and it was pitch black outside my bedroom window. My flatmate must have thought that I was being rude by not coming out to say hello to her. I was caught up in debating life, exchanging opinions about the workings of the universe and what path we wanted to take as individuals. It was an amazing conversation but I started to wonder time it was.

"Oh my gosh Andre! We've been on the phone for more than nine hours!"

We laughed and agreed to speak to each other later that evening. When we said goodnight, it was 3:11am.

Blossom Tree | Sharon Fevrier

Curiosity has struck me
Not sure what to expect
Should I take courage and get to know him?
Or is it my heart that I should protect?
The conversation lasted so long
Should I take it as a sign
Of good things to come?
And leave the past behind?

We had many more conversations during the rest of the week, but none lasted as long as the first. We continued to share details about each other. He was open and so was I. We discussed intimate secrets that I had not shared with anyone else and I felt very comfortable doing so. He felt the same so we decided to meet. We both had other commitments that weekend but we met the following Tuesday straight after work. As Andre didn't have a car, he asked me to drive to Elephant and Castle in South London. I wasn't sure about the location but he assured me that we would be going somewhere classy to eat for our first date. I parked my car and called to let him know I had arrived. I sat in the car and looked in the vanity mirror. I reapplied my lip gloss and tousled my hair. I wanted to squirt my perfume but thought the intense fragrance would knock him out as soon as he opened the passenger door.

I thought back to the night he came up to me. Handsome, tall with shiny, genuine eyes. I was really looking forward to seeing him. Though I was usually a confident woman when it came to dating, on this occasion, I felt a little nervous and wished I had carried my deodorant. I opened the window to let in the cool evening October air. I had already described my car to him so he would not have had any problems identifying my bright turquoise three door beauty. I wore khaki coloured boots, a hooded jacket, black leggings and a sparkly black sleeveless top. I felt I was appropriately dressed for the occasion — comfortable but sexy. To my knowledge he was taking me to a restaurant and a movie. I really had no expectations of the night or even my relationship with him. When it came to dating, my motto was usually 'easy come, easy go' as I was never short of suitors. However, we had connected in a very short time.

There was a gentle knock on the window. I unlocked the car as I recognised his face. He opened the passenger door.

"Hi Shantel." He sat down smiling, leaned over and kissed me on the cheek.

"Hi Andre. How are you?" I greeted him shyly.

"Good thanks," he replied. "It was a long day at work but glad it's over. Did you get here alright?"

"Yes, no problems. It was pretty straightforward." I paused and looked at his beautiful features.

"Wow. You're really good looking," I blurted out in awe.

As soon as the words slipped out of my mouth, I realised how corny I must have sounded, but I wasn't lying. His beautiful smooth skin glistened under the glow of the streetlamp that was just outside the car. His goatee beard was trimmed close. His hair was freshly cut to a sharp fade. He smiled at what I had said.

"Thank you," he responded. "And you're really pretty, if you don't mind me saying."

I was blushing and feeling awkward. I wondered if he could hear how fast my heart was beating.

"So, now that we've declared our admiration for each other, where are we heading?" I was conscious of the time and wanted to get the evening started, but not in my beloved car.

"Wandsworth. There's a great Indian restaurant that I want to take you to."

Andre had a plan. I loved men who knew how to wine and dine, were in control and could make decisions. I then realised I didn't know how to drive to Wandsworth from Elephant and Castle.

"Do you want to drive?" I asked. "I'm not sure of the route."

"No problem," he responded.

I was relieved that he was comfortable with driving. We swapped positions and he adjusted the driver seat and mirrors. I felt at ease with him behind the wheel. I felt as though I could trust him even though this was only my second time meeting him. The first had been so brief that it hardly counted. But, here I was, in the passenger seat, enjoying the journey.

Within thirty minutes we were at the restaurant, and being a Tuesday, it was quiet. The waiter showed us to our table. Andre was being a gentleman. He pulled out my chair and ordered a bottle of wine. Had I hit the jackpot? We then looked through the menu and made our selections. I enjoyed the meal and of course the company. The conversation flowed just as it had on the telephone and he was definitely eye candy.

It was almost 9 o'clock. We had a movie to watch so he paid the bill. We drove to the cinema which was thankfully only five minutes away. Even though we were both full after dinner, we ordered some snacks and then took our premier seats. I had told him that I loved scary movies, so what were we watching? A scary movie of course — 'Saw 3'. I don't think I had ever screamed so much in my life. Even though I had seen the first two films in the series and I knew what to expect, this instalment was on a totally different level. Scary wasn't the word. One scene was so gory that I shut my eyes tightly, grabbed his arm and buried my face in his shoulder. I'm sure he liked that. Throughout the film, he kept checking if I wanted to leave. I chose to stay.

The film finished and the credits rolled up. One by one the couples left their seats and headed to the exit. Andre and I held back; we were still glued to our seats. Something was coming. There was real chemistry between us and a strong physical attraction. The lights came on.

"Are you ready?" he asked.

"Yes," I answered. "What did you think about the film?" I asked as I stood up.

"Did you even see the film? You hid behind your hands most of the time," he laughed. "But yes, I enjoyed it. What about you?" he asked.

"You know what, that was gory. Even by my standards. There was too much blood, guts and horror. I think I will just watch romantic comedies for a while. Something to make me smile, not make me feel sick!"

Andre chuckled.

We walked towards the exit. Suddenly Andre pulled me to one side. I felt my heart beating rapidly. He looked so handsome with his beautiful brown skin, large hazel eyes and cheeky smile. Yes, I was smitten after the conversations we had indulged in. I realised how much of a gentleman he had been that evening. He towered over me. I had a thing for tall men. Something about their height made me feel as if I were cocooned in a protective shield. His face drew closer to mine and he leaned in. Butterflies in my belly fluttered frantically. Our lips parted and we looked each other directly in the eyes. His lips touched mine and we began to kiss. It was gentle, sweet and passionate. Thankfully he wasn't a sloppy kisser. That would have put me off immediately. The kiss went on and on and I felt as though I was melting. Eventually we pulled apart and smiled at each other. He took my hand and we headed out of the cinema. Andre drove to where he lived in Clapham, on Lavender Hill. We talked all the way. I wanted more time with him and I told him so. I was so curious about him.

"So, what kind of coffee do you have?" I wanted to explore him further, just as we had explored each other's minds in conversation. I had already told him so much about me that I felt he knew me already. I wanted to know more about him but I didn't want to rush.

"I don't have any coffee or milk." He'd declined my suggestion of continuing the night further. "If you come up, there is a high chance that we will end up getting into bed because I really like you. I want to spend more time with you before we get physical. You are a lovely girl, one of a kind and waiting a little while will make our first time very special."

I was stunned. Silenced. Never had I met a man who would decline a passionate moment with me. He had other intentions. He wanted more from me than just sex or a few dates. Was I ready for a man who could be more than a buddy to me?

"Ok," I said, slightly disappointed but flattered that he was considering a relationship with me, after just one date. The fact that he was strong enough to resist the temptation to go a step further that night intrigued me.

"I can wait. It's just that I need something to keep me going until I get home. You know it's going to take me a while to get home, right?" I said comically, but he wasn't budging.

When I took a minute to think about what he had said, I realised he wasn't blowing me out, but instead, offering me something that I had been too scared to accept before. There was the real possibility of a commitment with someone who was on my level. I knew I couldn't run forever and had to give myself a chance at happiness and a future in a relationship. I rarely took risks with my heart. Perhaps I chose to date men that I knew wouldn't deliver when it came to a serious relationship. Perhaps I had now met a man who ticked all the boxes.

Andre and I talked a little more, but I had to get home to my bed and sleep as I had work in the morning. We kissed again and said goodnight. It took thirty minutes to get to my flat in Dagenham from Clapham. My car was nippy. At that time of the morning there was no traffic and I literally flew through all the green lights. When I got home, I called him to let him know. That night, I fell asleep with a smile on my face.

Chapter Two:
Step Into Love

I continued to date Andre. He remained a gentleman. It was lovely being with a man who didn't want to rush into sex but would rather take his time to get to know me. That had to be a good sign. Still, I was a woman with needs but because I felt I had started something with him, I wasn't tempted to contact any of my exes, buddies or 'special friends' to fulfil my womanly needs. After a few weeks of dating, he invited me to his flat and suggested I pack an overnight bag. Woo-hoo! I dressed casually as it was a Friday night and we weren't planning on going out anywhere. He was cooking. Bingo — he was chivalrous and could cook! His mother must have taught him well.

I left work and drove to his place. I wore some green combats that were loose and comfortable, a red sports style vest and gold Nike trainers. No need to dress to impress as I figured he was already besotted. In no time I was parked outside his block. I took my bag out of the boot and headed up the three flights of stairs to his flat. I knocked on the door and heard some music playing but I couldn't quite work out what song it was. Andre opened the door with a smile. He also wore a red top with jeans and trainers.

"Hello," I said, a little nervous as I knew what was coming that evening.

"Hello, come in. Let me take your bag."

Andre put the bag in his bedroom. He had a small one-bedroom flat. It desperately needed decoration and modernisation, especially with the blue carpets and orange walls in the living room. In fact, the living room was cluttered with a flat-packed kitchen and a bathroom suite that were waiting to be installed. At least the bedroom was tidy and organised. Obviously, he had plans to upgrade his flat but I would find out more with time.

"Sorry about the mess but it's not been long since I moved back into my flat after renting it out to a friend," he explained.

"That's alright," I said in a reassuring tone though I didn't know where to sit.

He hadn't finished cooking so I went into the kitchen with him. He cleared a space for me to sit on top of the washing machine.

"I see you have plans. When are you going to get your kitchen and bathroom done?" I asked.

"I've got to get the money together to do that but I also have plans to knock down this wall between the kitchen and living room so it will be open plan. My dad is going to do the work but he's in Jamaica now so I have to wait until he's back. He's a builder so I know it will end up looking great. I've got a vision but I don't want to rush it as I want to get it right," he explained.

The conversation continued until we were interrupted by a knock on the front door. He looked surprised.

"Excuse me for a minute," he said and walked out of the kitchen.

"No problem," I replied.

After a couple of minutes, he came into the kitchen and following behind him was a tall and lean man. There was also a young woman with him. Andre introduced him as his brother Vince. There was no resemblance at all. I couldn't see how the two were brothers as they had no physical features in common. Vince had a nice genuine smile and his female friend was pretty. After a brief conversation, they both left the kitchen to go into the bedroom. I thought that was slightly strange behaviour but accepted that there was nowhere to sit down in the living room.

"I'm sorry. I didn't know my brother was coming. That was totally unexpected. He's staying for dinner and then they are going to go," he said as if to reassure me.

On first impressions, I liked Andre's brother but I wasn't willing to compromise our first night together.

"Cool," I replied.

As I walked to the bathroom, I smelt marijuana coming from the bedroom. I wasn't being a prude but wondered why they couldn't smoke outside the flat. I was pretty tee-total. Though I drank alcohol, I never got myself into an inebriated state. Besides, I drove everywhere and didn't believe in drinking and driving.

"Dinner is served," Andre announced as I came out of the bathroom.

I smelt the chicken and couldn't wait to eat as it was already 8:30. Andre asked me to take my seat in the bedroom. I sat on the bed, next to Vince's friend, while he sat on the floor. Andre brought my plate of food — chicken, rice and peas, salad and fried plantain — on a tray. It looked amazing. He told me to start but I said I would wait for him to come inside with his own plate of food. Once he returned, we all started eating and it wasn't long before the conversation stopped completely while we all concentrated on our food. Gospel music streamed out of the DVD player through the TV. We finished dinner and I asked Andre if he needed some help tidying up the kitchen. He said he didn't and that I should relax in the bedroom as his brother and friend had left soon after they had eaten. I lay on the bed listening to the soothing music in anticipation of his arrival.

The door to his bedroom opened. Andre had finished in the kitchen and brought in two glasses of wine.

"Thank you," I said before I took a sip of the chilled white wine.

Andre sat down at the end of the bed near my feet. I moved to give him space but he asked me to continue lying where I had been. I moved back to my original position and he took one of my feet, massaging it gently but adding pressure just where it was needed. This boy is good. He can cook and massage my feet! Now I was feeling chilled. We talked some more about our days at work while he started on the other foot.

"I need to come here more often so I can get this royal treatment," I joked.

He laughed, "Anytime."

I finished my wine. There was nowhere to put my empty glass so I put it on the floor. Andre had finished his wine too so he put his glass down and moved closer to me. We were facing each other, smiling, talking and joking. He had made me feel comfortable and relaxed. Then the moment happened. He leaned towards me slowly and gave me a peck on the lips that soon became a very sensual and passionate kiss. Andre held my face while we kissed. His hands were soft and smooth. We both wanted more. It wasn't long before our clothes hit the floor and we were rolling around on the bed enjoying each other. The first time was magical. I wasn't in love, but I felt that I could fall for a man who made me feel this special. This feeling was new to me. I rarely allowed anyone to get too close to my mind or my heart and now, here he was, more than close to my body. I enjoyed the sex and I knew that it could potentially change into love-making if we allowed ourselves that opportunity. He put his arms around me and held me closer. I was the kind of girl who needed her space to sleep, but on this night, I fell asleep in his arms, with a smile on my face.

The next morning, we lay in bed for a while, talking and laughing. We were both comfortable and happy with what had happened the night before. After our separate baths, we went to a local cafe for a late breakfast, which he paid for. I dropped him home and we agreed to speak later. As I was on my way home, Andre called to say that he had enjoyed spending time with me and hoped that we could see each other again soon.

"Of course," I replied. "I would love to see you again. I just need to catch up on my sleep though."

We laughed about the sleep that we had sacrificed for a night of great passion and romance. I was prepared to sacrifice my sleep again to repeat that moment with a man who oozed class and style, who was street yet sophisticated and educated.

"How about Tuesday?" he asked.

"I can do that," I replied. "Maybe we could go to the cinema but this time, no blood and guts."

He chuckled and said that he would like that.

Once at home, I relaxed for the rest of the weekend and spent time with my girlfriends. I went to the gym and before I knew it, it was Tuesday. Before work, I packed my overnight bag and prepared my body for another passionate night. I was so excited. We were beginning to talk every day, occasionally two or three times a day but I wasn't getting bored. I embraced our conversations and time we spent together. How lucky was I to have met a man who slotted nicely into my life? I had never considered settling down. I was happy just dating and having fun. The idea of being tied down forever to one man while I was in my twenties horrified me. But in December, I would turn thirty.

'*Go with the flow Shantel*' is what I told myself on a regular basis. So I did.

The evening approached rapidly. My heart was racing as I climbed the steps to his floor and knocked on his door. He opened it with a big smile and took my bag as he had the time before. Again, we had a wonderful time and we both felt that it was too short. We agreed that he would come to my home on Friday to spend the night. I knew I would spoil him, treat him like a king. I had already started to plan the night.

It was soon Friday and I picked Andre up from the train station. He still looked as good as he did on that first date. Andre had such beautiful skin with no tattoos or blemishes. Tall, a friendly face and a warm smile with perfect teeth. This man had it going on and I had him in my flat. My flatmate said she would be out most of the weekend which was perfectly timed as I wouldn't have to tiptoe around, trying not to make her feel uncomfortable. I unlocked the front door and Andre stepped into my flat. I told him I had a 'no shoes' policy which he didn't have a problem with.

"Your place is lovely. It's really comfy." Andre made himself at home with ease. The layout of my flat was simple. It was an open house to my friends and family. I loved company and entertaining, and here I was entertaining Andre.

"Make yourself at home. Would you like a glass of wine while I get dinner ready?"

I had already prepared our meal. I thought I would make him some steak, rice and sweet vegetables. I assumed that being a man, a chunky piece of meat on a Friday night would go down well. I wasn't a big red meat eater myself but didn't mind it occasionally.

"Yes please," he hollered from the living room.

I poured some red wine while the food was warming. I sat down on the sofa beside him and we talked for a short while until the food was ready. I set the table and asked him to take his seat.

"Wow, this looks amazing," he exclaimed excitedly.

"Oh, this is just something I rustled up." It felt good to say that but it was a recipe I looked at while I was browsing the internet at work searching for ideas.

"Enjoy," I said smiling.

I knew the way to a man's heart and I felt as though I had already won it. We ate, drank and talked for hours. Andre helped me to clear the table and I washed the dishes while he kept me company. We were both feeling a little tipsy but this didn't stop us from opening the second bottle. We took it into the living room and flicked through the channels to watch a film. The television was really on for background noise because we remained focused on each other. By this time, I was very mellow and decided to straddle Andre to give him a kiss. Andre was strong. No words had been said at that point. We kissed and kissed as he picked me up and carried me all the way to the bedroom. I was horny and ready for this man in my bed. He was now in my territory but I felt very comfortable sharing my space with him. Our clothes were soon off and we began a night of steamy, hot, passionate sex. It was amazing. He took the lead, and then I took over and made him succumb to me. The night turned into morning as the sun streamed through my linen curtains. After we finished pleasuring each other we decided to sleep. No need to set the alarm clock as we had planned to spend Saturday together. It was incredible how Saturday quickly turned into Sunday. Andre said that he didn't have any clean clothes and needed to go back home as he had work on Monday. I told him that I was happy to wash his clothes if he wanted to stay another night. He didn't need much persuasion.

Monday morning, Andre left early for work. He told me that he would come back on Wednesday and stay over again. We were becoming inseparable and actually seemed to fit like a hand in a glove. We loved each other's company. Our relationship was developing quickly and I didn't want to get off the ride. I felt comfortable on it and so did he. I knew that this was the beginning of a very special romance.

Wednesday came and after work I picked Andre up from the train station. He was suited and booted. This was attire that I hadn't seen him wear to work before.

"You dressed smart for work today. Job interview?" I said jokingly.

"Actually, yes," he replied. "If I'm thinking about a relationship with you, a long-term relationship I mean, then I have to try to get a job that pays me a decent salary at least."

Andre explained that he had taken a break from working in HR and was working as a financial assistant for a Local Authority. It was a break he needed as he revealed that life for him was a little stressful a few years ago. He just wanted a nine-to-five job that he could survive on. Now he was ready to jump back on the career ladder. I understood what he was saying as sometimes a career could completely take over your life and occasionally you need to take steps to reclaim it. Andre told me more about the interview when we arrived at my flat. We sat on the sofa after our dinner and chatted some more. Our conversations were always deep and meaningful but this one developed in a way that I was not expecting.

"Shantel, I've really enjoyed spending all this time with you. I've fallen in love with you," he announced.

I was in shock. I didn't expect that, not so soon.

"I love spending time with you. You're kind, genuine, and beautiful and I want more of this, of us."

"Wow, I don't know what to say," I explained. "I love you too. I love spending time with you and nothing is hard work. This feels good."

I knew we had only known each other for a few weeks and that it was very early to say the 'L' word. He said it first and if I hadn't, the moment would have been ruined. I couldn't leave him hanging and I didn't want to run away from another relationship just because of that word.

We kissed and I felt the weight slide off his shoulders. I had scared myself by telling him that I loved him. I didn't want to analyse the situation too deeply though I would happily have waited until we knew each other a lot longer before telling him. I went with the flow though and felt nervous for doing so but I wanted to know where this relationship could end up.

Chapter Three:
Keys

Three weeks had flown by. Andre and I spent nearly all our time together — talking, dating and living in domestic bliss. I felt so comfortable with him, almost as if we had known each other for a lifetime. He was becoming the perfect boyfriend: cooking dinner while I lay in a candlelit bath and buying me flowers and sexy lingerie. We went on romantic walks along the River Thames and in various parks. We were inseparable and I felt like I had all that I wanted and all that I needed. We laughed together, continued to converse into the night, sharing my secrets, history and desires for the future. I had not shared my inner most secrets with another man in many years, but he allowed and encouraged me to. I was now an open book, completely free and honest with him. Of course we made plenty of good love. I felt guilty about not spending time with my friends but they understood that I was caught up. Andre was fulfilling my mind, heart, body and soul.

It was a Friday in the fourth week of our relationship. Andre came over to my flat after work and we ordered a Chinese takeaway. He sat on the black leather sofa while I sat on the wool rug, sipping my wine while putting a DVD in the player.

"Shantel, you know I love you right?" Andre asked.

"Yes babe," I replied inquisitively. His tone was leading to a question. "Why do you ask?"

"Well, I'm curious." He paused. "You know you're an attractive woman and you mean everything to me. I just wouldn't want to lose you. But I'm sure I'm not the only one that wants you. I just want to know if you've seen any of your ex-boyfriends since we've been seeing each other."

I wondered where this line of questioning was going. Andre looked straight into my eyes, looking for the truth.

"No, I haven't," I smiled reassuringly. "I've hardly had time to see my own family and friends let alone an ex-boyfriend." I decided to throw the question back at him, though it had never crossed my mind.

"Have you been seeing anyone else?" I asked.

"No. You are all I want and need. I just wouldn't want anyone else thinking they had rights to you. I want us to be completely exclusive. We are, aren't we?" Andre needed reassurance for some reason.

I wondered if there was anything I had done or said to make him feel insecure.

"Since I met you four weeks ago, I haven't seen anyone else. I'm only interested in you. Ex-boyfriends are exes for a reason. You're in my life now and I am happy," I replied sincerely.

I hoped this was enough to satisfy his concerns. He had asked me questions about my past before. I wondered if my honesty was too much, too soon. Still, I felt that he loved me and wanted to make this relationship meaningful. Andre continued to ask me about my past relationships. It wasn't a past I was ashamed of. I had been in love before but hadn't always been an angel and I never needed to look back. I wanted to continue looking forward to new experiences and had the expectation that one day I would find the one. I had never been ready to settle down but with Andre I was seriously thinking about it.

"Do you still talk to your ex-boyfriends?" he asked.

"Occasionally, but I don't exactly have much time for them," I responded.

Andre was silent.

"Are you alright?" I asked.

"The wine is taking effect. It's cool. Press play. I'm ready."

We watched a film that night while lying on the sofa together. I really hoped he was happy with the way relationship was going. We planned to do some shopping early in the morning, so soon after the film we went to bed. That night, we fell asleep in each other's arms.

Perhaps we were now settling into our relationship and becoming a couple. I was excited by the idea even though this was new to me. The quality of time that we had spent together made the relationship like no other.

The following day, while we were having lunch, Andre confessed that he had not slept easily. He explained that he wasn't completely comfortable with my ex-boyfriends calling me as I was an attractive woman. He couldn't see how a man and a woman could just be friends if they had previously been intimate. I again reassured him that my friends were my friends and that I didn't spend a great deal of time with my exes. I had never been in a relationship with a man who wanted to keep talking about my past. I was happy to move on from the conversation completely as it made me feel a little uneasy. Why should he, or anyone else care? My experiences had made me the person I was, and if he loved me as he said he did, then my past shouldn't be an issue. After all, he had told me a little about his past but to be truthful, I wasn't even remotely interested.

The rest of the weekend was spent having fun and making love.

It was week six. I drove to Andre's flat on the Saturday morning instead of Friday night as I was really tired and needed a good night's sleep. He met me in the parking area, kissed me on the lips and told me he had a surprise for me.

"What is it?" I was intrigued. I had been to the gym that morning so I was energised and happy. "Come on, don't keep me waiting," I said urgently.

"Patience Shantel," he replied. "Let me take your bag."

I was grateful for his chivalry as I had worked extra hard on my arms and they ached. We walked up to his flat. He took the keys out of his pocket, and waved them in the air in front of me and smiled.

"These are yours. I want you to move in. I miss you when you are not with me. I am in love with you and want to be with you," Andre was still smiling.

I beamed a smile back at him.

"Are you sure?" I asked as he put my bag down.

"Definitely," he responded.

I took the keys and gave him a big hug. He lifted me up and spun me around. I was elated. This was a mature step and I was ready for it. I knew I hadn't known Andre for very long but the feeling was surreal. I started to imagine the possibilities as I opened the front door. I looked around the flat. It needed major refurbishment and decoration to be habitable. I loved walking around bare foot but the flooring as well as the walls needed a lot of work. Andre told me that as soon as his dad was back from Jamaica the following month he would start work on converting the kitchen and lounge into an open-plan space.

"Where would I put my clothes?" I walked into the bedroom and he followed me.

The room wasn't as big as my bedroom and he only had a small fitted wardrobe. The storage space was fine for him, but he didn't need half the amount of space I needed for my shoes, handbags, clothes, coats and other female necessities.

"Well, I was thinking we could look for a wardrobe for you. We can rent out your flat and work towards making this flat a home for us." Andre put his arm around my shoulders. "I can see a future for us and this is the beginning of our lives together."

"Andre, this place is going to need a lot of work and that will take a lot of time. It needs to be brought into the current decade at least."

Literally every room apart from the bedroom needed a complete facelift. I didn't mind how much work was needed as long as the end result was worth it. We talked about our ideas. I had already made my flat a home and I was precious about it, with its spacious rooms, wooden floors and cosy feel. I loved Andre and was looking forward to making a home with him, but it would take time. What he didn't know was I hated being in dusty and dirty environments. I couldn't stay in his flat whilst it was being refurbished, so we discussed moving dates. It was now mid-December. At least double glazed windows had just been installed and his heating worked a treat, so that was something we didn't have to update. We decided that in March I would give up my palace to live in Andre's kingdom in South London.

I had never considered living in the south before. The tunnels were always congested and the traffic was just horrendous. Andre's entire family lived here but I didn't have anyone. My family lived in east and west and Bedfordshire. The south was alien to me but I enjoyed being in Clapham, dining in the trendy, modern restaurants and bars. I saw the dream and I was prepared to take a leap of faith and make it my own reality.

Just one week until my thirtieth birthday party. One of my friends Tasha was helping with some of the party preparations and had already designed my champagne and brandy invitations. Andre and I met her in Peckham as she knew an off-licence that sold alcohol at a reduced price. As Andre knew Peckham well he drove us there.

"How many bottles of brandy do you want to buy Shantel?" Tasha asked.

"I'm not sure hun. Three bottles maybe?" I turned to Andre for his suggestion.

"What do you think babe?" I asked, though he had been rather quiet on this shopping trip.

"Probably three bottles. People are going to bring more. That's what you've asked for right?" he replied curtly.

After paying, I thanked Tasha for her help and Andre drove us back home.

や

"How do I look?" I asked my flatmate Anya. I had treated myself to a designer dress. It was white, cross-over style with a plunging neckline, revealing just the right amount of cleavage.

"Stunning," she replied. "That white dress really suits you!"

"Thanks babe." I was pleased with her response.

Anya was born into a Muslim household. She didn't wear traditional Asian clothing. Her dress sense was modern and trendy, and she always knew how to throw clothes together to create a unique look. I didn't quite have her flair, but tonight, I was on top form! I looked in the hallway mirror, just to ensure everything was in place. I was looking hot! Andre stepped out of the bedroom wearing silver cufflinks on his lime green shirt. He wore brown trousers that complimented his shirt. He was looking dapper.

"Very nice Andre," Anya commented.

"Thank you," he replied while continuing to look at his reflection in the mirror. I noticed that he didn't repay the compliment.

The doorbell rang. It was Andre's brother Vince. He was the DJ and had arrived to set up his equipment.

"Wow! You look amazing Shantel! Happy birthday!" he greeted me with a huge smile.

"Aww thanks Vince," I beamed.

Andre helped him with the equipment and within fifteen minutes, the harmonic tones of Jagged Edge were blasting out from the speakers. This was going to be a loud night. Thankfully, I had already alerted the neighbours. The doorbell rang and rang continuously until the party was in full swing. Champagne and brandy glasses were filling up and people were dancing. I was enjoying the music and having all my friends with me. This was the first time that my friends and family were to meet my new boyfriend. I made the introductions throughout the night. Andre was a handsome, charming man who was polite and smiled at the right time. So it was easy for him to get their seal of approval.

Daniel arrived at the party. We had been in a relationship before I met Andre. He had to be one of the most attractive men anyone had ever seen. He walked into the flat with an air of familiarity, carrying a beautiful bunch of red roses, dressed in a blue shirt and black trousers. He was six foot two, just like Andre. Daniel was eye candy, with his stature, high cheek bones and a caramel skin tone that was typical of a Carib descendant. I remembered the strength of his thighs as he cat-walked into the living room. His parents were also Dominican and his birthday was the day after mine. We had a lot in common, but our relationship didn't flourish. It was easy for Andre to come into my life, offering me more than Daniel could.

I could tell that Andre took an instant disliking to Daniel by the way he glared at him at the front door. I had decided that an introduction wasn't necessary. The party continued until five in the morning when the last guests staggered out. I had drank too much, danced excessively and was incredibly tired. Andre carried me to bed and I slept soundly into the afternoon. When I woke up, I smiled, remembering what a great time I'd had at my party.

Christmas flew by, as did Valentine's Day and soon March was right in front of us. I found a tenant for my flat and started to box up my possessions. I didn't realise how much I had accumulated in the four years I had been there. Time had flown. I clearly remembered the day I had moved into my flat. My best friend had driven the moving van because he was more comfortable driving it on the motorway than it was. I drove my car in front. Another friend was on hand to change my locks. It had been a long day but I cherished that first night in my flat by myself.

I sat all alone, packing everything away. Earlier I had to say a difficult goodbye to Anya. She'd been not just a flatmate but a true friend. Still, this was progress. I knew one day I wanted to get married and have a family. I couldn't do this unless I took a chance. The refurbishment of Andre's flat was almost complete with white walls, walnut wooden flooring, and brand new fitted kitchen and bathroom suites. All it would take to transform the blank canvas into a Picasso were my black leather sofas, my glass dining table and chairs, my TV and stereo set. My IKEA bed would go in Andre's bedroom and his bed would come to my flat. His bed had no character. Andre insisted we replace my mattress and I was happy to oblige. New beginning, new home, new mattress. All my kitchen items were also being transferred to our new home, from my teaspoons to my microwave. I left nothing in my flat, which was beginning to look like a shell but I knew that the new resident would be happy. I hoped she would love and cherish my flat as much as I did.

The move went as planned with all hands on deck to help transfer my worldly possessions from a large flat to a cosy one bedroom property. Nothing was broken apart from a crafted wooden walking stick that I had bought on my travels in the Caribbean. I shrugged my shoulders at seeing the pieces of the wooden carving. After all, this was the beginning of a new journey to a place I had never been before, living with a man.

I settled into the flat with ease. Andre helped me to organise my belongings. He had no homely possessions so there wasn't any duplication. I was still working in East London and Andre had switched jobs and was working in Loughton, with a better salary than his previous job, now that he was back in HR. I would usually drive him to his office in the morning before heading to work. Our daily routine was set. It was fun and we were happy. I couldn't wait to see Andre at the end of each working day.

We decided to go on a weekend break. After working long and hard to decorate the flat, it was to be a well-deserved treat. I was mindful about spending more money as I had virtually drained my bank account to decorate Andre's flat. He needed the support as his finances were low.

I justified spending the money for our break as I was getting rental income from my flat. I didn't want to travel long haul, so we chose a city break. Andre suggested Barcelona for the heat, the food and the Camp Nou football stadium. The football element didn't appeal to me, but I was happy to go along with anything. We booked flights from City Airport and accommodation at the Barcelona Princess Hotel. We were excited about the trip.

"This room is amazing!" I blurted out, scanning the scenery from the window.

Our room was on the tenth floor with spectacular views of the city. I could see for miles. The architecture and landscape were beautiful. Andre fiddled with the remote control to turn on the TV. Suddenly, the blinds descended, creating a blackout effect. He was impressed with the technology in the room. It was, without a doubt, the most modern room I had ever stayed in. We lay on the bed for half an hour, holding each other and watching Spanish television before we ventured into the city for food.

We spent the weekend walking hand in hand along Las Ramblas, riding on an open top bus touring the city, shopping, going to the football stadium, dancing in jazz bars and eating authentic tapas. It was a truly romantic break. I was now totally in love with Andre. He made me feel special. He protected me, like a man should. He provided me with comfort and professed his love for me. What more could I ask for? We had very quickly built our relationship, our home and our future. I felt that our holiday was just a glimpse of good things to come for us. We were young, free and happy.

Andre and I had now officially lived together for two months. After work one evening, we had dinner at the local Thai restaurant. The waitress arrived with our menus. But there was something very odd about her. She was dressed in traditional Thai dress but had a very visible Adam's apple. I discreetly pointed this out to Andre, who confirmed my suspicions. This was a real-life lady boy before us, asking me what I wanted to drink. Andre chuckled, but I was shocked. I guess this was what added to the experience of dining in Clapham restaurants. Andre then started the conversation by announcing that he had something to ask me.

"Shantel, you know I love you dearly," he started. "You know I have cut off all my ex-partners. I don't want or need to have any contact with them," he continued.

I put the menu down and looked up at him attentively.

"I would prefer if you didn't have any contact with yours. If we are serious about this relationship we need to just concentrate on us and not have any distractions or outside influences."

Andre maintained eye contact without blinking. He was serious. I wondered whether he had a sixth sense about my contact with an ex-boyfriend recently. I was not a liar and if he had asked me directly, I would have told him. But he hadn't asked me.

"Well, my exes should not be a concern for you. Babe, you know it's all about you. You know my every move. We spend all our time together so you really shouldn't be concerned. I respect that you have cut people off and that was your decision. I can't be that heartless babe. I love you and not my exes. I don't even want to waste time talking about them." I hoped that I had said enough to convince him that he was my priority.

"Are you still speaking to them?" he pressed on. We were still waiting for our starters.

"I can't remember the last time. Why?" I responded.

I was getting annoyed at the line of questioning. Was this a night of interrogation? I wondered what else I would have to do to convince him.

"I just want to feel secure that you love me and will cut off your exes for me. I'm a man and yes, I have an ego. I don't want other men having access to you. You're with me now. If you really love me and want this relationship to work then you need to change your mobile telephone number," he asserted.

I was shocked by his request. Why was he really saying this to me? I had packed my possessions and moved in with him. I had transformed his shell of a dated one-bedroom flat into a home with my money and my furniture. I had told him that I loved him and wanted to spend my life with him. At this stage of our relationship, I thought that we were secure in our love for each other. Why now, after seven months is he asking me to do this? I had treasured my 07956 number ever since I got it at the tender age of eighteen. My father had encouraged me to get a mobile when I started university. That telephone number had seen me through so many years. Why should I give it up? What would he give up for me? I didn't want a random number that I wouldn't be able to memorise, let alone give to my hundreds of contacts.

"Andre, you can't ask me to do that," I replied. "You know I love you and changing my telephone number won't change anything apart from my ex partners not having my number."

I tried to reason with him and yet again, reassure him so he was aware that this was love and that I had already changed so much of my life to accommodate him and this relationship. I assumed that we were on the same page.

I didn't say much more during our meal and really felt uncomfortable. Was this going to be a one-off or would there be more unreasonable demands? He didn't appear to be secure in the fact that I couldn't be swayed by another man. If he was threatened by an old fling from the past, then what about a stranger I bumped into in the local supermarket? But perhaps Andre was right? New beginnings, new phone number. Was I really that attached to those eleven digits? Throughout the rest of the evening, Andre was sweet and convinced me that he wasn't trying to change me but rather enhance our relationship as he didn't trust other men. I made a deal with Andre that night, I would change my phone number if he deleted his second line, also a 07956 number. He told me most people had that number but not many had his new number so he agreed. In the morning, we would call his mobile phone supplier to make the changes.

I was watching television one Sunday evening. Andre was on the computer. The house phone rang. It was my mother in Dominica. She sounded different today. I could tell there was something wrong.

"Shantel, I have some sad news."

I waited patiently for her to continue. "What's happened?"

"Granny passed away this morning." She paused. "She died while I was with her." My mum sounded distressed. I knew she needed me there. Dad took the phone from her and asked me if I was alright. I was but I knew my mum was devastated and I had to find a flight to Dominica.

Chapter Four:
Goodnight Granny

My grandmother had lived to the grand old age of ninety-three and her spirit was now at peace in heaven. She was a religious woman with a strong faith in God. I was rarely affected by the passing of relatives back home, but this time was different. I felt a void, even though I was thousands of miles away. I told my father that I would speak to my Aunt Sophie to co-ordinate our flights. I discussed the trip with my brothers but they both said that they couldn't make it. Guess it was up to me to do it alone.

The following evening Andre and I had dinner at an Italian restaurant in Dulwich. He wanted to take me out to make me smile and divert my attention from the recent news. As it was a quiet Monday evening the staff were attentive. I told Andre of the dates my family and I were considering for the trip. We hadn't booked our flights yet though. Andre sat opposite me with a sombre look on his face.

"What are you thinking?" I asked.

"Well, you're going to be gone for two or three weeks. I know you have to go, but I'm really going to miss you. That's a long time for us to be apart. Since meeting, we've hardly gone a day without seeing each other."

"Ah babe. I will miss you too," I replied.

We ordered our mains and drinks. I sat and thought about the situation in silence. I would only be away for a few weeks. Would Andre miss me that much? He would be free of me nagging about his socks being left in random places or the state of the kitchen. I had to go for my family.

"It's just a thought," I said, "but how about you coming with me?"

I thought that this could be an opportune time for my parents to meet Andre. By inviting him, I wouldn't feel guilty about leaving him behind. He didn't have to say yes.

"How much is the flight?" he asked.

"It's around six hundred pounds. It's the cheapest I've seen. The travel agency is in Hackney. Do you think you can afford it?" I asked feeling slightly excited at the thought of us going away together again.

"I haven't got six hundred but I can pay some of it if you lend me the rest."

"I think I can work it out. I'll have to use my credit card." I thought I'd better tell my parents as soon as possible that Andre would be coming with me.

I wondered how they would receive him. They had spoken on the phone numerous times but my parents were still from a different generation. Would they accept us sleeping in the same room under their roof? I would have to warn them of our intentions to share a room.

"Shantel, I love you and I just want to be there to support you." Andre was interrupted as the waiter served our food.

I smiled and felt comforted by his words. I knew he didn't have a credit card or any disposable money for his flight but I was happy to lend him the cash. We started to make plans for the trip. I had to consider that my mother may want me to buy her some essentials and after our meal I would have to phone my parents. Andre and I had been together for eight months and perhaps it was time that they met the person I wanted to spend my life with; the man who loved me and the man who promised to make my dreams become a reality.

Two weeks later we were ready to travel. My Aunt Sophie, cousins Mikey and Grace, Andre and I had all congregated at Gatwick Airport. Our bags were checked in and we were ready to board the flight to go and say goodbye to Granny. We travelled the eight-hour journey to Antigua where we would get a connecting flight to Dominica. At the airport in Antigua, the entertainment was non-existent. There were only a few shops that sold CDs, souvenirs and basic food. The staff weren't particularly friendly. Andre and I wandered off to a jewellery counter to pass some time. A sales assistant tried to engage us in conversation. Her name badge said Leylah. No doubt she was working on commission.

"You are a lovely looking couple. How about a beautiful ring for the gorgeous lady?" she enquired.

I wondered if she made many sales with that technique. We stopped and looked at the engagement rings.

"I love your name Leylah," I told the sales woman.

"Thank you," she replied with a beautiful smile.

"What style of ring do you like?" Andre asked.

Though we had talked about spending the rest of our lives together we had not actually looked at rings before. Andre hadn't proposed to me. We had previously discussed marriage but had not agreed on the type of wedding we would have. I felt there was plenty of time to discuss those plans once I was wearing a ring.

"That one is beautiful," I pointed out excitedly.

"Ah, you have taste," Leylah said in her beautiful Antiguan accent, pulling the diamond encrusted ring out from the locked glass display cabinet. She placed it in my hand. I took a breath and tried it on.

"This is a princess cut. It's white gold and I can do a deal for you." Leylah was pushy but sweet and inoffensive. "It looks lovely on your finger." She didn't let up.

Leylah went through some finer details about the ring with Andre. I zoned out and wondered what it would feel like to wear such a beautiful engagement ring. I knew it wouldn't happen today as Andre did not have that kind of money. At least now he knew what I liked. I wanted my ring to be a statement of style and individuality. I thought the classical style of engagement ring was pretty, but I wanted something unusual.

Mikey walked through the jewellery store. He cheekily grinned at us while we were engrossed in conversation with the shop assistant.

"Just pretend you didn't see me," he stated cheerily, with a smirk on his face and continued walking towards the souvenir shop.

I took the ring off after admiring it on my finger, in the mirror, hand up, hand down, hand through my hair and hand on my chin. I tried not to get too excited about trying it on. It was a good feeling but until an engagement ring was officially presented to me, we were only co-habiting without intention.

"Last boarding call for flight number LI0378," the tannoy announced.

We thanked Leylah for her time. As we rushed back towards the rest of our party, my mind wandered back to her name and how beautiful it was.

We fetched our bags and boarded the Liat plane. Andre was a little surprised when he saw our next mode of transport as he'd never travelled on such a small aircraft. After forty-five minutes in the air we landed in Melville Hall Airport, Dominica. My Aunt Rosalie was there to pick us all up in her pickup truck. It was a tight squeeze. Andre and Mikey rode in the back, while Grace, my Aunt Sophie and I rode in the passenger seats. The men fully embraced the warm Dominican air whipped up by the speed of my aunt's driving up the winding hills of the island. It was a long drive to Wall House where my parents waited patiently. We knew our schedule for the next few days was already organised with visits to family and the morgue to see Granny for the last time. After an hour and a half of some serious native driving we reached our destination. The exterior of my parent's house had been painted a different colour but everything else seemed to have remained as it had since my visit last year. Once the engine was switched off, the familiar sound of crickets began to ring in my ears. My parents were standing at the door.

Warm embraces were exchanged. I introduced Andre to my parents. I could tell that my mother liked him by her big smile. We were all shown to our rooms. Our room had a double bed, wardrobe and a chest of drawers. There was only one window, which meant the room was going to be a sweat box, especially at night time. There was a rug on the floor, possibly placed there for me as I never wore slippers.

Back in the sitting room, Mum and Dad served us cool drinks with ice and some light food. We weren't used to the sweltering heat of Dominica and it would take some time to adjust. Mum had laid towels on all the beds and one by one we showered. Andre and I used the bathroom and then said goodnight to everyone. We slept peacefully until the morning.

Time wasn't waiting for us and the jet lag had to be ignored. There were far more important issues to deal with. We showered, ate salt fish and fried dumplings for breakfast and were ready to make our way to the morgue. As Andre was gathering his wallet and watch he asked me to sit down.

"Shantel, last night something strange happened. I saw your Granny. It was surreal." He paused. "She came into our room."

I listened attentively. Andre described what he had seen and heard. I'd never told him what she looked like, nor had he seen a photograph. However, Andre described her so accurately that I had goose pimples on my arms and the back of my neck.

"She told me to take care of you. She told me to cover you with the sheets so that you didn't catch a chill. She then drifted out of the room."

His voice was low as he described the event. Andre wouldn't lie about this but why did my Granny appear to him and not me?

"Wow! And did you cover me?" I asked with a smile, trying to soften the intensity of his revelation.

"Yes, after we made love," he replied with a cheeky look on his face.

We both laughed as we walked out of the room through the hallway into the blazing heat. The family had gathered by the car, ready to go. My father and his cousin were both driving separately to get us all into town together.

I took a deep breath as we arrived at the morgue. We climbed the stairs to see Granny one last time. My heart was pounding harder with every step I took, as I was nervous about seeing her laying there, lifeless. I put my arm around my mother's shoulders. All her sisters were there together, supporting each other. My Aunt Sophie was the only sibling who had not seen her mother lying on the table in the cold clinical room. It was such an emotional time for her. There were so many tears. While the sisters were comforting each other, Andre supported me.

"Shantel, she looks exactly as she appeared last night," Andre whispered in my ear.

I smiled at Andre. How long would the family stay in the room? I had been there long enough and was ready to leave, so I told Andre I wanted to go outside. The building was so cold, though it made sense to keep the building's air conditioning on full blast. I needed the sun on my body to thaw the chill in my bones. Once outside, I slowly warmed up. My cousins were next to leave the morgue and join us. Though we were all sad, it was still an occasion that brought the family together. Granny was always a strong and inspirational woman and I hoped that I could be as strong and powerful as she had been. She had given birth to eight children though one had died. She held the family together and was supportive of all her children, near or far. She had nothing but love in her heart.

The funeral took place in a village called Delices, where Granny was born. It was another hot day and I was feeling dizzy in the blazing sun. I sipped the water I'd brought along to cool down. I stood behind my mother as her mother descended into the earth. I prayed to God that my mother and her family would be strong and that there would be no challenges during the division of the estate.

After the burial, we made our way to the house for the wake. I served drinks at the bar. Andre and Mikey helped when the requests increased with the afternoon sun. The food was served and most of the guests had eaten. Andre and I sat down on the steps to the kitchen. An unfamiliar man approached Andre.

"Yuh ignoring me? Why yuh nah sey hello?" the man snarled at Andre. "I curse you! I curse you for what you 'av done!" the man shouted.

"What?" Andre stood up. "I rebuke you! I rebuke you in the name of the Lord!" Andre yelled and instantly became angry. "You don't know me. Who the hell are you?" Andre demanded, walking towards the man. They had now created a scene.

"Oh, I thought you were somebody else. I sorry. Yuh look like somebody I know. Yuh look real familiar. I sorry," the man muttered sheepishly.

"I rebuke you!" Andre exclaimed angrily.

"You need to leave," I told the stranger. "Leave and don't come back. You're not welcome. Leave now!" I had to defend Andre.

Maybe it was a case of mistaken identity but I knew some village people believed in 'obeah'. I had heard stories about villagers wishing evil on others because of greed and hatred. Was this man one of them? Whatever the case, he needed to leave as he had upset my man. I personally did not believe in curses but Andre seemed quite shaken by the incident.

That night Andre and I stayed at my uncle's house in the neighbouring village. It was a modern house that could have been picked up from England and placed on a plot of land in the hills of this pretty landscape. While lying in bed we talked about staying in a hotel for a couple of nights. I decided to speak to my cousin Stella about getting a local rate rather than an extortionate tourist one for a room. I wanted to be pampered in elegant surroundings. Andre needed some time alone with me especially as the trip so far had been hectic and we had been consumed with the funeral. I was happy to spend some intimate quality time alone with him and became excited at the prospect of gourmet cuisine and a swimming pool.

Two days later and we were in town with our overnight bags. We had reserved a room at the Artillery Hotel. I had been there before for dinner and drinks but never to stay. I wasn't sure what the hotel was like beyond the bar and restaurant.

"Shantel, have you been here before with any other man?" Andre asked with an anxious tone.

"No Andre, I have only been here with family members."

I realised I had to be patient with him. He only appeared to be confident but needed constant reassurance that he was my focus and my future. With time, I knew he wouldn't need to continually question my loyalty.

"Sir, your room number is 312. The hotel is quiet so we have given you an upgrade. Make the most of it as a big wedding party is due in tomorrow. Enjoy! Would you like to be shown to your room?"

The receptionist was immaculately dressed with flawless hair, nails and make-up. I felt slightly self-conscious as my appearance didn't compare. My nails were unpolished, though my toes still looked pretty from the pedicure I'd treated myself to back in London the day before we flew out. Anyway, I preferred my hair to have body, not pressed paper thin. As we walked slowly to our room, I wondered if the romance of a Caribbean wedding would inspire us to explore our own ideas for our wedding day.

"Are you ready?" Andre asked as he slotted the plastic key into the lock.

"I'm ready."

He held the door open and I walked in. He followed behind me excitedly.

"This room is georgeous!" I bellowed excitedly from the balcony.

The white tiles on the floor and walls made the room feel tranquil. The bed was large and the decor was subtle and light. French doors opened onto a balcony with a stunning view of the Caribbean Sea and the swimming pool, which somehow seemed to merge into one. Was it my eyes? How was that possible? It was perfect. Our bathroom was splendid with a tub that we could both lay in. I was turned on by the thought of what we could get up to in that bathtub.

"Jacuzzi?" Andre asked suggestively.

"Definitely!" I answered.

Andre changed into his trunks while I looked for the sexiest bikini I had. I wanted to feel desirable. It was hot and the bubbles of the Jacuzzi would no doubt heighten the mood. Andre was always horny so I knew things would get explicitly raunchy. I brushed my hair into a pony tail. I didn't care if it got wet — after all we were staying in a luxurious hotel with a hair dryer in our bedroom. I had wrapped my sarong around my waist, applied my sun cream and lip balm, grabbed my sunglasses and was ready to enjoy the facilities. I looked at my reflection in the mirror one last time before we left the room.

We ordered our drinks at the bar and asked that they be sent to us by the Jacuzzi. We felt like royalty, like superstars. Andre was in control and being the man by organising our dinner for the evening. I removed my sarong to reveal my sexy gold bikini as soon as I saw Andre returning from the bar. He smiled. It was hot but the Jacuzzi was situated in a shady, secluded area of the grounds, just beside the swimming pool. There were no other guests in sight. I didn't mind. To me, that meant that the staff would be attentive and we could have some privacy. I had seen a German couple milling around the hotel earlier, but at that moment it was just us. I hoped they wouldn't interfere with our plans. The waiter soon arrived with our drinks in a wine cooler.

"Ah, champagne!" I observed delightedly. I needed some cold water to keep me hydrated but the idea of drinking bubbles while we were in bubbles amused me.

"A toast to us!" Andre's face was a picture of joy.

"May we have many more special moments like this Shantel. I want to spend the rest of my life with you. We can do this and make the rest of our lives together amazing. So, what do you say Shantel?"

"Of course we can do this. I'm so happy right now. I couldn't ask for anything more," I replied with genuine ecstasy.

This was the happiest I had ever truly been. Here I was with a man who was gorgeous, tall, caring and ambitious. He saw the potential in us. He wanted forever. I had only seen that vision with one other person before but I didn't have the emotional maturity to profess it then. That was in the past. He was my present and my beautiful promised future. Andre took the glass out of my hand.

"Sit on top," he requested with a seductive grin.

"Are you serious?" I asked sheepishly.

"Come on. Shhh," he replied.

I positioned myself on top of Andre, with my legs straddled over his. My arms were wrapped around his neck. He pulled me close and kissed me gently with his eyes closed. Andre was a risk taker, but I was nervous. I kissed him back and closed my eyes. The kiss became more and more intense. He leant into my neck and kissed it gently before nibbling at it. I was aroused and felt tingles shooting down below. I felt him get hard so I knew he was ready for me too. I swiftly unwrapped my arms from his shoulders, loosened his swimming trunks and gently eased his stiffness out. Andre flashed a grin as he pulled my bikini bottoms aside and lifted me up as I placed him inside me. He pulled my bikini top down to expose my pert breasts and gently caressed them with his tongue and lips.

"Make sure you keep your eyes open!" I panted.

"Mmm," he groaned.

I eased myself on top of him. The feeling was intense and dangerous. At any given moment, someone could have walked around the back of the Jacuzzi to see me exposed. We were so near to the swimming pool. Our intimate thrilling moment needed to end quickly as I didn't want to get caught. My heart was racing and I felt

Andre's racing too. I started to feel the excitement of making love in a public place, as we pleasured each other overlooking the turquoise waters. Suddenly, I felt free and didn't care who saw me.

"Oh babe!" I moaned in Andre's ear.

"I feel you," Andre mumbled through gritted teeth.

I could tell he wanted to orgasm louder but he restricted himself just as I had. We peaked at the same time. It was mind blowing. I quickly shifted my body from Andre's lap, adjusted my bikini and sat next to him, feeling flushed. He passed me my glass refilling it with more champagne. He filled his with what was left and placed the empty bottle back into the cooler. This was a moment of celebration. We didn't get caught!

"Thank you," Andre said smugly. He had a cheeky grin, almost like a child who had eaten all the jelly babies.

"No, thank *you*," I replied feeling as if we had committed a bank robbery and gotten away with the money.

We toasted again and sipped our drinks. I wondered if anyone had seen us carrying on with our 'outdoor activities'. The hotel industry must have been accustomed to this sort of carnal behaviour though.

We could hear voices. The German couple I had spotted in the hotel lobby earlier were making their way over to the Jacuzzi. I wished hard that they would turn around and go somewhere else. They smiled as they joined us. Damn, I wasn't in the mood for polite conversation. I was in the mood for more of Andre, naked and sprawled out on a king-sized bed! Nevertheless, we made some polite conversation with the couple even though we had other intentions. Andre then gestured for me to finish my champagne so we could go to our room. I quickly gulped the remaining drink and we headed up to continue what we had started moments earlier.

Time flew that afternoon and soon we had to get ourselves ready for dinner. Andre wore his white linen suit which I had helped him choose whilst out shopping. He looked handsome and stylish, and was glowing from the sun and the love-making earlier. I had never seen him look so happy. I knew I had skills in the bedroom so why wouldn't he be beaming? Andre was ready before I was. He said he was going for a quick walk and told me to take my time getting dressed. He suggested I listen to some music and enjoy the view on the balcony. He took the key and walked out of the room. I wondered what he was up to as he was behaving slightly suspiciously, though I knew he was a romantic at heart. I suspected he had planned some flowers or a bottle of champagne for the table. None of that mattered to me though as I was crazy in love with him. I didn't need material possessions or the grandiose gestures to keep me happy. I needed respect, trust, equality, love and kindness from my man. Andre was lucky that I was low maintenance. When I met him, he didn't have any money. True, he had remortgaged his council flat but I had to pay for the revamp. Now it was our modern, sleek and chic home that was to a standard I was more than happy with. I encouraged and supported Andre with his job search when he had decided to go back into HR. My positive energy was influencing him and he was progressing and achieving in his new job. I knew that God was on my side. Though I wasn't a regular church-goer, I knew that His presence still protected me.

I sat on the balcony sipping my cool tropical juice, contemplating life and the journey I had taken to get to this point. Through everything, I knew that I was embraced by God's love. I recalled a time a few years previously when I was in hospital waiting for an eye operation. I remembered sitting on the hospital bed in my gown, waiting to go into theatre. Though everyone saw me sitting alone, I knew He was sitting with me. It was surreal and when I told this to anyone I generally receive a confused, disbelieving look. I didn't care. When I had my car accident on the North Circular near Barking, God's arms were wrapped around me protectively, while the car was spinning round and round. The offending driver was drunk and he had managed to climb out of his overturned Mercedes to run off down the highway. That was a traumatic experience and Andre knew that I had undergone some counselling to help me recover from the accident.

Blossom Tree | Sharon Fevrier

I was a happy person with a good heart and I loved the idea of helping people to progress. Still, I wondered what my purpose in life was. Yes, I had Andre. We had been together for eight months and I wasn't trying to rush anything between us. I knew I was still learning about the beautiful man who I shared a flat with and hoped that the relationship would become fruitful. I was thirty years old and it was time for stability in my life. When I was younger, I had always imagined that I would be married by the time I was twenty-four and ready to start a family. None of my friends were in stable relationships or living with a good man. Maybe I would be the first to start the trend. So far it was good living with Andre. He did his fair share of housework and I did most of the cooking. We ate out a lot and partied frequently. It was a good life. While I was mid-flow in my thoughts Andre returned.

"Wow, you're stunning, my beautiful Queen," he commented whilst wiping the beads of perspiration from his forehead.

"Thank you, my King."

We were both dressed in white. I wore a halter neck dress which accentuated my curves in a sexy but classy way. My hair was loose and full of body as I had blow-dried it after our Jacuzzi experience. The moisture in the air performed wonders on my hair. My make-up was light and subtle. I had acquired a natural sun-kissed glow. I wore white sandals and was happy my pedicure was still holding up.

"Are you ready?" Andre asked.

"Yes, I'm famished. I could eat a horse right now."

I had that after-sex hunger that needed to be satisfied. I was looking forward to some seafood from the shores of Dominica. I loved eating out and Andre knew it. Though I wasn't a complete mess in the kitchen, I always appreciated being cooked for, or taken out to eat. Andre held his arm out for me, I linked it and we headed to the restaurant. The night was warm and the sun was just starting to set. We were escorted to a table overlooking the sea, but we could just about see the Jacuzzi. The sunset was glorious. The amber glow reflected on the waters, creating a breath-taking scene. Our waiter brought our menus and asked us for our order of drinks. Andre chose while I looked at the tantalising menu. I wanted the lobster, the crab and the king prawns, but I knew I couldn't eat them all.

"Have the lobster," Andre suggested knowingly.

He was allergic to seafood, fish and nuts but he encouraged me to order it every time we went out as I couldn't cook it in the flat. He was covering the bill and he wanted to make me feel special. So, I ordered the lobster. We held hands as we watched the sunset. We talked and discussed our future. I was happy with the way our relationship was progressing. When we were together, it felt as if I was walking on air.

Our food arrived quickly, possibly because the restaurant was quiet. I looked around at the other diners. They looked like affluent and well-to-do local people. The restaurant was known as one of the finest on the island. I couldn't wait to eat my lobster and use my fingers if need be. That's how lobster is supposed to be eaten! The food was delicious. The ambiance was mellow but refined. I felt as though we were in an exclusive club. We finished our meal and decided to stroll down to the bayfront to walk off our dinner. We were both so tired. The moonlight set the finale to a perfect day. We decided to go back to our hotel room, just to sleep. We wanted to make the most of our second day in the exquisite resort.

"Andre, wake up. Wake up!" I rocked Andre's arm gently at first, then vigorously until he was awake. "Something's wrong!" I exclaimed frantically.

"What is it?" he asked with a concerned expression on his face.

I didn't answer. I was in shock.

"Shantel?" Andre sat up in bed. "Shantel, you're scaring me. What is it?"

"I can't see!"

Chapter Five:
Changes

"What do you mean you can't see? What are you talking about?" Andre blurted.

My body was trembling with fear. I took a deep breath.

"I can't see. I mean I can see normally with my left eye but my right eye, my good eye...I don't know. There's a problem." I spoke calmly as getting hysterical wasn't going to help me.

"What can you see?" Andre's tone reflected my calmness.

"I can only see black," I sighed loudly.

I took deep breaths to remain composed because saying the words made my problem a reality. I wanted to cry, but my eyes were dry. I wanted to scream, but I could barely speak. I wanted to close my eyes and re-open them to restored vision. This was more than déjà vu. I had experienced a similar episode with my left eye, many years ago.

I was working a late shift in a four-star London hotel near the Houses of Parliament, as a front-of-house assistant. It was a part-time job I had whilst at university. I started the shift at 3 o'clock and as the evening approached, the rush had died down. The supervisor, Amy, was on another cigarette break. I was left alone to man the reception desk when I suddenly felt as though I was going to faint. I was hot and dizzy. I needed to use the toilet. The vision in my left eye had become distorted. I panicked. I called Amy to relieve me.

"But I haven't finished my break yet," she complained.

"I need you here now. I feel sick. I feel really ill!" I protested.

"Can't you wait five minutes?" Amy asked sounding disgruntled.

"No!" I blurted, and hung up the phone.

Within minutes, I had locked myself in a toilet cubicle. Everything I had eaten that day exploded out of my body. The distortion in my eye had almost completely diffused. After twenty minutes of sitting on the toilet, I was ready to stand up. I looked at my reflection in the mirror. Something was wrong; something was different. I felt and looked drained. I rubbed my eye, reassuring myself that I just needed a good rest.

My vision had never fully recovered after that especially as I hadn't sought medical advice at the time. I never had a thorough explanation as to why I almost blacked out either. Having sickle cell anaemia meant that I didn't have as much oxygen circulating in my blood in comparison to the average person. Some years later, I had to have surgery on my left eye and since then, my vision had been, thankfully, stable.

But now, I knew there was a bigger problem. I was scared. I didn't want to have poor vision in both eyes. Impaired vision in one eye was bad enough but I coped well. I had adapted and could still live a normal life. Andre knew my medical history since our very first telephone conversation. I didn't hide it and figured that if he couldn't handle it, he was not for me.

"We've got to go home," Andre concluded.

"Andre, I won't be able to see my consultant until Monday. It's Wednesday today. There's no point going home early. Nothing will change."

I was terrified of what could happen in the next few days. I wondered what my consultant at the hospital would say. What had I done to make this happen?

"Shantel, lie down and close your eyes," he suggested.

I lay down next to Andre, closed my eyes and prayed to God to restore my vision. The darkness cleared slightly. We discussed what we would do when we returned home. I began to mentally prepare for an operation. I described my vision to Andre, comparing it to seeing objects in distorted mirrors; the images were stretched beyond belief. I started to shift down the enormous bed.

"Where are you going?" Andre asked with concern in his voice.

"I'm just going to the bathroom. I'll be ok babe."

"Would you like some help?" he asked.

"I'm ok babe," I replied.

As I got to the end of the bed and stood up, I held my hands out in front of me to feel my way along the bedroom wall to the bathroom door. I struggled to find the door handle. Andre jumped out of the bed and flung the door open. He then held my arm to guide me towards the toilet.

"Here, let me help you," he said as he positioned me in front of the toilet.

"I'll be alright. I'll shout if I need you."

I flushed the toilet and stood up to wash my hands. I looked in the mirror with my distorted eyes. What happened to me? Why had this happened? I never missed an appointment. Didn't I deserve a break? Clearly not. I had to be tested again. Was this to see whether I had strength of character? The visual distortion was now disturbing. My peripheral view was non-existent as all I could see was a black tunnel with stretched images that looked as if they had been painted by a caricaturist.

"Are you ok babe?" Andre shouted from the bedroom.

"Yes," I replied quietly.

Andre came into the bathroom and brought me back into the bedroom. I didn't want to be blind. I had such a wonderful day yesterday but today was a complete contrast. We still had another day booked at the hotel. I told Andre I didn't want to waste it and we would go back to my parents' house the following day.

Andre looked after me. I couldn't have asked for anything more. We went to the swimming pool and spent time in the Jacuzzi. This time there was no sex, just relaxation. I wasn't sipping on cocktails or champagne as I had the day before, just water and plenty of it. I needed to keep hydrated. Perhaps that was part of the problem.

During the course of our second day, there had been a slight improvement in my vision but not enough for me to relax. That evening we ate dinner on our balcony. It was still a special evening. Our paradise trip would be over once we returned to my parents' home. Their concern would be overwhelming.

We left the hotel the following morning after breakfast to inform my parents. Predictably, they were worried about my eyesight. They felt helpless, but their prayers were a comfort to me. My father drove us to the travel agency, where we brought our flight forward by two days. The fee to change our tickets was irrelevant; it was worth paying for the reassurance of seeing an experienced eye specialist.

We arrived in London, dropped our luggage home, and drove straight to Moorfields Eye Hospital in Old Street. I sat quietly throughout our journey. It seemed to take a lifetime but I wasn't in a rush to learn about my fate. I felt as though I was having an out-of-body experience. Was this really happening to me? Though it had been three days since my vision had become distorted, there was no major improvement.

I hated what I saw, so much so that I preferred to close my eyes and see nothing. Everything was elongated and deformed. People looked ugly. The world looked ugly. I always saw the beauty in my surroundings, so this was a dreadful experience for me. Andre whizzed through the streets of the city. Every manoeuvre he made felt dangerous and scary. He found parking opposite the hospital. We made our way through to the A&E department. It was a Saturday afternoon and the waiting room was busy. Andre got some coffee from the vending machine and sat down beside me. The coffee was hot and strong. I was tired from the flight. I was normally an impatient person but I sat there quietly praying to God that my eyesight could be restored. Andre paced up and down the waiting room, speaking on his mobile phone. He was restless and tired too. Eventually, he sat down beside me after speaking to the reception staff.

"How are you feeling?" I asked, wondering how he was coping.

"I'm fine babe. I just want you to be alright. I want them to hurry up and call your name so we can see someone."

"No Andre, how do you feel about what has happened?" I asked inquisitively.

I wanted him to express his feelings. Surely it was better to talk openly about his fears so we could try to support each other.

"Well, we don't really know what has happened to your eye yet, so there's no point panicking. Let's just wait and see shall we?"

We sat in silence until my name was called by the junior doctor on duty. We walked into the cubicle, holding hands. I explained what had happened and then he started his examination. The bright light of the machine usually made me squint, but this time I barely flinched. After taking time to examine me, he said that he wouldn't be long and left the cubicle. I prayed silently while he was gone. He soon returned with his consultant, who after introducing himself, started to assess my vision. He took a deep breath.

"Shantel, you're going to need an operation. The blood vessel in your eye has burst and your retina has detached. You will need to come back on Monday to see the retinal specialist. His clinic is on Monday afternoon so please come at 1.30. I will inform his team that you will be seeing him as an emergency patient."

The doctor spoke some more but it was all white noise to me. I couldn't hear what he was saying and perhaps this was because I had heard enough. Andre interacted with the doctors while I imagined I was walking freely in a meadow, with the sun shining and without a care in the world. I was transported to heaven on earth. I focused on this beautiful place, a far cry from the concrete jungle of Old Street. Who had named it Old Street anyway? Weren't most of the streets in London old?

"Take care Shantel," the doctor said.

I didn't even realise the men had stopped talking.

"Thank you, doctor."

We walked out of the hospital back to the car. I took a deep breath in slowly, imagining that I was inhaling countryside air rather than the fumes from a congested main road. Then I exhaled.

"Are you ok?" Andre asked sweetly.

"Yes. I guess this is what I expected. I knew I'd have to come back on Monday. In the meantime, you have to cook!"

I joked with Andre about taking care of me while I put my feet up on the sofa. After all, that's what he usually did.

"Shantel, let's get a Chinese," he suggested.

I laughed. Andre was a good cook but he rarely volunteered to do so unless it was a special occasion.

"Besides, are you really going to watch TV?"

"Yep, I want to watch a good romantic comedy tonight, even if I can't see the screen properly. How about that?"

Andre knew I was joking as all I wanted to do was eat, shower and get into bed. We were both physically and mentally drained.

"You haven't lost your sense of humour then," Andre commented.

My motto sprung to mind: *'life is too short'*.

Two days later, I was back at the hospital with Andre. The black tunnel in my eye had disappeared but the distortion was still there. I was calm and ready for whatever the doctor had to say. I knew which consultant I was seeing as he had already performed two operations on my left eye. After a short wait in the clinic with eye drops in my eyes to dilate the pupils, my name was called. We both went into the cubicle.

"Hello Shantel. I understand that you visited A&E on Saturday. Let's take a look."

Mr Atward, the consultant, didn't waste time. He was the big chief and I was happy to see him. He assessed my eyes for a few minutes.

"Shantel, the blood vessels in the back of your eye have burst and detached the retina. You will need an operation to re-attach the retina. Unfortunately, I cannot predict how good your vision will be after that, but I suspect that it will be a vast improvement on your current vision."

"How did this happen?" Andre asked.

"It's because of a lack of enough free-flowing oxygen in Shantel's blood due to the sickle cell. So, it's called sickle cell retinopathy. There is no way of predicting if or even when this could happen. Some people are affected and others aren't. Shantel, my secretary will contact you to let you know the date of the operation. I'll see you soon."

"Thank you Mr Atward." I was confident that I was in good hands.

We left the hospital. The cool air hit me and I felt a little dizzy. I stumbled and held onto Andre's arm tighter.

"Are you ok?" he asked with a concerned tone.

"Yes. Just felt a little bit wobbly. I think I need something to eat."

Even though I had eaten a big breakfast of cheese and tomato bagels at home, I was still hungry. I loved to eat and it was a gift from God that I wasn't a plus size. I would have to stop going to the gym as I couldn't drive anymore and I wasn't confident enough to even make it to the corner shop by myself, let alone handle gym equipment. We got to Clapham and decided to have an early dinner at the local Thai restaurant. The food was hot and sweet. I slept well that evening.

Tuesday morning, Andre went to work and I telephoned my boss to relay the consultant's plans. I was exhausted. My health had taken a hit but I hadn't been over-exerting myself. I had spent a lot of time in the flat resting, cooking and doing the housework. I felt confined but I was comfortable. Outside the front door was the unknown. I was too scared to leave my haven by myself. Little Miss Shantel was now a hermit, locked up to keep herself safe. This wasn't me. I was a socialite. I enjoyed life and it enjoyed me. I still tried to make time to see my friends and family though Andre had to escort me.

The following week, on a Saturday evening, we were heading to a party in Bedford. My cousin Rachel was celebrating her thirtieth birthday. I sat on the bed, looking at my make-up, thinking about whether I should even attempt to put any of it on. This was the first social event since coming back from Dominica. I decided to just use lip gloss and forget everything else. I put on a little black dress and flat sandals. I figured wearing heels wouldn't help me if I couldn't see any cracks in the pavement or a raised kerb. I didn't want people to know the extent of my appalling eyesight. I was getting it fixed as soon as I could. Maybe after that my life would go back to normal. Andre walked into the bedroom with a towel wrapped around his waist. He had just finished his shower.

"Shantel, I've got something on my mind. I'm happy for us to go, but can you guarantee that none of your exes will be there?" He was serious.

"We've discussed this already," I huffed. "No one has been invited."

Andre warned me that he wouldn't go to the party if any of my ex-boyfriends were invited. I didn't have the energy to fight him on his issues about men that he didn't know and who probably weren't even interested in me anymore. I had already contacted Rachel to ask if any of my previous partners were invited. Rachel had confirmed that she hadn't invited anyone from my past and I gave Andre the green light.

Even though my vision was limited, I still wanted to go out and hear some good music, eat some tasty food and see some familiar faces. What better remedy for a woman going through a life changing experience? Here I was, dependent on Andre. He loved me though his insecurities bugged me and I couldn't understand his mentality towards people that were no longer in my life. Surely, he would be proud to have me on his arm. Why not show me off to rub the noses of anyone who had lost me? That would be my angle. But everyone had different takes on these things. All I needed was for Andre to support and care for me.

"We need petrol," Andre said

I told him to fill up closer to home, but Andre knew best. We ended up stopping at a petrol station in North London. Our journey was awkward. Not only were there major road works which prolonged the drive, but our conversation was stifled. Andre was painfully quiet.

"What's wrong Andre? You've hardly talked to me since we left home.

"Nothing. I'm cool." Andre gave me very fake smile and turned the music up.

We continued listening to some hip hop but I wanted to listen to something a little more soulful. There was clearly something bothering him but he wouldn't share. I stopped trying to engage him in conversation and let him concentrate on his driving. There were more roadworks on the M1.

"I think we should turn back. This journey has been one from hell!" He was hassled by of the queue of cars in front of us.

Forty minutes later, we finally arrived. Andre parked the car. There was no point looking in the mirror to check my make-up and Andre was in no mood to give me reassurance. We walked to the party. As we approached the community centre, I heard Rachel's voice. She was on her phone, giving directions. Andre and I waited in silence for her to finish her conversation.

"Hi Shantel, how are you? Hi Andre!" Rachel looked stressed but greeted us both with a hug and a kiss.

"Happy birthday babes," I said and handed over her gift.

"Shantel, you know the thing you had asked me on the phone? Well he's here," she whispered.

Burn

Chapter Six:
Depleting Pleasure

"Oh." I was surprised. Andre overheard Rachel's disclosure.

"I knew it! Why did we bother come here? Shantel, let's go. We're not going in there." Andre was so angry, he was unrecognisable.

"I'm sorry. I didn't know he would turn up and I don't even know who he came with," Rachel explained.

I turned to Rachel and apologised. I was embarrassed by Andre's reaction. What could I do?

"Hun, you should go back inside," I encouraged her to enjoy her party. She didn't need to hear the impending argument between Andre and I.

'I'll call you tomorrow." We hugged and she went back inside. Andre and I stood outside the entrance.

"Andre, we came all this way and I think it's only right we go in and say hello! If you don't want to stay, then we won't. I really can't see what your problem is!" I was feeling disappointed and embarrassed by his reaction.

Why was he so insecure? Here I was, barely able to see and totally dependent on him. I told him I wouldn't go out of my way to say hello to my ex. My heart sank. My ex was in there. I hadn't seen him for years. This was the man who had stolen my heart and I would always care for him. I had memories of a great relationship but that was all it was now — memories. The relationship was not perfect by any means. I had shared my feelings about my past to Andre. Perhaps I was too honest with him. I wanted Andre to concentrate on us, not a man from my past. If I was supposed to be with my ex-boyfriend, then surely, I would still be. I loved Andre and I needed him. Why would I be swayed by any other man? I was too scared to go into the building alone; it was dark and I wouldn't be able to see anything or anyone anyway. Andre was my eyes right now.

"If you go in there you can make your own way home!" he barked.

"How do you expect me to get home Andre? I came with you so I have to leave with you!" I was distraught. "You need to be stronger Andre! All I can see right now is a weak man. Why are you so pathetic?" I was now angry.

"Let's go. I'm not staying. You're not going in there. I don't want you coming to Bedford again by yourself from now on. Rachel knew he was going to be there. She had planned this all along. I blame her! Does she want you and your ex together again?" Andre was furious.

I was convinced Andre was suffering from paranoia. He was jealous and insecure, but this was extreme. Ok, my ex-boyfriend was in there and I could understand why he would be uncomfortable, but he was so wrong about Rachel. How dare he blame her for this? Rachel, like me, couldn't see why this was causing such drama. I hoped that this hadn't ruined her big evening.

"I wouldn't be so bothered if we had gone somewhere and one of your ex-partners was there!" I shouted.

This was disastrous. We had driven all the way from London to my hometown, only to return home again. I sat in the car upset that I was missing my cousin's birthday. I wanted to stay and celebrate with my friends. This was my car but I couldn't drive it. I was vulnerable and needed him. I felt helpless. I wanted to take the keys from him and tell him to make his own way home. How dare he? Andre turned on the engine of my car and proceeded towards the M1. We had been on the motorway for five minutes arguing about what had just happened.

"I'm so disappointed in you. Why do you hate the idea of being around a man I've had a relationship with? You have exes and I don't care about them at all!" I exclaimed.

Andre had not lived the life of a saint. He had told me just how he had treated women in the past. At one point, he had been with a string of women, sometimes three or four at the same time. There were women all over London, Manchester and even Paris that he had used for his own selfish pleasure. I accepted his past but he didn't want to accept mine.

Within minutes we were on the M1. Only two lanes were open southbound. We were in the slow lane, picking up speed. The vehicles travelling in the fast lane raced past us. The hard shoulder was shut because of road works. Andre slowed down. Cars and lorries whizzed past us. The car had now stopped in the slow lane.

"Andre, why have you stopped?" I asked, feeling nervous.

He stepped out of the car without saying a word, slammed the door and walked off towards the rear. I was glued to my seat. I couldn't move. I couldn't breathe. There was no escape. He had parked so close to the roadworks that I couldn't open the passenger door. I looked out of the rear window. All I could see were bright lights coming quickly towards me. My vision was further distorted by the lights. I knew I couldn't get out of the driver side as it was too risky. My heart thumped in my chest. I started sweating though my hands were cold. My head hurt and I felt dizzy. Was I about to faint? That would have been better than seeing a forty-foot truck ploughing into the back of my car. Then, I smelt cigarette smoke. The stench intensified as he walked closer to the passenger side.

"Andre, what the hell are you doing?"

He didn't answer. I opened the window and shouted again.

"Andre, what are you doing?!"

He strolled behind the orange and white road work barriers. He pulled on his cigarette and I sensed him glaring at me.

"Andre! What the fuck are you doing?!" I bellowed.

The situation reminded me of the horrific car accident I had been involved in not long before meeting Andre. My car had been written off. I recalled the car spinning, turning several times and then slamming against the central reservation of a motorway. Andre knew I still had awful flashbacks about the accident and was now a nervous passenger. But here he was, tormenting me, deliberately. How sick was this man? I opened the window further.

"I'm finishing my cigarette." Andre stood beside the car. I put the hazard lights on to indicate that there was a problem. I took out my mobile phone and called Rachel.

"Rachel, I'm on the M1. I'm scared. Andre drove us onto the motorway and has stopped the car. There are cars speeding past me. He is outside the car having a fucking smoke. I need to be picked up!" I uttered in panic. "I don't feel safe!" I yelled so that he could hear.

"What the fuck? Where are you on the M1?" Rachel shouted in fear.

"We literally joined it five minutes ago, so not far. I'm so sorry but I need your help."

I said it loud enough so that Andre could hear my anguish and that I was telling Rachel about his evil, irrational actions. How could a man who loved me and was fully aware of my anxiety about driving at night do this? How could a man who claimed he wanted to spend the rest of his life with me put me in danger? Andre pulled on his cigarette for the last time and climbed back into the car. This man and his tobacco stench were like poison in my car. I wanted to vomit.

"What's the matter with you? You're an idiot!" I was so angry.

"Take me back to Bedford now!" I demanded.

"No, I'll take you home." He seemed calm. Perhaps he had realised the danger he had put me in for his selfish need to have a smoke.

"If you choose to put your life at risk, then that's your prerogative. What gives you the right to jeopardise my life?" I needed answers.

"I'm taking you home." Andre started the engine, turned the hazard lights off and began to drive down the dark, unlit motorway.

I still didn't get the answer I wanted from him. I called Rachel.

"Andre is driving down the motorway now. He says he is taking me home. I will call you when I get in." I was scared and didn't trust the man sitting in the driver's seat.

"Shantel, are you sure. We're making our way to the car as we speak." Rachel was sniffing. This arsehole had upset the birthday girl.

"Babe, I'm so sorry. Please don't cry. This man is taking me home. I will contact you later but please try to enjoy the rest of your evening. I'm so sorry. Love you." I was deeply apologetically.

The phone call distracted me from the danger on the road, and now I saw that we were on a clear stretch of the motorway. I was still angry beyond words.

"How dare you stop the car on the motorway for a smoke? Are you insane?!"

I wanted to lay into him. He was an evil bastard. His stench filled the car and I simply wanted to get out. We were now in the Brent Cross area. I could tell by the familiar lights.

"Pull over and let me out!"

"No, I'm taking you home."

"Let me out!" I ordered. "You can't imprison me in my own car. Let me out."

"No," he repeated sternly.

We were driving in slow moving traffic through Cricklewood.

"I said let me out!"

I threw a punch at his shoulder, then his neck. I started slapping and punching. Punch after punch landed on his head. He tried to drive while defending himself from the blows. I didn't stop. I couldn't stop. I saw red and wanted him to feel physical pain for the emotional trauma he inflicted on me. The tears flooded down my face. He then managed to pull into an industrial estate. I thought he would stop driving but he continued to drive further and deeper into the deserted space.

"Stop the car so I can get out!" I yelled at him.

He finally stopped the car and I scrambled out. I couldn't see. It was pitch black. I started to run in the direction we had driven from. I wasn't sure where I was but I needed to get away from him.

"Shantel, it's not safe here. I promised I would take you home." Andre said, walking quickly behind me.

I could hear his steps speed up until he also began running. He tugged at my arm to stop me. I pulled loose and punched his chest. I threw more punches as I tried to get away.

"Leave me alone!" I screamed. "I'll find my own way home. I will go somewhere, anywhere away from you!"

This was an anger that I'd never experienced before. Andre gripped my jacket and in a swift movement, I released the zip and took it off. He held the jacket in his hand. I would have taken all my clothes off to get away from him if I needed to. I imagined myself running to the main road and finding a taxi rank so I could get away. But it was difficult. I could hardly see my feet as the estate was poorly lit. There was no one around. There was no point screaming for help. Fuck.

"Shantel, I promise I will take you home and then I will leave you. I won't stay in the flat tonight. I just want to take you home. You won't be able to travel by yourself Shantel. You can't see.'"

I hated him for making the obvious apparent.

"I have never hit anyone before in my life. You put me in danger and have not even apologised. I hate you. You put on this pretence, going to church on a Sunday, praising God, yet your actions tonight were so disgusting. Is this how you handle your emotions? I hate you for what you've done."

The tears poured down my face and clothes. I had never been in such a hostile situation before. This was alien to me. I started making my way to the car, realising that I needed to get back to the flat to pack a bag and leave. Andre took my arm to escort me back to the car.

"Leave me alone. Don't fucking touch me!" I barked.

I got into the car and sat in silence for the journey back to the flat. True to his word, he took me back to Clapham and escorted me to the front door. He pushed the heavy door which squeaked as it opened. It was a familiar sound I was happy to hear. I took two steps into the flat, turned around and slammed the door in Andre's face. I clicked on the latch and walked into the living room. I went to the kitchen to shut the blinds. That would stop him from looking in.

"Shantel, can you open the door please?" Andre asked politely through the letter box as if this whole ugly episode had never happened. He was unbelievable.

"No! Go away!" I shouted.

Andre banged on the front door.

"Shantel, can you please let me in?" He sounded less calm and more agitated.

I walked towards the front door so he could hear my words clearly.

"Leave me alone. If you continue banging on the door, you'll wake up the neighbours and trust me, tonight, you are not stepping foot in this flat. So, fuck off you shit-head." I felt nothing but hatred towards the man.

I needed time to plan my next step. The banging on the door had stopped and Andre had gone. I didn't care where he went. No man had ever treated me so appallingly. I struggled to see the screen on my phone but I managed to send Rachel a text to tell her that I was home. I couldn't bring myself to talk to her as I was ashamed of Andre's behaviour. I sat on the sofa in the living room. I needed to consider my options one by one. One — I'd rented out my flat. To get the tenant out would take at least two months. Where would I go in the meantime? Two — I needed an operation but the hospital hadn't confirmed a date. I knew my pre-op assessment was due in the next few weeks. Three — we'd only just returned from Dominica where my parents were living. They couldn't look after me after an operation as there was nowhere for them to stay. Four — I needed support but who could I get it from? It's all very well having friends that I could party with but when it came to the crunch, who would take care of me after the operation? Everyone had their own lives. Some of my friends had confided in me that Andre had not always made them feel welcome and slowly, one by one, they had stopped visiting me. Even Julie, who had introduced us, didn't bother to call me anymore.

I dragged myself to the bedroom, stripped off my clothes and chucked them into the linen basket as if I were a basketball player. I flopped on the bed and sat there feeling dazed and drained. I was tired and wanted to forget the entire embarrassing night. I went into the kitchen and poured myself a large glass of red wine. I drank it quickly. The second glass of wine I took to the bedroom and placed on the bedside table while I chose my nightwear. I was starting to feel the effects of the fruity, sweet alcohol. It was a feeling I needed to dissolve the pain, even if it was temporarily. I put the TV on and flicked through the channels. Distraction was what I needed tonight. I would deal with my issues in the morning.

My mobile phone was ringing. I looked at the time. 10:30. Maybe I'd drunk too much wine last night, but I had to drown my sorrows. It was Andre calling. I didn't answer. The house phone rang. There was no handset in the bedroom, so I didn't answer that either. I wasn't getting out of bed for him. My mobile phone rang again. I took a deep breath and hesitantly answered.

"Shantel, I'm sorry. I'm downstairs. Can I come up please?" Andre sounded meek.

"Why?" I questioned, wanting him to suffer immensely for his behaviour.

"I want to talk to you, just talk. I need you to listen. I am so sorry Shantel." Andre sounded genuine, but I was so unsure about who he really was now.

"Come up," I replied, wondering what bullshit reasoning he had in store for me.

I pressed the 'call end' button on the phone, put on my dressing gown and went to the toilet. There was no point talking to him with my bladder full. I glanced at myself in the mirror, washed the sleep out of my eyes and dried my face. I was unsure about what I wanted to do. Andre had revealed a very ugly side to his personality that I didn't care for. Could this relationship come back from the brink? If I wasn't living with him and waiting for an operation, there would be nothing left to say. I was vulnerable and he had used my weakness against me. This was a scenario I had chosen to avoid previously by only getting involved in relationships that I knew would never materialise. I took a risk with Andre and let myself down.

Andre knocked. He didn't use his key probably because he knew I'd left my key in the lock. One of my favourite films as a teenager sprung to mind — 'The Lost Boys'. There was a particular scene where Michael, the head vampire tells Sam, 'Don't ever invite a vampire into your house, you silly boy. It renders you powerless!'

Andre was becoming impatient and knocked again. He should thank me for not cutting up his clothes or painting the flat red. I walked into the hallway to open the door. I didn't even greet him as he wasn't worthy. I walked into the living room as he shut the door behind him and followed me. He was still wearing the same clothes from the night before.

"Hi," he said softly.

I sat on the sofa in my usual spot. He pulled a dining chair and sat down facing me. He was still wearing his shoes but at least they weren't on the rug.

"What have you got to say for yourself?" I was still seething and embarrassed by this man who just a few weeks ago was looking at diamond engagement rings with me.

"I'm sorry Shantel." Andre was staring at me intently, trying to gauge my feelings and whether I had softened towards him.

"I should have handled last night differently. I didn't want to go into the party. I didn't want to be in there with your ex-boyfriend." Andre looked remorseful.

"Why?" I needed the truth, a real explanation.

"We discussed this before. I didn't want to be put in that position." Andre avoided the question.

"What did you think he would do to you?" I asked feeling exhausted.

"Nothing. I just didn't want him looking at you and reminiscing about the past."

"Don't you trust me?" I asked. This was the only conclusion I could arrive at.

"It's not you babe," he stated.

"Don't call me babe. Carry on," I instructed.

"It's not you Shantel. It's men. I don't trust their intentions around you. Men that say they want to be your friend really don't, because they'll always want something from you."

Andre was a university graduate, but I wondered why he was so clueless.

"Of course, if they're my friends they are going to want something from me. It's called a friendship Andre. Don't you understand that? Not everyone has an ulterior motive. Why are we talking about friends? This is not about friends. Andre, this is about your actions last night."

He was deliberately swaying the conversation in a different direction. I wanted to focus on last night and him to explain why he had acted so selfishly.

"I'm sorry for what I did. I shouldn't have stopped on the motorway. Rachel was in the wrong as she invited your ex." He still didn't get it.

"Whether she did or didn't is irrelevant. I was with you. No one else. Do you think that I want to be with anyone else? Am I so weak that I would just run off with an ex? Do you value yourself as a man? Do you love the person you are? If you did, you wouldn't be here now telling me this bullshit! I wanted to kill you last night. You were pure evil. I've never acted like that with any man."

"Shantel, I don't want to lose you. I love you and I am so very sorry for my actions. I wouldn't hurt you. I want you to be happy." He spoke with a panic in his voice.

"Love is knowing I have an issue with night driving, that I am a nervous passenger especially at night, and being understanding about that. Love is not leaving me in a car in the middle of a busy motorway, while you go off and have a cigarette."

"Shantel, please tell me, are we ok? I don't want to lose you. I will do whatever it takes to make things right," Andre pleaded.

"You scared me. You were disrespectful to Rachel. You need to call her to apologise. You ruined her night and I will never forgive you for that." I was firm and clear about what I wanted from him. I wouldn't budge until this was done.

"Shantel, Rachel disrespected me knowing your ex was invited. I can't apologise for that." Andre was being stubborn.

"Andre, if you want to rectify this situation you need to speak to Rachel to make amends. You can't blame her for your actions and insecurities."

We talked more but kept going around in circles. I was still appalled at his behaviour and didn't want him around me anymore. I was feeling nauseous, probably from a combination of the red wine and his presence.

"I don't want you around me today. Do what you need to do and leave."

I was amazed at my strength. Ever since my vision had deteriorated, I had lost confidence but after this, I wouldn't be a pushover. I wanted to be at home alone so I could think and put everything into perspective.

"I'm just going to have a shower before I go. Can I come back tonight?" Andre looked like a sad puppy dog.

"I don't know." I responded.

He wasn't getting off the hook that easily. After his shower, he said goodbye and that he would call me later. I wished I'd taken the car keys from him.

I spent the rest of the day talking to my close friends about last night's events. I finished the day with a long hot soak in the bath whilst listening to music and sipping on more red wine. Andre called me at 10 that evening.

"Can I come home?" he asked.

"Ok," I answered.

I've backed down, I've given in
This man has got me in a position where I can't win
Why right now? I'm at a disadvantage
I need my vision sorted
I've seen a side that I don't like
Give up the relationship, or do I fight?
Maybe I just need to forgive, be patient and await a new day

Chapter Seven:
Three

My feelings for Andre were hardened by the recent events. I'd never had my safety compromised at the hands of a boyfriend. How could a man who claimed to care about me, hurt me in the way he had? Andre was being extremely cautious around me, said he needed me and didn't want me to leave him. He fractured our relationship with his insecurities. I was torn, but I decided that we could work through our issues. I prayed that the pending operation would restore normality for me. I felt scared and lost.

One week after the drama of that night, my pre-op assessment appointment letter arrived through the post. I collapsed on the sofa, distraught. I could see the letter was from Moorfields but I couldn't read the print. This was frustrating, but I just had to sit tight and wait until Andre came home from work to tell me the date. I was now used to Andre's offers of help, though I didn't want to depend on him. Being reliant on a jealous and insecure man to help me with some of the simplest chores didn't feel good at all. I loved him but he had let me down. Had I let myself down? I had to shake off this line of questioning and focus on getting better. I kept busy during the day to distract myself from the reality of what would be revealed to me later that evening. He came home at 7 and I asked him to read the letter.

"Your pre-op assessment is next Wednesday. I'll come with you," he added, matter of factly. "It'll be fine."

"Ok. A week to go." I spoke more to calm myself down.

I got up and headed to the kitchen to dish out our dinner. Conversation that evening was limited and I was happily zoning out in front of the television, watching programme after programme, none of which involved any mental engagement.

Wednesday soon arrived. I said a silent prayer as we walked arm in arm into the hospital. It wasn't long before my name was called. I took a deep breath as we followed the nurse into the cubicle. My legs buckled slightly beneath me but Andre steadied me by putting his arm around my waist.

"Are you alright?" he asked tenderly.

"Yes, I'm fine," I lied. I had a slight headache but put it down to tension from the anxiety and stress of my predicament.

The nurse checked my oxygen levels, blood pressure and temperature.

Do you have a sore throat?" she queried.

"No." I replied.

"Is there any chance you could be pregnant?" she asked.

"No." I replied. Unlikely I thought to myself. "Out of curiosity, if I were, what would happen?"

Andre raised his eyebrows.

"Well, you wouldn't be able to have the operation until the second trimester," the nurse answered.

"If you're not sure then you should do a pregnancy test. If anything comes up, then contact the consultant's secretary with your results. We cannot do pregnancy tests here anymore due to a change in policy." She smiled sweetly at me while taking the blood pressure cuff off my arm.

"Oh, a pregnancy test? I'm not pregnant." I wanted to continue with the rest of the assessment. I wondered if I had been slightly short in my tone with my response to the nurse, but I could only focus on having the operation and getting better so my life could go back to normal.

"Everything is fine. You'll have to wait for your appointment letter for surgery. Hopefully it won't be long." The nurse then told us we were free to leave. I thanked her and we headed out of the hospital.

Blossom Tree | Sharon Fevrier

Closer. Closer. Closer. This was my mantra. My life was just around the corner. I said another silent prayer in the car, asking God to keep me strong and guide me through this journey. I wanted my eyesight to improve so that I could be in control of my life again. I used to be funny and confident. I used to see my world clearly. All my life I feared being a burden yet here I was, helpless and incapable.

A week went by as I occupied myself with washing, cooking, waiting for the letter, watching television, chatting on the phone and waiting for the letter some more. My mobile rang as I headed to the toilet. I picked it up from the sofa and continued to the loo.

"Hi babe," Louisa greeted.

"Hey darling," I tried to stifle the fact that I was on the toilet.

"On the toilet, again Shantel?" Louisa knew me too well.

"Yes" I giggled. "Though, I've got this period pain that won't go away and my boobs are still achy," I revealed.

"Babe, I don't mean to scare you, but you should get a test." Louisa sounded concerned. She was always my voice of reason. I had known her since we were both nineteen. We'd met through a mutual friend at a seventies disco night in Stoke Newington. She was not just my friend, she was my sister and Andre seemed to like her. We spoke almost every day and she knew me better than most.

"What do you mean?" I asked. I understood but refused to acknowledge her words.

"Shantel. Get a pregnancy test babe," she said in exasperation. "I know you don't want to think about it but the symptoms you describe are so similar to other women I've talked to when they were pregnant. Surely you've thought about this?" Louisa wasn't beating around the bush, but I wanted to hide behind the bushes.

"I'll get a test, but being pregnant...wow...I don't even want to think about what that means. Right now, I feel like going out, getting a little tipsy and facing the real world." I sighed.

"Honey, that's not a good idea. Tonight. Do the test tonight. Go to the chemist, pluck up the courage, pick up a test and do it," she encouraged.

"Okay. I'll do it today. I'll wait for Andre to get home so he can read the frigging stick. I'll call you later babe."

"Okay honey. You take care," she replied.

Louisa was my rock and was keeping me sane throughout my ordeal. I needed her friendship and was happy that she was strong and there for me no matter what. There was that word again. *Need.* Why was that such a struggle for me to need someone, to be dependent on anyone?

The key turned in the door. Andre was home from work. I counted his steps into the living room from the front door. One, two, three, four, five. I sat patiently on the sofa.

"Hi babe." Andre greeted me with a kiss on my lips.

"You ok?" I replied. "How was work?" I thought I would soften the blow with the pleasantries before I dropped the bombshell about my recent purchase.

"Yeah, good thanks babe." He washed his hands in the kitchen and sat beside me on the sofa. "What have you been up to?" he enquired. Normally, my day would be filled with a mind-numbing routine. This day was different. I was nervous.

"Andre. I bought a pregnancy test. What with my achy boobs, my period pains and being extra tired, I had to."

I stopped talking as Andre's expression changed to a look of shock and horror. I stood up and pulled out the pregnancy test from a bag on the dining table.

"I can't deal with this right now."

He stood up and went into the bedroom. I followed him. He took off his suit, tie and shirt. He pulled out a T-shirt and tracksuit from his wardrobe and dressed swiftly.

Blossom Tree | Sharon Fevrier

"Andre, we need to talk about this and I need to do this test. Please Andre!" I pleaded as he busied himself with getting dressed.

"Shantel, you're not pregnant and I'm going to the gym." He put his trainers on and headed towards the front door.

"I'll see you in a while." He opened the door and slammed it shut behind him.

There I was, in the flat alone with my pregnancy test. Ironically, I had held my pee until he had returned home but now I needed to release. So I did. After the bathroom call, I helped myself to dinner and called Louisa. Her number was easy to dial as I had memorised it years ago. I recounted the evening's events and decided I would tackle the subject again once he had returned from his workout. I realised he needed time to digest the possibility and repercussions of what the stick could show. He was scared. I was scared. I understood that we handled our fears in very different ways. I wasn't prepared to ignore the signs and brush them under the carpet though. I needed to know if the changes to my body were in my head, due to stress or because I was pregnant.

Two hours later, Andre returned home. I sat still on the sofa watching television. I didn't turn to look at him but I felt his eyes on me.

"Where's this test then?" he asked casually.

I pointed to the dining table but didn't speak. I could tell he'd been for a swim and not a gym workout because of the smell of chlorine that wafted past me as he sat down. I was upset that he had chosen to go out and leave me hanging with such an important issue to talk about.

"Are you ready now?" I asked sarcastically, feeling annoyed.

Andre reached over to the table and removed the white stick out of the packaging. He took my hand and led me to the bathroom.

"It's all yours," he said and walked back into the living room.

I pulled the lid off the stick and sat on the toilet. My heart was thumping in my chest. After a few minutes, I slowly walked back into the living room and sat down on the sofa with the white stick in my hand. I handed it to him. We waited and waited for what seemed like an eternity. My heart was still racing so I took a deep breath to calm my nerves.

Andre took a deep breath too. "Two blue lines Shantel. You're pregnant."

I sat there in silence. Pregnant? Me? Pregnant? I was taking my birth control pills religiously! No breaks, and when there were breaks, we were careful. This was poor timing. My life had already been turned upside down because of my visual disturbance, by not being at work and by a man who could only be described as jealous and possessive.

"How could you be so stupid?" Andre barked angrily. He stood up and walked to the window.

"What are you talking about? I asked, equalling his hostility. "Do you think I've planned this? It takes two to make a baby Andre, so you're equally responsible!"

"Were you trying to trap me?" Andre was on the attack. "Are you going to get rid of it?" he asked as he sat down beside me.

Trap him? Get rid of it? Those words cut me like a knife. The tears started rolling down my face. I couldn't believe my ears. Why couldn't he be supportive? He wasn't the only one in shock. I needed to be alone. I stood up, went into the hallway and put my jacket and trainers on.

"What are you doing?" Andre asked.

"I need to get away from you. I can't believe you. How dare you think I would have an abortion? I need to be by myself, far away from you."

I grabbed the keys from my handbag and then decided I should carry my bag, just in case I needed to pay for something. Maybe for a hotel room or a cab somewhere. Where? I didn't know. I took my mobile phone from the charger and headed towards the door. Andre started putting his trainers on.

"Don't follow me!" I blurted out as the tears began to stream down my face.

"Where are you going?" he asked as I slammed the door behind me. I took a deep breath. If I stayed in well-lit places I'd be fine. My vision was worse at night but this did not stop me from wanting to escape the cold and hostile environment of what was my home. I walked steadily down the stairs to the exit of the building. Freedom. I walked along the main road. It was a typical Friday night in Clapham. How I wished I could laugh and joke like the hordes of people I walked past on Lavender Hill. The air was buzzing. I decided to walk towards Clapham Common and pulled my mobile phone out of my pocket. I wasn't ready to make a call. I was still in shock and wondered why I was in this mess. The cool air helped to relax me a little. A baby. Me, a mother? Well, it wasn't unheard of, a 30-year-old being a mother. I could do this. Things had to change with my vision but this would put a hold on my operation.

"Shantel!" His voice bellowed close behind me. I turned around and saw Andre running fast towards me. I was already opposite Clapham Common underground station. I turned around and continued walking.

"I need to be alone!" I shouted at him.

Andre was stubborn and chose to ignore my request. He was now walking alongside me.

"I told you to leave me alone. Why are you here?" I asked, suddenly feeling exhausted.

"Shantel, we need to talk about this." Andre explained.

"I need space. It sounds like you're blaming me."

"Shantel, you need to sign a contract." Andre blurted.

"A contract?" I looked at him, shocked at what he had said and wondered what his intentions were.

"Yes, a contract," he repeated.

I stopped walking and turned toward Andre. I wiped away the tears with the palm of my hand. I didn't need to cry anymore. I couldn't be any more shocked after hearing his venomous words. Andre was being a fool, a scared rabbit, and if he thought I would sign any contract, he was deliriously mad.

"Having a baby is not a business deal. You're being a complete idiot. I have asked you to leave me alone. If you don't, I will do something drastic. Do you understand me?"

I didn't even know what I would do, but it sounded good to say it. Andre had told me that he'd had a girlfriend who had tried to kill herself when they were together. I bet he was the driving force! Perhaps he didn't want a similar experience and that may have been running through his mind. No, I would never do that. There would be a different type of punishment for him.

"I'm going back to the flat. I don't want you there tonight. In fact, I'm going to think long and hard about our relationship because right now, you are not being a lover or a friend. You're a stranger to me, you arsehole! You're full of shit!" I shouted firmly.

I was pregnant. I needed time to think. I didn't want to have a baby alone because I didn't know what my vision would be like once the baby was born. I needed Andre to be the man he'd proclaimed to be when we had first met. Not the scared mouse he was now. Perhaps this was the reason I always dated men that were older than me, with experience and who could handle any situation with maturity. Here I was, staring at a thirty-year-old, mentally under-developed boy, the father of my unborn child.

Andre took a deep breath as his eyes widened. "Shantel. Ok, I'll go to my brother's house tonight and will come tomorrow when we've both had time to think. I'll walk you back." Andre tried to take control of this situation.

"Andre, right now, I want you to go to hell. I want nothing to do with you. Just leave me alone."

I knew I was being harsh but I also wanted to claim back my independence. I knew it had been slipping away and because of the pregnancy it would continue to do so.

"I made my way here and I'll make my way back!" I shouted.

I watched the people around us, too preoccupied with their need for alcohol to notice our quarrel. This man I thought I'd loved was suddenly so very unattractive to me. I chuckled at the thought of it — Andre was becoming ugly. Was my vision so distorted or was it now becoming clearer?

"What's so funny?" Andre snapped.

"Andre, I just want peace, so please go. I'll take a slow walk back to the flat and I want to be alone when I get there."

"Ok." Andre agreed reluctantly, sounding exasperated as he headed back towards the flat.

I made my way over to the common and sat on a park bench. I watched the world go by for what felt like an eternity. Cars driving along the one-way system, couples walking hand in hand, queues of people lining up to get into bars and busy restaurants. I touched my stomach.

"It's me and you kid," I reassured the mass of growing cells in my womb. "Mummy will love you forever."

I sat there for a little while longer and realised I was hungry. If I was hungry, the baby was too. I didn't want to go back to the flat and cook, so decided to stop at the Chinese take-away on the way back. I ordered my favourite salt and pepper prawns with special fried rice. I couldn't wait to get home, turn on the television and demolish the mound of spicy food. I opened the door and to my relief Andre was nowhere to be seen.

"It really is just you and I kid!"

I was beginning to feel somewhat maternal. This felt good. I now had something positive to focus on. A little baby growing inside me, needing me, dependent on me. This marked the beginning of change in my life. Monday morning, I would book an appointment to see my GP. I locked the door to ensure we would be alone, just me and my baby.

The following morning, I woke up to the sound of my mobile phone vibrating. I didn't want to answer it. Why would someone want to disturb me from my sleep? I reached towards the floor to pick it up. I slowly began to remember that something was different. Oh yes, I had a baby inside me.

"Hello?" I answered sleepily.

"Hi," the voice replied.

It was Andre. There was silence as I didn't respond.

"I'm sorry Shantel. I didn't mean the things I said last night. I was in shock. I didn't expect this would happen now. I thought we would have more time together first and that the operation would have fixed your eye." Andre sighed. "I'm sorry."

"Andre, I can't understand why you would think that I would get pregnant deliberately," I replied.

"I'm sorry. I know you wouldn't. I was in shock and I reacted badly."

"Why would you think I would want to trap you? If you don't want to be part of this baby's life, then don't. I wouldn't try to force you."

This was a conversation I shouldn't be having. I was scared too. He didn't consider my feelings at all. Andre was yet again consumed with his own emotions.

"Shantel, let me take you out for lunch so we can talk about this. I am sorry and I want to make this right. We're going to be parents and we will have to find a way of working this out. I love you. I'll pick you up in one hour."

"Ok," I replied and then ended the call.

An hour passed and I was on my way down to the car. I wore a sun dress, strappy flat sandals, lip gloss and perfume. I didn't eat breakfast. I also didn't realise I'd slept until 12:30. Clearly, I was exhausted. The shower I had was revitalising and gave me the energy I needed. Andre was waiting outside the car with a bunch of flowers in his hand. As I got closer I realised they were my favourite flowers.

"Lilies. Thank you. They're lovely." I managed to be gracious and polite.

I needed to hear what he had to say before I made a life changing decision. A song by The Clash came to my mind — 'Should I Stay Or Should I Go?' Andre opened the passenger door for me and I got into the car. He was trying and wanted forgiveness.

"Where are we going? I asked.

"It's a surprise," Andre announced.

We drove in silence as soulful music played from the stereo. Andre had organised a playlist of my favourite love songs. He was pulling out all the stops because he knew he had work to do. He didn't know that I was already smiling inside, not because of him, but because of the angel growing inside me. Was it a boy or a girl? Whatever the case, it was my angel. We arrived outside Battersea Park. I was beginning to dread the forthcoming conversation. Andre paid for a parking ticket and placed it on the windscreen. He then walked around to the passenger side and opened the door. He offered his hand to help me out of the car. Next, he opened the boot and pulled out two plastic bags full of groceries, grabbed the blanket from the back seat of the car and held his arm out for me to take. We strolled into the park full of playful children and yapping dogs. There were lots of other people in the park with the same idea as Andre. He had organised a picnic where we could be alone to eat and talk in the fresh, warm air of a sunny summer's afternoon. The romantic gesture had softened my heart.

We discussed our hopes and fears about having a child. I had no idea of how far gone I was and so we couldn't predict when the baby was due. This was without a doubt the most adult situation I had ever found myself in. We would be transformed from a couple to a family. I wasn't sure what reaction I would get from my family and friends once I'd told them about my pregnancy. This would be my parents' first grandchild. Andre was already an uncle to his brother's and sister's children. We lived in a stylishly decorated one-bedroom flat, suitable for a young, trendy couple wanting to just eat, drink and be merry in Clapham. It wasn't suitable for a family. We had a lot to discuss.

It was now July and Andre accompanied me to my GP and first pre-natal appointments. My GP confirmed that I was six weeks pregnant. I chose to have our baby at St Thomas' Hospital as this was where I had appointments for my sickle cell. The staff knew me well and would be able to provide the care I needed. It was now an exciting time for me. The baby gave me something positive to focus on. I was nurturing a little life. I'd heard that a woman's emotional state through her pregnancy could transfer to the baby. Though I wasn't sure whether it was true or not, I tried to keep in good spirits. As time went on, I did become happier but remained anxious. What would be of this little life inside me? Would the baby be happy and healthy? Would I even be able to see the baby? I was worried that my eyesight wouldn't improve enough to see my baby's little features. Would he or she resemble me in anyway, or would he or she take after Andre? There were so many questions.

I had to go back to Moorfields to have a discussion with the consultant about my pregnancy and upcoming operation. He confirmed I wouldn't be able to have the op until the second trimester and the surgery date was rescheduled.

It was a Saturday morning and we were both in bed. I was awake though Andre was still asleep beside me. My bladder control was now almost non-existent. I slid out of the bed and headed to the toilet. After a very long pee, I wiped myself but I felt something different. I looked at the tissue. Red. There was blood.

Chapter Eight:
Two Steps Back

"Andre, come here please," I asked in a calm but assertive tone. "I need you now."

I could hear Andre shifting out of bed.

"What is it?" he replied as he stood at the bathroom door.

"There's blood Andre. I'm bleeding." I stood still because I was in shock and too scared to move.

"Let me see." Andre looked at the tissue in my hand then peered into the toilet bowl.

"I've got to go to the hospital," I said.

We quickly got ourselves washed and dressed, drank some coffee and made our way to Waterloo for a train to A&E. We were directed towards the antenatal department where I was immediately put into a bed. Andre was silent and hadn't spoken to me since we had left the flat. As I lay in bed, I turned to Andre.

"Are you ok?" I asked, disappointed that he hadn't asked me how I was feeling.

"Yes, fine," he replied sternly, flicking through a newspaper.

Perhaps I shouldn't have dared interrupt his thoughts? What on earth had I done to deserve that response? I was feeling vulnerable, scared and in need of some love, comfort and reassurance. Instead I was given nothing but the cold shoulder. It then dawned on me that I was alone. I needed emotional support but I wasn't going to get it from him. He wanted to sit beside me in the hospital but he didn't want to either talk, acknowledge or show me any affection. Inside I was hurting but decided to hold it together. I suddenly wanted him to go, and turned my back to him. I called Louisa for the support I needed. I wanted him to know that I did have other people to turn to. In reality though, I knew I wasn't alone. I spoke to God the whole time, telling him my fears, my hopes and my dreams. As always, he listened and gave me the comforting arm I needed.

The silent wait was painful but eventually a doctor entered the cubicle and pulled the curtain to give us some privacy. After introducing herself, she started to perform some tests, poking and prodding my belly gently. I didn't feel any pain. She informed me that I needed a scan and proceeded to rub the cold gel on my stomach and probe for any signs of life.

"There we are. Heartbeat. Everything looks normal." The doctor smiled.

I breathed a sigh of relief.

"It's common for some women to experience bleeding at this stage of pregnancy. The bleeding should stop but if it continues you'll need to come back."

Andre hadn't asked the doctor a single question. He just listened. He looked like he was holding his breath. I knew he was worried but I couldn't understand how he could be so distant towards me. The doctor instructed me to get plenty of rest and not to lift anything heavy. I thanked her and slid out of the bed. I looked at Andre, whose eyes appeared vacant.

"Are you ready?" I asked him.

"Yes. Let's go." he replied. He took my arm and we walked out of the hospital, again in silence. The drive home was awkward but thankfully, the car stereo filled the silence with the sounds of Mary J Blige's 'What's The 411?' album. I was also grateful that it was a quick one as I wanted to discuss Andre's lack of support once we were indoors.

Andre opened the front door and allowed me to enter the flat first. I kicked off my trainers and he followed me into the living room.

"Why didn't you talk to me at the hospital?" I asked.

He looked uncomfortable and took a seat at the dining table facing me. He didn't answer at first, but I needed to understand.

"I was worried about losing the baby," he replied quietly.

"Ok, but what about how I was feeling? Did you consider me?" I quizzed.

"I know," Andre sighed. "But the idea of losing the baby worried me. I was scared and froze."

"Ok, but while you were busy freezing, the baby and I needed you. You weren't there for us." I wasn't about to let Andre off the hook so easily.

"I was there for you both Shantel. Don't say that. I took you to the hospital and I waited with you. Don't be unfair." Andre looked hurt by what I had said.

He didn't know how to articulate his feelings to me and so, emotionally, we were strangers. Yes, he was there for us physically, but that wasn't enough. I was already attached to the baby and so was he.

I felt alone
He was there, but not
I saw him there but I didn't feel his presence
I heard him turn the pages of the newspaper but he hadn't read a word
Not a hug, not a touch
Not a kiss or a gentle squeeze
Maybe he needed me more than we needed him?
RUBBISH! I wasn't there to reassure him!
But the baby and I make two, so weren't we in the majority?
He didn't even get me a cup of tea
What was really important to him?
Is this a sign of things to come?
I have to be strong. Strong enough for me and the little bump
We're ok baby, my emotions I can handle
You're a fighter, my tiny little bundle

September soon arrived and I was in my second trimester. The Bio Oil was becoming my best friend. I wasn't planning on getting ugly stretch marks. I carried that precious bottle wherever I went and carefully rubbed copious amounts of the oil on my belly morning, noon and night. My skin was smooth and I was desperate to keep it that way. The pregnancy had progressed well. The operation had been scheduled. I was feeling nervous about the procedure but ready all the same. I wanted to see my baby — all of my baby. That was so important to me. How could I have a baby and not be able to see her eyes, eyebrows, hair, fingers and toes? I knew that I was being protected by a power much bigger than I was. The prayers were streaming in from so many different directions. I felt a warm glow and was happy about the possibility of seeing the world in a new light. I called my parents the night before I went into hospital for my operation. They were naturally worried about me. I put a brave face on and reassured them that their baby girl was fine and that no harm would come to their grandchild. They knew that Andre would take care of me. My father asked to speak to him. I could hear the conversation was heavy but Andre seemed to be able to handle it.

"Well, the procedure should last about an hour," Andre said.

"Of course, I will call you when she's back on the ward."

"That's my job. I have to look after her."

"Yes, we will speak tomorrow. Goodnight."

Andre handed the phone back to me. I understood why they felt Andre had to be the one to answer their questions. After all, he was the man who was looking after me. He was the father of my unborn child, their soon-to-be first grandchild. Besides, I needed Andre to support me and take the reins. Deep down inside I was still an old-fashioned girl, who wanted a man to take the lead. He needed to take care of his family as we were now the most important people in his life. We were dependent on him.

Andre escorted me down towards the operating theatre. He held my hand all the way through the long corridor of sterile white walls until he couldn't walk with me any further.

"Well, I'll see you on the other side," Andre said, putting on a brave face.

"Not if I see you first babe," I replied, adding a little humour to break the tension.

I followed the theatre nurse into the room and climbed onto the bed.

'*God, protect me and the little one.*' I said my silent prayer while the theatre staff were milling around.

The anaesthetic was administered and, before I knew it, I was counting backwards from ten. I decided to take the challenge and fight the hold of the drug. I wanted to reach at least number four or three but I could only remember counting down to six. I guess I had been through the anaesthetic process a few times and each time I tested myself to see the lowest number I could reach.

"Shantel, you're in recovery now darling," a Scottish voice murmured sweetly. "Would you like some water?" the voice asked.

I nodded but my eyes were still closed. I touched my stomach to let the little one know that I was ok. I could feel the eye patch. The nurse held the straw against my lips and I sucked the water out until I had drunk enough. My throat was sore from the intubation tube and the water temporarily soothed the irritation. As I lay in the bed, I wondered how long it would take for my eye to heal and how well my vision would improve. I prayed that when my baby came into the world I would be able to see her face clearly, if not perfectly. Soon, the porter came to wheel me back to the ward where Andre was waiting.

"Eye, eye stranger!" Andre said with a relieved tone in his voice.

"Eye, eye captain!" I replied.

Andre pulled my right hand from my stomach and squeezed it tight. My left eye was still closed as I was too scared to open it. I knew that if I opened it the right eye would also open.

"How did it go?" Andre asked the nurse.

"As expected," she replied. "She's doing well." I heard the nurse walk away as Andre sighed with relief.

"Can I get some water babe?" I wanted him to focus on something else.

"Sure babe." He opened the water bottle and put it to my mouth. I took a few sips.

The consultant arrived onto the ward and informed us he was happy with the way the surgery went. After checking me over, my dressing was changed and my eye drops were delivered to the ward. I was now ready to be discharged. Andre packed my belongings, helped me to get dressed and led me out to the car park across the road from the hospital. The cool air felt refreshing against my skin. I felt as if I was floating inside a bubble and letting the wind take me on a journey. That bubble kept me strong. I had faith so riding with the wind was not an issue.

It wasn't long before we arrived home. This time, I was happy Andre was with me. I wouldn't have wanted to go through the operation alone.

"Right. I'm going to get us a take-away. Is that ok?" Andre asked.

"Yeah babe, sounds good," I replied feeling tired and tender.

"The usual?" he asked.

"Sure," I confirmed as I took my jacket off and laid on the sofa.

I heard the front door shut. I picked up the remote control from its usual position on the arm of the sofa and turned on the TV. I flicked through the channels and found a music station for background noise. My mobile phone rang in my jacket pocket. I felt for the green answer button, hoping that I was pressing the correct key.

"Hello," I answered.

"Hi babe. How are you?" It was Louisa.

"A little sore but I'm ok," I replied.

"Where are you? Are you home now?" she quizzed.

"Yes, I'm at home hun. Andre has gone out to get some food. I'm really hungry so I hope he doesn't take too long."

"So, how did the operation go?" Louisa asked.

"As expected, according to the doctors. It will take a couple of weeks for the irritation from the stitches to go and then about six weeks until I have an idea of how much the vision has improved. I feel ok, but this baby needs some feeding. Ah, I've just remembered. There are some cheese puffs in the kitchen."

"What is it with you and cheesy puffs?!" joked Louisa.

"It's not me, you know. This child of mine needs them and what kind of mother would I be to neglect the baby's needs?" I giggled.

I stood up and walked slowly and steadily into the kitchen feeling my way with my hand, one eye open but squinting slightly.

"Be careful hun," Louisa sounded concerned.

"Babe, this place isn't big and, besides, I've already got my cheesy balls." I laughed as I sat back on the sofa, removing the remote control from underneath me.

We chatted more until Andre came home. I'd almost demolished the large packet of crisps, but still had space for my shredded beef with chilli. There really was nothing I loved better than food, but my appetite had grown even more. Andre dished up the takeaway and brought it to me on the sofa. He poured two glasses of water and sat beside me. He seemed happy we were home in one piece.

"A toast." Andre raised his glass.

"To?" I asked.

"A toast to your recovery and to our family. Let's toast to happiness and love. I do love you Shantel, with all my heart," Andre whispered sincerely.

"I love you too babe," I replied.

We clinked our glasses together, sipped some water then started to eat our food. Andre had taken two days off work to look after me and would return to work on Friday. I knew by then I would feel stronger and probably only need to use my eye patch at night. Even now, I almost felt normal.

Friday and I was on my own. I didn't mind being in the flat. It meant I could finally take possession of the remote control and be free of sports. I slept late most mornings and started on the road to recovery. I watched daytime TV and each evening Andre returned home to a cooked meal. I enjoyed being a housewife. I was still receiving pay from work so money wasn't an issue. My clothes began to feel tighter. I didn't see the point of buying maternity wear so I chose clothes in my wardrobe that were loose fitting. I would occasionally look in the mirror and wondered if I was still attractive. I really didn't care to know the answer. My hair was braided with extensions and brown highlights. My body was still the same apart from the bump at the front. The baby was being kind. My skin still felt the same. I just couldn't see the detail. Nothing was crystal clear. The vision in my left eye wasn't perfect but it was now my stronger eye. The vision in my right eye could only be described as looking through frosted glass but day by day I could see a very slow improvement. With time, my eye became less irritable and I wore my sunglasses to protect my eye from the elements when I went out. Autumn in London was particularly windy so I didn't feel out of place wearing my shades. I looked no different from the many stylish girls walking around in Clapham.

I considered life as a new mother with limited vision. What if I couldn't work and was wholly dependent on Andre to support me? My feelings towards him had now changed, affected by the commotion in Bedfordshire and my treatment on the motorway. The disrespect towards Rachel was unbelievable and he continued to blame her for something she hadn't done. His insecurities and jealousy overshadowed everything. Still, he was looking after me. Maybe it was because I was carrying his child. He told me he was still in love with me, but I didn't have that 'in love' feeling anymore. Perhaps after the honeymoon period, that feeling dies out? It wasn't supposed to fade so quickly, surely? Our relationship had been under a lot of pressure in the short time we had been together, though it had felt like years. Would that feeling ever return though? Did it need to? I loved Andre and wanted us to be a family, so I decided I would try to support him through his insecurities. I wasn't a healer or counsellor. I wasn't here to be his saviour, but I would do my utmost to make it work.

Christmas was steadily approaching. It was always an exciting time of year, though of course this year was different. People seemed happier, hopeful and remembered the importance of family. I was going to be pregnant on my birthday which was a week before Christmas and wondered how and if I would even celebrate. I was turning thirty-one. My baby was due in mid-March. Surely this was a good age to have a baby? I kept up my appointments at Moorfields. There was a little improvement in my eyes but not as much as I had hoped. My consultant informed me that I needed further surgery once I'd given birth. I took the news in my stride. I was a strong person, even though I was feeling exhausted and weak. The baby gave me something to focus on.

I often talked to the baby about my hopes and dreams. I chanted another mantra of mine: *'we were able, we were strong'*. The baby loved mangoes as much as I did. Every time I ate them, she had a party inside, wriggling, dancing and poking me. No one else in the world felt what I did. I updated my parents with weekly health and pregnancy reports. Back pain was a regular problem but I was doing all I could to alleviate the aching. My parents were due to arrive in the

New Year to support me through my last trimester. They were excited but worried all the same, and they continuously encouraged me to rest and relax. I was doing that in abundance as I had no choice. I missed interacting with the outside world. I couldn't use my laptop as the words on the screen were too small so I couldn't email or browse the internet. No driving either, so when I wasn't with Andre I relied on public transport and foot patrol. Thankfully, Clapham Junction had shops so window shopping became a favourite pastime. The Christmas decorations were already up giving me a warm, rich feeling. I had asked Andre to get the Christmas decorations from our storage so I could focus on decking the halls. It was the 1st of December and I was too impatient to wait for the weekend to decorate. I wanted fairy lights, tinsel, stockings, a tree and bells to transform the white walls of the flat. Andre was going to see the flat decorated in a way he had never seen before.

'Perfect!' I told myself. It was 5 o'clock and I had finally finished. I cooked a dinner for Andre. I slipped on my trainers and coat. I pulled my hat over my braids, grabbed my purse, keys and mobile phone and then headed out of the door. Sainsbury's Local was just a two-minute walk away.

The shop was busy with commuters. I took a basket and whizzed around to find turkey steaks, basmati rice and sweetcorn. While queuing I noticed my mobile phone was ringing.

"Hello?" I answered not knowing who the caller was. I still couldn't see the name on the screen of my phone.

"Hi babe. Are you out?" Louisa asked.

"Yeah. Just paid for my bits in Sainsbury's, but going home now.

I started to waddle up the road with my phone in one hand and shopping bag in the other.

"I put my decorations up today," I told her, as that was the highlight of my day.

"Really? That's early!" she laughed.

I told her about my decorations, then was interrupted by a deep voice beside me.

"Hello Shantel." The voice was familiar.

"I turned to my left and saw my ex Mason walking past me.

"Hiya Mason," I replied as he continued walking.

"Who was that?" Louisa quizzed.

"That was Mason. Remember him from university days?"

I explained that Mason's daughter had a childminder in the same block that we lived in. A few months before, Andre and I had bumped into him. Andre was unhappy that Mason knew where we lived. I recalled Andre's face of thunder when I introduced them to each other. Andre sulked for days afterwards. Louisa and I continued our conversation about Christmas decorations and what I would make for dinner. Before long, I was back inside the flat seasoning the turkey steaks to grill. The front door opened so I told Louisa I would call her back the following day.

"Hi babe!" I greeted him excitedly.

Andre didn't reply and slammed his keys down on the glass dining table. He loosened his tie and took of his suit jacket.

"Did you have a nice conversation with Mason?" he alleged with a raised voice.

"Excuse me?" I uttered, stunned.

"I saw you talking to your ex. Was it a nice conversation?"

I wondered where his line of questioning was going.

"I didn't have a conversation with him." I paused and thought about what he was saying to me. "Were you spying on me?" the fury rose inside me. "You were spying on me!" I shouted. "Why?"

"I saw you talking to him. What were you saying to him?" Andre asked angrily.

I felt my chest tighten and started to shake with fury.

"How dare you?" I began. "Here I am cooking food for you. I've decorated the flat and you've not even noticed. I am practically blind and pregnant and you are concerned with my very brief encounter with an ex? Are you for real? Are you stupid?"

My breathing quickened so I held onto the kitchen counter to keep my balance. I felt a shooting pain in my lower back. I was not prepared to have a crisis over this. Was he deliberately trying to cause me and the baby harm with his words?

"I saw you talking to him," he repeated.

"Firstly, I was on the phone with Louisa. Secondly, I'm not rude like you. I will say hello if someone says hello to me. Is that why you've been smoking? Are you feeling stressed because my ex said hello? Why don't you smoke some more? Hell, buy another pack of twenty and smoke them too. You stink, you shithead."

"I saw you talking to him and I told you not to." Andre looked furious but I was becoming enraged.

Was this his intention? He couldn't handle his jealousy, so he wanted me to suffer too? Didn't he realise that he was also hurting the baby? I took the seasoned turkey steaks and threw them in the sink. I looked around the kitchen and thought about turning the whole flat upside down. I wanted to break the windows, throw knives, smash glass and turn everything upside down, but what was the point? I would be the one who would have to tidy it all up anyway. Perhaps I was being too irrational. I breathed in long and slowly while closing my eyes. I felt a vein in my head start to throb. My purse was still on the kitchen counter with my keys and mobile phone. I wasn't staying here with him. I had to leave. I wondered where I could go. I felt so isolated and didn't want to impose my troubles on anyone, but I had to leave the flat. I took my things from the kitchen counter, walked into the bedroom and threw them into my handbag.

"What are you doing?" Andre asked.

"I'm leaving you," I replied. I put some clothes into an overnight bag. I picked up some toiletries from the bathroom and pushed passed Andre who was deliberately being obstructive by standing in the doorway.

"Where are you going?!" he asked, panic in his voice.

"As far away from you as possible! I can't be around you. You're not a man. You're a stupid immature boy with issues. I don't need that. I'd rather be blind, pregnant and alone than be with a jealous, possessive boy who can't handle his own emotions. Now get out of my way!" I spat my words out through gritted teeth.

How could I let him wind me up so drastically? I was furious that he had disrespected me. I was playing the 'good little housewife' for nothing. I put my trainers on, grabbed a warm coat, my overnight bag and headed towards the front door. Andre started to put on his trainers. I turned towards him.

"Don't get in my way and don't follow me. If you do I will call the police." I opened the front door and slammed it shut behind me.

He was bound to follow me, but I wanted to get away from the flat as soon as I could, so he wouldn't know which way I was heading. How the hell did I get myself into this position? Here I was desperate to get some air, desperate to breathe. I wanted to run but my body wouldn't allow me. My sight had cruelly restricted my pursuit of freedom. I cautiously manoeuvred around the neighbourhood. No matter what time of day it was, the streets were always busy. My physical circumstances made me slow and before long I heard him behind me, calling me.

"Shantel."

"Andre, I asked you to leave me alone. I don't want to be around you and right now, I'm realising that this baby and I are all alone. Go away or I will make a scene and this situation is going to get ten times worse for you. Don't harass me, please!" I yelled.

"Shantel. I've packed my bag. Please go home. I will go to my brother's house. Please!" he begged.

"That's a big risk for you, isn't it? Don't you think I'll call Mason round to rub my feet and belly? Andre, your head is too screwed up for me. Any real man would have more sense to know how to treat a pregnant woman, a woman who can barely see, carrying his child! Fuck you Andre. You don't have a brain or even a heart! You don't deserve me. Leave me alone!" I screamed.

I suddenly focused on my surroundings. I had been walking on autopilot and had reached Clapham Common underground station. There was a line of black cabs, waiting to pick up customers. I walked to the front of the line and opened the door to the first cab. Andre was still behind me. He wasn't backing down.

"Shantel! Where are you going?" Andre sounded worried.

"To hell with you!" I shouted. "Leave me alone and stop trying to stress me out. If you care about the baby, then you will just go away!" I climbed into the cab and pulled the door shut.

"Drive, just drive please," I sniffed, fighting the tears. I could feel Andre's glare boring into my body. I had to think quickly but I knew I would end up at Louisa's flat. I pulled my mobile phone out of my bag and dialled her number.

"Babe, are you at home?" I cried.

"Yes, babe what's wrong?" Louisa asked, concerned.

I gave the driver the address and within 20 minutes I was in her living room, exhausted. I told her about the evening's drama while sipping on a cup of camomile tea. Gone were the days of a glass of wine to mellow my mood. My phone rang but I didn't answer it. It was no doubt my crazy, stupid boyfriend. I turned it off, hoping he would get the message.

"Babe, I don't know if there's any point turning your phone off as he's going to call everyone in a mad panic to track you down." As soon as Louisa had said that, her mobile began to ring.

"It's Andre," she confirmed. "I'm going to answer it babe so at least he knows where you are and that you're safe.

"Ok," I replied.

"Hi Andre," Louisa began. She was silent, so it seemed he had a lot to say to her.

"She's here but she doesn't want to see you," Louisa said. "I'll call you back."

"Babe, he's outside and wants to talk to you," she said, sounding concerned. "This is completely up to you. He can come in here. I will go into my bedroom and you two can chat."

I didn't want to talk to him. I wanted to be left alone.

"Babe, I really don't want to have to bother you with this. I didn't know where else to go. I just want peace and quiet. I just want to sleep."

I knew I'd have to be the one to make him leave. He was stubborn and wouldn't take no for an answer.

"Ok, I'll speak to him," I replied calmly.

He was being selfish as usual. I told him what I wanted tonight but his needs were clearly greater than mine and his feelings were his priority. It was now 11 and Louisa was working the following day. I had to consider her too. I felt as if I was imposing on my dear friend. Inside me was a baby, who could feel what I was feeling. This baby breathed what I breathed. This baby ate what I ate. This baby lived in me. But I was in pain because of its father's misdirected emotions. I just didn't want to listen to his pathetic words and emotional pleas. He was in the wrong and we both knew it.

"OK, let him in please."

Louisa opened her front door. I could hear Andre exhale loudly. He greeted Louisa, removed his trainers and walked through the hallway into the living room. Louisa shut the door.

"Make it quick as you are inconveniencing my friend."

Had other women in his past accepted his behaviour? I sighed and waited for a response from the inconsiderate man in front of me.

"I'm sorry. I saw him walk past you and I freaked. I didn't want him to talk to you." Andre explained and held out his hand to take mine.

"You're pathetic!" I blurted.

I was in my friend's flat and needed a place of sanctuary. Why was he continuing to invade my space?

"Ok. I know you're upset Shantel, but please, hear me out," Andre begged as he heard the hostility in my voice.

"Speak." The quicker I let him talk, the quicker he could leave so I could plan my next steps.

"I know it was wrong and completely innocent. I just want you to be mine." He sighed and looked sincere. "It's hard for me to think he had you before me and he could be thinking anything about you. You looked like you were talking to him and I just don't like the idea of you two being friends or anything else." Andre gave his usual lame excuse for his unreasonable behaviour. He waited for me to respond. I didn't.

"Shantel. Talk to me please," Andre pleaded.

"I'm waiting for you to finish. You see, I can't understand your mentality. Right now, I don't want to waste time trying to understand your behaviour. I just want you to leave me alone." I stood up and opened the door to let him know his time was up.

"Shantel, listen. I'm sorry. I'll pack a bag and go to my brother's house. Please go back to the flat where you'll be comfortable. I won't bother or disturb you in anyway." With that, Andre stood up, walked to the hall, put his trainers on and left the flat.

Louisa popped her head out of her bedroom. "Has he gone?" she asked.

"Yes, he has," I replied. We walked back into the sitting room to chat.

"He wants me to return to the flat. I'll go back tomorrow but if you don't mind, I'll just crash here tonight." I had very little energy to think about doing anything else.

"I'm really not sure how I got myself into this situation. Why am I with such an insecure man?" I paused. "I don't even have tears to cry right now."

"Babe, you've got to be strong for your health and for the baby's sake. I know it's hard but you've got to block out his behaviour and find a way to keep going. You're going to have to focus on the baby and then your eye operation. I don't know why he's being such an idiot. I really can't believe he's treating you so badly. He's so useless."

"I know. I don't think he's considering this baby at all. It's not about anyone else but him and his feelings. I just need some time out from him. If I didn't need these regular hospital appointments I'd be with Mum and Dad."

I shifted on the sofa, shaking my head, wishing things were different. We talked a bit more but it was late and I had to sleep. I crawled into Louisa's bed; we ended up talking some more before we both fell asleep.

The following morning, I returned to Clapham. There was no sign of Andre which was perfect. I turned on the shower. The water was hot which relaxed my body and mind. I felt the baby moving around inside me. Was that a sign? I knew I didn't want to give up on the relationship. We needed time to be a family. The relationship was hard work and undoubtedly the most challenging I'd ever had to deal with. I just wanted an easier life. I knew in a few days Andre would make contact and ask to come back. Not now though, I wasn't ready for any communication with him.

I visualised myself on a beach, rubbing my belly, walking on warm golden sand and staring at miles of blue sea. I imagined walking slowly along the shore and feeling the waves of the sea splash against my legs. The water was warm and relaxing but I was jolted out of my fantasy by my mobile phone. I opened my eyes to see the white tiles of the bathroom rather than the sea. Eventually I climbed out of the shower, dried myself slowly and got dressed. I wondered who had called. Although I couldn't see the screen of my mobile phone clearly, I could just about work out some familiar names. It was Louisa. I called her on my way to get a Caribbean takeaway. She wanted to check on me and whether that insecure man had left me alone. I reassured her that all was well, especially as I was about to indulge in one of my favourite past times.

Back at the flat, I put the TV on and ate. This was the beginning of a new-found strength I had discovered. I enjoyed being alone and something inside me was guiding me and telling me that I was going to be fine. I knew God was working on me, empowering me to be strong and supplying me with the ammunition that I needed to have the baby, to have the operation and to deal with Andre. Andre came back at the end of the weekend as predicted. We talked. I didn't accept his behaviour but I was prepared to keep trying to make our relationship work.

That Sunday night we went to bed early. We were both emotionally exhausted from our fight.

I was woken by a shooting pain in my back.

"Wake up Andre." I nudged him to wake him up.

"Hmmm?" Andre shifted on the bed.

"Wake up! I'm in pain!!" I croaked weakly.

Chapter Nine:
Penguin Walk

"Andre, I don't feel well. I need to go to hospital." It was the middle of the night and I had excruciating back pain.

"Hmm?" Andre moaned again, still half asleep.

"Andre! Get up, now!" I shouted as I rocked him awake. He sat up swiftly.

"The baby?" He asked while turning on the bedside lamp.

He stood up and switched the ceiling light on.

"Where's the pain?" he panicked.

"I'm having a crisis!' I said through gritted teeth. "My back again. Call an ambulance." I wanted to cry but the pain was so unbearable, I couldn't breathe. I wanted the window open but I knew it would be cold outside. Andre was on the phone.

"Ambulance please. No. Sickle cell crisis. She's pregnant." Andre ended the conversation and started to get me ready for the hospital. He knew the drill. I needed clothes, flip flops, water.

"I need my phone charger!" I cried out as he walked into the sitting room. He came back with a glass of water.

"Don't go," I whispered.

My back began to throb intensely.

"Rub my back please."

I wanted Andre to take the pain away. I needed to relax. The paramedics had to be quick. I became frustrated as I couldn't move and Andre's massage was not taking the pain away. I tried to lie down but that didn't help.

"Help me sit up," I requested. "Actually, I need to go to the toilet."

Andre helped me to stand and led me to the bathroom. As I sat on the toilet, the paramedics arrived.

"Where is she?" a female voice asked.

"She's just in the bathroom,' Andre replied.

"I'm finished," I announced as I flushed the toilet. Andre opened the door as I stood up to wash my hands.

"I can't take the pain," I said, as Andre led me to the sitting room where the paramedics were waiting.

"Hello love," greeted the female paramedic. "Can you tell me what's happening?"

"I need pain relief. I need something quickly. I'm having a sickle cell crisis. My back. I need something," I reiterated.

"Ok, let's get some Entonox," the female paramedic instructed her male colleague, who started to take out the canister of gas and air which would take the edge off the pain. I began to tune out of the conversation taking place between Andre and the paramedics. Andre began to rush around the flat gathering the essentials for my unplanned visit to the hospital.

"We just need you on the chair love," the female paramedic requested but I was concentrating on sucking in the powerful gas.

"Ready?" she asked.

I nodded.

Andre pulled me up and helped me to sit on the ambulance chair. I was still floating. My back was still so painful but the Entonox helped me to escape. My mind was somewhere else. I was walking along the beach with a bikini and a sarong listening to house music that had a trance-like beat. It moved me. The sky was blue and the sand was warm. It was paradise. I could hear my heart beat. Andre opened the front door. Reality hit me as the cold air disturbed my fantasy. I could still hear the house music while I inhaled the gas as the paramedics wheeled me to the lift. The ride was bumpy and made me feel even more uncomfortable but the gas was my lifeline. I was dancing to the house music but it was so cold. I needed to get onto the bed in the ambulance. The paramedics helped. Andre appeared and spoke to them. He waved. I waved back. The ambulance doors were shut and I could still hear the house music.

"I'm just going to check your blood pressure," the female paramedic said.

After she'd finished, we were on the move. Ten milligrams of morphine was all I needed. I prayed for God to take the pain away. I was going to get through this. I closed my eyes and listened to the house music until the ambulance stopped. We arrived at St Thomas'. The driver opened the door to the ambulance and they wheeled me into A&E. It was bright. I closed my eyes. The beat of the house music stayed with me as I continued taking deep breaths of gas and air. My head was fuzzy but I needed that feeling as a distraction from the pain. I could hear the paramedics checking me in. If only this was a hotel with room service. There were voices and moans of pain around me. Nurses quickly shuffled up and down the corridor. I was wheeled to my cubicle. The male paramedic switched the Entonox canister to one that belonged to the A&E department. They said goodbye and left. I knew Andre was on his way, but I was alone, rubbing my belly and walking on the beach listening to house music. My sarong was blue. It was hot. My hair was up in a loose pony tail. I breathed in the warm air while watching the waves carve pretty patterns in the golden sand.

"Hello Shantel." A nurse appeared with a needle.

Shit!

"I have a needle phobia!" I hissed in between draws of gas.

"Ok love," she replied. "You'll just feel a little scratch."

I didn't believe her and inhaled even deeper. Why did they always say it'll be a little scratch? I knew she was taking a blood sample but I couldn't look. I felt sick at the thought of it.

"I'm just giving you some pain relief love. You're having some morphine. Pretty soon you'll feel better. I need to get you some oxygen. You can't have too much gas. It's only for short-term use, ok?"

Couldn't the nurse see I was in desperate need of the feeling the gas and air gave me? She wasn't taking it. It was mine. I was beginning to feel a little more comfortable. I shifted on the bed just as Andre appeared. He told me that I was moving to the high dependency ward. Before long, the nurse had returned and disconnected me from my beloved Entonox and replaced it with an oxygen mask. The pain relief had started working and I was feeling tired. I closed my eyes and fell asleep until the porters arrived and took me to the new ward where I would be receiving more treatment and closer monitoring — for both the baby and I. She was fine though. She? I realised then that I'd been referring to the baby as a girl. Just then, I had a vision of a baby girl wrapped in a bright pink blanket. The nurse introduced herself and I immediately asked her for some more pain relief.

"Ok. I will see what the doctors have signed off for you." The nurse walked away with my chart.

Andre sat beside me.

"Babe, the pain is coming back thick and fast," I told him with a groan.

"Keep breathing deeply. Let me see what's happening." He walked out of the ward.

There were two other patients in bed sleeping. I worried about disturbing them, but I wanted more gas and air. The pain came back with a vengeance. Did my baby know I was in pain? Finally, Andre and the nurse were back.

"I can give you some more morphine," the nurse said.

"Morphine?" Andre questioned.

"Yes. It'll take the pain away completely," she pointed out, smiling.

"No. No morphine!" Andre instructed. "Won't it affect the baby?"

"No," the nurse replied. "It's fine for the baby."

"Just hold on. Shantel, don't agree to this. Give me a minute." Andre pulled out his mobile phone and walked off the ward.

The nurse looked at me, baffled. I was still in pain. I didn't know what to do but the medical staff were the professionals. They knew what was good for me and what was fine for the baby. They wouldn't put the baby at risk and I trusted them. Stress wasn't good for me or the baby.

"Listen Shantel, it's your choice to have pain relief but the doctors wouldn't have prescribed morphine on your medical chart if it would harm the baby. In the meanwhile, I can get you some paracetamol but I don't think it will help much. I'm going to call the doctor." She smiled warmly and walked away.

I was embarrassed but unsure about what Andre was trying to do. Here I was again, left with my pain and needing help. I wanted to call the nurse to come back. I looked for the buzzer but couldn't reach it as I was now paralysed by my pain. I didn't want to disturb the other patients on the ward. It was Andre who had created this commotion. The tears began to roll down my face. Here I was, in hospital, needing care but no one was there. If I was left without pain relief my crisis could get worse and surely that was harmful for the baby. I wondered what Andre was doing and who he was calling. Maybe he was surfing the internet to see if morphine could harm the baby. This was bread and butter for the medical staff. Why couldn't Andre trust them? Right now, he cared about the baby and I understood that, but why didn't he care about me? Didn't he understand that I was having a crisis and needed pain relief? Who was he to dictate what I should and shouldn't have? Andre was being overprotective without cause. I was doing my best to protect the baby but leaving me in pain was not going to help either of us.

A familiar face came to the ward. It was Nick from my sickle cell clinic. I wondered why he was here, because he didn't have any drugs on him. I needed drugs or Entonox.

"Hi Shantel," Nick greeted with a caring voice. "I heard you were here."

I started to cry again. It was good to hear a warm, familiar voice. I was physically and emotionally drained.

"Shantel, that dose of morphine won't harm the baby. Is that what you're worried about?" Nick asked sympathetically.

"No, I want the pain relief. I need it. But Andre has a problem with it. He thinks it will hurt the baby."

"Do you want me to speak to him about it? There is other pain relief we can give you but you know that morphine works well for you." Nick could see I was getting stressed by the situation and the pain was continuing to increase.

A nurse arrived with the paracetamol. I took them quickly.

"Shantel, if Andre being here is stressing you out, you can ask that he leaves so we can continue with your care. You need to rest," he advised.

The tears continued to flow. Andre should have been my support. I shouldn't have had to ask him to leave so I could rest and relax. Why was Andre taking so long? This was becoming an emergency that needed a quick resolution. If my pain wasn't managed, I would end up staying in hospital for longer than was necessary.

Andre walked back onto the ward.

"You can't have any morphine. It's not good for the baby. My sister is a nurse and she told me, so I don't want you to have it. She's not having it," he said, glaring at the nurses.

"Andre, your sister deals with mental health. She doesn't specialise in pregnancy or sickle cell." I was becoming more agitated. The paracetamol eased the pain but I needed more.

"Andre, Shantel can have a small dose which won't harm the baby. In fact, it will calm her down and take the pain away. Her distress may impact the baby." Nick tried to reason with Andre but he was adamant that he didn't want me to have it.

The nurses stared at Andre in disbelief. I closed my eyes and wished away the pain and my dictating boyfriend.

"Can I please just have something to make me sleep?" I begged.

I wanted to block out the noise and be alone. To save the conflict and tension it was better not to have any morphine. There was no relief with more paracetamol. I simply had to toss around in the bed until I became comfortable or tired, whichever came first. Andre sat in the chair beside my bed with his arms folded, like a security guard, keeping the night watch to monitor the drugs given to me. I didn't want him there but I didn't have anyone else. He was useless. It was all about the baby. He didn't care about my pain and stress, which he had caused. I eventually closed my eyes and fell asleep.

Three days later, and I was finally discharged. The nursing staff were extra thoughtful and caring, and their kindness strengthened me. After Andre's behaviour during my stay, they must have realised that I really needed some kindness.

Andre picked me up. We barely spoke on the way home. I just wanted peace and quiet.

I was eight months pregnant and beginning to feel stronger. The baby was doing fine and kicking the life out of me. I had spoken to my consultant about being induced. There was no way that I could go the full forty weeks. As the baby was getting bigger, the sickle cell crises became more frequent. I needed my parents with me. There was nothing more comforting than their compassion, love, understanding and help. I needed them to take over and baby me again. Andre had a one bedroom flat so it would have been impossible for them to stay with us. My mother's sister was welcoming enough and offered her spare room for them to stay for the duration of their visit. The birth was scheduled for the end of February, two weeks before the due date.

"Shantel, we're here!" Mum said excitedly.

"Aww, that's good news Mum. Looking forward to seeing you," I replied wearily.

"We'll come over to see you tomorrow, ok darling?" She sounded chirpy despite the long haul flight.

"Sure Mum. That would be nice. I will cook lunch." I was excited about making them a nice meal so decided to go to the supermarket later in the day.

"Shantel, your father wants to speak to you. Hold on Sha-Sha," and she passed the phone to my dad.

"Sha-Sha, you ok?" he asked with a cheery voice.

"I'm fine Dad. A bit tired but I'm sure I'm not as tired as you right now," I replied.

"Don't worry about us Sha-Sha. Are you taking some tonic? You have to look after yourself you know," he instructed.

This was a familiar lecture from my father. I told him that I now had a planned delivery date. I needed plenty of stress free rest in order to not to have another crisis. It was winter and very cold. My body wasn't always aware of the falling temperatures outside as I was cooped up indoors, virtually bed ridden. I was looking forward to the pampering though. Andre did the best that he could, but he had to work. Fortunately, I liked my own company. Sometimes there was nothing better than having a long soak in the bath, listening to music. I used to love reading and felt a huge part of my world was now missing without books. I would spend hours in my flat reading in the bath, topping up the hot water as I immersed myself in a novel. How things had changed. Still, I remained hopeful that I would regain some sense of normality. How did blind people cope and work? If they could get on with it, so could I. I couldn't really talk to Andre about my feelings. He was scared too but he handled his emotions by not talking about things that frightened him. I had to confide in others. This would all pass. In a year from now, my life would be very different. I would be a mother. I didn't know if I would be able to return to work though. That part was a mystery to me, but one way or another, I'd be fine.

My parents arrived and before I knew it, were straight in the kitchen, preparing lunch. Rachel called and said that she and her daughter would come to visit too. I was looking forward to having all this love around me. I'd missed Rachel immensely and was relieved our relationship hadn't suffered after Andre's outburst at her party. We had lived on the same road, attended the same nursery, infant, junior and secondary schools. On top of that, we were distant cousins through my mother and her father. So, of course my parents were also excited about seeing her and her daughter. I had asked Andre on many occasions to make amends with Rachel but he refused. I had become emotionally drained by the hostility towards her. Still, she hadn't forgotten me and was finally coming to visit. I felt honoured and grateful for her company, especially as I was so isolated.

Andre called at 1. I took the call in the bedroom for some privacy while my parents milled around the kitchen.

"Yeah. Mum and Dad are making lunch. I got a call from Rachel. She's coming down with her daughter to see me. I'm not sure what we will do but it's a nice day so we might go for a walk."

I wanted Andre to know that he would need to get over his issues with Rachel as she was going to remain in my life.

"I don't want her in the flat. Do not let her in the flat Shantel. Do you understand?" Andre seemed panicky.

"What's wrong with you?" I asked, annoyance escalating.

"I don't want her in the flat. Whatever you do, she is not coming into the flat!" he barked.

"Andre, this is my home too and I don't like the way you are speaking to me. Rachel has just called a few minutes ago to tell me her daughter needs to go to the toilet. Are you really telling me you don't want her daughter, a child to come into the flat?" I was dumbfounded.

"No, she can use the toilet in the pub. Rachel is the one who lied about your ex being invited to her party. She's a liar. I don't want her in my home. I'm coming home now." Andre ended the call.

I sat on the bed in disbelief. Did he really hate her that much? How would I explain to my parents that she wasn't able to come inside? Worse still, how would I explain to Rachel that she and her daughter couldn't come into my home and her innocent daughter couldn't use our toilet? This was barbaric. Did he have no compassion in his heart for a child? My head and my heart couldn't take much more. I wanted to cry but my parents would see my red eyes and know that there was a problem, which I didn't want to explain. No, crying wasn't an option. I took a few moments and lots of deep breaths before I called Rachel to tell her about my shocking conversation with Andre.

"I am so sorry babe," I said with a broken heart.

"Oh, don't worry hun. It's not your fault." I could hear she was being guarded about what she said, especially in front of her daughter.

"There's a pub just before you turn into the close. Just call me when you're nearby and I will come down to meet you."

I felt so embarrassed about telling her Andre was coming home to ensure she didn't come inside. I told my parents that he'd be coming home for lunch. My mother started to prepare some extra food. I wanted to tell her the truth about what had just happened. I'm sure after that revelation, making lunch for him would have been the last thing on her mind.

Minutes later, Rachel called my mobile to say she was downstairs. I explained to my parents that she couldn't park so had to stay with the car. They accepted this as a reasonable reason for not being able to come upstairs. The three of us headed down the three flights of stairs to see Rachel and her daughter.

"Hello Rachel," my Mum said warmly as she have her a hug. "Is this your daughter? She's beautiful!" Mum gave her a hug too.

"Hello Lina. Hello Randall. It's good to see you both." Rachel greeted my father with a warm embrace.

"Hey girl. You got here alright then?" I asked Rachel covering up my hurt with chirpy tones.

"Yes, no problem. It's pretty straight forward." She smiled wryly.

Was Rachel disappointed with me? Maybe I should have been stronger and told Andre I wasn't accepting his pathetic issues. I should have never tolerated his behaviour. Was my fire completely smouldered? I was so tired. I wish I was standing tall, strong and wise in this game of love and life. Instead, I continued to endure his shit. It seemed he had a plan to change me. Was I letting him? This was all too heavy for me emotionally. I should have been flying, but instead I felt like crying. My wings had been clipped. I was supposed to be happily in love as a mother-to-be, but I had to continue travelling along this pot-holed path in pursuit of happiness.

I told my parents I wanted to spend some time with Rachel before she headed back home. My parents were happy to stay in the flat and relax. I reassured them that I wouldn't be long. The three of us then headed to Nando's in Clapham Junction. We ordered and sat down. Rachel could see that I was distraught. She tried desperately not to focus on Andre's manipulative behaviour. Instead, she asked about the baby, about how I felt about becoming a mother and the other changes going on in my life. Seeing Rachel and her daughter felt like a breath of fresh air. A real distraction from my depressing situation. She also talked about some of her problems. I knew she hadn't found being a mother easy, especially in the early days. She always seemed so tired but I guess that was the effect of being a parent. I was already going through physical, emotional and mental fatigue, though my baby hadn't even arrived yet.

After eating, we walked around the shops. I enjoyed the female company and suddenly realised how much I missed my girlfriends especially now. However, my confidence was low and the few friends I now had unwittingly pitied me. I didn't need that. I was still me, happy Shantel. I had just grown a very fat belly and my vision was blurred. Things would return to normal though. I had a wonderful afternoon but after a few hours I was really tired, and so we headed back. I apologised to Rachel again for Andre's behaviour and thanked her for coming to see me. She could have abandoned our friendship because of him, but she recognised that he was the one with issues, not me, and certainly not her.

When I got home, my mother told me Andre hadn't even come home for lunch. The plate of food was still covered on the kitchen counter. He'd have to eat it for dinner as there was no way in hell I was cooking anything for him that evening.

Chapter Ten:
The Arrival

Two weeks later.
My bag was packed. It was time for my induction. I had been thoroughly pampered with fresh braids, a manicure and pedicure. Last thing I wanted was dry, crusty feet in the midwives' and doctors' faces. I wanted to hold my baby with beautiful fingers. My heart had been beating rapidly all day because I was so nervous. I milled around Clapham shopping for a few last minute bits. At times I felt as if I was in a daze. Was this really happening to me? Though I had attended all the antenatal classes available, I still felt unprepared and unsure about what to expect. The next day would bring a dramatic change in my life. But it was exciting. There wasn't a booklet or DVD that could prepare me for my new role. Mid-afternoon shoppers and traders bustled past me. I looked at them. Would their lives also change tomorrow?

I slowly walked back up Lavender Hill towards the flat. It was a beautiful sunny day, a perfect one to spend as my last day being a pregnant woman. The next time I would walk this route, I would be a mother pushing a bright blue and orange Bugaboo buggy with my bundle of joy, snugly laying inside. My clothes would fit me better. My ankles hadn't swollen much so I lived in my trainers and boots. These were ideal for my defective spatial awareness and peripheral vision. My freshly braided hair made me feel good. I still felt pretty although I wasn't sure if others saw me in the same way. Maybe one day, I could look in the mirror again and recognise the person I used to be. I took a deep breath and walked into the block of flats.

My obstetrician had told me that I'd probably spend a couple of nights in hospital. They wanted to make sure that I was well after giving birth with a low risk of having a sickle cell crisis. Now inside the flat, I checked my packed bags. Reality hit. I would be coming home with a baby wearing miniature nappies and wrapped in the John Lewis blanket I fell in love with. It had blue stars all over it. Blue was my favourite colour, so even if my baby was a girl, she'd be swaddled in the soft cosy blanket. I turned on the stereo to listen to music. Gospel was my choice of the day. I needed to hear positive spiritual vibes. My circumstances weren't perfect but it was natural for me to persevere; perhaps this was part of my DNA. I disconnected my iPod and docking station and carefully packed them into my handbag. Music would be a distraction from the uncertainty of the planned delivery of my baby. I was due to have an epidural which was almost guaranteed to take the pain away. Anyway, I knew about pain. A sickle cell crisis was no walk in the park — a throbbing, crippling pain that made every joint in my body seize up. Still, why waste time worrying about the effects of a crisis when a simple shot of morphine rectified the situation? I sat on the edge of the bed reminiscing about the times I had been to hospitals abroad where they clearly didn't meet black people often. The A&E staff would question how genuine my pain was presuming I was a junkie, looking for my next fix.

I went into the living room, turned off the music and prepared to watch the next episode of *Charmed*. Those three witch sisters had cast a spell on me and I was hooked. It was entertaining and I loved the characters, their magical gifts and predictable storylines. Andre was getting a Chinese takeaway on his way home from work. I took my seat on the black leather sofa and started nibbling on some barbecue Pringles while I watched the show. Before long, I heard the key turn in the front door. Andre was home with the food.

"Hey darling, you ok?" Andre called out from the doorway.

"Yeah. I'm good. You?" I replied, not budging from the comfort of the four-seater sofa.

"I'm good babe. Have you finished packing?" he asked as he placed the food on the dining table and planted a kiss on my lips.

"Yeah. I'm good to go. I'll dish up," I offered, as he removed his shoes and headed to the bathroom.

"Cool babe," he replied.

The nerves had increased and I was starting to feel the butterflies. I was a few hours closer to labour. Shredded beef with chilli, kung po chicken, special fried rice, Singapore noodles and crispy seaweed were all on the menu. Andre had exceeded himself. I started nibbling on the shredded beef as he entered the sitting room. He removed his jacket and tie, pulled off his trousers and draped them over the back of a dining chair. We sat at the table to eat our last meal as a couple. The food temporarily distracted me from the reality of my hospital visit. After clearing the dishes, we watched EastEnders. I had a shower and started preparing for our departure. Andre did the same. Few words were spoken between us. It didn't bother me as I was meditating, drawing upon the strength that God had given me. I'd be coming home with my baby, as a mother, and I had to be prepared.

Andre drove cautiously to St Thomas'. We headed towards the maternity ward. I checked in at the reception and we were directed to the waiting room. I was stunned at the number of security doors we had to pass through but I understood the reasons. Who would want to give birth to a baby only for some random stranger to walk away with it? There were lots of couples sitting in the waiting room. One by one they were called into the ward. After half an hour of waiting, my name was called. I took a deep breath. Andre carried the bags and we followed the midwife into the labour room, which was small but pleasant. I wished my room overlooked the river, but I wasn't so lucky. The midwife gave us a tour of the ward. We entered the Green Room. It was cold, but stunning, with a variety of beautiful plants in every corner. I walked to the window and was blown away. This was the amazing view of the Thames and Houses of Parliament I'd wanted! I had never seen Big Ben from such a height before. It was an awesome sight. I considered returning to the room later, with a cup of tea and a blanket. After showing us the rest of the ward, the midwife showed us back to my room. I sat down on the bed. Andre sat next to me.

"Not going to be long now," he stated.

"Yep. I guess they'll be inducing me soon," I replied nervously.

Andre hugged me. It felt reassuring and comforting. I could have rested my head on his shoulder for the rest of the night, but I was feeling tired. Just as I decided to lie down, the midwife came in to induce me. It was just after midnight.

"Hello Shantel. I'm Debbie, one of the midwives tonight."

Debbie spoke calmly while explaining the process. I lay still and took a deep breath as she started the procedure. It was slightly uncomfortable and intrusive but necessary to kick start my labour. Why hadn't all those pineapples my father gave me done their job and induced me? In the end, I was sick at the sight of them.

"Ok. All done," she confirmed.

"So, what happens now?" Andre asked.

"We wait. It takes a few hours for you to go into labour. Every woman is different. You should try to sleep. Would you like some more blankets dear?" she asked.

"No thanks Debbie. It's quite warm in here," I replied.

"Well, we're outside if you need anything," she assured us and left the room.

Andre took his position on top of a mat on the floor. I covered myself with the blanket and closed my eyes. I tossed and turned but I couldn't get comfortable. Within minutes, Andre was already sleeping. Great, at least he was comfortable. I sighed and thought about the bundle of joy that I would have by tomorrow. I wondered when the labour pains would start. The deep breathing wasn't helping. My back started to throb. I tried different positions to find comfort. Nothing worked and I was becoming frustrated.

"Andre. Andre, wake up"

"What is it?" he asked sounding dazed.

"My back hurts," I explained.

"Mmm, ok," he muttered, rolled on his side and fell asleep again. Was this an ordinary day for him? Had he experienced this situation before? I hadn't! He was of no use to me. I was carrying his child and about to give birth! How about a back rub? I needed some pain relief. The throbbing pain felt like a sickle cell crisis. Not again. I took deep breaths, stood up, slid on my slippers and headed out of the room. I glanced back at Andre but he didn't stir. The nurses were talking at their station. I wanted someone to talk to but decided to head to the Green Room for sanctuary, peace and the view to distract me from the pain. Rubbing my back wasn't going to be enough. As soon as I walked in the cold air hit me, and I knew I wouldn't last long in there.

I sat on the wooden bench, gazing in wonder at the river and the architecture. The agony, coupled with the cold, were too much for me to handle. I left the room and headed straight to the nurse's station.

"Hiya love. Are you alright?" asked one of the midwives on duty.

I wanted Debbie.

"No, my back hurts," I sobbed.

I felt so alone and needed some company but I knew the staff were occupied. The screams of women in labour were frightening. The loud echo of pain haunted me. I knew I would be going through the same until the epidural took effect.

"Let's get you back to bed and I'll bring you some pain relief." She helped me back into bed.

Debbie came into my room after us, looked at my chart at the end of the bed and walked out again. She returned shortly afterwards with tablets and passed me one of my bottles of water.

"Thank you" I said, feeling grateful for the painkillers and the attention.

After a few minutes, I felt more comfortable and closed my eyes to sleep.

I woke up to the sounds of bustling midwives. Why did hospital staff always have to be so noisy? I checked the time on my mobile phone. 6:30. Surely it was better for patients to sleep. I tried to sleep again, but before long I was being offered tea and toast for breakfast. I ate it quickly. Andre ate the snacks that he'd packed in the overnight bag. My back was still feeling achy but I wanted to shower and brush my teeth. I headed to the bathroom while Andre made some phone calls. When I came back into the room, I phoned my parents at my aunt's house to update them that I was alright apart from my backache. I was looking forward to seeing them later. Within minutes, the pain intensified.

"Andre, my back! I'm in serious pain! I need something. Call a midwife please."

I started to breathe deeply. I was in labour and the pain was like nothing I had ever imagined. I took short and quick breaths. The midwife came in and hooked me up to my beloved Entonox. I breathed it in deeply and closed my eyes. I didn't hear anything apart from the familiar sounds of house music. The beat was hypnotic. I was in a trance again. I moaned loudly and sucked in the air even harder. After about a minute the pain had stopped. I was fine again. I pulled the gas pipe out of my mouth and smiled at Andre.

"That wasn't so bad," I told him.

"Really?" he responded. "So why is my arm and neck feeling so sore from your grip?" he chuckled. He sat beside me the whole time I was in my trance.

"I don't know...whaaaa!!!!" I yelled as the pain returned with a vengeance.

The gas and air was my friend again. I breathed it in, deeper and deeper until I returned to my zone. The pain was excruciating. The midwife left to get the doctor. The house music was back and then the pain stopped again, after about thirty seconds. Was this how it was supposed to be? I relaxed again as I knew the next time would come soon enough.

"I need some water babe." Andre passed me the water and I took a quick sip.

"Oh no, not again! Aaarrrgghhh!" I groaned and puffed on the magic gas again.

The midwife came in, closely followed by an unfamiliar doctor. He talked to me and I responded as best as I could. He explained the procedure for inserting the epidural and the risks involved. I agreed and signed a consent form. The midwife already had the needle in a tray ready for the doctor. I tried not to look at it. The painful contractions had momentarily stopped.

"Are you ready?" the doctor asked. "I need you to swing your legs round the edge of the bed and hold onto your partner. You need to lean forward and do not move. If you feel a contraction coming on you need to tell me straight away," he said firmly.

I did as he asked though I hated needles, but at least this wasn't a dreaded blood test. This was an injection of essential pain relief. Damn, the contractions were painful. The needle wouldn't be anything in comparison.

"I'm just going to insert the needle now. Please don't move," he said one more time.

I followed his instructions and held on tightly to Andre who held me tightly too. I felt the sharp prick enter my lower back and held my breath.

"Oh dear," the doctor said. "That didn't quite go as it should have so I will have to try again."

My calm quickly turned to annoyance. What the hell was this doctor doing? The contractions were starting again.

"Gas and air. I need it!" I shouted at the midwife.

I shifted on the bed in pain. The contractions were coming thick and fast.

"Awww!" I cried out in pain.

I sucked the air in desperate urgency. After a few deep breaths of the gas, I started to feel some relief. I released my tightly shut eyes and glanced at Andre standing in front of me, looking helpless. I needed real love and to float away with the happy house music. I wasn't sure if Andre really knew what love was so I concentrated on the love between me and my baby. Was she actually going to be a girl? The baseline of the music was thumping. Couldn't anyone else hear it? The contractions slowed down. I started to tune into the conversation in the room.

"Ok Shantel. We will have to try again now," the doctor announced, as the midwife took my favourite toy away from me.

I gave her an evil eye when her back was turned.

"Lean forward please."

I did so, but apprehensively. This was my spine. I wasn't pleased that he missed it the first time. I needed to speak to God for his protection. I said my silent prayers as Andre held me tight. I hoped that he was praying for me too. I held my breath as the needle went in.

"That's it. I have just given you the epidural. In about twenty minutes to half an hour you should feel some relief. If you need a top up please let me know. You'll need to remain in bed now as you'll feel numb from the waist down."

"Ok," I replied.

The doctor patched me up and left the room. Another contraction quickly approached and I asked Andre to pass me my beloved pipe. The relief from the gas was almost instant. I wondered if this was because the injection in my spine was beginning to take effect. As the doctor had predicted, the painful contractions had stopped and I couldn't feel anything from my waist to my toes. I had no pain but I was bedridden. There were hours ahead of lying in bed with nothing to do, no TV, or books or magazines that I could read. I only had Andre to keep me company and calls on my mobile from friends and family, checking for updates.

Chapter Eleven:
Forbidden Delights

The time passed quickly, with midwives and doctors popping in and out of my room to check on the progress of my labour.
Four centimetres dilated.
Eight centimetres dilated.
I wondered how much effort I would have to put in to pushing if my body was numb. The staff advised me not to eat, but I was ravenous.

"Babe, I'm really hungry. Pass me those Pringles." I fancied a sneaky feast when the midwife wasn't looking.

"Are you sure Shantel? You know they said not to eat," Andre replied as he popped open the tube and started tucking in.

"Andre, I need something. I need food. Where's that Lucozade?" I stretched out for the crisps.

I licked the flavour off before devouring them, then guzzled the fizzy drink. Andre opened the shortbread biscuits and we demolished the packet with ease.

"Let's put this lot away babe before she comes back. I'm fine now."

He finished the crisps and put the rest of the forbidden foods away. Shortly afterwards the midwife returned. She checked how far I was dilated.

"I think you are pretty much ready to start pushing soon, my love. I will be back in ten minutes."

She left the room.

"Oohh, scary times," I said to Andre and took a deep breath.

"You'll be fine Shantel," he said reassuringly, giving me a passionate kiss on the lips and a big hug.

He comforted me which was a complete turnaround from just a few hours earlier when I needed him, but he needed sleep more.

"Shantel, our family seem to have taken up most of the waiting room. They all want to say hello. Are you up for it?" he asked.

"Of course," I replied.

"Ok, I won't be long."

Andre left the room and returned with my parents and his mother. I was so pleased to see them. I wondered how they felt about their daughter giving birth. The moment was surreal. After the hugs and goodwill, they left the room so the other visitors could see me. The midwife returned and said it was time. I prayed to God for the safe arrival of my baby.

"Ok Shantel, I just need to adjust the bed so we can get things moving now." She pressed a button on the remote control. My body shifted into a vertical position. The midwife looked at the monitor that timed the contractions.

"Shantel, you're having a contraction right now so I am going to need you to push as hard as you can. Push down love."

The nurse was very sweet but didn't inspire me to push a baby out of a body that I couldn't even feel.

"Come on, push, push, push, push, push, push," she instructed.

So I pushed.

"Come on baby, push our baby out. You can do it." Andre held my hand as I pushed though the contraction.

"Well done. Take a break love and we will start again when the next contraction begins," she said.

The room was silent apart from the sound of the iPod playing some hip hop. It was The Game's album, 'The Documentary.' Did I really want to listen to gangster rap? Andre put it on to inspire me to push. I wanted to hear songs of love and tranquil lullabies.

"Babe, can we change the music? I need something else."

"Ok. Let's see what we have here." Andre flicked through the different albums on my iPod and found one he was happy with. "Corinne Bailey Rae? How's that?" he asked.

"Perfect," I replied.

"Ok, you're having another contraction," the midwife said as she looked at the monitor. "Start pushing Shantel. Push hard darling."

So I pushed again.

"Come on babe," Andre squeezed my hand and encouraged me to push harder. I did, but it was tougher than I had imagined, especially as I could not see any results.

"Shantel, push, push, push, push, push," the midwife belted out. "Ok love, relax now."

This process was repeated a few more times but I was becoming tired. My energy levels were rapidly diminishing. The obstetrician arrived. He checked to see the progress.

"Shantel, I may have to assist you with your delivery. Labour has lasted longer than expected. I will give you ten more minutes to push unaided but if the baby still hasn't come out I will have to help with some forceps. I'll return in ten minutes, ok." The doctor left the room.

I looked at Andre feeling quite worried. My baby couldn't enter the world with a squashed head.

"Ok Shantel. Let's go again." The midwife seemed even more determined to get the baby out quickly. "You have to push harder than you have done before."

"Come on Shantel," Andre said sternly.

I pushed and pushed as hard as I could.

"Ok, I can see the head!" the midwife exclaimed.

Andre went to the end of the bed to look. I continued pushing through the contraction until the midwife told me to take another break.

"I feel sick. I'm going to vomit," I said, as I started heaving.

The nurse gave me a cardboard dish which Andre held. I heaved again. I felt awful. I regretted eating all those Pringles and shortbread biscuits. This was bad but there was no vomit.

"Ok, ok, the baby's coming!" the midwife declared excitedly.

I heaved again but I wasn't sick. The baby had shot out. Andre was beaming. I was in shock.

"You have a beautiful baby girl!" the midwife announced.

She cleaned the baby and wrapped her in a blanket, then handed her to me.

I held her in my arms.

"Welcome to the world baby. God bless you," I whispered. I gently kissed her on her forehead.

She had a full head of hair. My tiny bundle of joy.

"My turn, my turn," Andre requested excitedly.

I handed our baby to him and he held her, smiling and kissing her cheeks and forehead.

"You have to feed her now," instructed the midwife.

What?

This was too soon. Andre handed our baby back to me. I held her tight. They were both staring at me. Was I really supposed to do this now? I had no choice.

"This will help with the bonding Shantel," the nurse reasoned. Perhaps she could see my fear.

"Ok. Here we go. Time to feed baby girl." She latched on straight away. It was an odd feeling but she seemed satisfied.

"How long should I do this for?" I asked.

I didn't have a clue. I hadn't researched breastfeeding. I couldn't access the internet or read books because of my eyesight. I didn't even speak to anyone about breastfeeding. It was the last thing on my mind throughout my pregnancy. I did want to breastfeed though and was told it would help me lose the baby fat, but I hadn't thought about it properly. After about fifteen minutes on one breast I moved her onto the other until she seemed content. We had bonded. Life would be very different with a baby, someone who was dependent on me. But I was also dependent on her. I had something good and positive to focus on.

I named her Leylah.

It was 11 and we had to consider the family members patiently waiting outside to see the new arrival. Andre fetched them in the same order as before. My parents and his mother came in first to greet their grandchild. This was a very happy moment for my parents who were holding their first grandchild. I was thirty-one years old and they had hoped that I would be married first. Well, the possibility of marriage with Andre was there. After all, I had now given birth to his first child. I'd always dreamt that I would be married with two or three children, but this fairy-tale wasn't written by me. I was going with the flow. It had been a bumpy ride so far but I was hopeful that it would finally smooth out. Perhaps the past would eventually seem more like speed bumps rather than the mountains we had climbed so far.

One week later, I was in hospital again, this time for the eye operation. I wanted to see clearly again, but I would be happy with any improvement. I left it in the hands of God. My baby was at home with her father who incidentally chose to pick an argument with me the night before. I felt myself becoming withdrawn from the relationship. I kept my negative feelings to myself, hoping that we could rekindle love. I was dependent on Andre to look after me through this period. I didn't want to be a blind single parent on benefits. I didn't even know whether I could get help. I had never considered how blind people coped with day-to-day living, let alone work. Surely help was out there. I had no answers apart from perseverance. At least my first week with the baby allowed me to bond and get to know her. I was in love and I found my sanctuary in her.

The consultant was happy with the operation. Later that day, I was allowed to go home. My parents and I took a black cab. I'd been through this recovery process before. I had four different eye drops. With time, the eye became less irritable. My baby helped to take my mind off the discomfort. Breastfeeding became routine. I hated leaky boobs but she loved the milk so I didn't complain. I still couldn't read print clearly. I tried squinting but that didn't help a great deal. Still, I remained positive. I was looking forward to my follow-up appointment at Moorfields, and was confident that the doctors would tell me that my vision could improve further. It was still early days after the operation but I felt positive that I would see more clearly.

The doctors were friendly enough even when they informed me that my vision wouldn't improve much more than it already had. They referred me to the Low Vision Aid (LVA) department. I didn't know exactly what this department could do for me but I wanted a chance to see something, anything, a little clearer. A chance to be able to read again would have been perfect. I missed the intrigue of a good mystery novel. I loved reading magazines on hair, beauty and fashion just like any other woman my age. I had to put all of my books in storage. I didn't need painful reminders. However, I had come to the realisation that my entertainment options in the future would be limited.

I was amazed at the variety of tests that the LVA department performed. I could read print with magnifying glasses. This was exciting. I could read again! I wanted to scream, shout and tell the world. I wanted to hug the optician but decided that wasn't appropriate. I would be able to wear glasses and see my daughter's eyes clearly. This was going to be life changing. I found a pair that were perfect for me. I'd be able to return to work. The optician informed me about magnifying software for computers and other devices that would be useful to me and how I could access them. My heart was beating rapidly. I left hospital feeling overjoyed, so I called Andre to share the good news. He was as happy and excited as I was. This was a great development as I'd be able to resume work after maternity leave. We would have two salaries again, rather than struggling to survive on one. We started discussing getting a bigger place together as Andre's flat only had one bedroom and the baby would eventually need her own. We could now plan a future together.

I enjoyed my maternity leave. It was a hot summer and Clapham Common was lively with sun worshippers. I pushed my baby girl in her Bugaboo practically every day. I would park the buggy in a quiet spot and lay a blanket on the grass. I used an umbrella to shade her and we would lay in our spot, at peace, in the beautiful summer sun. I played music from my iPod while watching my little one fall asleep. These were our special times together. No one else had this. It was bliss. I couldn't have asked for more. Andre would occasionally meet us in the park when he finished work. It was the summer of love. Even my parents were hands on and loved looking after their granddaughter.

An old friend of mine, Denise, invited me to her birthday meal. It was now June, the sun was beaming, and I was in high spirits. My parents had offered to babysit so Andre could also have freedom for the evening. I had taken the baby to my Aunt's house where my parents were staying. Naturally they wanted to feed me, even though I was going out to eat. To appease them, I had a small amount and was in two minds about going home to get changed or go straight to the dinner. I could have gotten away without changing but I wanted to look good as it had been a while since anyone had seen me. Denise had given birth to her baby boy in December, two months before I had my daughter. It was going to be nice to see how she was finding parenting. These were the early days of motherhood and I had spent almost every moment with my daughter. This night off was special and I was looking forward to it.

I called Andre when I arrived in Clapham to let him know I was coming home to freshen up.

"Ok, where are you now?" Andre asked.

"I'm just walking up from Clapham Common. I'm about five minutes away now."

"Oh, ok. I didn't think you were coming back." Andre sounded distracted.

"Yes, I am coming home. I'll be there in a few minutes but I'm not stopping, ok?" I reiterated.

"Ok babe, see you in a bit." Andre hurried me off the phone.

His behaviour was strange but I put it down to him having issues with me going out. He clearly felt threatened, especially when he thought other men would be on the scene. I wouldn't let his negativity and insecurities spoil my night out on the town. I wanted female company and I didn't want him to ruin it for me as he had done so many times before. I ran up the stairs to the flat and quickly pushed the key into the door to let myself in. I could hear music. It was Brian McKnight playing on the stereo. This was not Andre's usual choice of music. In fact, he would rather watch TV than play any kind of music. Why was the living room door shut and why was the music so loud? I opened the door and saw the room full of pink and silver balloons. This was odd. Andre was sitting on a dining chair facing the door. He was smiling but also appeared nervous. The flat was tidy. There was a bottle of champagne on the dining table with two champagne flutes.

"What's going on?" I asked.

Andre turned Brian down with the remote control.

"There are eighteen balloons. One for each month we have been together. There are eighteen roses for the same reason. Here's a pin." He handed me a needle.

"Pop the balloons until you find something special inside one of them." Andre was still smiling when he handed me the needle.

"I don't want to pop them. They look lovely," I told him.

"Ok, pick a balloon that you think might have something inside it." Andre waited eagerly.

The balloons looked so pretty. The moment was romantic and I could sense Andre had planned it for some time. I guessed he hadn't expected me to return home to change. If I had made my way to the birthday dinner, I wouldn't have seen this until much later in the evening. I picked a silver balloon and hesitantly popped it. The bang was loud and I didn't want to pop anymore.

"Tell me what I'm looking for," I said.

Andre breathed deeply and took a small jewellery box out of his jeans pocket. He knelt on one knee. I couldn't believe my eyes. Andre was proposing to me.

"Shantel, I love you with all my heart. I'm still in love with you and want to spend the rest of my days with you. You have made me so happy and I want you to be my wife. Will you marry me?"

He opened the small black box and took out a beautiful engagement ring. I answered him the only way I felt was appropriate. I wanted to be happily married. Despite our relationship issues, I wanted to be settled with Andre. We just had to work at making our relationship stronger and I felt it was achievable. I had no doubt about our love for each other. He was tall, handsome, educated and wanted a future with me. He knew I was a forgiving person. All the pain and heartache that he had caused had flashed before me but I could never hold a grudge. We had a child together so we would always have a connection. Why not tie the knot with him?

He's bending down on one knee
Speaking in terms of simplicity
The love he professes to have for me
To provide and protect for all eternity
He promises his heart and a future to me
A life fulfilled, bringing happiness and ecstasy
Though I know there have been indiscretions and imperfections
I am still willing to give this union my long term blessing
He loves me he says and bought an engagement ring

My heart is alight, inside I'm dancing
I want a future, a dream, my desire
Surely, I deserve love that spreads joy like wild fire
To have the freedom and peace in a relationship with this man
Never have I opened my heart to another who has claimed they can
I've been so guarded and never allowed another in
But I have come this far, and it's a beautiful ring
I'm not really swayed by the amount of diamonds or carats therein
He has the ability to please me and to be head of this family
I can work with that, so here is where I'm laying my hat.

"Yes, I will marry you," I replied excitedly.

Andre put the sparkling ring on my finger, stood up and kissed me. We hugged each other to the sounds of Brian McKnight. This was a blissful, romantic moment. I felt so happy and I could visualise our relationship blossoming into something solid and everlasting. We sat on the sofa and continued to hug each other.

"Oh my gosh! I'm supposed to be going out! I've got to call Denise and tell her I can't make it!"

"No, you still go babe. I don't mind," Andre replied.

"I can't do that. You've just proposed! I'm going to call her." I reached for my phone, put my glasses on and dialled her number.

"Hi babe, I'm really sorry but I'm not going to make it tonight," I said smiling.

"Oh no. Why?" she asked inquisitively.

"Well...Andre has just proposed to me."

"Oh wow! Congratulations!" she responded. So how do you feel and what's the ring like?" she asked.

"I feel great babe. It was a real surprise. The ring is stunning. I can't believe it!"

I was still in shock because this was not what I had expected. I looked closely at the intricate design of the ring.

"Ok darling, I'll let you continue with your celebrations. Let's speak tomorrow."

"Thanks hun. I hope you have a lovely birthday celebration too. Speak tomorrow. Bye babe."

"Bye darling!"

I took off my glasses and turned to Andre.

"Well, as you're not going out we'd better organise some food. Do you fancy going out? Andre asked.

"I'd rather stay in. Shall we just order a Chinese?" I asked.

"Sure, let me call them." Andre held my face between his hands and kissed me gently.

I didn't want to share this moment with anyone else but him. I wanted to stay at home, eat some food and make love to my fiancé.

Andre and I left the flat to get the takeaway. This was our first time out as an engaged couple. We happily bounced down the road hand in hand beaming at each other. I was engaged to the father of my child. We were to be married and my title would change from Miss to Mrs. I was looking forward to calling my parents and friends to let them know that I was going to be Andre's wife. My closest friends knew of the troubles we had overcome and those that we were still dealing with. I hoped they would be happy and supportive towards me, though deep down I knew they had their reservations about the relationship.

As we strolled, I started daydreaming about our wedding day. I imagined myself in a beautiful white gown, with bling and embroidery, looking beautiful and elegant. In recent months, my confidence in my looks had dwindled to an all-time low. Deep down I knew that my physical appearance hadn't changed, but I didn't feel pretty anymore. Maybe it was because I couldn't see myself in as fine detail as I once had. I used to wear eye liner, mascara and eye shadow, but there was not a trace of these beauty enhancers to be found in my flat. I simply couldn't see well enough to apply them correctly. The most I would use was lip gloss. I started to relax my hair again, though it had been braided throughout my pregnancy and for three months after giving birth. At least my hair was in a healthy state.

I hadn't been on any shopping sprees either, something I used to do frequently with my girlfriends before my vision took a blow. Clapham had a few shops that I frequented but I knew my wardrobe needed an overhaul. I used to turn heads as I walked down the street, but now I couldn't tell if anyone was even looking at me. Well, Andre was in love with me and told me I looked beautiful, but I wanted to feel good about myself. Wearing a wedding dress and getting my hair and make-up done professionally would make me feel beautiful. I reminded myself that other people saw something that I couldn't. I was still me. I was still Shantel. I still had my brain, my heart and my feelings. I was an emotional woman that concealed my insecurities and uncertainties about my future. I didn't want to rely on anyone, but Andre was happy to love me and look after me.

"I will look for some wedding fairs for us to check out. We need to get some ideas," Andre said excitedly.

"Wow, I can't believe we're going to plan our wedding!" I screamed happily.

"I don't want a big wedding Shantel. I want our guests to be the people that are part of our lives, not people that we hardly ever see." Andre's tone was serious.

"Well, we can talk about our guest list when the time is right. Let's just get home, eat some food, drink some more champagne and celebrate." I didn't want to get into an uncomfortable debate about who to invite.

I wanted to make love to my fiancé for the first time. That night, Andre and I wiped the slate clean. I forgave him for all he had done and he started to look forward to sharing a future with me. We sealed our commitment with passionate love-making. Andre made love to me in a way he had never done before. I was finally being treated as his woman, his lady, his family. That night I didn't feel like an outsider looking in. I was in the midst of creating a family life with the man I had agreed to spend the rest of my life with.

I said I was ready to forgive his unjust treatment
So I'll put the past behind me where it belongs
I am longing for a fresh start, a new beginning
I have given my all and I demand all back
He has vowed to give me his future
I put my faith in this relationship and forecast good feelings
I ask the universe to guide, protect and select love and happiness
for me
So, I continue to commit my love to Andre

The colours are shining brightly
There's a light that I am walking towards
A future sheltering me, persuading me, changing me
A status, a reason, a being, conceiving the woman in me
Enduring obstacles, climbing those mountains
Despite the odds, believing in we
Learning to forgive, God is blessing me
Knowing this wasn't tailor-made perfectly
Bespoke? Hardly!
Never refraining from achieving my will, my desire, my destiny
To be living happily in a green tranquillity
Prepared, forever we will be
Him, baby, me
Us, three.

Chapter Twelve:
Sparkles Dimmed

After the proposal, things moved at a rapid pace. By August, we were in a house where I spent the rest of my maternity leave caring for the baby and becoming a true housewife. The semi-detached house had three bedrooms, with a hundred feet of mature garden. The walls of both reception rooms, the bedrooms, the bathroom and the hallway were all blue. The carpet in the bedrooms, the hallway and the sitting room were also blue. Though it was my favourite colour, this was blue overload. The house was on a hill with a panoramic view of Canary Wharf and the Thames. These were sensational views of London. The back of the house faced the woods of a conservation area with a beautiful mature landscape. Foxes, squirrels and magpies were regular visitors to the garden, but I was the lady of the manor. The trees were tall and leafy. I knew I would enjoy many hours in the dining room looking out at the scenery. I planned to buy garden furniture, especially as it was the middle of summer. Maintaining the garden would be challenging, but my parents loved working outdoors and offered to help tame it. Andre and I discussed colours that could transform the walls. We chose magnolia in the hallway and sitting room as a temporary solution until we had time to consider a colour scheme.

A few days after the move, Andre returned to work. There were still so many unopened boxes and crates. My parents volunteered to help paint the blue away. All hands were on deck as I cooked and my parents displayed their decorating skills, transforming the blandly decorated house into a lighter, subtler, less offensive colour scheme. When Andre came back from work, he helped my father paint the hallway and the sitting room. We both decided to replace the carpets and before long we'd transformed the house. My parents were proud of my achievements. I had given them their first grandchild and here I was in my own house.

The summer was hot and the days were long. By the time Andre came home in the evenings, the washing, cooking, cleaning and gardening were done. I wanted to embrace childcare while we had it, as once my parents had returned to Dominica, we would be juggling our different responsibilities.

"Babe, why don't we go out tonight?" I asked when he came home from work one day. "My parents will babysit."

"I just want to stay home babe. You don't mind, do you?" he replied dismissively.

"Oh, it's just that when my parents have gone we won't have this opportunity again."

"Maybe tomorrow. I just want to lie on the bed and watch TV tonight." He flicked through the channels.

My mum had cooked a hearty dinner but I wanted to go out, put my glad rags on and have fun. Our baby was on the bottle as I was weaning her off breast milk. I was at home all day, but Andre wasn't interested as he had been out all day. His routine consisted of eating dinner downstairs and then putting his plate in the kitchen, unwashed. Perhaps he expected someone would wash up after him but I couldn't understand why he didn't use the dishwasher. His actions frustrated and embarrassed me. My parents thought Andre was lazy and I had to agree. What did he do around the house? He still had boxes in the dining room that he wanted to unpack himself as they were his private possessions. I had no interest in the boxes, apart from having them removed from our dining room to either his wardrobe or the loft.

"Andre, you've stopped saying thank you for dinner. What's that about?" I asked bluntly, feeling annoyed that he had been rude once more.

"I do say thank you. I thanked you in the kitchen, didn't I?" Andre said looking like a child who knew he was in the wrong.

"You know my Mum cooked dinner. Doesn't she deserve a thank you?" I wondered if this man had any appreciation or just expectation.

"Shantel, I said thank you to you as I thought you cooked dinner but from now on, when I know your Mum has cooked, I will say thank you to her. Is that ok?" he asked sarcastically.

"Ok, and please try not to put your dinner plate on the floor in the sitting room. The dishwasher is just in the kitchen and it doesn't look good. Can you at least try to put it in the kitchen? Then we can relax without dirty plates lying around."

I wanted to get my point across that we should be making the most of being a couple, rebuilding our relationship to become stronger again. We had a fresh start in the new house and I wanted to revitalise our relationship by re-enacting our first date, not by sitting on the sofa day after day.

The next evening, Andre returned from work while my parents and I were eating. The baby was in her swing, enjoying rocking with her attention flitting between us and the TV. Andre shut the front door as my father was putting his plate into the kitchen.

"Ah hello Andre. You're home," my father greeted Andre cheerfully.

"Yes, I'm home, in my house!" Andre replied.

There was silence. I couldn't believe my ears. Andre took his shoes off and entered the dining room.

"Good evening, good evening," Andre declared.

He kissed me on the cheek and smiled at my mother. Andre glanced at the now dozing baby, then strolled into the kitchen to wash his hands. My mother looked at me in surprise. She could tell I was fuming. What was Andre trying to insinuate? What was he trying to achieve? I saw my father walk silently up the stairs, looking defeated. I heard the bedroom door shut. Andre emerged from the kitchen to pick up the stirring baby. I was disappointed by the harsh words he'd thrown at my father. He sat down beside me. I shook my head at him. My mother gave me a look that suggested that I leave it alone, but I couldn't. This was complete and utter disrespect to my parents. They had spent weeks making our house a comfortable home. I didn't expect him to speak to my father with that tone

"Andre would you like some dinner?" my mother asked politely.

How she managed to be so accommodating, I didn't know. Though she was wise and experienced, she knew I was unable to accept that behaviour from my fiancé to my father. He was supposed to be respectful, humble and grateful for the support we had received since they had left their home to support me, to support us. I had suffered a minor crisis while they were with us, and was grateful for the tonic they'd bought over, and their help with picking up prescriptions. They looked after the baby while I rested and cooked copious amounts of high iron and energy foods for me. Didn't we all benefit from my parents being around? If I became sick, my parents would nurse me to good health.

"Yes please. I'm hungry," Andre stated, without even looking at my mother.

She looked at me, stood up and went into the kitchen. I followed her. She could tell I was fuming. She knew me too well.

"Shantel, don't say anything to him. Just leave it," she whispered.

"Mum, you know I can't leave this alone. I have to address this. That was uncalled for and disrespectful." I was, yet again, embarrassed by Andre's antics.

"Shantel, don't worry darling," she said calmly.

"I'm going to see what Dad's doing."

I knocked on the guest room door.

"Come in," Dad replied.

He was sitting on the bed, reading a newspaper.

"You okay Dad?" I asked.

"Yes darling. Come and take a seat," he requested.

"I heard Andre's comment about this being his house. I'll speak to him when I've calmed down. I can't believe he was so rude to you."

"Shantel, don't worry about it. I heard what he said. I am disappointed, but don't make a fuss about it."

I left the room feeling saddened after the brief conversation. I went downstairs to find my mother clearing the kitchen. I knew she would join my father once she had finished. It was time for a discussion with Andre, so I joined him in the living room, closed the door and sat on the sofa opposite him. The thought of sitting next to a man who had just insulted my parents repulsed me. I looked at my daughter sitting in her rocker, with her eyes darting between me, her father and the bright lights of the TV. Could she sense my frustration?

"Andre, I need to talk to you." I sat forward on the sofa.

"What is it?" Andre asked with a smug expression.

I took a deep breath. This man was unbelievable. Was he that oblivious to the hurt he had caused?

"When you came home my dad said hello to you. You replied, 'I'm in my home!' What did you mean by that?" I was annoyed and upset but didn't want this feeling to turn into anger.

"What?" Andre rolled his eyes at me.

"I'll repeat myself, as clearly you didn't understand me. You told my dad you had arrived into *your* home. My home! What did you mean? Were you deliberately trying to make my dad feel uncomfortable?" I asked.

"Shantel. I don't know what you're talking about. You're being too sensitive. Besides, it is my home," Andre stated.

"Andre, may I remind you, this is *our* home. My parents are guests here. Furthermore, they are here at my request to help in the house. Do you have a problem with that?" I felt my blood boil.

"Shantel, I don't know what you are talking about. Yes, this is our home. I didn't say it wasn't your home," Andre replied.

"I would appreciate you not making them feel uncomfortable in our home, Andre. They do so much for us in this house. They've painted and fixed the garden. All of this means that the pressure is taken off you when you come home from work and on the weekends."

Andre had to realise that he ought to be more gracious and humble.

"Shantel, I didn't ask your parents to do anything. You did." Andre's response was cold.

"You need to look at the bigger picture and realise they won't be here much longer. They'll go back to Dominica and I'll go back to work. You can't expect me to do the gardening and the decorating while I'm looking after the baby. My eyes aren't what they used to be so I don't exactly think I'd be useful at painting. I'm grateful for the help. Are you saying that you don't want dinner when you come home from a day's work? If that's the case I will tell my Mum not to bother leaving food for you. You can sort yourself out. Your choice. Just let me know." It was too late. I was angry.

"Shantel, there's no need to be like that. Sometimes I just want to come home to you and our baby. I don't always want your parents to be here. They have other children they can spend time with. Why don't they go to one of your brothers?" Andre asked.

"Well, neither of my brothers have just had a baby or moved into a house that needs work. They don't have a massive garden. You wanted this house as much as I did, maybe even more, but still I've hardly seen you pick up a paint brush or mow the lawn. My Mum is cooking dinner almost every day because I'm still weak. I thought you'd have more compassion. I've even suggested we use the opportunity to go out while my parents are here as they have no problem babysitting their granddaughter." I ranted quietly so that my parents couldn't hear my anger and disappointment in my fiancé.

"All I'm saying is I want some time alone with my family in my home, our home. I don't think I'm being unreasonable. Is it too much to ask? My family is here in this room and after a long day at work, I just want to spend time with you."

"No, it's not unreasonable, but right now my parents are here. They are also my family. You can't isolate me from them. That's not fair. They only have a few weeks left before they leave. Four weeks left Andre and they have plans to spend time with other family members. Do you really think they want to be working on this house? When have you ever said thank you to them for all they've done? They're making me happy being here Andre. Can't you understand that? If I'm happy and they're taking the stress of the house from me why can't you appreciate that? My parents want to make sure that our home is comfortable before they leave and you're being selfish because you want the house to yourself."

I didn't let up. I couldn't understand why Andre didn't appreciate the support we were getting free of charge.

"It's just how I feel Shantel," Andre stated bluntly.

"I'm going upstairs to feed the baby," I said. I picked her up out of the rocker and shut the living room door behind me, leaving him alone.

I was utterly disappointed in him. I held my baby tightly and took her upstairs to my parents' room. I chatted to them for a few minutes, trying to create a smile out of hurt, but they saw through it. I went next door to my bedroom to feed my angel in peace.

A shift in my emotions
A change in my direction
An unsatisfied notion
A constellation of disappointments
A partner oblivious to his actions
A fabrication of happiness
An illusion of a perfect family to outsiders
A desire for genuine happiness
An uncertainty of this reality
An unpredictable future that lies ahead

The bedroom door opened. It was Andre.

"You alright?" he asked

"Fine." I responded dismissively.

I thought back to what my manager had told me fine stood for 'feelings inside not expressed'. Andre needed to understand that I didn't appreciate him being disrespectful to anyone I loved. It was embarrassing and, of course, this wasn't the first time. I should not have let this behaviour go unchecked. He didn't have to call my parents his mum and dad; he had his own. They were separated but he still communicated with them periodically. Perhaps his actions towards my parents were a reflection of his own difficult relationship with his parents.

"Do you want to go out?" Andre asked.

"It's almost nine o' clock. I'm about to bath the baby and put her to bed. Besides, why do you think I would want to go anywhere with you right now? I've never known a man so selfish and ungrateful. Anyway, I want to be left alone. I'm feeding the baby and trying to calm down." I was still fuming and he knew it.

"I won't disturb you then." He turned the TV on and stripped off his clothes.

He laid on the bed with just his shirt and boxer shorts on. This frustrated me even more. He flicked the channels on the remote control to watch Top Gear. There I was, sitting in my tranquil peaceful sanctuary, for it to be disturbed by the sound of roaring cars and men enthused by the new technology that Audi had developed. I didn't share their excitement. I removed the baby from my breast. She looked at me with a puzzled expression. I fixed my clothes, stood up and left the room, closing the door behind me with the baby in my arms. I didn't turn back to look at Andre. He could have laid there all night by himself for all I cared. I wanted to sleep in the baby's room but there was just a cot in there. I continued to breastfeed her downstairs while flicking through the music channels. I didn't want to hear R&B or soul music. I sat on the sofa and realised that I was no longer interested in listening to love songs. Love songs and slow jams weren't real anymore. They were probably written and sung by artists who were just in the business to make money, not by people who really felt the emotion. All that wailing and deceitful words of pseudo-affection were not what I wanted to hear. Hip hop was my choice for the evening. Love songs were so overrated.

The next day, my parents packed their bags and went to Auntie Sophie's house. I didn't know how long they would be gone for, but I knew it would be for more than a weekend. Andre had caused this. I knew where my loyalties lay. If they were going to stay at my aunt's house until the remainder of their visit, then I would stay there with them as much as possible. If Andre wanted the house, he could stay in it alone.

I paid my parents regular visits. At least everyone was comfortable and Andre didn't feel as if his territory was being invaded. We were in a difficult place. He wanted to be with me and Leylah in isolation, with no interference from what he called 'outsiders'. How could our parents be outsiders? He was always ready to follow advice from his sisters, but our parents had more experience and wisdom. My parents were supportive and dedicated to ensuring my life was stress free. Andre couldn't comprehend that and clearly, he didn't understand, or care about my medical condition.

Chapter Thirteen:
Trapped

I needed to get away for a night or two. I was becoming depressed and needed to find solace. I wrote Andre a letter to explain that I was taking some time to myself. I packed a weekend bag and headed off to North London with Leylah before the busy Friday rush hour. I was going to stay with Anya, my old flatmate. We had barely seen each other since I had given up my flat. I needed peace, a confidante and, more importantly, the time and space I knew she could give me. She now had a two bedroom flat in Finchley. I was finally getting away from my misery in South London. On my journey, I contemplated my life and wondered whether it was really that dire. I thought about the facts.

- I was thirty-one years old.
- I was engaged to a tall, handsome man who had emotional problems but claimed he loved me.
- My baby was almost six months old.
- My body had suffered a little from the strain of pregnancy but I was bouncing back. I had been hospitalised a few times since giving birth. My consultant put me on a trial medication that had so far worked miracles. I hadn't had a crisis since.
- Was I still attractive?
- My confidence was low.
- We lived in a comfortable three-bedroom house in Greenwich.
- I was expected to return to work in a couple of weeks. That thought frightened me but it was positive progression from where I had mentally and physically been just a few months before.

I was scared but left my fear in God's hands, allowing him to guide me. I wanted love, or was that a thing of the past. I needed breathing space but Andre wouldn't give it to me. I felt stifled and smothered by his desire to keep me close. That side of him had tarnished my feelings for him.

I must have been travelling on autopilot, as I suddenly found myself at East Finchley station. I called Anya to pick me up. She arrived in no time and we decided to go to the supermarket for nibbles. It was likely to be a long night of conversation, which required the essential cheesy puffs and onion rings. Anya would not accept any money, saying I was her guest. I carried the baby in my sling as I didn't bring the buggy on the journey. I wanted to be care-free and enjoyed her being so close to me, even though she was getting heavier at six months old. My mobile phone rang in my handbag. I'd check the missed call at a convenient time. Five minutes later, it rang again. I ignored it. This was my time. If it was Andre, he'd have to wait until I had fed the baby once we were at Anya's flat.

In the car, I put my phone on silent as I didn't want the distraction and stress of an irritating man, nor did I need my daughter to pick up on my frustrations. Once at the flat, I fed and put her to sleep. I took my phone out of my bag and saw calls from Andre, his sister Shelly and his mother. I hesitantly listened to the voicemail messages.

'You have four new voicemail messages. To listen to your messages, press one.'

Message number one from Andre.

"Shantel, where are you? Call me as soon as you get this message."

Message number two from Andre's sister.

"Hello Shantel. How are you? It's Shelly. Just calling to find out what's happened. Call me back when you can, please. Take care, Shantel."

The pearl of all wisdom, Andre's mother. Message three.

"Shantel, where is my grandchild? Where have you taken her? She should be at home."

Message four. Andre.

"Shantel, can you call me back as soon as you get this."

Blossom Tree | Sharon Fevrier

He sounded even more agitated than he was in the first message. The friendliest voice was Shelly's. I'd planned to spend time with my friend and was not wasting my evening chatting on the phone. Anya left the room to give me some privacy. I called Shelly first.

"Hi Shelly. I saw your missed call." I wanted to keep the conversation brief.

"Shantel, how are you?" she enquired.

"I'm ok. So is Leylah. I take it you've spoken to your brother?" I asked knowingly.

"Yes, he said you left him a note. What's happened?" she quizzed.

"Shelly, I need time out from your brother. Andre is just too much for me right now. When I'm ready I'll go back home."

"Ok. Well, take care of you and baby." She said sounding relieved that we were safe.

"Thanks Shelly. Take care. Bye." I hung up.

Reluctantly, I made the next call.

"Hi Felicia, I got your message." I wondered what comment she would come out with.

"Where are you and where is my granddaughter?" she asked sternly.

Did she even know her son? Was his behaviour anything to do with his upbringing? She raised him. Was there enough love? Was it a happy environment? I wanted to tell her that I was on a plane to Timbuktu but resisted the temptation.

"I'm at a friend's house. Why?" I played ignorant curiosity.

"Did you tell Andre where you were going? Leylah should be at home. You shouldn't just take her without Andre knowing where you are." She seemed annoyed.

Felicia was getting involved in our relationship so I decided to let her know a few truths about her son.

"Felicia, your son is selfish, arrogant, jealous, possessive and worst of all, disrespectful to my parents. Do you want me to continue? I need time away from him. Your granddaughter is safe and fine. I am her mother Felicia." I was getting agitated and annoyed with this woman.

"Andre is her father and he should know where his baby is. You should take her home," Felicia instructed.

"I will take her home when I'm ready. Thanks for your concern. Goodbye." I hung up.

I couldn't believe the audacity of the woman, not caring about me or my feelings. She only cared about her precious son and his daughter, without having a clue about the type of man he had become. He was cold, but clearly learned from the master.

I was ready to make my final call.

"Andre. You called."

"Where are you Shantel?" Andre asked with a softly spoken voice.

"I'm at a friend's house Andre."

"Which friend Shantel?" he asked calmly.

"Look Andre. It's not important. Just know that your daughter is safe and tucked up in bed. I need some time alone so can you please give me that. I'll either come home tomorrow or the day after. I just want to be alone."

I wasn't about to give in and tell him where I was. He didn't need to know. I didn't trust him. He had treated my friends badly in the past, so what was to stop him from disrespecting Anya?

"Can I call you in the morning?" he asked.

"Ok. Bye." I replied and hung up.

Anya and I spent the night discussing my predicament. I knew when I went back home, it would be more drama. Andre needed to experience life without us. His actions were destructive. He wanted me to himself. Not even my parents could share my time with him. Anya was a comfort to me. I didn't want to keep my hurt and pain to myself anymore. I needed to talk. I didn't want to be this depressed and isolated woman. I wouldn't hide behind a smile. 'Tears Of A Clown' was my favourite Smokey Robinson song, but I didn't want to be the subject of the lyrics. We hadn't long been engaged, but sadly I couldn't visualise a happy ending.

I decided to go back home the following day, so as not to delay the inevitable. I sent Andre a text in the morning to let him know that we were coming home that afternoon. Anya cooked breakfast and in the afternoon Leylah and I travelled back to Greenwich. I was still so angry with Andre after he contacted his family, as if I had kidnapped our child. I needed a break and he couldn't give me one. I didn't know what the day would bring. Maybe we would kiss, make up and he would apologise to my parents. Maybe he would continue to play the victim, abandoned in his beloved home, crying to his family. Who knew? I was going to tell him how I felt. He had to understand, otherwise we were done and I really didn't want that. I was sure we could make our family work, but I couldn't sacrifice my dignity, personality and soul for a man who had issues. Maybe he fooled himself into believing he was ready for a relationship when we met. It was too late to turn back the clock though.

I took my front door key out of my bag. The porch door was already unlocked. I stepped inside, took a deep breath and opened the front door. Andre stepped out of the sitting room.

"Hello," he said. I put my overnight bag down on the floor just behind the front door. Andre came towards me and helped me unstrap Leylah out of the sling. He pulled her out and hugged her as if he hadn't seen her for years.

"Oh baby, I love you so much. I've missed you. Daddy loves you. Oh, my pumpkin. You're home. I love you, I love you, my love."

That show of affection was so unnecessary. It had only been one night! What would he be like if we went on holiday?

I took off my coat and shoes and headed upstairs to use the bathroom. I walked slowly back down the stairs and went straight into the kitchen to organise a bottle for the baby. She wasn't hungry, but I was keeping myself occupied before the discussion. I let him have his precious time as despite the theatrics, I was sure he had missed her. I contemplated going for a walk to get some air. How would he cope with the baby by himself for a few hours? No doubt he would take her to his sister's house for assistance. After getting a drink, I went into the sitting room.

"Where did you go?" Andre asked, pacing up and down with Leylah held tightly in his arms.

"I told you. I was at a friend's house. Why? I thought you were concerned about Leylah's wellbeing?" I wanted him to get to the real point.

"Of course I was concerned about Leylah's wellbeing. I am always concerned about our daughter. I always want to know where she is Shantel!" he responded sternly.

"Well, unfortunately you won't always know where Leylah is because you'll never be strapped to her twenty-four seven. You can't install her with GPS. When Leylah is with me, she is safe. I am her mother and I will always make sure she's safe. If I need a break away from you, no doubt I will take her with me. But there may be occasions I'll leave her with you. Do you think you would be able to care for her if I wasn't here for a couple of days?" I blurted in a patronising tone.

"Where would you go?" Andre asked cruelly.

"I'm not that insignificant. Do you think I've lost all my friends and no longer have a family? You haven't destroyed all my relationships yet Andre. That is your plan isn't it? Tell me!" I demanded.

Andre put Leylah down in her rocker. He was getting agitated. She sat peacefully for a moment but then started crying. Perhaps she sensed the tension in the air. I was so angry with him.

"And what was with you running to mummy, like a boy who's lost his toy? Did you really think she could help the situation? And your sister too? Really?"

What possessed him to involve his family in our private matters?

"Shantel, you took my daughter. You went away and I didn't know where you were. You're not supposed to take my baby away from me and not tell me where you're going." Andre sounded as if he were reading a script.

Leylah started to cry. Andre didn't flinch and remained seated on the sofa. I went to pick her up as she needed cuddles and so did I. Instantly, the crying stopped. Andre stood up. I slowly walked around the sitting room with Leylah in my arms. He stood by the door.

"I'm going upstairs to feed her." I walked towards the door where Andre stood on guard. He slammed the door shut.

"No, we'll finish this conversation now!" he demanded.

"No, I'm going upstairs." I paused. "Are you really trying to stop me from leaving the room? Who do you think you are?" I barked at him. I was becoming increasingly agitated.

I stood in front of him, with the baby on my hip. I had one hand free to try open the door but he blocked me. How dare he try to trap me in the room? Who was he? I saw him as a monster and he had triggered the fighter in me. Andre didn't move.

"Why are you being such an idiot Andre? Are you really trying to barricade me in this room? Really? Do you think that's sensible, you idiot?"

I'd lost complete respect for the man. Andre moved closer to me, but I didn't back down.

"You'll stay here until we finish our conversation," he said, towering over me. As he shouted words of venom and control, I could feel his spit on my face.

"Why are you spitting on me? Get out of my way Andre. Now!" I demanded.

"No!" he said as I felt the spray from his mouth.

My rage overwhelmed me. I spat back in his face. He slapped me in my face and I went flying into the middle of the sitting room, just managing to hold onto the baby.

"You slapped me?" I reacted surprised. I was in shock.

"You spat in my face," Andre wiped my saliva from his cheeks with the same hand that he had slapped me with. He looked shocked.

"I'm calling the police!" I yelled, walking over to the cordless house phone.

"I'm leaving!" Andre said, opening the door and rushing up the stairs.

I raced to my handbag in the hallway for my mobile phone. His family were about to get some news. The same people who, less than twenty-four hours ago, were happy to interfere in our relationship. I went upstairs to see what Andre was doing and sat in Leylah's bedroom. She sat quietly on my lap.

"Hello Shantel," Andre's mum answered.

"Hi Felicia. I thought you should know that I came home today with your granddaughter but your abusive son hit me. He actually slapped me while I was holding our daughter in my arms! I'm about to call the police on him if he doesn't leave the house within one minute." I waited for a response from the wise woman, who was so eager for the family reunion, without hearing the facts about her precious son.

"I need time to get my head around this Shantel. You do what you have to do. Let me call you back. I'll call you back." She hung up.

I was shocked at her response. But onto the next call. Andre's sister.

"Hi Shelly."

"Hi Shantel, how are you?"

"Your brother slapped me, in my face, while I was holding Leylah in my arms. So much for coming home today. You need to speak to your brother. He's violent. He trapped me in the sitting room. He's deranged. I'm calling the police on him!"

"Stop lying Shantel. Tell the truth!" Andre yelled from our bedroom. I could hear him shutting his wardrobe door.

"I am telling the truth!" I bellowed as I stood up.

"I've got to go Shelly." I ended the call.

Andre had changed his clothes and left our bedroom carrying his rucksack. He began walking down the stairs. I put the baby on her bed and arranged the cushions so she would feel comforted. I moved swiftly to the top of the stairs. I hadn't finished releasing my anger.

"You're just filthy, abusive scum Andre, and everyone is going to know about you!" I yelled.

I stood there and watched him put on his trainers. The front door slammed behind him, then the porch door opened and closed. He was gone. I ran down the stairs and rummaged through my handbag for my keys. I locked the porch door and left my key in the lock. He wasn't coming back uninvited. I locked the back door and did the same. I needed to feel secure and I didn't want my daughter to witness any more violence. My relationship with Andre was volatile, to say the least, and no longer for me. I deserved better. I didn't need or want this relationship. I didn't want that man anymore. The physical pain of the slap had disappeared, but the anger was raging. I was vengeful and wanted to hurt Andre in ways he couldn't imagine. How dare he treat me so badly? I wanted love, but was full of hate.

A feeling, no healing, compassion is lacking
A pain everlasting, conflicting, hands trembling
With anger, so vengeful
Protecting my offspring
My heart is defending
You did this, you monster, you hurt us, destroyer
I'm lost now, confused now, unsure of the ending
What's written in our future? I can't take more of this saga
I need to be stronger, controlled and secure
Oh what does God have for me in store?
My barriers are up, it's too late to draw back
Our love you've destroyed, with a knife you've hacked it
So what happens next, can I possibly be independent?
God show me a sign that's heaven sent
Is he really the best I can do?
What more in this relationship should I endure?
Surely there's more to life than these dramas, no more!
Show me a sign, I beg of you
Make a miracle happen, open a door

I warmed a bottle of milk for Leylah, sat down and fed her, trying desperately not to transfer any emotions to her. At least if she was satisfied she wouldn't be too demanding. I was still shaking and terrifyingly angry. Worse still, he slapped me with the baby in my arms. Even if I accepted Andre back home, the love I had would never be enough. I switched on the television in the sitting room and put Leylah into her rocker. She was happily distracted by the colourful characters on CBeebies. I called Louisa.

"Babe, I'm coming over," she announced. "See you within the hour."

I was glad Louisa was making her way over. I needed to keep myself busy. The housework wasn't going to do itself. I loaded the washing machine, tidied the kitchen and changed the bed sheets. Last thing I wanted was to lay in the same bed as him. I wanted everything fresh, with the smell of fabric conditioner and the feel of newness. I put Leylah to bed for her nap, now late as a result of the argument.

Love was supposed to make a house a home. Andre's idea of love involved restrictions, isolation and control. Perhaps he wanted to transfer his insecurities to me? A secluded lifestyle wasn't on my agenda. He met me as a sociable and open person. Not even my visual impairment could stop me from enjoying my life with family and friends. His smothering had led to our relationship smouldering. Isn't love about allowing your partner to be free to be themselves? Andre hurt people to keep them away. I now realised that he didn't have an honest or truthful bone in his body. He kept people, even his own family at bay.

Before I knew it, the housework was finished and Louisa was outside. Thank God. I rushed to open the door and she hugged me in the hallway. The floodgates opened and the tears flowed. Louisa removed her shoes and we sat down in the sitting room. I offered her a drink.

"Cup of tea please," she replied.

I went into the kitchen while she made herself comfortable. I walked back with her tea and some cold water for me.

"I'm not going to cry again. I can't give that arsehole any more power," I affirmed.

There was no way this man would ruin my life. Romance had blurred my vision at the start of the relationship. Ironically, though now partially sighted and dependent on Andre the situation was more clear than it had ever been. I was no longer in love with Andre but I had a child with him.

"You ok babe?" Louisa asked.

"Yes hun. The baby's sleeping but I'll have to wake her up soon. I've told my brothers and parents. I don't know what's happening now, or who's speaking to who. All I know is he is not coming to sleep here tonight, tomorrow, the day after and the day after that. I've told his sister and his mother too."

"What did they say?" Louisa enquired.

"Nothing really. Shelly said we shouldn't be spitting and hitting each other and his mother told me she needed time to think about what I had said to her. Unbelievable!"

I rolled my eyes and giggled at what I had said. The idea of someone thinking about their son hitting a woman, rather than being proactive and speaking to her son baffled me. The apple really didn't fall far from the tree. Anyway, that wasn't my concern. The relationship was spoiled by the afternoon's drama but Andre would still try to worm himself back into my good books. This time, that was an impossible task but he was too blind to see it. I hated him, but at the same time felt pity for him.

"She's crazy. Forget her and forget him. You need to concentrate on you and Leylah. You need to do what's best for the two of you. You've only just moved into this house, but you still have your flat. You'll be going back to work in a few weeks. Your parents are still here so they can support you while you decide on your next move." Louisa always gave constructive advice.

"What are you going to do?" she asked.

"I don't know. He needs to be taught a lesson. Hitting me was not a good move and maybe he needs to feel what a slap is like from a man. But I'm not like him. That bastard is the father of my child." I sighed. "Didn't I pick well?"

I smiled at my question, but realised whatever decision I would make, I would have to consider our daughter. She was the most precious person in my life. I had given Andre too many chances. He didn't deserve any more.

Louisa and I discussed and debated my options. Whatever the case, I didn't want that man anywhere near me. Louisa took care of Leylah while I had a long soak in the bath. I could hear my mobile ringing, but I had asked Louisa to answer my calls. I told her if Andre called she should ignore him. I needed time-out. After my bath, Louisa bathed Leylah and put her to bed, while I cooked dinner. She had to go home soon after we ate.

"I'll be fine. I'll lock the door after you leave. The police are on speed dial. Anyway, he won't do anything stupid. He's worried about my next move," I said reassuringly.

"Ok, well I'll call you when I get in. I want you to lock this door as soon as I leave. I'm going to watch you lock it," Louisa insisted.

"Ok, bye babe. Thanks for coming around." I took the key and locked the door. It was late but I decided to watch TV until I was ready to sleep.

Leylah woke me up with her early morning call. She was ready for a bottle. At least, if I walked away from the relationship, I would be leaving with my baby. She was worth it. Andre was a charming man and could cunningly twist reality to accommodate his truth. How well did I even know the man? I didn't even really know his friends. He seemed to only spend time with his siblings. They were his only advisors and confidantes, but their perspectives were similar.

I wasn't a woman who kept her feelings to herself or internalised my emotions. I wasn't going to cower in a corner; I was opinionated and I had a voice.

My parents and brother Calvin came around in the afternoon. "You look like you've lost weight Shantel," my dad remarked. "Don't stop eating because of that boy. Lina, see if you can make some food in the kitchen," he said to my mother.

"We bought some chicken Sha-Sha. I'm going to cook now." Mum stood up and went into the kitchen.

"I am eating. I always do. Mum, don't go overboard for me. I'm really ok." I shouted towards the kitchen where Mum had already started searching through the cupboards to prepare the banquet.

I was wearing jeans and a black vest top. The reality was I had lost a significant amount of weight. A lot had happened and my body had been through a lot. It was just a matter of time before I recovered though.

"Why does he feel he can put his hand on you? I don't understand." My father was angry.

I told them about the note, staying at Anya's overnight with Leylah and the events that took place afterwards.

"He shouldn't be putting his hand on you. What kind of monster is he? I don't like him. I really don't like him." My father expressed his vexation, but remained strangely calm.

"I think Ray spoke to him yesterday. He said he didn't mean to do it but couldn't take the spitting in the face," Calvin my brother added. Ray was our older brother.

"Actually, he spat at me first, so I gobbed in his face." I smirked as I said the crude words.

Mum came into the sitting room after hearing what I'd said.

"He deserves more than spit after the way he's treated you." Mum smiled too. We shared a similar sense of humour.

"Fact is though, I was still holding Leylah in my arms when he did it. He stood by the door and wouldn't let me leave the room. It was bound to end badly. At least I wasn't waving a knife at him like his last girlfriend did!" The room went quiet in response to what I had said.

"What do you mean?" my father asked.

"Well, he told me that his ex-girlfriend tried to stab him in the back. She accused him of rape and entrapment." My family stared at me in astonishment.

"Apparently, he cheated on his girlfriend with her best friend. He says his girlfriend had mental health problems. He tried to leave her but the night he told her the relationship was over she ran out of the house naked and went banging on the neighbour's door. The police were called and arrested him. He was charged with rape and entrapment but the charges were dropped." I stopped talking to see what their reaction would be to Andre's history.

"Do you know why the charges were dropped?" Calvin asked.

"Andre told me that somehow his people found out what safe house she was in. They knew where her family lived. She had two children so after the threats, she decided to drop the charges." The story sounded like something from a thriller but this was Andre's life before me.

"Safe house?" Calvin asked amazed.

"Yep. He told me he had to give up his job in HR as the case went on for over one year. He needed a job that was easy and not taxing on his brain. When I met him, he was doing admin for a local authority but decided that he needed to get back on track when he met me. He got a job in HR but his CRB showed he had been charged for the offences, though they were dropped." My family were sitting in silence listening to this drama.

"Did you know about this when you got with him?" Calvin quizzed.

"Nope. He revealed bits of the story as time went by. I guess he's good at fooling people. He can be charming when he needs to be, but really, he's covering up some demons inside. I'd love to hear his ex's side of the story but I doubt I will."

I continued talking about the relationship quite openly with my family. They needed to know what the issues were. Ultimately, I had to reconsider the future between Andre and I but more importantly, Leylah. We ate the dinner that was lovingly prepared by my mother. I played some music to lighten the mood. After the dishes were washed and the kitchen was cleared, my parents decided to make their way back to my aunt's house and my brother went home. It had been another long day. I was glad I hadn't heard from Andre, but I knew he would send me a text message soon enough. I put Leylah to bed and watched TV, wondering if I had said too much. If I decided to try and mend our broken relationship, again, I didn't want my parents to hate him. I had so much to think about. I lay in bed, flicking through the channels when I noticed my mobile phone vibrating. There was a text. I put my glasses on to read the message from Andre.

Hi Shantel. Can I come home and get my clothes for work tomorrow please?

I thought about saying no meaning he would have to buy a suit before he went to work in the morning but I wasn't that cruel.

You can come but you only have two minutes to get your things and leave otherwise I will call the police.

Ok. I will be about 20 minutes. I will text you when I'm outside.

Twenty minutes later, the phone vibrated again.

I'm outside. Can you open the door please?

I alerted Louisa to let her know he was coming and I would text her again in five minutes to confirm we were safe. I went downstairs and opened the front door. I struggled to see through the porch window as it was dark outside but I knew he was there. I unlocked the door. Andre stepped into the house.

"Hi."

"You have two minutes." I spoke sternly, holding my mobile phone and the house keys tightly in my hands.

Andre took off his trainers.

"Don't disturb Leylah either," I uttered quietly as he walked up the stairs.

I heard him push the bedroom door open and rummage through his wardrobe. I stood at the bottom of the stairs wondering what happened to the life I was supposed to have with him. I still loved him but I wanted things to be different. Could it get any better? I couldn't help myself and thought of his warm embrace. What was I thinking? I couldn't ask for that. He assaulted me. He had to pay for the hurt and pain he had inflicted on our family. Sorry wasn't enough and I hadn't even heard it yet. I didn't care where he was sleeping, and was just glad that I had my own space. I was sleeping in a super king size bed, without my king. It was my bed now and I was the queen he didn't appreciate.

He walked down the stairs with an overnight and suit bag. He put his trainers on and walked towards the front door.

"Sorry." He apologised and walked out the door.

I locked the porch door and went back up to my bed. I sent a text to Louisa letting her know he had gone, turned off the TV and fell asleep.

Chapter Fourteen:
Sorry

Monday morning, I woke up to a text message from Andre. *I'm sorry Shantel. I still love you.* No response necessary. Leylah was already awake. I picked her up and gave her a long hug while thinking about what we would do for the day. I had food in the house so didn't need to go shopping. The sky looked gloomy but no rain was predicted so I planned a walk after breakfast.

She looked so adorable in her buggy. I was glad I'd spent the money on it. Why put my baby in a Ford when she could ride in a Mercedes? I received two calls on our walk, one from my parents and the other from Louisa, both checking that I was fine. I convinced them that I was and told them that Andre had texted an apology. This was how he always showed some remorse for his actions, but he couldn't change his personality. There was a limit to how long I could stay in such a destructive situation. Relationships needed continuous work, especially when perspectives on life were as miles apart as ours were.

The walk was good exercise for not only my body but also my mind. I could see things more clearly. As much as I was angry with and disappointed in Andre, I still thought about how we could repair our broken family. We needed some help. Not from his friends — he really didn't have any he could count on anyway. I saw how they treated each other and their counsel would definitely not work for me. We needed professional help to get through this war zone. If Andre wanted this relationship to work, he would have to accept that. The problem was that he thought he knew it all. Such a stubborn man. I just wanted to live the dream and get married. I still thought that he could be the one, but never did I think I would be in this position.

Still, I was determined to succeed whichever way my life panned out. Whether I stayed with Andre or decided to quit, I would be okay.

Would I end up being a disabled single mother?
Would I be able to do the same job or would I be demoted?
How much will I earn?
How much money will I need?
My parents were preparing to leave and return to Dominica.
Would I end up alone in South-east London, without any
friends living nearby?
My brothers had their own lives to lead and I didn't expect them
to support me.
I had to support myself but didn't know how well I could until I
went back to work.

My parents and aunt had agreed to look after the baby until I had settled back into work but eventually I would have to find a nursery for her. We'd only lived in the house a few months. At least we had the furniture which, when looking around the house, I realised that I had bought, not him. I'd even paid for all the kitchen appliances. The mortgage was high and I wouldn't be able to afford the payments by myself. I had taken out extra money from the equity of my flat to pay my share of the mortgage while I was on maternity leave.

I did what I wanted with my day, waking up when I needed to or when the baby needed me. I got on with the housework and made the most of the garden. Occasionally, my sickle cell flared, but I'm sure that was because of all the stress my body and mind had been through. The wonder drug I had been prescribed, though working well, couldn't counter the stress of my domestic situation. My mind wandered to what the long-term side effects might be.

That evening, I received a text from Andre.

Can I call you?

I wasn't sure if I was ready for the conversation.

Yes, but I'm going to bed soon.

The phone rang. I answered.

"Hello," said Andre.

"Hi." I responded.

"How are you? How's Leylah?" Andre asked.

"Fine." I answered reluctantly.

I didn't want to talk to him but the conversation had to take place eventually.

"I'm sorry Shantel. I shouldn't have hit you and I promise you, it will never, ever happen again. If we're in a difficult situation like that again, I'll just walk away." Andre paused for a response.

"To be honest Andre, I'm pretty fed up with this relationship. You are who you are and I don't know if you will ever change. I can't breathe in this relationship. We won't be able to survive the way we are." I needed Andre to understand that I wasn't happy.

"I know Shantel, I know. I know things have to change. Can we meet and talk? How about tomorrow? Please say yes." Andre pleaded.

The last thing he wanted was for me to have the time to think about and decide on separation.

"It depends on whether I can get a babysitter. I'm not confirming anything yet." I wasn't going to inconvenience anyone because of Andre and his selfish ways.

"Can't you ask your parents?" he asked.

"You don't have the right to ask anything of my parents. Don't you dare!" I answered firmly.

I wasn't impressed with him even considering my parents to babysit when just a few weeks ago he had disrespected them so blatantly in our house.

"Ok, ok. I'll organise a babysitter. If it's not tomorrow, it'll be the weekend. Let me work on it, ok?"

"I've got to go." I wanted to end the call.

"Ok. I'll let you know tomorrow if I've organised a babysitter."

"Fine. Bye." I hung up.

By Saturday he had organised a babysitter. I wasn't excited about meeting him at all. In fact, I wondered if I was doing the right thing by going anywhere with him. Talk? Did I have any more talk left in me? He picked us up at 5 o'clock. His mother was the babysitter. I hadn't spoken to her since the day she told me she would call me back after I had told her that her son had hit me. She hadn't even called me back. I was disgusted with her. This was a woman who was happy to get involved in our issues when it suited her but she couldn't handle the reality of her son's behaviour. She had a degree in psychology but didn't know how to use it appropriately in real life family situations. She was disingenuous and unsupportive. I no longer respected her or her son. I hated, yet still loved him. I finally understood the saying, 'there's a thin line between love and hate'.

The journey to Norbury was long because of the traffic. Leylah slept in the back of the car for most of the journey. She woke up just as we pulled up outside her grandmother's house.

"Wait here. I'll just drop Leylah off," Andre instructed.

He took her out in the car seat and grabbed her bag. He walked up the steps to the house and used his keys to open the door. I sat there for a couple of minutes though it felt like an eternity. I realised I hadn't kissed my daughter goodnight. I needed to. So, I got out of the car and walked up the steps to the house. The door was left open, so I walked in and followed the voices. Andre and his mother both turned around surprised to see me standing there.

"I didn't say goodbye to my daughter," I said as I reached over and took Leylah out of her grandmother's arms. "Bye-bye baby. See you in a few hours." I handed her to Andre and started to walk down the stairs.

"Err excuse me Miss. How dare you enter my house and not greet me. I don't have anyone come into my house and not greet me." She was annoyed.

I wanted a rise out of her and she took the bait.

"Up to now, I'm still waiting for you to call me back. You were quick to get involved and call me when I decided to take a break from your son. How come you weren't quick to react when your son slapped me in my face while I was holding your granddaughter?" I demanded an answer.

"You can't talk to me like that," she replied.

"I just did Felicia," I responded.

"From now on you will call me Mrs Cane." She spat back at me.

"I won't call you anything." I started walking down the stairs to leave.

Andre didn't say a word throughout the exchange, but I honestly didn't expect that he would anyway. No backbone whatsoever. Why should I respect his mother when he didn't respect my parents? He needed to know just how it felt. My behaviour was so out of character, but it felt good. Andre had to know that I was now unpredictable. And you know what? He had made me that way.

"And don't come back into this house!" Felicia yelled in fury.

Andre followed me down the stairs after handing his mother the baby. I could tell he wasn't happy but I didn't care. He now had a taste of his own medicine. I got into the car and Andre soon followed.

"Why did you do that?" Andre asked.

"What? Kiss my daughter?" I was being facetious.

He and his family needed to know my pain. Andre's mother was a huge disappointment. I had enjoyed our relationship prior to that event. I saw her as a friend, advisor, confidante and a mother figure. Instead, she was nothing but a real life Ice Queen. I could never have her back in my life. There was no point as she simply couldn't be trusted.

"You know what I mean. You came in the house and didn't even say hello to my mum. Shantel, that's really not on, is it?" Andre took the moral high ground.

"Andre, I hardly think you have the right to tell me what you think is right and wrong. You know what? Go and get Leylah. I want to go home."

I didn't want to talk to him or go out with him. It wasn't going to be a good night. It had started off badly and would only get worse.

"No Shantel. We have to go out. Let's just carry on with our plans."

He started the engine and drove off. I sighed with exhaustion. This was not what I wanted from a relationship with Andre or any man for that matter. Anyway, was I still attractive? I knew my appearance hadn't really changed, but because I couldn't see properly, how could I be sure? If I left Andre, would I be able to find someone else? Why was I thinking about being single anyway? What would it take to make my relationship work? Damn, I was confused, but I was all dressed up and about to go to a bar with Andre. I guess he figured that sitting face to face in a restaurant would create further tension between us; what better way to avoid working through our difficulties than to sit in a bar listening to music? Andre knew I loved music, though my taste had changed since my feelings for him had died. I just wanted to listen to hip hop, garage, house — anything I could dance to and that wasn't about love. I wanted a beat to move to. Getting tipsy was out of the question. Besides, I only wanted to go out for a few hours, then get my child and go home without him.

Instead, we pulled up outside an Italian restaurant in Dulwich. We had eaten there before in happier times. I was hungry and bar food wouldn't have satisfied me anyway. I ordered the seafood linguini and Andre the lasagne. We shared a bottle of white wine, which I needed to take the edge off.

"Shantel. I don't want us to have a heavy night. I just want us to try and enjoy each other's company. Can we try?" he asked.

Andre wanted to have a peaceful night, but I wasn't feeling at peace.

"Andre, it's hard for me to switch off as if nothing has happened. You disrespect my family and show no remorse. I take a break from you and when I return you slap me in my face. Do you really think I can just brush this under the carpet? You know I can't do that Andre."

I downed half my wine. He gave me a refill. Perhaps he wanted to get me drunk and kiss me, then all would be forgiven. He knew I was a forgiving person, but this I would never forget. He continued to cut open the same wound, how could I not forget?

"I've missed you Shantel. You and Leylah. How have you both been this week?" he enquired.

"We've been fine. My parents have brought food around for us, even though we didn't need it. Leylah and I have been on long walks. I've had a hospital appointment. It went well. It's been a nice relaxing week and we've made the most of our time." I wanted Andre to know that life went on and we didn't pine after him.

"What did your consultant say?" Andre asked.

"Everything is fine and the tablets are making improvements, so it seems as though I'll stay on the wonder drug for a good while. The only thing I can't do while I'm on the tablets is get pregnant and that's not going to happen now, is it?" My words were harsh.

"But I'm happy if it stops me from getting sick. My priority is to look after Leylah. That's all I want to do. She is my priority and I love her more than anything or anybody else in the world. All I want to do is protect her, and that doesn't involve exposing her to warring parents. She needs to see what love is all about.'

Our food arrived. We ate quickly and in silence. Andre clearly had a schedule and wanted us to move onto the next part of the evening. He knew I was a woman that liked to eat out and socialise so he played on that. It was his way of making sure that he still had a relationship. I wondered what was next on the agenda but ordered dessert anyway. After all, the dinner was on him. Andre paid the bill and acted like a complete gentleman, opening all the doors — out of the restaurant and into the car. We drove for about half an hour, listening to some Brian McKnight. He knew I loved this music though I hadn't listened to him in months. His game plan was in full swing. We pulled up outside a bar in the city. It was modern and classy with a lot of bouncers on the door. At around 9, a few people, all elegantly dressed, were milling about the entrance.

Andre told me the dress code so I wore an appropriate outfit that I also felt confident in. It was the dress I had on the first time we had met, well over a year ago. I was slimmer now and my hair was still thick. I wore light make-up and had applied it as well as I could. I didn't want to appear to have made too much effort.

We walked into the bar. The music was loud. The sound was amplified with every step I took through the foyer. The bass thumped through my chest, almost rattling my insides. The DJ announced that there would be a live performance later that evening. It was a popular reggae artist from Jamaica. He announced the other artists performing that night. The line-up was amazing. Andre was definitely trying to make me forget our woes. He knew I loved live music and the artists were some of my favourite. I smiled at him. He smiled back. This, by no means, was forgiveness, but I felt the tension ease. My shoulders dropped and I exhaled. I was going to dance, drink, sing and be very merry. This was my night and I knew Andre would get me home. The revellers in the venue were mature, sophisticated and elegant. The atmosphere was vibrant and energetic. The band was excellent and the artists performed all their popular hits. I was amazed at how well I knew the songs. The night drew to an end and my feet were aching from all the dancing. We had even managed a slow dance. I had to admit that it was a romantic evening. My feelings shifted. My heart softened. Maybe I could try again, at least for our daughter's sake. We went home together, made love and I fell asleep on his chest.

The following day we went to pick up the baby.

"Don't take long!" I shouted to Andre as he left the car to go inside his mother's house. Last thing I wanted was to be bored sitting in the car waiting for Andre while he engaged in a lengthy conversation with the Ice Queen. I pulled out my mobile phone and updated Louisa on last night's events.

"Just don't rush things. You need to have a proper discussion about all of this." Louisa stated the obvious.

"We're going for counselling babe. There has to be some change. He needs to acknowledge that he has a problem. No one can do that for him. We haven't resolved anything yet, but at the end of the day, I have to try again despite him continuing to chip away at our relationship. He doesn't recognise the damage he's causing though." I sighed.

"Hun, it will work out. One way or another. You'll get through it," Louisa reassured.

"Thanks darling. He's coming back now. We'll catch up later." My baby was on her way back to me.

"Ok babe, take care of you and Ley-Ley," she replied.

"Will do. Bye."

"Bye babe," Louisa said.

I opened the car door to see my baby sleeping in the car seat. She was so beautiful and at peace. I wanted to pick her up but didn't want to wake her. My angel slept all the way home.

Sunday flew by. Andre called me on Monday afternoon from work. He told me that he had arranged six sessions of relationship counselling through his work; it was an employee benefit. I accepted.

Louisa babysat for our first session. Andre and I made our way to the home of the counsellor. We arrived at a Victorian house in the middle of a quiet cul-de-sac in Greenwich. A middle-aged lady with short dark hair answered the door. She invited us into one of the reception rooms. It was a family home, with colourful ornaments and photo frames on the side-table in the hallway. The counsellor introduced herself as Bianca. She started by asking us what we wanted from the sessions. She looked at me as if to suggest that I answer first. I did.

"There's a lot of friction in this relationship. We're different people, but ultimately we want the same thing. I find Andre difficult to live with and to be in a relationship with." I paused.

"Sometimes I can't breathe. I need him to loosen his grip. I've been through so many changes since we've been together. He disrespects my friends and family and expects me to accept his behaviour. I can't accept it so we clash. I feel isolated and don't want to feel that way anymore. I want Andre to see how his behaviour is upsetting me. This relationship won't last unless things change. I want things to change." I concluded.

"Thank you Shantel," Bianca said and turned to Andre for his objective.

"Well, we do clash. Sometimes I ask Shantel to do things and she doesn't. I don't disrespect her family and friends but I think it's important that we have time to ourselves, as a family. I don't mind her family being around, just not all the time. I've explained this to her but she hasn't made any changes. It's our house but sometimes it feels like it's taken over by other people. That's the crux of it." Andre shifted in his seat.

"Thank you Andre," Bianca said, as she made some notes on her pad. Once she finished writing she looked up at both of us and explained the next steps.

"So, Shantel, you've told me that you want Andre to be more respectful and give you time and space for you, your family and friends. Andre, you've told me that you'd like more family time. There has to be a way to compromise so that you can both benefit from change. That is what we will work on. Can you both explain what has happened recently that has brought you here?"

I started to talk about the recent events. It felt uncomfortable sharing my story but I needed to talk freely so that this stranger could provide a solution to our problems. I needed this impartial woman to hear what I felt about our relationship. I wondered what Andre would say in defence. Andre was a charming man and had the ability to make strangers believe anything. The difference now was that Bianca had six hours to get to know us. That was enough time for Andre to reveal his true colours. After I had portrayed our history, Andre started to tell her his version of events.

"There should be no hitting or slapping," she said to Andre. This cannot happen again. It's important that if your discussions get heated you walk away and come back together when you have both calmed down." Bianca was a straight talker.

I was happy to use this forum to express my concerns without Andre talking over me or making me feel as if everything was my fault. The six sessions came and went so quickly. Unfortunately, it felt as if nothing had changed. There was no resolution. Andre did not see the errors of his ways. I knew Bianca had made every effort to highlight some of his insecurities. At least that was obvious to her. However, it wasn't obvious to Andre that he was the thorn in our relationship. He felt that the problem was still with me.

Our relationship continued despite the ineffective counselling sessions. Life slowly reverted to normal. My parents returned to Dominica and it was time to return to work.

Chapter Fifteen:
Work To Fly

S uddenly, my maternity leave was over and I was declared fit to return to work after my eye operations. I was extremely apprehensive about going back to the office. My visual impairment had shattered my confidence. It felt as if I would have to start again with a new set of limitations and fears. I was happy in my bubble of the hustle and bustle of Clapham, even with the many drunken party goers spilling out of the clubs and bars at two in the morning. Living in Greenwich was very different — quiet and peaceful — and my home had become my sanctuary. I wished I could have had more sick-leave but I was down to half pay and the mortgage was now a struggle. My reserves of cash had dwindled away to nothing. So, I had no choice but to start work again. There was no alternative. I probably needed to get back into the real world and learn to live as a disabled woman anyway. There. I'd said it — the 'D' word.

I confirmed a return date with my manager. An appointment was also arranged with Occupational Health. I had no idea what they would say. I knew there was a woman at work who had visual defects but I didn't know the extent of her disability. She had specialist equipment to help her work. If she could do it then surely I could too. She used a white stick when she walked around. I didn't have to. As daunting as it felt, I could cope.

"Welcome back Shantel. It's good to see you. How are you feeling?" asked Peter, my manager.

"Hi Peter. Good to see you too. I'm okay. I'm adjusting to one or two changes. Life is a little different," I replied.

Peter asked about what I could see. He told me about an agency that could assess my needs, with a view to providing specialist equipment that would make work easier. I felt reassured after that meeting and made my way to the Occupational Health appointment.

The doctor was pleasant and made me feel confident about my return to work. It seemed there were others in the same boat and lots of help was at hand. I said a silent thank you to God as I now knew everything would work out. I opted for an assessment by someone from the Royal National Institute of Blind People. I wanted a specialist who knew what equipment would be useful for me. Fortunately, there was one who turned out to be really helpful. There were magnifiers to use at my desk, portable magnifiers, a mobile phone that spoke to me and magnifying software for my PC and laptop. The equipment came within two weeks and I was given a demonstration for each item. There was a lot to learn, but I had time and there was support at the end the phone. My job involved home visits, going to meetings and extensive note-taking for literally everything as I sometimes had to prepare cases for court. My patch was modified so that I was within walking distance of the office. In no time, I was fully functional again. The sense of empowerment and confidence I felt made me feel as if I could conquer anything.

My daughter was developing nicely. She was approaching her first birthday and needed additional stimulation. We decided to get her started in nursery. I was worried about her being looked after by strangers but I had to let her socialise. Other mothers did this so I could too. It wasn't long before we found somewhere suitable. The routine changed again. Even though dropping off and picking Leylah up was exhausting business, I had a little more time to myself. By the time Andre came home in the evenings after work, I had already cooked and got her ready for bed. All he had to do was turn the microwave on to warm up his dinner. Weekdays became monotonous, but such was domestic life.

An opportunity arose at work for an office-based role. My field job had ensured that I had remained slim and fit but it was time for a change. The job was in a different team but I wouldn't have to trudge through the streets of the borough, doing home visits in houses that smelt of wet dogs and meeting parents of children who were just simply wayward. I needed a new challenge and to expand my knowledge and repertoire of skills. I was always good at selling myself in interviews, so, I got the job and started straight away. My confidence was growing and I had even gone out with my colleagues for the occasional drink after work. Andre wasn't one hundred per cent comfortable with that but he soon realised that I didn't care. After all, I encouraged him to go out, which he did on a regular basis. He spent most Fridays with his brother, and I had no reason to doubt him. In any event, my Friday night routine was sorting out the baby for bed, catching up on some TV and then getting a good night's sleep, knowing that the next day, an early start was inevitable. Andre would arrive home at some point during the night. Unfortunately, he wasn't always of great use to me on Saturday mornings so I rarely had a lie in. Our relationship was now a far cry from the early days. I preferred my quiet time and space. He was there to take me shopping and occasionally vacuum the house on the weekends. That's all he did despite the numerous debates we had about his lack of interest and pride in our home. As a result, I had no desire to personalise our house. The walls were still magnolia and unlikely to change anytime soon.

We rarely had sex. In fact, I wasn't interested. He now didn't have a clue — instead he was acting like a male porn star. The passion was gone. Foreplay was minimal and I had no desire whatsoever to pleasure him. I no longer felt motivated to tell him what I liked and what I wanted. We had been together long enough for him to know. I found myself reminiscing about past relationships and the close intimacy we had. When did it become so bad? In fact when we were having sex, I found myself fantasising about doing it with previous partners. I felt awful about it, but it got me through. I became even more withdrawn from the relationship.

I had endured pain in the relationship, so it shouldn't have been a surprise to either of us that my feelings had changed. Andre claimed he was still in love with me, but I wasn't in love with him anymore. I loved him as the father of my child and for wanting to build a future with me. For that, I was prepared to try and make things work. He suggested another round of counselling as we were still arguing. I still didn't have any insight into the core reason for his insecurity and jealousy, but I knew that I didn't want him to continue blaming me for our problems. Despite everything, I was still dedicated to him. I had this need to make him understand that I was his and was not going to stray. In turn, he continued to tighten the leash. I resented paying half of the mediation fee. Why should I when he was the one with the problem? The sessions would cost fifty pounds each. We had already been through counselling and it didn't help, but at least it was free. Eventually, I agreed as the tension was through the roof. We had six sessions. At the end of it, I was one hundred and fifty pounds down and still, there was no resolution.

The stress of the relationship meant I continued to have crisis after crisis. Stress was the prime suspect. I discussed my relationship issues with my friends openly but there was nothing they could do to help. I received counselling from the haematology psychologist attached to the clinic. She asked me questions that made it easy for me to disclose my feelings about the problems at home. Of course, she nailed the stress down to my relationship and she spoke about how important it was to try and work through the issues, which, in turn, could help my health to improve. She wanted Andre to come with me to my next appointment with her. I discussed this with Andre.

"Why do I need to be there?" he asked.

"Well, I guess it's because I'm still getting sick so often and they want to work out the cause."

Why did I have to explain this to the man who was my fiancé? He was supposed to know me more than anyone else in the world. Didn't he realise stress made me sick, and if I was really unwell he would have to look after our daughter alone?

"Ok, fine. I'll come," Andre agreed reluctantly.

I wondered how charming he'd be in front of the psychologist and whether she would be able to see straight through him. I had no expectations but hoped for a resolution of some kind. I booked the appointment for the following Friday.

I met Andre in Waterloo and we travelled to the hospital together. It was a short distance from work. He was dressed smartly in a grey suit and blue tie. I was also dressed for work in my usual smart casual look. We arrived on time for our appointment and were seen straight away. This was the first time Andre had met my psychologist. She introduced herself.

"Hello Andre. I'm Helen. How are you?" she asked politely.

"I'm fine thank you. And you?" he replied.

"Good thanks. Please take a seat." Helen opened her file with my case notes. I had been seeing her for a few years so she knew me well. The session began.

"So, I wanted to explain that this clinic doesn't see patients with their partners, but Shantel has been getting very ill quite frequently. I thought it might be beneficial to you both if I could help in any way." Helen had a soothing voice, with a calming effect.

"Shantel, do you think you can highlight what you think the issues are at the moment?"

This felt like déjà vu, I was trying to be optimistic. This was a service courtesy of the NHS to stop me from getting sick so often. A useful resource that I hoped Andre would take advantage of. I took a deep breath in and started my constructive moan.

"Ok. At the moment, we're doing alright. I guess there are some underlying issues that haven't been dealt with. Andre feels that I am going to cheat on him with any man that turns my head. He thinks I can be sweet-talked by anyone. Fact is, I've been faithful since the beginning of this relationship and will continue to be, but this is exhausting. Andre has picked fights with my friends, so they don't come around or contact me as often anymore. He's disrespected my parents. He created a big issue when they were last here because he felt they were spending too much time at our house. They were helping me with the baby through my maternity leave. He didn't appreciate the support they were giving me. Now they're gone it's down to us to do everything and obviously it can be quite tiring. I'm not saying that I can't cope but I do get tired. Sometimes I just want to know that Andre will encourage me to go out and be with friends. Instead, he creates obstacles and indirectly lets me know that he's not happy about me socialising. I miss having girly fun. I miss having my own space. I know I have a new title as a mother, but that shouldn't stop me from still being a friend to my friends and a daughter to my parents. I feel like Andre is constantly looking over my shoulder to see what I'm doing."

I talked about the numerous occasions I'd been surfing the internet on my phone or texting someone in the living room when he would creep around the house, silent as a mouse, just to catch me out. I wasn't supposed to be in a relationship like this. I shrugged my shoulders to indicate to them both that I had finished. At that point, I didn't feel I really needed to say anything more.

"Ok, thank you Shantel. Now Andre, would you like to talk about what you're feeling?" Helen looked at Andre.

He took in a deep breath, with his hands on his knees and started to talk about our relationship.

"First of all, I'd like to say that our relationship isn't quite as bad as Shantel makes it out to be. We have our good times and bad times. Shantel doesn't always listen to me when I ask something of her. She kept telephone numbers of her ex-boyfriends, even after I had asked her to get rid of them and change her phone number. As far as I'm concerned, she shouldn't be in contact with them. I got rid of one of my phone numbers for her. I have explained to her that there are men out there who don't care that she has a fiancé. All they care about is trying to get with her. Well, I don't want any problems in the future. My motto is 'prevention is better than cure'. I would rather Shantel avoid situations where someone can tempt her. That's not what I want." Andre finished his monologue, with a satisfied look on his face.

Helen took a moment to digest what Andre had said. She was making notes throughout and once she had finished, she looked up and summarised his thoughts.

"Thank you Andre. That was clear. Well, it seems to me that there are some issues around trust between you. I'm just wondering what we can do to help you both." Helen paused again and looked at her notes.

I didn't dare look at Andre. I just wanted her to make Andre see the error of his ways. Helen looked up at us again.

"What I'm going to suggest is that I speak to my colleague to find out whether we can offer you both separate sessions. This is not a service that we usually provide at all, but it could help. Is that something that you would be happy trying Andre?" Helen asked.

"Yeah, fine," Andre responded with a surprised tone.

Can you both just give me a few minutes?" Helen stood up, took the file and her pen, and left the room.

"You ok?" I asked.

"Yes, I'm fine." Andre rubbed his face in exhaustion. "I've got a busy schedule when I get back into the office. There's a meeting at 2:30 that I can't miss."

He looked at his Rolex, which we bought together. Andre told me that his ex-girlfriend had destroyed his Breitling watch in anger. I wondered what drove her to do it. Andre's issues with me were related to his previous relationships, and they had unfairly spilt into ours. His past had never been my concern until now. Helen walked back into the room with another woman that I didn't recognise.

"Ok. Let me introduce you to Dionne. Dionne is another therapist. As Shantel is my patient, Dionne will be happy to see you Andre."

We all exchanged pleasantries. Dionne and Andre exchanged telephone numbers. She told him that she would be in contact in the next few days to arrange an appointment. The session was over. Andre had to rush back to his office. I kissed him goodbye, then we went our separate ways.

That evening, at home, Andre seemed more quiet than usual. I had served dinner. Leylah was in bed so we were having a peaceful meal.

"How did you think the session went today?" I asked tentatively as I didn't want him to shut down on me, or dismiss the importance of the day.

"It was fine. She listened but didn't tell us anything. Time will tell I guess. Anyway, shall we watch a film tonight? I bought some DVDs today," Andre changed the subject.

That was ok. I was a patient person. I hoped Andre would accept the opportunity of support. There was no longer a stigma attached to therapy. Andre needed it. I decided I wouldn't raise the subject again and leave it until he was ready to talk. After all, I would only frustrate myself. What was the point in that? In the meantime, we would carry on as normal, though normality with Andre wasn't necessarily a happy existence. I was still in the relationship because I didn't want to feel like a failure. I wanted a father for my daughter. I wanted to build a home and a life with Andre, but the issues in our relationship made it a challenge for me to focus on marriage and a future. The reality was that I couldn't even decide on a colour scheme for the house, home, whatever it was. I just let day-to-day living take over the planning for a future.

I continued with my counselling sessions. Helen gave me strategies I could use to de-stress. Just talking to her helped me to refocus on the elements of my life that were working. I had my parents who were supportive from afar. I had family. I had friends that hadn't abandoned me when the going got tough. More importantly, I had my beautiful angel who needed me. My emotional state would affect her wellbeing and her welfare was more important than trying to maintain a relationship with her father. Did I want to be a single parent? No. But my new-found confidence made me realise that I could do all things. I would need a little help occasionally and had a trusted few I could turn to when that time arose. I was becoming stronger every day and Andre knew it.

Two months later.

I arrived for my scheduled haematology appointment, with my counselling session booked straight after. Needles. Ugh. My therapist had given me strategies to cope with the dreaded metal intruder. Having a blood condition and a phobia to needles wasn't a good combination at all, but I had to get a grip, because I was stuck with both...forever. After the dreaded deed and a discussion with my consultant I was ready to meet with Helen.

"So Shantel. How have you been since we last met?" she asked.

"I've been fine. Not been sick. The tablets are still working well. My home life hasn't changed a great deal. Maybe I'm just floating and getting on with things. I guess if there isn't a great change then I have to start considering another way to make myself happy."

I had already thought about whether the future with Andre could be different. I didn't want to be alone but there had to be a different kind of love. I wanted to remember what it felt like to be in love. I wanted a man to not just profess love, but also trust, honour and respect me. The words sounded like the lyrics of an RnB song. Not that I knew which one — they all sounded the same to me now. But truth be told, I fantasised about real love, a relationship to be cherished. I deserved it because I was a good person. I had given Andre my heart and soul, but he lost both and was now left with my physical shell. I thought about the older generation. Through thick and thin, they stayed together. They were troopers, battling through hurt, pain, devastation, good and bad times. They made it. I wasn't prepared to battle though. My health was more important to me than status.

"Well, what do you think it would take for you to be happier Shantel?" Helen's questions always made me think about my life in ways that I had been afraid to.

"Well, my relationship isn't sustainable, unless there is some change. I don't want to suffer because my partner has trust issues that he refuses to deal with. He tries to isolate me. That's not working for me. The unknown is a scary thing though." I smiled as I thought about what the unknown could be. "I may have to do it alone. I practically do it alone anyway, so what difference does it make?"

"I take Leylah to nursery in the morning and pick her up after work. When I get home, I rush to put her in the bath and cook dinner. I clear the kitchen, put the washing on and she's practically in bed by the time Andre gets home. I'm tired, but I do my best to maintain the house." I paused and thought about Andre's relevance in my life. Limited.

"I'm not really sure what the impact would be if Andre wasn't around and we weren't in a relationship. I think he'd still want to see his daughter, but I'm not really sure that I would miss him. I think I need time to think about it."

"Well, you should. Don't make any rash decisions. You need to do whatever is right for you and Leylah. Your health and your daughter are your priorities." Helen was talking sense to me. I understood her.

"Were you aware that Andre is using the services of the other therapist, as we had discussed at our last session?"

"No. I suspected he might be, but didn't know for sure. I'm glad he's having therapy. That's good. When he's ready to talk about it I'll know."

The hour soon passed and my session with Helen was over. I made my way back home contemplating the discussion and my emotions. I needed time to think about everything, but this was hard to do with all the distractions of life and my hectic routine.

Two days later.

Andre spent Saturday evening with his brother and had come home in the early hours of the morning. Leylah and I went to church, while Andre had a lie in. I kept my mind occupied by cooking Sunday dinner. Roasted vegetables and grilled chicken was on the menu. After dinner, he escaped to the computer in the dining room, no different from every other night. His beloved PC had more quality time with him than I did. I put the baby to bed and returned downstairs to lie on the sofa. After a couple of minutes of settling down and getting comfortable with the remote control, Andre came into the living room. If he thought he was getting sex, he had another thing coming.

"You alright?" he asked as he sat down on the adjacent sofa.

"Not really," I replied. "Andre, I'm not happy. I'm going to take Leylah to Dominica. I need time out." I wondered what his response would be.

"When are you thinking of going?" he asked in a quiet and suspiciously composed voice.

"As soon as possible. I need to let my parents know. I have to go Andre. This isn't the life for me anymore."

"Are you coming back?" he asked.

"Of course I'm coming back. I'm going to call the travel agent in the morning and I'll confirm time off with work."

"Ok. I can help with the flights if you like. Let me book them for you. It's probably a good idea. You need some time out in the sunshine. I want you to come back feeling refreshed. You deserve it."

"I'm going to bed. Do you want me to turn the TV off?" I asked as I shifted myself off the sofa.

"No, I'll just watch it for a while. I'll be upstairs soon."

"Ok, goodnight."

"Goodnight babe."

I didn't want Andre to come upstairs while I was getting ready for bed. I knew he'd return to his cherished computer so I figured I would have at least fifteen minutes to sort myself out. I was tired after my busy week. It wasn't long before I fell asleep, on my own, on my side of our super king size bed.

I woke up to the annoying sound of the alarm on my mobile phone and pressed the snooze button for another nine minutes of sleep. I sensed Andre in the bed beside me. I rolled onto my right side, body turned away from him. The alarm went off again. I pressed snooze again. Andre got out of bed.

"Good morning babe. Coffee?" he said as he put his dressing gown on.

"Yes please," I replied, as he made his way downstairs. I got out of bed and headed to the baby's room to prepare her for another day at nursery. I gave her a quick wash, fresh nappy and dressed her. I put her on my bed and switched on the television to keep her occupied while I had a two-minute shower. Communication between us that morning was limited. I didn't have a great deal to say. I just wanted to get out of the house and to my office as soon as possible so I could start checking prices for flights. Andre acted as if we hadn't even discussed my going away. I don't think he really got the reason I was going. Still, at that moment, it wasn't about him. It was about me, my strength, my health and my happiness. My job had exposed me to the effects of dysfunctional families and the negative impact on innocent children. My child wouldn't be a statistic. I wanted her to be emotionally healthy and not scarred with memories of fighting and crying.

I'd been at work for just over an hour when Andre called.

"Shantel, I've booked your holiday. Four weeks for you and Leylah to Dominica. Leaving in two weeks' time." He sounded pleased with himself.

"What do you mean?" I was in shock.

"I said, I've booked your flights. Four weeks. I want you both to go away and have a great holiday. I don't want you to worry about a thing. Just go and spend some time relaxing."

"Andre, I can't spend four weeks away. I can't take all my leave at one time. I only want to go for three weeks. Can you change the return flight?" I asked.

Part of me was happy that I didn't have to pay out for the trip as my bank account would have been wiped out. Flying to Dominica was not cheap at all. But most of all I was shocked that he'd actually done that. I didn't want him to hijack our holiday. This was my plan, my escape and I didn't want it being organised by the person I was running from. However, I didn't want to appear ungrateful for his gesture.

I waited patiently for his call to confirm the new dates. I thought about my parents. They would be happy to see their only daughter and grandchild. He finally called and confirmed the change. We were due to leave late October and return mid-November. It was becoming cold in London. I needed a happy, warm and secure environment. Andre and our home didn't provide that. I was looking forward to being somewhere that soothed my physical and emotional state.

The Sunday before my mid-week flight, I woke up extra early. The baby was still asleep and Andre was in bed after having had another late night with his brother. I took the opportunity to have a long revitalising shower. As the water cascaded down my body, I started thinking about the rain in Dominica and how cooling it was. I soon jumped out of my reverie and the shower, got dressed, brushed my teeth and hair, and went downstairs for the essential black coffee. Just as the kettle boiled, I heard the doorbell ring. I bet it was the unwanted Jehovah's Witnesses. As I walked towards the door I thought about what I could say to get rid of them. My coffee was important to me and these persistent evangelists were not going to spoil my morning caffeine fix. I opened the door.

"Hello Shantel."

It was Andre's mother, Felicia.

Chapter Sixteen:
History Revealed

"Hi Felicia. I wasn't expecting you." I was surprised at her unannounced visit.

"Come in," I said. "Are you ok?" I asked concerned.

"Yes, I'm fine. I just wanted to talk to the both of you. Where's Andre?" she asked as she took off her shoes in the hallway.

"He's upstairs. I'll get him. Do you want a cup of tea? The kettle has just boiled."

"I'll make it. You get lazy bones out of bed. Where's Leylah?" she asked.

"Still sleeping," I replied as I quietly made my way up the stairs. I entered the bedroom to find Andre lying in bed, awake. The curtains were still drawn.

"Your Mum's downstairs. You need to get up. She says she wants to speak to us."

Andre looked at me with a blank expression. Was he as baffled as I was or did he know what was coming? Andre shuffled out of bed and wrapped on his dressing gown.

"Ok. I'm just going to the loo first. I'll be down in a minute."

I made my way downstairs, hoping the baby would continue to sleep while the discussion took place. I took my coffee from the kitchen and joined Felicia in the sitting room. She was sitting on the two seater leather sofa. I sat on the three seater, leaving plenty of space for Andre to sit close to his mother.

"Hello Mum." Andre greeted her with a kiss and then sat beside me on the sofa. He glanced at me, expressionless.

"I wanted to talk to the two of you together," Felicia started. "Shantel, I know you're going to Dominica and I wanted to say something before you travel. I don't know whether Andre has told you about his past, about a previous relationship. If he hasn't, I think you should know."

I glanced at Andre, but he didn't look back. He was staring intently at his mother. He knew what was coming. I didn't.

"Andre was with a girl. She accused him of all sorts. She made his life a misery. She had him arrested. Because of her, he lost his job. His life wasn't his own for a whole year. Andre got so stressed that he even lost his hair. It was like she wanted to kill my son," Felicia revealed.

I looked at him. I was shocked by what I had just heard.

"She accused Andre of assault. She was the one with mental health problems, but the stress of it all gave Andre problems. He wasn't the same person. He didn't speak for months. It was so difficult for us all. His sisters helped take care of him even doing things that a grown man should have been able to do himself. I'm telling you this because I don't think Andre will and you have to understand him."

Felicia didn't want a discussion, she just wanted to say her piece. I wondered why she hadn't told me this before. I wanted to tell her that it was too late but her manner made it clear she wasn't up for a conversation. Her purpose was to inform me of Andre's past, which clearly had an effect on his present. Andre sat quietly, not saying a word. Why didn't he speak? Didn't he think it was appropriate that he did?

"I just think you should know that Andre had a difficult time in this past relationship and if you knew some of what happened, you would be more understanding of his ways." Felicia picked up her bag.

"You need to talk to each other. I'm going now." She stood up and put her empty cup in the kitchen.

Andre and I stood up and headed to the front door where Felicia was now putting on her shoes. I was happy Leylah was still sleeping. She must have been tired, but perhaps she sensed her parents needed time to talk. We said our goodbyes and then headed back into the sitting room. We sat down in the same position as before.

"Why didn't you tell me?" I asked Andre, feeling frustrated.

"I wanted to tell you, but I didn't know how you would react. I didn't want you to reject me, especially as I had fallen in love with you so quickly. I am sorry for all the pain I've caused. I'm sorry for treating you the way I've treated you." Andre paused for a moment. He was in deep thought.

"My ex accused me of attacking her and trapping her. I didn't. I tried to end the relationship but she got upset. She knew it was ending, but she couldn't let go. The relationship was difficult towards the end. I hardly saw my family. I spent a lot of time with her. She had mental health problems and had tried to kill herself. She had two children but didn't think about them when she decided she wanted to take her life. I admit, I wasn't an angel. I slept with her best friend. I knew it was wrong but our relationship was coming to an end. I didn't realise her friend would tell her and it would send her over the edge. I hurt her, so she wanted to cause me pain too. I did things I wasn't proud of. When I was arrested, my life changed dramatically. To be truthful, I don't remember much about what happened that year after I was arrested. I knew I was facing prison. I couldn't work. I didn't want anyone to see me, just my family. Even then, I couldn't talk. My life was totally upside down. I was a mess." Andre seemed relieved to finally disclose his secret to me. I was surprised by his confession and frankness.

"Her payback was to make my life a misery. She told the police that she didn't feel safe and I was harassing her. The police put her in a safe house. I truly don't know what happened after that. I couldn't work, I didn't want to eat and I became a totally different person. You can't imagine the stress I was under. It lasted a whole year, police gathering evidence, the whole lot. She destroyed me. Eventually she dropped the charges. I think she was encouraged to. It wasn't difficult for people to find out where she was staying. Once, she tried to stick a knife in me while I was lying in bed with her. Then she accused me of raping her. I didn't Shantel. She consented to sex, but because I overpowered her and grabbed the knife, she claimed that I attacked her. Slowly, I got my life back together again, but I guess I worry that someone will try to take you away from me. I'm worried that you'll cheat on me."

What a revelation!

"I'm happy I finally know the root of your problems, but you should have told me a long time ago. We're now almost three years into this relationship. That's three years of unnecessary pain and grief I've endured because you hid your past. I've been totally truthful with you as I thought we'd be able to make a good go of this relationship. I knew there was something. But all this time you've blamed me for the problems in our relationship when you haven't recovered fully from the last one. I'm sorry it all went so badly for you but you chose to transfer the problems into this relationship. It's unfair." I was feeling all sorts of emotions. Angry, frustrated, annoyed and pity for my fiancé. Here sat the man I was going to marry but wondered if there were more secrets and lies.

"Shantel, I love you and I am sorry. You know I'm still getting counselling. I want things to get better. I want you to be happy. I want us to get married and have a happy life together. Please give us a chance," Andre pleaded.

"Andre, you know I'm not happy at the moment. I can't guarantee anything right now. All I know is you failed to share an important truth. I entered this relationship with an open heart. You entered it with secrets. This is all coming out now because you told your Mum I was going to Dominica. You told her that things weren't right between us. The truth shouldn't have come from her. It should have come from you. I need to think about all of this. I need some time out to digest it all." I felt deflated.

"Can I get a hug?" Andre asked, needing some reassurance.

"Sure," I replied.

We both stood up and gave each other a warm embrace. I knew Andre was worried about our future. I loved Andre so I was prepared to try again. I heard the baby stir. She was finally waking up. I pulled myself away from him.

"I better get her. You need to shower." I walked away holding my nose while fanning the air in front of my face. Andre laughed.

"Cheeky. Listen, let's go out to lunch. Let me treat my girls."

"No problem," I replied.

"Passports?"

"Check."

"Tickets?"

"Check."

"Sun tan lotion, mosquito creams?"

"Check, check"

"My heart?"

"Check." I replied to Andre's checklist.

My suitcase was packed. I was getting excited. It was Wednesday morning, 5:30. Andre packed the suitcases in the boot of the car. Leylah's stroller went in as well. I figured I'd need it as she wouldn't be able to walk very far. Andre was driving us to the airport. The journey would take about forty-five minutes. Part of me thought that he might somehow sabotage our journey and I really didn't want to miss our flight. I tried to think positively and prayed before I left the house. I held my baby tightly before Andre put her in the car. It wasn't just a physical journey but an emotional voyage. We were going back to the place where Leylah was conceived. It was a place of new beginnings, a place of sanctuary, protection and escape from Andre. I needed the three weeks away to see how I would cope without him. I wanted to know whether I would be strong enough to survive without the man who was the father of my child. I wasn't running away because I was definitely coming back. I just needed the time to think and become the person I used to be. I sat in the front seat of the car, looking forward to my journey ahead. October in London was cold but in Dominica it would be hot.

It wasn't long before Leylah had fallen asleep again and I was glad for that. She was still tired. I had packed her a few cartons of milk for our trip. She was 18 months old so she would need to eat too. I had plenty of reserves for her in my rucksack. We would be able to get breakfast at the airport so I wasn't worried. I was nervous about travelling alone, without an accompanying adult but this was a challenge that I was prepared to take. It would convince me that I had the ability to get on with it...alone. I knew I would have some difficulties but there would be people to ask. Asking was not something I liked to do. It wasn't in my nature but I had to prove my ability despite the changes in my life.

We arrived at the airport having hardly spoken on the way there. However, the car was warm and love songs were playing on the stereo, all enough to keep me relaxed and enjoy the ride. We parked and Andre escorted us to the Virgin check-in desk. I handed over the tickets and passports and our suitcase was weighed. I didn't want to carry too much, though I had a rucksack, one suitcase, a baby and stroller. I hoped I would get some help along my journey.

"Right. You're both checked in," Andre confirmed.

We walked away from the desk and headed towards the security gate.

"Yep! We are," I replied happily.

I was looking forward to walking around duty free. I needed some perfume and fancied a treat. Finally, it was time to say goodbye. Andre took Leylah out of the stroller and gave her a hug.

"Oh Leylah. I'm going to miss you. I love you so much pumpkin. Have a lovely holiday. I love you, I love you, I love you!" he exclaimed.

Andre put Leylah back into her stroller and smiled.

"Have a great holiday. Please let me know when you've arrived. I'll miss you." Andre threw his arms around me and gave me a hug. It was a sincere one. I wished my feelings towards him were filled with the same and not disappointment.

"Speak to you on the other side," I said, pulling away from the embrace.

"Ok," Andre replied.

He kissed me, then kissed his daughter goodbye. I put the rucksack on my back and pushed the stroller towards the security entrance. The queue was moving slowly. We turned, waved goodbye and entered security. He disappeared from view.

Leylah and I approached the metal detector and thankfully walked through without a bleep. We gathered our possessions and made our way through to the shopping area. The hardest part was going to be checking the departure screen. Luckily, the announcements were loud. I looked for an information desk but couldn't see one. Anyway, I knew we wouldn't board for at least an hour. That was enough time to get something to eat and browse through the shops. Leylah needed some sweets to munch as she watched the children's entertainment on the on-board TV. She would have to sit on my lap for the journey as she was still classified as an infant. My legs would probably get tired even though she didn't weigh that much. I would give my angel hugs and kisses on our journey to keep her comforted. We ate toasted sandwiches in one of the airport restaurants. Once I knew Leylah was full, we used the ladies and then hit the shops.

"Flight number VS33 to Antigua boarding at gate 24. Flight number VS33 boarding at gate number 24."

"That's us Leylah. Let's go baby."

We headed towards the gate. It was a longer walk than I had anticipated. Why did my gate have to be at the far end of the airport?

"Boarding pass please madam," said the check-in clerk.

I dug around in my shoulder bag and found the passes and passports. I handed her everything as I hadn't had a chance to separate the inbound from the outbound. She smiled at Leylah, pulled out two sheets, handed me the stubs and the two inbound tickets.

The stroller was taken away at the airplane door. I was directed to my seat. A steward came over with a baby strap. We sat comfortably. I sent Andre a text to let him know we were on the plane. I guess I did it out of courtesy. He replied saying that he loved us both very dearly. I texted Louisa to let her know I was on board and would text again when we got to our final destination. I switched my phone off and said a silent prayer for a safe journey.

Dear God, thank you for getting us this far. That you for all of the blessings you've bestowed upon us. Without you, nothing is possible. Please protect us on our journey. Help Andre to realise what he has while we're away. Help him to understand what he could lose if he doesn't start to treat me properly. Help me to know which path to take. Help me have clarity about this relationship and to make the right choice. Allow me the time and peace to remember who I am and what I want for my future. I pray that we return to our home safely. Amen.

Eight hours later.

The pilot announced twenty minutes until touchdown. I organised my hand luggage and popped a chewy sweet in Leylah's mouth, just in case her ears were affected by the descent. She started chewing straight away. Typical. I kept them out as it was obvious she'd get through a few more before we landed. We were strapped in and ready to land on the tropical island. We both looked through the window and could see the beautiful green landscape, fringed with golden brown sand. The sea was turquoise and calm. The temperature in the cabin began to rise quickly. The stewards took their seats and strapped themselves in. I took out some more chewy sweets and shared them with Leylah. Before we knew it, we had touched down in Antigua.

After a few restless hours, we were ready to depart for Dominica. Before take-off, I said another prayer for a safe journey. The plane was tiny and the journey short and bumpy. Within what felt like minutes, we were collecting our suitcase and the stroller that was looking a little worse for wear. It had only cost twenty-five pounds and clearly couldn't handle being thrown around from airplane to airport. I made a decision to throw it away as soon as we returned home.

It was hot and humid. I fanned my baby down and made her sip some water before we headed outside to the arrivals lounge. There were so many people lingering, waiting for loved ones.

"Sha-Sha!" a familiar voice greeted.

"Li-Li!" the same voice exclaimed, waving.

It was my father.

"Hello Dad. We're here!" I replied excitedly, though I was tired. My dad kissed and hugged me.

Then I saw my mum.

"Hello Li-Li," my Mum cooed, as she bent down and kissed the baby, beaming a smile so wide. She then gave me a big cuddle.

After the reunion, we headed towards the car to start another long journey along the winding coastal roads. Darkness quickly fell and Dad appeared a little nervous. He hesitated and drove cautiously. The large lorries literally threw themselves around the concealed corners, blowing their horns as they sped down the scary clifftop roads. Why weren't there more barriers to protect vehicles that got a little too close to the edge? I now understood Dad's fears of night driving. I prayed again for a safe last leg of our trip. An hour and a half later, I woke Leylah up to let her know that we had arrived. She was dazed and tired. I lifted her out of the car and carried her into the house. We were greeted by the sound of crickets chirping everywhere.

The house had changed since my last visit. It was more homely. The furniture hadn't moved but the tiled floor in the lounge was now covered by a warm rug. The windows were fixed with mesh to stop mosquitoes and nasty bugs from overtaking the house. Leylah looked around our holiday home, investigating her new adventure playground. She looked happy. Mum said that she needed to feed the cat.

"Suzie! Suzie! Where are you?" Mum opened the back door and Suzie came running in.

Leylah's eyes lit up when she spotted the furry animal and her two kittens. She was bound to have fun over the next three weeks. As promised, I sent both Andre and Louisa a text to let them know we had arrived safely and then put the phone away in our bedroom. Leylah and I sat down on the sofa and had some refreshments while talking to my parents. Before long, it was bedtime.

"Good morning darling," I looked over at my baby.

She was stirring. She smiled. I leaned over and gave her a cuddle. This was pure love. No other love could match this feeling. Before long, Leylah had remembered that she was in a different environment. She climbed out of bed and opened the bedroom door. She stepped outside to be greeted by her grandmother.

"Good morning Li-Li! How are you? Did you sleep well? Come and give me a kiss!

I could hear my mother picking her up and giving her a cuddle. Leylah then ran back into the bedroom followed by my mother.

"Good morning Sha-Sha. How are you darling?" Mum asked quietly with a beaming smile.

"I'm fine Mum. How are you?" I beckoned for her to come in the room and patted the bed so she could sit down.

The three of us chatted for at least half an hour about our plans for the day and some recent events. I wasn't ready to get up as I was tired from the journey. The bed was comfortable and I felt at peace. I needed a shower though and my daughter some breakfast. Mum went in the kitchen to organise food, and I heard her pulling some plates out of the cupboard. I pulled on my silk dressing gown and followed Leylah into the dining room.

"Morning Dad." He was sitting at the dining table. I could smell the cocoa tea he was sipping.

"Good morning Sha-Sha. Li-Li, you ok darling?" he asked.

"Yes. We had a good sleep didn't we Li-Li?!" I replied, as he pulled a chair out for Leylah to sit down.

She looked tiny on the grand dining chair. I sat down beside her and waited for Mum to come into the dining room. The house was open plan, from the lounge to the dining room and kitchen on the far end. The dining furniture was a warm mahogany which complemented the terracotta leather sofas. The floor was tiled throughout the house but accessorised with colourful rugs from England. There were curtains on each window, trying to disguise the burglar bars. The house was flooded with the sounds of CNN. Those female news presenters always looked immaculate. I compared them to the ones in the UK. For some reason, they didn't have that star quality look about them, or maybe it was because they didn't use Botox.

Warm, soft white bread was on the menu. I started with a black coffee to wake me up, while Leylah had some fruit. Dad put the classy newsreader on mute and turned on the radio which was already tuned into the local station, DBS. The DJ was full of life, as most morning presenters around the world were. After breakfast, we showered, dressed and prepared ourselves for our first day in Dominica. We heard familiar songs from England as well as some local bands.

My bag was packed with essentials for our visit to Roseau, the capital of Dominica, which was a ten-minute drive from my parents' home. I didn't think there would be a major risk of mosquitoes feasting on us but sprayed our arms and legs just in case. The smell of mosquito repellent made my baby cough. Next time I'd spray it on in the veranda rather than our bedroom.

The road to Roseau was bumpy. I remembered the last time I was in Dominica with Andre. He took control when my retina detached. He had literally become my eyes. He'd made me feel special when we stayed in the hotel together, arranging champagne and a candlelit dinner. I remember feeling secure in the fact that I could rely on him in an emergency. Back then, I loved him for all the support he had given me.

This time, I was with our daughter and my memories of him were not so rosy. Andre had become controlling, and had made every effort to isolate me because he wanted me all to himself. Selfish. Stubborn. Insecure. Disrespectful. I tried my hardest to remember the positive aspects of his character but it was difficult. He was now like a dark cloud that hovered persistently, regularly pouring down a thunderstorm on anyone that crossed his path. Did I really want to remain in a relationship with a man like that? I needed space to grow in, not stifled by his love.

My ruminations came to an abrupt end as my dad pulled up the handbrake. We had parked near the bay front. I needed to change some money before heading to the shops. I took Leylah in the buggy with me, wondering if it would be a help or a hindrance. The bank was air-conditioned. The cashiers looked like air hostesses with fresh, slick hair styles and slim figures. The men were tall, handsome and immaculately dressed. I wondered if a prerequisite for working in a bank was being blindingly attractive. The queue moved in typical Caribbean fashion — at a snail's pace. After twenty minutes of waiting, I was finally served my Eastern Caribbean dollars. I was good to go. As we headed towards Dad, I noticed that he was chatting on his mobile phone. I wondered who he was talking to.

"Sha-Sha. The phone for you," Dad said with a puzzled look.

I took the phone.

"Hello?" I said tentatively.

"Hi baby. How are you?" Andre.

"We're good. We're just in the bank," I replied.

"How is Leylah? How was the flight for her?" he asked.

"She was fine. I gave her sweets for her ears. She's sleeping in the buggy at the moment." I looked at my parents. They wanted to go. Andre wanted to talk. "I have to go now. We have things to do."

"Ok, ok. Before you go, I just wanted you to know that I love you both so much and I really miss you."

"We only left yesterday." I coolly stated the obvious.

This was not what I wanted to hear, especially as my feelings towards him were so mixed up. I needed breathing space and I hoped he would allow me that over the next three weeks. I needed to know who I was again.

"I know baby, but I want you to know that you're in my heart and I love you both so much."

"Ok, got to go. Speak to you soon."

I had heard enough sweet talk and was feeling a little embarrassed by the words of affection whilst standing in the quiet bank. You could practically hear a pin drop. I felt pressurised.

"Ok, listen. Shall I call you tonight?" he tried desperately to draw things out.

"Ok, ok. Bye," I agreed.

"Ok. Bye." I ended the call.

Escape to paradise to be free
To release the tension in me
To find my reality, sanctuary, normality
To be encompassed by love that's meant for me
The calls have already started
Crowded, smothered, covered
A break I requested
My request you rejected
My time now infested
You didn't listen to my wishes
Your selfishness overrules

True to his word, Andre called the house phone later that evening. My parents were in the kitchen when I answered the phone.

"Hello, good evening?" I had long learnt how polite the Dominicans were when they greeted each other. It was a far cry from the way Londoners behaved.

"Hello Shantel. How are you?" Andre asked.

"I'm fine. How are you?" I replied.

"I'm good. Tired from working late, but I'm ok. How's Leylah?" he enquired.

"Sleeping. The sun has knocked her out. It's really hot here. She's had a good day though. We spent the day in town, shopping and had some lunch too. We've already had dinner so I'm going to bed soon myself."

My dad came over to the living room to see who was on the phone. I mouthed to him that it was Andre. He acknowledged me and walked away to give me some privacy. We talked for another ten minutes about nothing important.

"I miss you!" Andre suddenly blurted out. "Have you missed me yet?"

No! I hadn't missed him. It was too soon. Didn't he realise I needed some time out?

"Not yet. I guess I've been busy."

"Ok, ok. Enjoy your day. Speak to you soon babe," he responded.

"Bye Andre." I ended the call.

The following morning, we woke up early. The sun was bright. A cockerel made his morning calls. I could hear the TV. Leylah stirred beside me in the double bed.

"Good morning darling." I kissed her on the forehead. "Are you ready for another day?"

She blinked, smiled and began to suck her thumb, just as she had on the ultrasound scan. After a few minutes of giggling and chattering, we heard a knock on the door.

"Good morning!" Mum called out.

"Morning Mum. Come in."

She walked into the room with an enormous smile, visibly overwhelmed that we were with her. Three generations in one house. Leylah was their first grandchild. The second would be due in a matter of days. My brother Ray's wife was already forty weeks pregnant, so good news was imminent. I wondered if she'd had news of the birth. Mum greeted us both with a kiss and then sat at the foot of the bed.

We talked about our plans for the rest of the day. She then ushered us into the dining room for breakfast where my trusted black coffee awaited me. Dad was already dressed and ready to go out.

"Morning Sha. Morning Leylah. Did you both sleep well?" he asked.

"Yes, we did. Are you going out?" I asked, wondering where he was going so early.

"'I'm off to the health centre. I need to get some more medication. I'll be back soon." Dad sipped his coffee, put his cup in the kitchen and sped off out of the house.

We had finished breakfast and showered by the time he returned. He was quicker than I thought he would be, bearing in mind this was the Caribbean. We were now ready for a day of visiting family in the village. It was an hour's drive away, through winding, pot-holed and quite frankly, dangerous roads. Dad had to take time travelling there. The roads in Dominica were either right next to the coast or a cliff top — no middle ground. I recalled previous journeys to the village and how I held my breath as I looked down the precipice below. The locals were used to the roads, but I was used to concrete roads that had yellow and white lines, not these narrow roads that were fertile ground for tragedy. I took a deep breath as we climbed into the jeep. The house phone rang, but we were already in the car. No doubt it was Andre. He had my parent's mobile number if there was a problem. But it was only eleven in the morning so he was up early. We were on our way when the mobile rang. Mum answered the phone, made small talk and then passed the phone to me. I wondered where he was making the call from. I hoped I wouldn't face a hefty phone bill on my return to London. We talked for a short time before I passed the phone to Leylah for her to hear her father's voice. After a short exchange, I told Andre we had to go and ended the call.

The next two weeks of our holiday comprised of trips to the White River, dips in the sulphur springs and the Caribbean Sea, short hikes, visits to the Emerald Pool and spending time with extended family and friends. The time flew by. Three weeks felt like three days. I wanted more time especially as Andre had called every day. Before I came on this holiday, I had written a list of my objectives. I wanted to return with answers to my questions.

Objective number 1: To understand me again.

What did I want out of life? How strong was I? How dependent on others was I? How independent was I? What did I value in my life? What could I discard? How could I turn negatives into positives? Where could I be in a few years' time? Would I still be working in the same place? How was I limited with regards to my work?

Objective number 2: To understand my relationship with Andre.

Could my feelings towards him go back to the way they were before? Could I trust him to be my confidant, my lover, my friend, my partner and one day, my husband? Would he ever be transparent? Would I ever really know him? He had omitted so much of his life. What else was hidden? Would he give me the freedom to be myself without him fearing the men that cross my path? Will he ever accept that he has a problem and would need help to break the chains that restricted him? How else could I support him to change? Was his change my responsibility? Would he ever accept his contribution to the state of our relationship?

Objective number 3: To choose the right family set-up.

Could I see a future where we lived together? Could we make a marriage work? If we separated, where would I live? Would I move back to my flat in East London or could I afford to continue living in the house? Did I have enough of a support network in South London? Would I cope financially as there was no guarantee he would give me any maintenance money for his daughter? Would I feel like a failure if I decided to end the relationship? I had lost friends because of him. Would I ever get those friendships back? I didn't know if my friends really understood my relationship and how manipulative Andre could be. How would Leylah cope with the separation?

What would she gain from living in a tense family home? She was still very young. How much longer could I keep trying to make the relationship work? How much more of myself and my life could I give to a relationship peppered less with love and more with hate, erratic and irrational behaviour, fear, jealousy and possessiveness? Did the negatives outweigh the positives?

I sat on my bed looking at my list of objectives and questions. Leylah was watching the Disney Channel in the living room. My parents were in the kitchen. We only had a few days left in paradise. This was the only window of opportunity to consider my future. Then, I heard the house phone ring.

"Shantel! It's for you!" Dad shouted.

"Ok! I'm coming!" I shouted back.

I kissed my teeth and shook my head. No time for me. He might as well be here with me. I folded away my typed list and put it in my suitcase. I didn't want my parents to see my issues. They were aware of some of my concerns but not all.

"Hello."

"Hi baby. How are you? How's Leylah?" he asked.

"We're good. Leylah's just watching Disney and laying on the sofa. How are you?" I asked feeling hot and tired.

"I'm good babe. Just come in from work and about to go to the gym. Thought I would call you first."

He sounded tired.

"Ok, that's cool. I was just taking some time out while Leylah was engrossed in her cartoons."

We talked for ten minutes. I prised Leylah away from her beloved cartoons to talk to her dad. Dinner was on the table, so I told Andre that we had to go. He asked if we could speak later that evening. I told him we were supposed to be going out so it was unlikely. I didn't know whether we had plans to go anywhere but I knew I didn't want to talk to him. I hadn't had enough time to reflect. It felt like he was keeping tabs on me and that frustrated me. As I hung up, I promised myself that I would think about my situation in bed with Leylah sleeping beside me.

That night, I lay in bed, but the only thing I remembered was waking up the next morning. I was clearly too tired from the sun, the previous day's activities, and probably Andre's calls to think about my future.

One more day of our holiday left. Our suitcase was packed. Andre had all the flight details and was excited about picking us up from the airport. He would work from home on the day of our arrival so that he could spend time with us. I had decided that I would give our relationship another go, as despite our turbulence, Andre still loved me. I knew he needed a lot of work, some therapy and time but I was prepared to be a little more patient and understanding. After all, I was now armed with the knowledge of his history and the least I could do was try to learn to be more understanding.

Later that evening, as I was packing, my mother joined me in my room. Leylah was happily watching the TV in the living room.

"Sha Sha, here's some clean clothes from the line," she said, as she lay them on the bed and sat down next to them.

"Thanks Mum," I replied.

"I noticed that Andre called a lot. He must have missed you," she said softly.

"I don't really care if he's missed me. He's probably going to miss a lot more in the future. I'm feeling disappointed with the relationship Mum. I just don't know anymore." I sighed. I felt an urge to change the conversation; reflecting on my doomed union with my daughter's father shouldn't have been a priority. "Anyway, it was still great, being here with you guys. We've both had a lovely time."

Just then, Leylah burst into the room and flung her arms around me. My mother was smiling at our embrace.

Blossom Tree | Sharon Fevrier

"Well, you have to do whatever is best for you and that little girl," she gestured towards Leylah. "Always remember who you are."

"I know Mum, I know."

After a long ride we finally arrived at the airport. My parents were soon hugging us and saying softly how much they would miss us.

"Everything will be alright Sha Sha. Have a safe flight and call us when you get back home," my dad consoled me.

"I will. Love you both." I sniffed, feeling as though I was leaving home.

"Love you too," they responded simultaneously.

The flight was smooth and Leylah slept on my lap for the majority of the journey. I reflected on my mother's comment, telling me to remember who I am. There had been so many changes and disappointments. But through it all, I would aim to turn those disappointments into blessings; I just wasn't sure how but I knew the answer would be revealed eventually.

"There's your daddy baby!" I sang to Leylah as we came through customs to arrivals at the airport.

Andre walked towards us with a huge grin on his face and arms open wide, ready for an embrace. We hugged each other. That warm bear hug was so comforting. We kissed. I had missed him. He then leant down to kiss and cuddle Leylah who was sitting in her now completely battered stroller which was really looking the worse for wear. A second bout of being thrown about in the plane was just about all it could take. It was now on a one way trip to the bin. Andre took care of the luggage while I continued to push the stroller to the car park. We were tired, but travelling home in the car rather than the train was a blessing. Brian McKnight, again, serenaded from the CD player.

Andre had organised drinks and snacks for us in case we were hungry. We'd had breakfast on the plane so we were full, but I welcomed the thoughtful gesture. Before long, Leylah had her thumb in her mouth and fell into a deep sleep. I would have loved to join her but wanted to shower and wash my hair first. I couldn't wait to get home. I was sure the house would be tidy and clean. Andre wouldn't want me to come home after three weeks to a dirty house. The journey was smooth and we were home within an hour. It felt good pulling up outside the house. I was home with my fiancé and my baby. I was prepared to keep trying. I didn't know what would happen, whether we would stay together, get married or separate, but I knew I wanted to try again. It would be difficult to forget all the hurt and pain, but I could forgive. Holding grudges was against my nature.

Rise

Chapter Seventeen:
Inbox Me Surprise

Within days, I was back at work and our routine had resumed. The holiday was well and truly over but home life was different. Andre was no longer a spectator and receiver, but an active member of the household. First, he made every effort to repair our damaged relationship. He told me that he had taken advantage of a few more sessions with the psychologist and so felt stronger and more in control. I was happy he had continued to get help. Second, he was more involved with caring for his daughter. He was even more helpful around the house — vacuuming, doing laundry and cleaning the kitchen, all without even being asked. This was a new and improved Andre. Perhaps the time apart made him value all I did to maintain our house and our lifestyle. I could sit down and relax more often now. I started reflecting on what kept other couples together. Was it largely tolerance? Could I tolerate and accept Andre, for better and for worse? I was still prepared to think positively about our future, and even considered the possibility of getting married and having another child.

Disappointingly though, I found it difficult to make love to Andre; it was literally just sex. There was no passion or intimacy and it all felt like a chore. Whenever I found myself positioned on top of him, I imagined someone else beneath me. I remembered how that someone else made me feel. I remembered love-making. Why couldn't I experience that with Andre anymore? Why couldn't he treat me like his queen and not his adult movie co-star? Love treated me like his empress in the bedroom, the living room, the bathroom, the car and the park! Oh, I remembered what Love did. I felt guilty reminiscing, with Andre underneath me, but those memories of Love made me happy. Dwayne, a previous partner, was Love and there was no comparison. I held such precious memories of our happy days, but our timing was always poor. Soon, I couldn't focus on being intimate with Andre anymore. Memories of Love continuously flashed before me. Love made me climax and Andre didn't. Andre had never taken the time to learn the simple things that turned me on. I had taught him, time and time again, but he reverted back to his ways. So, I started imagining Love's way. Did Love ever think about me? I would never cheat on Andre, but I could enjoy my private memories. Would my feelings ever return? I guess it was hard to make love to a man who had repeatedly hurt me.

I imagine the gentle kisses on my neck
In return, my vampire bite would send him to heights of
indescribable pleasure
Could he remember how his glare sent me to feelings unknown?
I became submissive, succumbing to his wishes
He knew what to do to excite me

The gentle grasp of my arm, teasing with his teeth along my
wrist to my shoulder
I'd pull my arm away, reaching heights of indescribable pleasure
He knew where to kiss me, to send my pulse racing
He knew what to do to excite me

He would look into my eyes, watching my every reaction
To his actions and seduction
He would make me squeal and wriggle on the bed
But he'd capture me every time
He knew what to do to excite me

He placed gentle kisses from my toes up to my inner thighs
My eyes would water as his kisses reached higher and higher
Foreplay was thrilling, daring, electrifying
He took time with flawless passion
Hands soothing and massaging
He knew what to do to excite me

Blossom Tree | Sharon Fevrier

I remembered how he would lick and suck my fingers, one by one
He would breathe his sweet words gently into my ear
Oh, the anticipation
He would sprinkle gentle kisses all over my tummy
And make me giggle with sweet pleasure
He knew what to do to excite me

He would stand me up, gently pull my hair and kiss my neck,
lips and face
Holding me by my hips, planting those soft lips in that place
Explicit moments of engagement, feeding my desire
Standing behind me, hard muscles ripping,
My heart was on fire!
Oh, I remember
How I remembered
He knew what to do to excite me!

Perhaps he too had sensed that the passion was lacking, because out of nowhere, he bought some sexy lingerie for me to wear to spice up our nocturnal activities. I tried. I wore them, minus the whore stockings. There were too restricting. I hated wearing tights during the day, so why would I wear them at night? He loved stockings. In fact, most of the lovely ladies in his porn collection wore stockings so I knew this was his fetish. It wasn't mine. I wore them occasionally for him though, but my heart wasn't in it. Why should I dress like a porn star for him when he didn't know how to make love to me? He became disheartened when I didn't follow his lead and enthusiastically participate in his role plays. Perhaps I should have written it all down. Maybe then he would have understood and satisfied me. Still, I had my memories to satisfy me.

Leylah was becoming more mobile. Some modifications to the house were necessary to ensure her safety. For one, the banister had horizontal panels with large gaps, a clear danger. We needed a carpenter to modernise and secure it. Eamon was recommended by our plumber. He gave us an estimate and said he would do the job in December, just a couple of weeks away.

I took annual leave for the two days he would take to get the work done. On the first day, Eamon arrived right on time at 8am. We talked for a little while before he started the work. I plied him with tea, wondering why workmen loved drinking tea as much as they did. Why not coffee or water? Anyway, he removed the old planks of wood then headed out with them telling me that he would be back shortly. When he left I looked at the work he'd done. I was sure the new banister would add style to our house. He was back within the hour, carrying matching natural wooden poles. I wondered whether we would varnish it or paint it white to match the rest of the banister downstairs. That was a discussion I would have with Andre when the work was finished. The day went quickly. He finished at five-thirty in the evening and told me he would return the following morning. I left to pick Leylah up from nursery and then back home to organise dinner.

Andre arrived just as I was putting Leylah to bed. That evening we chatted, watched television and had an early night. I knew the carpenter would return promptly at 8 the following morning, so Andre had to get Leylah to nursery. I still had to get her ready for another day of fun and play while I spent the day with the carpenter.

That next morning, I showered as soon as they left. The doorbell rang exactly at 8. Right on time. I made my way downstairs in my blue jeans and vest. I'd combed my hair but had not yet brushed my teeth. Last thing I wanted was to greet the carpenter with frowsy breath. I didn't want him to pass out so I decided to keep my distance until my breath was minty fresh.

"Hello Eamon," I greeted him, opening the door.

"Hello Shantel. How are you today?" Eamon asked in his strong Irish accent.

"I'm good thanks. Cold this morning, isn't it? How are you?"

The cold winter air flooded the house as I stood at the door. I contemplated getting a jumper as my vest was nowhere near warm enough.

"I'm fine. I've just got to get more tools out of the car."

Eamon put his toolbox down in the hallway and made his way back to the car. I ran to the bathroom to brush my teeth. When I came back downstairs, he'd unloaded his car into the hallway. I stepped over the worksite into the kitchen.

"Cup of tea Eamon?" I flicked on the kettle.

"Yes please Shantel." I heard Eamon walk up the stairs.

My laptop and mobile phone were already in the sitting room. I had made Eamon's tea and my black coffee. I left the door slightly ajar in case Eamon needed to talk to me. As I was flicking through the channels, I heard a knock on the living room door.

"Hiya," I said, wondering what he needed so soon.

"Shantel, I know it's your birthday soon, so I've got you something." Eamon handed me a small brown envelope. I looked at it with curiosity.

"You don't have to open it now, but you can if you want to," he said.

I was baffled. I had told him yesterday that my birthday was just before Christmas which was why I enjoyed December with the double festivities.

"Can I open it now?" I asked excitedly.

"Sure. Let me explain."

I opened the envelope and pulled out a small green cardboard tree. I smiled at the carpenter.

"Shantel, if you turn the tree around, you'll see that the tree is bare. There's nothing on it. No fruits, no birds. It's lifeless. I have received a message from God for you. I can't tell you why. I don't know why. All I know is that this side of the tree reflects your life as it is now."

I looked at the carpenter, puzzled.

"I'm a Christian Shantel and God has given me a message for you. I just need to pass it on because God is telling me that you need to hear it. If you turn the tree around, you'll see that there are birds and berries. There is life. That is freedom. The tree is blossoming. It's a blossom tree. That is where you're headed. You'll have freedom Shantel. I know I don't know anything about your life but God is telling me that your freedom isn't far away."

I started to cry uncontrollably. The tears wouldn't stop. I was so embarrassed. How did this man, the carpenter, know I was so unhappy? I couldn't believe that God had sent me a message. What did this mean?

"Thank you Eamon," I slobbered, with trembling lips that barely opened wide enough for me to speak. "I'll cherish this little tree."

"I don't know what you'll have to do or how your freedom will come, but it's got to be a good thing. God says it is," he smiled as he walked out of the room and pulled the door behind him.

I stood up to get the tissue box and slumped down on the sofa looking at my blossom tree. I turned it around, looking at the bare side, then the side in bloom. It had a gold string at the top. I could hang it up. I kissed the tree and said a prayer to God.

Dear God,
Thank you for my blessings.
You are a mighty God.
Thank you for sending your messenger to me.
But what does it mean?
What is this freedom that is coming my way?
Can you give me a clue? I need something.
But at least I think this means that my life will change for the better.
Does this mean that Andre and I will have a better relationship?
Does it mean that we will no longer have a relationship?
God, I will leave it in your hands.
At least I know that freedom is coming.
Thank you for sending me a sign.

This situation was difficult for me to process. One minute I was watching Jeremy Kyle on TV, next minute I'd received a message, through my carpenter, from God. Jesus was a carpenter. I chuckled

Blossom Tree | Sharon Fevrier

and pondered over that coincidence for a moment. Was I easy to read? Was my life so transparent? My relationship with Andre wasn't as challenging, so why was I being given this message? Who was this carpenter? Who was he really? Was he really sent by God? Why would God bother with me? Didn't He have lives to save across the globe? What was special about me? Did my ancestors have anything to do with this? Was my Granny in on this? Did she speak to the Big Man upstairs, requesting his help? I didn't know. I just had to accept that God was watching over me. My heart was racing. I couldn't hear the angry guests on the TV anymore. I could only hear my thoughts and the messenger working upstairs in my house. I stood up and looked outside of the window. The sun was shining and the sky was bright blue. Suddenly, I felt a sense of power. I knew that I could do anything. I had God's guidance and now could feel the positivity running through my veins. I smiled. I was prepared for life and wherever it would take me. Freedom, whatever it was, was on its way.

Finally, the job was complete. The banister was safe, secure and looked great. I thanked Eamon for the work and most of all, for the blossom tree.

"You're welcome Shantel," the Irish man said. "I'm glad you love the work. Remember, good things happen to good people. Your freedom is coming. Embrace it."

I smiled sweetly, wondering if I should give the carpenter a hug. I decided against the full-bodied embrace and settled for a hand shake. Then, just before 5, my blossom tree bearer had gone. I wondered if I should have asked him more questions. Were there any other messages I needed to know about? I was already overwhelmed by his revelation. Would my brain and my heart be able to process and accept anything more? No, that was enough. I didn't need to hear anything more. I just needed to be thankful for what I had received.

I didn't tell Andre anything about my encounter with the carpenter. That was my secret. The message belonged to me. Freedom sounded good. I didn't want to be trapped like my ancestors in chains. I wanted to run to the mountains for safety. Until my aching brain could decipher the message, I would continue as normal. There would be no immediate changes.

Christmas was soon approaching. We had planned to put the decorations up tonight. Andre wanted us to decorate together, so when Leylah woke up in the morning, she would have a colourful surprise. I had already chilled the wine and prepared a lamb supper. Leylah was ready for bed and waiting for her father to read her a story.

"Is she sleeping?" I asked, sipping my chilled wine.

"Yup. She was tired. She's fast asleep. I could easily join her," he chuckled.

Andre was still wearing his work shirt, with two buttons un-done and his boxer shorts on. He was in his comfort zone. I was in my silky nightgown and had started decorating the tree.

"So, the banister looks good. What time did Eamon leave?"

"Four. I like it. It might look good painted. What do you think? Paint it or leave it?" I asked.

"Let's just leave it. At least it will match the other banister that the council installed after your eye operation," he suggested.

As I thought — he wasn't prepared to paint it. That would be a losing battle.

"So, what did you do today?" Andre asked.

"Not much. Watched TV, cooked, picked up Leylah. Nothing exciting to report," I replied, while flicking through the channels on the TV.

"How's Louisa? Did you speak to her today?"

Damn, he was good. How did he know?

"Yes, she's fine. She's doing her last-minute shop for Christmas. She might come and visit this weekend, but she didn't confirm which day."

She was one of the few friends that Andre liked. As Leylah's godmother and my best friend, she was there whenever I needed her. It was rare for anyone to visit me, for fear of the wrath of Andre. He had alienated so many of my friends and isolated me, but I knew I wouldn't feel that way forever.

"Ok, that's nice. She hasn't seen Leylah in a while," he responded.

We finally finished the decorations. The house sparkled with beautiful soft lighting. I had inherited the festive decorating bug from my mother. She would have tinsel hanging from the ceiling, multi-coloured balls hanging from the tree and flashing lights that were comparable to those in Blackpool at night. Those were the good old days. I tried to recreate the same ambiance but there were only three of us in this family and one was a baby. My brother was coming over for Christmas though. I had asked my Aunty Sophia and cousin Grace to come, but they passed on the invitation. Too cold my aunt had complained.

"It's looking lovely now," I exclaimed, as I slipped into the sofa, sipping my wine.

Andre poured more wine into his glass and smiled as he looked around the room.

"We should leave early in the morning to do our shopping," he suggested.

I shuddered at the thought of waking up early. "Yup! Bed then!" I agreed.

"I'll come up in a while." He turned the TV off and kissed me goodnight as I stood up.

Andre went into the dining room and turned on his computer. I put my glass in the dishwasher, poured myself a glass of water, and then went upstairs to prepare for bed. Half an hour later, he was still downstairs, playing computer games, or whatever. What about a loving hug? We were almost at Christmas and I was hoping for a new beginning. I decided to close my eyes and think about my baby to put myself to sleep. I thanked God for all his mercies and the message he had sent me through the carpenter.

Leylah woke me up from my blissful dream. I was tired, but like most days, I had to tend to the baby. Andre never woke up when she did. He always wanted a lie-in, but I never got one. I looked at the time. 7:23. I got up and walked around the super king size bed, trying not to stub my toes or knock my knees on the solid wooden frame. I opened Leylah's door to be greeted by my happy child. I was ready to take her downstairs to show her the colourful Christmas decorations that had appeared overnight.

"Mummy, Kismass! Bootiful!" she squealed.

"Thanks baby. We saved the best for you to do. When Daddy wakes up you can put the star on top of the tree."

I turned it on so she could see the flashing multi-coloured lights. I wanted her to have a good Christmas. She was almost two years old. Last Christmas she was too young to get involved. This year she would be able to sit at the table with us, go to church and open some presents. Andre and I hadn't decided on gifts this year, but we were working on it. I opened the curtains and put the television on so she could be entertained while I went to prepare breakfast. As the kettle boiled, I remembered the days of the lie in. To be honest, my life wasn't fulfilling then. My daughter meant the world to me. If it meant waking up at the crack of dawn every morning, then I would do so. It was just a shame that Andre didn't feel it was also his responsibility take the lead when Leylah woke up early. I didn't even know what time he came into bed last night. The cheek of it, telling me we had to get up early to go shopping but he couldn't get up early with the baby.

An hour later, I heard Andre walking down the stairs. He opened the living room door wearing his blue towelling robe.

"Morning," he mumbled.

"Morning," I replied, as he kissed me on the lips.

He knelt on the floor to kiss Leylah, who was transfixed by the television. He sat on the sofa.

"What time did you come to bed last night?" I asked.

"Oh, not much later than you did."

Really?

"Ok, well we're going to get ready. We've both had breakfast."

I took Leylah upstairs. I didn't know what Andre was doing on the computer last night and frankly didn't care. We were going to the local supermarket to buy the food for Christmas day, I knew the queues would be horrendous, but was prepared for the madness.

The following day, we couldn't drive to church because of thick snow. It had come from nowhere. It was so exciting, trekking the short journey with our snow boots. We laughed and threw snowballs at each other all the way to church which was packed and lit all around with candles. We took a seat towards the back, not our usual spot near the screen by the overhead projector. Anyway, the words for the carols were on the sheet even though I knew most of them by heart. Leylah began to feel tired so Andre sat her on his lap and rocked her to sleep. It was a short service but it was almost midnight before we were done. I began to question whether it was a good idea going to midnight mass while she was so young. I felt blessed being able to be in church that evening though, but was also looking forward to putting Leylah to bed.

After service, we trudged our way home through the fresh layers of snow. The roads were pretty, with every rooftop and car covered. Andre carried Leylah all the way home. She continued to sleep when he put her to bed. I pulled out the champagne. Two crystal glasses and some nibbles were laid out on a blanket on the living room floor. We were going to have a romantic moment to bring in another Christmas together. Before long, he was sitting beside me on the floor and we raised a toast to continued happiness and love between us. I didn't believe his words. Something was missing for me but I was prepared to agree and keep an open mind. That night we finished the bottle of champagne. I was tipsy and Andre was tired. He had fallen asleep on the sofa. No chance of any action for me tonight. I cleared the glasses away and told Andre I was going to bed. He grunted and said he'd be up in a minute. I prepared myself for bed and fell asleep as soon as my head hit the pillow.

Christmas morning! The doorbell rang. Andre was busy in the kitchen preparing dinner, so I opened the door. Leylah ran behind me to see who the first guest was.

"Heyo Uncle Calvin!" She jumped for joy.

"Come in, come in," I beckoned as the cool air wafted through the house.

"Merry Christmas!" my brother greeted. "What's on the menu today?"

"Well, I'm cooking the meat. We have lamb, chicken and duck," Andre answered.

"Quack quack!" Leylah screeched, running into the sitting room.

Calvin made himself comfortable. It wasn't long before the next guest arrived — Andre's mother.

"Hello Felicia. Merry Christmas." I welcomed her, holding the door open.

It was time to let bygones be bygones. Yes, I was still unhappy that the family had kept dark secrets which had drastically affected my relationship, but I had to move on. Felicia made herself comfortable with a cup of tea, while Calvin was playing with Leylah. I had just finished laying the table when the final guests arrived. It was Andre's sister Sarah, her husband Alan and their two children. Their cooker had stopped working just one week before. Christmas wouldn't be the same without a roast dinner, so we were happy to have them over. In fact, I was thrilled at the idea of a busy Christmas day. It meant I would be distracted from my thoughts and the status of my relationship. I didn't want to think about the future. I just wanted to enjoy the moment. Focusing on our relationship potentially meant change. Today was all about good food, entertainment, family and Jim Reeves singing his Christmas hits on the stereo. I put all my feelings to one side and concentrated on creating a festive experience for the family. My daughter's happiness was paramount today but, at some point, in the future, I would have to think about my fulfilment, health and happiness.

Andre said grace and we all ate, playing happy families on the decorated dining table. Everyone enjoyed the meal. Duck, lamb, roast potatoes, rice, fried plantain, salad, garlic bread, stuffing, Yorkshire puddings and gravy were set out on the table. Both Andre and I were praised for our efforts. I was happy that Andre had made the rare effort to cook. After the main meal, we changed the music to mellow reggae. We ate our dessert, shared gifts and before long, our guests had departed. We were left alone to relax. The kitchen was clear and the dishwasher was in full motion. Leylah looked exhausted, lying on the sofa with her thumb in her mouth. I kissed her goodnight as Andre took her to bed. It was my time to relax. I sipped on some port and flicked through the channels. After a few minutes Andre returned to the living room and sat on the sofa beside me.

"That went well, didn't it?" he confirmed.

"Definitely. I think everyone enjoyed it. We hardly have any leftovers."

I was tired but relaxed. Andre put his arm around me and we cuddled on the sofa. I stared at the television, but wasn't watching it. I was comfortable being held by Andre. I wanted the feeling of security to last forever. There was nothing like the feeling of being embraced by a man that loved me. I didn't always feel that Andre was genuine but this embrace felt real. That night we went upstairs to our room and continued holding each other.

The New Year came and went in a flash. February was soon approaching and we wanted to celebrate Leylah's third birthday with a party. So I started planning. My brother Calvin would be the DJ, and Andre would do the games. I didn't find the organising stressful. My socialising generally revolved around my child anyway. However, I missed the friends I had before I met Andre. I tried to fill the gaps with new acquaintances, but I didn't want to lose my old friends so tried to keep them close.

The day of the party soon came. The children were all so adorable, playing with competitive enthusiasm. I found myself consoling my daughter when she didn't win all the prizes. She was a single child so I made allowances for her, as at home, she practically had everything she wanted. Seeing those beautiful children made me feel happy and slightly broody. Once all the guests had left, we were back to being just us.

The next few months flew by too, with work being busy and me accepting almost every invitation to socialise. I grew in confidence with every passing day. I no longer perceived my vision as being a hindrance. Yes, it was challenging at times but I could cope. I knew my limitations and what I could achieve independently. Andre saw the change in me, as I was smiling more. I was happier in myself, and more so because my parents were back in London, dealing with their property business. My mother was also turning sixty at the end of May. I was so happy that my parents were staying with us again. I couldn't quite work out Andre's feeling about it but this was my family. He just had to bite his tongue and be accommodating, even if it were just for my sake. However, after their last visit to our home, my parents had decided that they would keep their distance from him. They rotated between my brothers, aunt and I, and were happy exploring London visiting family members.

The end of May was warm, so we planned a garden party for my mother's birthday. Andre put on his 'man-apron' and volunteered to cook the chicken on the barbecue. At least that kept him busy. He had a role. My role was to be a good host. My parents just needed to enjoy themselves and mingle with their guests. It was a good day. Food and drink was flowing and calypso music was playing loud enough to be heard by the neighbours. A few days after Mum's party, my parents returned to my aunt's house. That evening, Andre and I were downstairs watching EastEnders. It was late so Leylah was already in bed. I sensed Andre wanted to speak to me about something as he seemed quiet and distant.

"Shantel, can I ask you something?" he asked.

"Sure," I replied, concerned about what he was going to bring up.

"If any of your exes tried to contact you, would you please tell me?"

Here we go again. After a good run, the insecurities were surfacing again.

"Andre, really? What's wrong now?" I retorted feeling frustrated and exhausted.

Where was this coming from when I had done absolutely nothing to stir things up?

"I just want you to tell me if any of your exes try to contact you."

"Listen, I know your views on that, but I'm not rude. I'm not like you at all. Exes mean nothing to me, so why are they your concern? Are we ever going to move forward from this? Do you want a relationship with me or with any of my exes?!" I exploded.

How had a peaceful evening turned into this nonsense again?

"Shantel, I'm not after an argument with you. All I want is for you to tell me if any of your exes try to contact you. That's all."

"Fine!" I spat out, standing up and leaving the room.

My body trembled with anger. After over three years, I still had to deal with his issues. I went into the kitchen to get some water and made my way upstairs, leaving him alone in the sitting room. I was happy there was a large screen television in the bedroom. I grabbed my nighty and went into the bathroom. As I sat on the toilet, I felt my hands start to shake. I was so upset. What was I doing here? I felt a sharp, throbbing pain in my back. Shit. I wasn't going to have another crisis for this man. The tears started rolling down my face uncontrollably. This man was not for me. The pain in my lower back worsened. I freshened up for bed, put on my night dress, went into the bedroom and took some pain relief. I pulled some tissues out of the box on my bedside table to wipe my eyes and blow my nose. My mind flashed back to the time Andre used to visit me at my flat when we started dating. He said that a box of tissues on the bedside table made him think about the men I had in my bed before him, using the tissues to wipe away the aftermath of a night of passion. Bastard. How messed up was that? The only wet thing I was wiping away now was the unhappiness that he had, yet again, inflicted on me. I was tired physically and emotionally. I remembered my encounter with the carpenter. What did he mean? I needed answers but more importantly, I needed the pain to go away so I could sleep.

The following morning, I woke up feeling tired, but at least pain free. I prepared for work in silence; I had no more words for Andre. Once we got to the train station, we said goodbye to each other and went off in separate directions to work. I sat on the train and decided to open Facebook for my morning entertainment.

One new message.

Hi Shantel. How are you? Long time I know. You ran across my mind recently so I thought I'd drop you a line to see how you are. Hope to hear from you soon. Dwayne.

Dwayne!

Was it a sixth sense? I sat on the train, feeling really puzzled. Did Andre have a premonition? How did he know? I read the words again.

Dwayne used to love me. Damn. I used to love him
Our timing was never right, my heart would skip a beat at night
And in the morning and in my dreams, for Dwayne
Dwayne smelt like the sea breeze at sunset
He walked like the leaves blowing in a gentle breeze
I breathed in his love, which flowed through my veins
I loved him with such intensity, such uncontrollable desire
But we were never meant to be
I was a realist
Lust, love, pleasure, purity
It ended with a dwindling fantasy
Uncommon territory
That was the love I felt for Dwayne

I was in shock. We hadn't communicated for years since I wrote him a message on Facebook informing him that my current beau didn't want me communicating with any of my ex-boyfriends. I respected Andre's wishes and cut off my past. It hurt me to do that because Dwayne used to be my confidant. So, we didn't work as a couple, but we did as friends. I had let him go for the promise of a relationship with Andre. The train pulled into the station. I put my phone in my bag. As I walked to work, I wondered whether it was a coincidence that he contacted me. I recalled the conversation with Andre just the night before. How bizarre. I smiled when I thought about Dwayne. I missed our friendship. He was so comical and caring. He often made me laugh uncontrollably until the tears ran down my face. If I was sad, he'd always find a way to make me happy. A glass-half-full kind of man.

But Andre charmed me away from all that. He promised me a future, a family and security. He loved me and took care of me, sometimes in an unorthodox way, but it was a mature love. My love for Dwayne was dangerous, while my love for Andre was real and rational. However, the relationship with Andre was becoming dangerous though, not in a passionate way, but in an unpredictable painful one. Andre seemed to be intent on stripping away my love for him. What had he learnt about love before me? Clearly, not much. His relationship with his mother was uncomfortable. Come to think about it, I didn't see him having any positive relationships with any women apart from his sisters but he was often too stubborn to listen to their opinions. Dwayne had positive relationships with everyone. He was a lovable character. Andre was an acquired taste, ostracising himself from others because of his insecurities. Anyway, I didn't want to compare the two men. They were so different. I was so upset that Andre made an issue about contact. Couldn't any part of my life be private? God knows Andre kept secrets from me. I didn't know anything about his friendships. He shared nothing with me. That's what frustrated me the most, the fact that he expected me to share everything with him yet he never did with me.

For the next few days I thought about the message. I didn't respond straight away. Eventually, I plucked up the courage to reply.

Hi Dwayne,
I hope you are well. I'm really sorry but I can't keep a friendship with you. My partner doesn't want me to have contact with any of my exes and I have to respect his wishes.
I hope you understand.
Take care of yourself.
Shantel

My eyes started to well up as I pressed the send button. I was ending the possibility of communication from someone who grounded me, appreciated me and loved me. I had let him go all these years without any real communication. I thought about the carpenter's message again wondering what it meant.

Hi Shantel,
That's ok. I respect your wishes.
I hope everything goes well for you. Even though we won't talk, we'll always be friends.
Take care,
Dwayne

I decided to come clean with Andre and tell him about the message. I was an honest person and had to tell Andre the truth, as I told him I would. After putting Leylah to bed, I disclosed the written encounter.

"Andre, I need to tell you something. You asked me to tell you if anyone of my exes contacted me. Well, Dwayne contacted me on Facebook a few days ago." I was nervous as I didn't know what to expect from Andre.

"What? Who?" Andre blurted.

"Dwayne," I replied.

"A few days ago? What did he say?" Andre quizzed.

"He was just saying hello. Nothing more. I guess he just wanted to see how I was."

"So why are you just telling me now?" Andre stared at me intently.
"You asked me to tell you. I've dealt with it anyway." I responded.
"How?" Andre spat out.

"Well. I sent him a message letting him know that you weren't happy with me communicating with any exes and that I had to respect your wishes."

"Why did you respond to him? Why didn't you tell me before?" Andre stood up from the sofa and started pacing.

He was angry. I wondered what he was going to do.

"I'm going to get in contact with him. How dare he contact you! You told him before not to contact you. Obviously, he's not taking you seriously. Maybe I should have a word with him myself. Maybe I should pay him a visit." Andre's eyes were almost bulging out of his head with anger.

"What the hell are you talking about? This is not a big deal Andre. I've dealt with it. I'm not interested in him. Why are you making a big deal out of this? You asked me to tell you, but you can't seem to handle the truth. Why?"

I became increasingly frustrated and scared. I'd never seen Andre act this way before. He looked like he was about to explode with hatred. He sat down again.

"Isn't he into sports? Doesn't he need his knees for his sports? Maybe I should pay him a visit. He wouldn't even know what was coming. All he'd know is that he'd never be able to walk again."

Andre stared at me to see what my reaction to his threats would be.

"If I hear anything about you hurting him, trust me, you'll feel pain too. If I hear anything about him having an injury then I will tell him what you've said.'

I was no longer scared for my ex. Now I was angry. How dare he make threats to hurt someone who had a pure heart? Andre's heart was riddled with demons. How could he profess to love God one minute, raise his hands in church to worship and in the next breath, threaten to break my ex's bones. I took a deep breath and remembered what I had been told about his ex-girlfriend — the entrapment, accusations, safe houses and threats to her family if she went ahead with the case. Andre had contacts. He was a South Londoner with connections. I wasn't prepared to take a chance on someone who meant so much to me, even if it was in the past. My ex had a new life and I was not part of it. Ok, he tried to reconnect, but communication wasn't an option for us. Even though I couldn't talk to him, he would always be my friend and I would protect him in whatever way I could.

"You need to think about what you've said."

I stood up from the sofa, clutching my mobile phone and feeling the fear, hatred and anger swirl around inside me.

"In fact, I will tell him what you've said. You embarrass me so much. You're not a man. You're an arsehole." I walked out of the living room and slammed the door behind me.

I went upstairs to our bedroom, grabbed my nightwear from my drawer and threw it on the bed in the spare room. That's where I would be tonight. I called Louisa. Even though it was late, I needed to speak to her. If I couldn't speak to Dwayne directly, I could ask her to pass on a message. I wasn't going to keep this to myself. My world, my relationships were nothing to Andre. Why was I really here? It wasn't for love or friendship. I was here for the baby, the house and the financial security. I didn't want to move back to East London, but I would if I had to. I didn't want to feel like I was going backwards, but I had to think about my future and protecting my child from any psychological pain that she would see her Mummy go through. I told Louisa about Andre's threats to Dwayne. Her words oozed sympathy and concern for me.

"Shantel, you know when the time is right that things will change. This is not a good relationship. There is too much hatred and anger and it's not going to improve. You'll have to make some decisions. You have to think about your health babe. You can't be a mother to Leylah if you're sick. Andre is not taking your health into consideration. He's only thinking about his own pain, that he doesn't even know how to manage. Babe, I can't tell you what to do, but eventually you will know what to do.'

"Thanks hun. I hear you. I know." I sighed loudly, like a broken woman.

"The house. My flat being rented. I'd have to give notice to get the tenants out if I moved back there." I thought out loud.

"I know babe, but it will all work itself out. You know, if I had a two bedroom flat you and Leylah would be welcome to stay as long as you needed."

"Thanks," I replied, "but this is my mess that I have to sort out. I'm not sure what's going to happen but right now Dwayne needs to be aware of this fool. Empty threats, I know, but I'm not taking that chance. He must think that controlling a woman is how to keep her loving him."

"But Shantel, do you still love him?" Louisa asked.

"No, I don't think so," I confessed.

Louisa agreed to contact Dwayne via Facebook as I no longer had a telephone number for him. She would ask him for his telephone number and speak to him about Andre. He would know that I was in an abusive relationship. I should be doing better than this. I should be with a man who could give me more than any ex ever did, but instead I was hurting.

Shortly after my conversation with Louisa, I heard Andre coming up the stairs. I held my breath, hoping he wouldn't open the door. The door handle creaked and then turned. He stood at the door. He flicked the bedroom light switch on.

"Get out!" I said firmly.

He came in anyway and shut the door behind him. 'Shantel, we haven't finished talking." Andre sat down on the bed.

"Leave the room or I will take Leylah right now and leave this house." The frustration was building up inside me. I was becoming angrier. "Get out now!"

"You're not leaving the house with Leylah. You're not going anywhere!"

"Really? You don't think I am? Watch me!"

I got out of the bed, went into our bedroom and started pulling on my jeans then a jumper over my night dress. We would go to a hotel. Which hotel? It didn't matter. Any hotel I could afford and that was local. How dare he? I pulled the small suitcase from the top of the wardrobe and began to fill it with clothes, cosmetics, underwear. Andre stood at the door, watching me as I packed my things. I went into Leylah's room. I started to pull clothes out of her drawers. Nappies, night clothes, day clothes, shoes and her coat. I went into the bathroom to get her creams, pushing past him as he stood in the hallway. I wanted to do more than just push him, perhaps shove him down the stairs.

"Leylah isn't going anywhere."

I went back into our bedroom and put the items into the case. I pulled my mobile phone out of my back pocket, scrolled down my contacts until I could see his brother Vince's name and pressed the call button. He answered.

"Hi Vince. I just thought I should let you know that Andre is once again being a prick and needs to let Leylah and I leave the house. If he doesn't, I will call the police. I feel no way about doing that. My bag is packed and when my taxi comes we will be leaving. Can you please speak to your brother so he knows that I'm serious? I'm sorry for contacting you at this time, but someone needs to know that this situation could get messy. Please speak to your brother for me while I call my taxi."

"Shantel, don't do anything hasty. Don't leave yet. I'm going to call Andre and I'll call you back in a few minutes. Where's Leylah?" he asked.

"In her bedroom. I'm about to wake her up so we can leave."

"Don't wake her up yet. Give me a few minutes."

"Ok." I hung up. Andre's mobile phone rang. He went downstairs into the sitting room and shut the door. I went downstairs and opened the door so I could hear his side of the conversation.

"Ok, ok," he responded to whatever Vince had said. "I'll leave."

"You go, you wanker. Get out, you arsehole. Leave us alone. Idiot! Go wander the streets!" I didn't care what I said.

Andre didn't respond. He grabbed his jacket from the porch and walked out of the door. He shut the porch door behind him. I rushed upstairs to retrieve my house keys from my overnight bag. I was relieved that Leylah was still asleep. I hurried back down stairs to lock the door and left the keys in the lock. There was no way he was coming back in here uninvited. I wouldn't be able to sleep easily knowing that he could walk in at any time and act irrationally. No, not in this household. Not to me and my child. I recalled stories of psychotic men that would hurt or even kill their children and the mother. I didn't think Andre was capable of that, but I wasn't taking any chances. I was prepared to do whatever I had to, including calling the police. They already knew Andre because of the charges that were held against him after the dramas with his ex. Well, he didn't want his current to do the same. I was so angry, I could have hurt him. How dare he act like a buffoon, beating his chest and threatening the life of someone I cared about? Dwayne was worth twenty of him. This relationship was not about trust. His actions always made me think about Love. Love that was faithful and kind, patient and understanding. Genuine and honest. I missed Love. I missed Dwayne.

That night I cried and cried. I closed my eyes and imagined Love holding me and telling me that everything would be fine. He'd always tell me not to worry or stress about anything, as it would all work out in the end. That was Love. It was time for God. I prayed to the Almighty for guidance and support. I prayed for a path, an open door and strength to get me through this train wreck of a relationship. I wasn't praying for a new love. I was praying to be happy, just me and my girl. I would never cheat on Andre but his mistreatment of my heart made me revisit my past and hope that one day, love, in whatever size or shape, would revisit me.

Leylah. She was crying. I picked up my mobile phone to look at the time. 7:55. Baby girl couldn't give me one more hour? I got out of my bed and went into her room.

"Good morning baby. She stopped crying, I picked her up and gave her a cuddle. "Good morning angel. How was your sleep?"

She rubbed her eyes and rested her head on my shoulder. That was love. I gave her comfort and she reciprocated the feeling. My heart was bursting at the seams. She was the only thing that Andre had given me that I cherished, whilst he appreciated nothing I had given him. I carried Leylah into my room and turned on the television. I didn't mind if she wanted to watch Peppa Pig. She needed normality. I cuddled her while she lay on my shoulder. She gazed at the television while I planned my day. I didn't want to leave the house in case he came back. There was enough food and entertainment for Leylah and while she watched television, I could cook, clean and do housework. Anything to detract from the fact that my relationship was breaking down.

After breakfast, we washed and got ready to enjoy a relaxing day indoors. We were going to do some arts and crafts. I started to lay the newspaper down though it didn't matter how much I did — the paint would always find the carpet. Anyway, the floor needed shampooing.

Suddenly, Leylah looked up at me.

"Mummy, where's Daddy?"

"He had to go out early this morning darling. Now, what colours would you like to use today? Shall we paint a face baby?" I replied.

Distraction would only work for a short time. She knew this was a weekend. During the weekdays, she was used to not seeing her dad until late evening, if at all. Fortunately, the day went quickly. I wanted to put Leylah to bed early so I could rest. I was expecting his call but I didn't know when it would come. He would probably need some clothes for work. I didn't want to see him and I didn't want Leylah to either. She would want him to stay and play with her. I wasn't prepared to sit through the ordeal of Daddy showing excessive affection to his child to prove a point. No, he would come in only after Leylah was asleep. She needed to sleep peacefully and not be interrupted by our arguing. He was a nasty piece of work with a heart twisted by hurt, pain, evil and distrust. Why didn't he trust me? What had I ever done to make him feel that he had to hurt anyone I had history with? History was all about *his* story and not really mine. Our issues were a direct result of his past. When I met him, I was happy to put my past to bed. He resurrected my history, time and time again because he was incapable of leaving his own buried, as it should be. He hurt, so I should hurt but our daughter was *not* going to hurt. This mess was going to stop with us.

My mobile phone pinged. It was a text from him. I had already spoken to my friends during the day to inform them that I was safe from the crazed partner the universe had matched me with.

Hi Shantel. I hope you and Leylah are ok. I won't get in your way but I need some clothes for work. Is it possible to come round and get some clothes?

No, go to hell. Go and buy a new suit. I wanted to scream.

I put the phone down. It was after 5pm. Leylah would be in bed early but I wouldn't allow him to come in until 9pm. He would have to wait for a response. I knew he would try damn hard to resolve our conflict. I responded to his message after dinner.

9 o'clock is a good time. Leylah should be sleeping by then. Text me to let me know that you're outside and I will unlock the door.

He replied straight away.

Ok great. I will text you when I'm outside.

Another text.

Thanks Shantel.

There was enough time for Leylah and I to go for a walk without worrying that he would return unexpectedly. She really needed to spend enough energy to sleep through the night. We put on our coats and I grabbed our scooters. We were out for at least an hour. The temperature had dropped but we were wrapped up. Being out was really a breath of fresh air. It was important to carry on with our routine so that she didn't suffer because of her parents' problems. She was a child and adult problems were not her concern.

By 8, Leylah was fast asleep. I went downstairs and turned on the TV for background noise. I browsed through the channels but there was nothing to watch. 8:15. I knew Andre would be prompt. No doubt he was staying at his brother's house. He needed to stay for at least a week or so. At that point, knowing me, I would probably let him back into my life and into my home. I wasn't ready to do this alone. Leylah needed a father and I needed security in my home. Those things were priority. Ugh, I was already giving in again before he was back.

8:45. The phone rang. It was Louisa.

"Hey girl. You alright?" she asked.

"I'm good babe."

"Call me as soon as he leaves. I need to know you're ok." She sounded worried.

"I will. Don't worry. I'll be fine. I'll call you as soon as he's gone."

"Ok, speak to you soon."

"Yes, babe. Speak soon."

9pm. I received a text. It was him.

I'm outside.

I got up from the sofa, turned the TV off and turned on the porch light so I could see him at the front door. I unlocked the door and stood aside so he could enter.

"Hi." he greeted.

"Hi. Please be quick."

"Ok." Andre took his shoes off and went straight upstairs.

I took my keys out of the door and shut it. I stayed downstairs so that I wouldn't get in his way. I prayed he wouldn't disturb our daughter as I would be the one to put her back to bed.

After five minutes, he returned downstairs with a holdall filled with his possessions and a suit carrier. Andre put his bags down and sat on the stairs to put his trainers on.

"Thanks Shantel," he said looking broken.

"Ok. Bye." I held the front door open for him. He walked out of the door.

"Goodnight Shantel."

I shut and locked the door.

He was gone. I felt relieved. I thanked God that he'd come and gone with no drama. After speaking with Louisa, I prepared for bed.

The following morning, we got ready as usual. I took Leylah to nursery then made my journey to work. My mind flitted from the events to wondering what would become of us. Love. What did it really mean? In my relationship, I couldn't see that it meant much. Andre's way of loving me just caused pain. I wondered if he had ever truly felt love before. His relationship with his mother was dysfunctional, to say the least. I wasn't stupid. I knew that not everyone received the kind of love as a child that stabilised them as an adult. What kind of love did he get growing up? Had that love created this dysfunctional personality? I couldn't let his past ruin my or our baby's future. He loved me and his daughter, but did he know how to love himself?

More love
Control, demand, no need to understand
Hurt, pain, history
His story, geography, sociology
Lessons learnt, abandoned, forgotten
Reminiscent of who? Your father, ancestral burden?
Similarities in physique, features language and thought
You were a child, perhaps not your fault
But we're grown, leave the past alone
My past, your past, their past, book burnt!
You had a chance at family love
The percentage has dwindled, work out the math
I'm walking to the light, you're no longer in sight
Baby girl, holding hands, she's my sanctuary

Deep down I knew the relationship was over. I had felt love before and this was not it. I needed to be with someone who had a pure heart. Andre's heart was scarred and I was suffering the consequences of his disastrous life. This life was too stressful for me. There had to be immediate change. Andre didn't protect me. He was all about self-preservation. I gave so much to him. I even wanted another child and to be married to him, even though he hadn't made enough effort to meet my needs and fulfil my desires as I had his. He couldn't allow himself to break free from the chains that held him back, yet here I was prepared to give the relationship one last chance. I didn't want my baby to be an only child. I never imagined that I would be an unmarried mother of one. If we could get over this hurdle, our relationship stood a chance. Or did it? Right now, I just needed to have peace, by myself, with him gone.

The following week was refreshing. I felt stronger, self-sufficient and capable of managing a work-life balance. I rested in bed early after putting the baby to sleep. I spent time talking to friends and catching up. I even got to watch some adult TV, a rarity these last 3 years. I felt Shantel was coming back. The disaffected mother, struggling with all the burdens that life had thrust upon her was slowly disappearing. I had coped with all that life had given me so far. My man was supposed to be supportive but, instead, he created unnecessary drama. I wasn't sure if he could change. There were so many complexities in our relationship. I didn't know one couple that didn't have their fair share of ups and downs but our challenges seemed to be in abundance. The negatives greatly outweighed the positives. Why were we continuing on this merry-go-round? I couldn't help Andre to become a better person — he had to do that himself. But here I was, prepared yet again, to have a discussion with him and try to make things work. One thing for sure, he would need more counselling.

By the end of the week we'd spoken. He agreed to more therapy, and came home that weekend.

Chapter Eighteen:
Disco Therapy

So for the umpteenth time, I decided to forgive Andre. I genuinely felt that the end goal was worth the effort. I didn't want to be alone and I still felt love for Andre despite the pain he had put me through. We started to attend church more frequently. God knows, we needed his blessings! I was happy to be prayed for and be guided by the scriptures. We could be better and we could achieve happiness. Andre told me that he had received counselling from the Pastor. That reassured me about our future. God needed to be involved.

One evening, when Leylah was asleep, Andre said he had something to discuss. He turned off the television and sat on the sofa beside me. He held my hand.

"Shantel, I've been thinking. Why don't we try for another baby? I know you're on the tablets. Why don't we go to see your consultant and have this discussion? I want to have another baby with you. What do you think?" he asked.

I was taken aback.

"Well, I wasn't expecting this. You know I would love another baby, but I'm scared of what might happen," I replied.

"I know. That's why we should speak to your consultant. I'll come with you for your next appointment and we can see what our options are." Andre sounded sincere.

This would add a new dimension to our relationship.

"Well, my next appointment is in two weeks. I'll give you the details. Are you sure you want to do this?" I asked. I needed to feel sure he was ready to embark on fatherhood for the second time.

"I want this Shantel. I don't want Leylah to be an only child. I think it'll be good for her. Once we've had the second child we could concentrate on the wedding. Let's see what the consultant says."

"You know I have to be off the drugs for three months, right? Do you remember the consultant said I couldn't get pregnant on those pills? I don't want to get sick and I might if I stop. But I don't want the baby to be affected."

I explained my fears to Andre and remembered the crisis I'd had while pregnant. He'd thrown his weight around the ward, telling the nursing staff that I wasn't to have any morphine for pain relief. Would the baby be worth all that grief again? Yes, it would. In my heart I doubted Andre and I would last forever, but I was swayed by the possibility of another child. Two was all I wanted. My hopes of a large family had dwindled away due to my age and my medical condition. I prayed that one more wouldn't affect my health because I really wanted one man to father my children. If my relationship with Andre ended and I was fortunate enough to find love again, I potentially would have two baby fathers. I hated that term but the thought of it being my reality made me shudder.

"We could make it four months, just as a precaution. We'll get you really healthy. Lots of vitamins, exercise and good food. We'll rearrange the spare room for the children. It might be a boy this time. I don't care. Boy or girl, it makes no difference."

"Ok." I replied, beaming from ear to ear.

There was finally something happy to focus on in the relationship. All the bad blood from the past was history and the autumn breeze shot through, clearing away the pain.

The following two weeks flew by. I thought about the idea of another child in the house. The idea two babies taking up my time and the bonus of maternity leave was really appealing. Two children calling me Mummy. That would be my family complete.

Andre and I walked hand in hand through the foyer of the hospital. My heart pounded in my chest, wondering what the consultant would say. I went through the usual rigmarole of the blood test, blood pressure, temperature, oxygen level checks and urine testing. The consultant popped her head out of her office.

"Shantel." She beckoned with a smile.

Andre and I stood up and he followed me into her office.

"Take a seat," she requested. "How have you been?"

"I've been well. No problems. A little bit tired from the usual running up and down but generally ok," I replied.

"Everything looks fine with your results."

"Great." I answered. "I wanted to talk to you about something. We're thinking of having another baby." I waited for her response with anticipation.

"That's great news. From a medical perspective, I see no problem. You need to be off the medication for three months. It needs to be out of your system completely, then you're good to go." she advised.

"So, what do you think is the risk of my eyes deteriorating, or anything else?" I didn't want my vision to get any worse. "What about the stress and pressure of labour?" I asked inquisitively.

"Well, you'll be closely monitored by Moorfields and continue regular appointments with us," the consultant reassured. "Is there anything specific you'd like to know?" she asked, looking at Andre.

"No, I think we know all that we need to know for now," he replied.

"Do you need another prescription or are you thinking of stopping the medication?" she asked.

"No, I think I will stop taking them now," I answered, smiling at Andre.

Andre and I were getting on well. We had started date nights again. He would organise a babysitter, so we could have some fun time together. He had even resumed helping with the housework. We started spending more time together as a family. Andre didn't seem to hover over my shoulder as often when I used the laptop or when my phone pinged. I had magnifying software on my computer so he could usually see what I was doing anyway. Besides, I had nothing to hide. Andre continued spending many of his evenings in front of his computer in the dining room. I couldn't see what he was doing as the door was usually closed. Still, if he was entertained, I could rest. He regularly spent his Friday evenings at his brother's house. I didn't mind. Once Leylah was in bed, I then had 'me' time. It was a given that Leylah would wake up early the following morning, so I had to be fresh to keep up with her demands. He would always return during the night but would have a lie in until late morning. That was our routine. Monotonous, but it seemed to work. I started socialising with friends more. My close girlfriends all lived north of the river, so I would always travel alone. None of my friends wanted to stay overnight at my house and we knew exactly why. Still, I cherished the moments we were able to share and enjoyed the escape from the titles of mother and fiancé. Sometimes I just wanted to be Shantel. I could never go back to the girl I was before I met Andre. There were far too many emotional, physical and mental changes in my life since then. I wanted to focus on my blessings, not my burdens. Though my friends didn't agree with me potentially having another child with Andre, they were supportive in their own ways and could understand my plight.

My cousin Anita, had asked whether Leylah and I would like to spend the weekend with her and her daughter Anna, at her home in Berkshire. Andre had made so many positive changes but I was unsure about how he would react to us spending the night away from home. He had previously made a huge deal about sleeping out, causing major arguments. I decided to broach the subject one Saturday afternoon after shopping. Leylah was on the floor in the sitting room, eating pancakes while watching cartoons. Andre brought a bottle of wine and two glasses and sat on the sofa next to me.

"Pizzas are almost ready," he said. He opened the bottle and started pouring.

"Thanks babe. Listen, Leylah and I will be going to Anita's for the weekend in two weeks," I announced assertively.

"Oh, ok. That's nice."

"Anna's getting older and I need to be a bigger part of her life," I explained.

"Ok, I'll take you both to the station when you want to go."

"Thanks," I replied sipping the wine.

That was easier than I had anticipated. Ordinarily he would have created a fuss and the insecurities would have shown. Was it that Anita lived in a town where I didn't know anyone? Did he think I was no longer attractive to others? Or did he finally realise that I wouldn't cheat on him because it just wasn't in my nature. Perhaps he now trusted me, bearing in mind that I was preparing my body to carry one more child for him. Whatever the case, I was happy that my plan for a girlie weekend wasn't challenged.

That evening, once Leylah was in bed, Andre told me that he was going out with his brother Vince. He ironed his black shirt and put on his tailored black trousers. He wore a gold necklace and his sparkly diamond earring. The Rolex was blinging. He looked and smelt gorgeous. In all the madness, I'd forgotten what a good-looking man he was.

The following morning, Leylah and I went to church and he slept in.

Two weeks later and I had packed a small suitcase for our overnight stay with Anita.

"Where do you want me to take you babe? North Greenwich or do you want to go on an overground train to Waterloo?" Andre asked.

"North Greenwich is fine," I replied.

"So, what are your plans then?"

Here we go. The interrogation I was expecting. He wasn't asking because he wanted me to have a good time. I suspected he was asking to keep tabs on me and make sure that there wasn't another man involved.

"We might do some shopping, get some food, go back to her house and open a bottle I guess," I replied nonchalantly. "What are your plans while I'm gone?"

"No plans. Will chill at home. Might see Vince later, but not fussed really."

I knew Andre would go and see his brother. I didn't mind as I liked Vince. He was an honest man with a genuine heart. I liked him because he talked to me openly. He was a positive influence in Andre's life, despite his own run-ins with the law. He was charming and had a way with the ladies. A sweet talker with swagger. His appeal wasn't necessarily his looks, it was his gentle voice and sweet personality. Guess that accounted for his eight children, by almost as many women. Andre didn't have the personality of his brother. He had the looks but I could no longer say he had the charm.

I was ready to go and was excited about the girlie time ahead, doing what women did with their daughters. We were going to eat some tapas and drink sangria. The children, despite the eight-year gap, would entertain themselves whilst their mothers conversed. Andre put our bag in the car and strapped Leylah into her car seat. She was excited about the sleepover, especially as my cousin had a tiny puppy. Andre locked the house and drove us to the underground station. He parked at the drop off point, got out the car and started to unbuckle Leylah from her seat. I opened the boot of the car and retrieved my bag. Andre gave us both a heartfelt hug.

"Have lots of fun. Call me when you arrive, ok?"

"No problem," I replied, kissed him goodbye and made our way down the escalator to the station.

An hour and a half later, we had arrived. It was so refreshing being away from London and seeing my cousin. How I missed female company. I had turned to Anita when I was on a high and in love and similarly, when I was caught up in the misery that my relationship with Andre had caused me. She knew that I was trying to make the relationship work and the changes he had made. We greeted each other and set off towards the restaurant for lunch. The walk through the town centre took ten minutes. I had called Andre on his mobile, but it went straight to voicemail. I left a message letting him know that we had arrived safely. Just before we reached the Spanish restaurant my mobile pinged to let me know I had received a voicemail message. I took the phone out of my bag and listened.

Hi, I'm at the O2. Where are you? I'm waiting for you. Call me back.

Andre had left this message on my phone, but it wasn't for me. He wasn't meeting me. Andre had said he was tired and was heading back home. So why was he going to the O2? What was he doing there and who was he meeting? I replayed the message. Anita looked at me, puzzled while I held the mobile phone to my ear. I handed it to her and asked her to listen to the message.

"Who is he supposed to be meeting? I thought he told you he was tired and heading back home?"

"Yes, he did." I replied with venom in my tone. I felt the betrayal, as anger start to crescendo inside me. Anita saw my mood switched instantly.

"Let's go and sit down," she suggested.

We started walking towards the restaurant. The children weren't close enough to hear our conversation. Anna knew which restaurant we were heading to so the children led the way.

"He's going to ruin my weekend. Maybe this was deliberate to make me think that he was seeing someone." I was annoyed and disappointed.

"Well, it seems obvious that he's planning to meet someone Shantel. He lied when he said that he was going back home. Do you suspect that there could be anyone else?" she asked.

Anita's ex-husband had cheated on her. She suspected her ex-partner of five years had also done the same. She knew the signs of a dishonest man.

"I don't suspect anything. Don't get me wrong, I know he goes out, but he tells me he's out with his brother Vince. Occasionally he gets dressed up to go out. He doesn't come in the house to jump straight into the shower," I said bitterly, thinking that perhaps he showered elsewhere.

"Then again, I don't usually know what time he gets home and what he does. He could wash before he gets into bed. I can smell when he's had a cigarette, but..." My heart began to thump in my chest.

Anna held the restaurant door open, as we all walked in.

"Thanks Anna," I said. The waitress came and showed us to our table.

"Let's get a jug of sangria. I think you need a jug for yourself," she whispered.

I chuckled. I'd been through worse things.

"I'm going to call him to let him know that he's left me that message," I replied.

"No, leave it for now," she suggested. "In fact, turn your phone off. He's going to do what he's going to do, despite you calling him. Take some time out and call him when we get back home."

I took her advice and switched off my phone. At some point, he would try to call me back.

"Food makes Mummy a very happy woman Leylah!" I exclaimed. "Let's order lots of food!" I tried to lighten the mood.

We ordered so many different dishes. I was in my element. The girls were spoilt for choice and picked at the food until they were full. Two jugs of sangria later and my woes were a distant memory. Did I even care if Andre was cheating? We had a pathetic sex life anyway. I wasn't in the least bit interested in having sex with him. He might as well be giving it away to someone else, as I didn't really want it anyway. Another baby. Was I fooling myself? The idea of Andre lying had left a bad taste in my mouth. He signed up to life with me, one of honesty, love, friendship and sincerity. Cheating was a cop out. I didn't cheat! He spent years practically accusing me almost on a daily basis and now this? Oh no! I wasn't having it. I had to think about my next steps. My thoughts were slightly blurred by the copious amounts of sangria I had consumed. I needed a clearer head and the restaurant was warm. The children were happily playing, running around the restaurant while their tipsy mothers were engrossed in conversation. I was oblivious to the stern looks that Anita said we had received from the waiting staff.

"Honey, visually impaired mammas can't see shit!" I laughed.

"Guess that's one way to look at it," she giggled.

"We better round up the kids before the manager calls social services to take our kids away!" I joked.

We paid the bill and headed back to her house. It was only a ten-minute walk but the fresh air instantly sobered me. I was tempted to turn my mobile phone on but decided to wait until we got to the house and the children were occupied with the puppy.

I took a deep breath and turned on my mobile phone. I looked at the phone Andre had given me two years ago. This was the phone he used, but since he upgraded, I accepted his hand me down. I didn't need glasses with it as everything on the phone was big. It wasn't difficult to see his number, even with alcohol in my system.

The phone rang.

"Hi babe. How are you? I've been trying to call you but the phone kept going to voicemail," he said.

"Really?" I asked with sarcasm.

"Yes, really. What's with the tone?" he asked.

"Andre, don't you know that you called my mobile phone earlier? You left a message on my phone saying that you were at the O2 and you were waiting for someone. You asked them to call you back as you were waiting for them." I was prepared to hear bullshit.

"Yes...," he paused, "...went to meet someone about a... a TV. You know, the TV in our bedroom isn't working and I... err... went to meet someone to get a new one." He stuttered, further fuelling my suspicions.

"So why didn't you tell me about your plans? Why lie Andre?" I caught the bastard.

"Because I just wanted to surprise you."

He was good, but not that good. Trusting Andre again was proving to be an impossible task.

"I don't believe you. TV or no TV. I've not lied to you, but if you choose to lie to me then that's your concern. Enjoy your night, whatever you've got planned." I hung up and switched the phone off.

"Yaay, well done you!" Anita cheered. "What was he saying, that he was going to buy a TV from someone at the O2? Surely, if you're going to buy a TV from someone then you're not going to do that in such a public place." Anita clearly had a point.

"I know. The devil is a liar babe, and he is definitely that. He must have met some woman. You know, all this time he's accused me of cheating, yet he's the one who's been at it." I felt deflated. I knew I was wasting my time with Andre.

"Look at it this way Shantel, he knows that you've caught him out. What's he going to do next? Lie some more to cover up another lie? Do you realise that you're in the driving seat? Look at the way he's treated you, your family and your friends? How much more are you willing to take? Now he could be cheating on you? Is he really the type of person you plan to spend the rest of your life with?" Anita frankly stated the obvious.

I got up from the sofa and looked out of the window into the garden, sipping my water. I no longer needed to be sober. I needed something to make me high but I didn't do drugs. I wanted a drink. And music.

"Let's open the wine and play some tunes!"

Anita had a selection of house music. She jumped up out of her seat, found a CD in her collection and pressed play on the stereo. Beats filled the house and the speakers started thumping the only way house music could. I was glad there were no love lyrics streaming out of the speakers like daggers to my heart. Love was out. Wine and dancing were in. Our daughters ran downstairs when they heard the music blaring. The four of us danced for hours. The sun was setting and the party was in full swing. I didn't need Andre. I just needed my girls, house music and wine.

The following morning, as predicted, I woke up with a throbbing headache. Leylah was still sleeping beside me. I was dehydrated and so glad I'd bought a bottle of water up to bed. I sipped it while looking for the paracetamol in my handbag. I popped two and finished off what was left of the one litre bottle. My thoughts drifted back to the conversation I'd had the night before with Andre. My mobile phone was still switched off. Luckily, he didn't have Anita's phone number or address so he couldn't hound me. I took the phone out of my bag and turned it on to see what he had to say. Whatever words came out of his mouth were to be taken with less than a pinch of salt. I wasn't interested in a barrage of lies.

I had stopped taking the 'wonder drug' in preparation for the second baby. But could I really have another baby with him? There was just too much drama and he would never ever grow up. He was nothing but an immature prick. I turned to look at my princess lying on the bed. I decided to join her. I wasn't overly tired but my mind was exhausted as I mentally debated staying with Andre versus doing it alone. Could I be a disabled, single parent, working full time? But I was also beautiful, stronger, wiser and determined not to fail. I had the inner strength, but wasn't sure if this time was the right time. I was still scared about what the future would hold and how the potential changes ahead would affect my child and I.

Leylah started to stir. She opened her eyes. "Mummy?" she called.

"Yes baby," I replied, looking into her eyes. I gave her a cuddle. "Good morning darling."

"Morning Mummy. Where's Anna?" she asked and shifted out of my arms to sit up in the bed.

"I don't think she's awake yet baby." I said quietly.

Anita was an early riser. I had heard her boiling the kettle for her morning dose of strong black coffee. The puppy barked.

"Mummy, can I go downstairs?" she asked.

"Ok babe. Put your slippers and your dressing gown on. It's cold in the house and you've just woken up."

She rummaged through the bag for her dressing gown and slippers, then put them on.

"Are you coming Mummy?" she asked.

"Yes baby," I smiled and got out of bed. I would have much preferred to stay in bed longer, deliberating over my life, but needs must and my daughter was enjoying her time. For her it was like a little holiday. Perhaps I should make it the same for me.

"Morning love. Do you fancy a coffee?" Anita offered, as she saw us coming down the stairs.

"Morning hun. A black coffee, one sugar please. How are you feeling?"

"I'm alright. I've dosed up on paracetamol and caffeine so feeling better than I look. Go and sit down. I'll bring the drinks in. What would you like to drink Leylah?" she asked.

"Just juice please," Leylah replied, playing with the puppy.

Anna skipped down the stairs.

"Good morning," she smiled. She immediately sat down with Leylah on the floor and began playing with the puppy.

Anita handed me my coffee and sat on the sofa next to me. It tasted good.

"So, have you turned your phone on yet?" she asked quietly.

"I've turned it on. There are some messages, but I haven't listened to them yet." I sipped my coffee again. I needed the bittersweet taste in my mouth after last night's shenanigans. "I know what he'd have said in the messages, so there's no rush to listen to them. I'm just going to concentrate on enjoying the rest of my time here before I make my way back."

"Well, make sure you call, or text me later to let me know you're ok. Remember, you're in control and you're a strong woman. He's made the mistakes and he needs to rectify them but you have to decide where you go from here. I've done this myself. Anna's dad is a complete waste of space but you'll be able to cope doing it alone. I promise you. You deserve a man that'll love you wholeheartedly. Not a man that's tried to change you from the minute he's known you. He'll never be happy Shantel. Let's face it, you've done everything to please him but what have you had in return?"

She had a point and it was nothing I didn't already know.

After lunch Anita and Anna walked us to the train station. We said our goodbyes and headed back to Greenwich. I still hadn't listened to the messages.

Chapter Nineteen:
Exit Plan

Andre called my mobile while we were on the train approaching Waterloo Station. I rejected the call. I looked at the time. 4:25. Thirty minutes later, I opened the porch door to be greeted by him, dressed in house clothes and with a slightly worried look on his face.

"Hello Daddy!!" Leylah skipped through the door.

"Hello Pumpkin. I've missed you. Did you have a nice time?" he asked.

"Yes Daddy. I played with the puppy. I had so much fun," she replied and ran into the sitting room.

I could hear she had turned the TV onto something more appropriate for her. I walked in, put my bag down and shut the porch door. I took my coat off and hung it up.

"Did you get my messages?" he asked.

"I didn't listen to them," I answered without looking at him.

I removed my boots and went straight into the kitchen. I was thirsty and still dehydrated from the alcohol consumption. The water from the jug in the fridge was perfectly chilled. I needed it. I poured a second glass and asked Leylah if she wanted a drink. She didn't so I took my glass, walked past Andre, who was staring at me in the hallway, took my bag and headed up the stairs. I heard his footsteps follow me. I went into our bedroom and pulled off my jeans. I glanced at the new television mounted onto the chimney breast and then looked at him.

"So, this is the TV you bought?" I asked feeling tired of the lies and wondered what line he'd give me.

"Yes, I wasn't lying Shantel."

"Maybe you weren't lying about the TV Andre. Anyway, whatever." I continued to strip off and changed into comfortable clothes. "Who were you meeting at the O2? I see the bed sheets have been changed."

I didn't even care about his response. I just wanted him to know that I'd noticed.

"Is it a crime if I wash the sheets so that it's all nice and fresh for your return?" Andre asked.

I walked out of the bedroom, into the bathroom and shut the door. I didn't need him spectating. I wanted ten minutes to myself.

"Shantel." Andre called through the closed door.

"Go check on Leylah!" I shouted.

There was no need for any other words that evening. Andre said he was going to cook. I let him and I let him tidy up too. He offered to put Leylah to bed. I kissed her goodnight and lay on the sofa, flicking through the channels, no longer caring about his feelings, but constructing an exit plan.

Later on, he came downstairs to the sitting room. I said goodnight without looking at him and went upstairs to prepare for bed. Our relationship felt doomed and was continuing down the slippery slope to the crash at the bottom. I took my tablets out of my medicine box one by one. I stared at my wonder drug, fondling the packet for a while and threw it back into the box. I sighed, took my medication and lay down on our bed. I was glad it was so big, as it meant that we were unlikely to touch each other in the middle of the night.

I awoke in the morning to Andre's alarm, screeching unpleasant tones. I hated that alarm, despite it having the desired effect of waking me from my slumber. Andre pressed snooze and sat up in the bed. It was the beginning of another week of grind. Winning the lottery would be a huge solution, for many different reasons. I lay in bed thinking of how a million pounds could change my life dramatically. I wouldn't have to get out of bed so early. I would have a chauffeur. I could sleep in the day and devote more time to my child. Oh the possibilities were endless.

"Good morning," Andre said.

"Morning," I replied. He was still an arsehole.

"Coffee?" he asked.

"Please," I answered.

As he shifted off the bed to go downstairs, I started to get ready too. I put the radio on and headed to Leylah's bedroom. She looked so peaceful.

"Wakey, wakey baby girl!" I sang.

Leylah shifted and twisted in her bed. I flicked her light on. The bright light coupled with the music on the stereo was enough to arouse her from her sleep.

"Let's get up baby girl. Time to go to nursery." I kissed Leylah and started to get her ready for a wash. Andre came up the stairs with my coffee and greeted his daughter with a kiss on her forehead.

"Wake up sleepy head. I'll put your coffee on the bedside table," he said, walking into our bedroom.

I quickly finished up with Leylah, then showered and grabbed some clothes out of the wardrobe. Andre went into the shower while I dressed in the bedroom. Leylah's eyes flicked between me and the new forty-two-inch TV that hung on the bedroom wall. Was the TV really worth a lie? Our relationship was not working. We were a partnership of sorts but the fundamental aspects were missing. What had happened to our spiritual connection? Was it ever really there or were we blinded by the fantasy of a relationship? What happened to the emotional ties? There weren't any anymore. We just existed in this partnership. The physical aspect of our relationship had dwindled away to nothing. I didn't even want him to touch me because he wasn't genuine. Andre cheating on me was expected because of the type of person he was. His heart was never pure and I suffered as a consequence.

Your sweet smile and charm fooled me
Your pretty eyes and words, now cruel to me
I signed up for love, trust, a best friend
You gave me pain, lies, tears, emotionally I could not depend
Who soothed my hurt? Who mended the break?
I prayed to God for my soul to shake
To revive and repair the strength I once had

Make me smile, sweet Jesus, please make me glad
I want to hear colours and see the wind
I want to fly and encapsulate sound
I want to breathe love and smell happiness
That's my future, I need nothing less

I felt nothing for Andre. I searched and searched myself but there was nothing. I reflected all day. The love had truly and completely gone. How could I possibly have another child with him? I didn't want Leylah to be an only child but I was no longer prepared to stay in this relationship for the sake of a baby. I had to look at the bigger picture. I couldn't see myself being tied to Andre for nine more months. I was scared about what my future would hold, but I knew I was blessed. I knew God had granted me strength. After all, he'd sent a messenger! The journey ahead was unpredictable, but I knew Andre wouldn't and couldn't be by my side. I couldn't be hasty as I needed to plan an escape route. I no longer wanted to share a bed with him. The one in the spare room was originally mine from my flat and I was happy to return to my Japanese style double bed. It was comfortable and I was guaranteed a good sleep. The spare room would be my sanctuary. I returned to it when I needed peace and an escape from my heartache. How could I happily lie down next to a man I no longer loved or even wanted? Forget the pretence, tonight this was where I would sleep. I needed to embrace the strength, guidance and messages God had provided me with. His purpose for me was unknown but I had to go with my gut and physically distance myself from this relationship.

Andre came home that evening, just after 7. Leylah had already eaten and it was soon her bedtime.

"Evening," he greeted.

"Hiya."

"Hello Daddy," Leylah greeted in her sleepy voice.

"Hello Pumpkin. Let me take you upstairs and read you a story. Would you like that?" he asked.

"Yes please!" she answered.

They both went upstairs while I poured myself a glass of well-deserved rosé. His dinner was prepared and on the counter. I plonked myself in front of the TV and flicked the channel from the mind-numbing children's television to an adult show. I wanted comedy or a soap to entertain and distract me from my own current state of affairs.

I still had my wonder drugs in my medicine box. I knew that once I'd taken the first tablet, the relationship was definitely over. I heard Andre come down the stairs. He opened the sitting room door. I sipped the last of the wine, thinking that it went down too quickly.

"Leylah wants to say goodnight to you," he announced as he sat down.

That basically meant that I would be putting Leylah to bed myself as he couldn't finish off the job. At least I had ten minutes to myself to sip the wine and relax.

"Ok," I replied, as I got up to put my glass in the kitchen then head up to Leylah's room.

"Night night baby girl." I kissed and hugged her.

"Stay with me for a little bit," she asked sweetly.

I couldn't refuse her, and besides, I wasn't in a rush to sit downstairs with the liar.

I watched her as she drifted off into a deep sleep. She was so beautiful and the reason for my existence in this dreadful relationship. She would also be my catalyst out of this relationship. I had never cried in front of my daughter and didn't intend to. I wanted her to see me as being resilient and a positive role model for her. She was three years old and needed to be protected from this emotionally dysfunctional relationship. She couldn't pick up on my pain and anger towards her father. I was angry because of the lies and the way I had been mistreated despite all that I had given. He had skilfully mastered the art of carrying weighty baggage, without anyone knowing. I was caught off guard and it was now too late to go back. It wasn't Leylah's fault, she just needed to be happy and I hoped that I could make her happy as a single parent. So many women were doing it solo. Why couldn't I? I could have a work-life balance. I worked hard at my nine to five and at being a mother but I wondered if my health was going to withstand the potential stress that was coming my way. I considered the possible scenarios:

Andre could accept that the relationship was over and leave.

Andre could fight for the relationship to work and resume counselling.

He had a malicious streak and could get nasty and cruel. My mind wandered to all the news reports of the crazed men whose relationships had failed leading to vengeful attacks on their wives hurting and sometimes killing them.

Andre was unpredictable. I realised then that I'd never quite known what lay behind those eyes. I knew some of his past, but needed to guard myself against him and the changing future. There would be no guarantee of his participation with his daughter. Would he just disappear? The mortgage was high. Would he continue to pay it with me or would I be left to struggle? These factors were important but my sanity, health and happiness took priority over the unknowns. I looked over at Leylah, now fast asleep. She looked so peaceful. I wondered how she would cope when the storm hit. I prayed silently.

Dear God. Thank you for all the blessings you have bestowed upon me. I don't know what the future will hold but please help me and Leylah to be strong. Help the transition to be smooth and not traumatic for my little girl. Keep her happy and knowing that she is loved by all. Dear God, please keep me strong through the transition. Father God, please help me to be free. Amen.

I went to the spare room. It was free of clutter. My wardrobe had always been in here, so it was my room and an Andre-free sanctuary. He had never slept in this room. Every time we argued recently, I would sleep here. He would never volunteer to do the same because he was so selfish. This time I was prepared to give up our bedroom for clutter free surroundings. I went to get my medicine box.

I remembered Andre's reaction to the offer of morphine when I had that crisis in pregnancy. Andre created such an embarrassing fuss. I was in excruciating pain and he was trying to stamp his authority, which inadvertently caused me more stress. I wasn't going through that again. I popped two pills and sipped some water. They were gone, into my body, putting a full stop on the possibility of a future with Andre. I checked my mobile phone for messages and emails. There were none. I put my phone on charge, flicked off the light switch and collapsed into bed, pulling the thick duvet over my exhausted body. I anticipated Andre opening the door and wanting to talk, but I wasn't in the mood. I breathed in the smell of fabric conditioner from the pillow case and exhaled. I closed my eyes and prayed again for God to watch over this household.

No sooner had I started to relax in the bed, could I hear footsteps coming up the stairs. I started to count, awaiting his entrance into the room. One, two, three, four, five. The door opened and the light came on.

"Shantel, what are you doing in here?" Andre asked standing in the doorway.

Wasn't it obvious?

"I'm sleeping in here."

"Why?" Andre questioned.

"Please turn my light off. I'm trying to sleep," I replied.

Andre stepped into the room, shut the door then sat on the bed. I really didn't need his presence distorting the karma I had created in the room.

"Andre, I need my own space. Can you please leave the room so I can be alone to sleep in peace?" I was getting frustrated at the resistance to my request. I could see by his body language and facial expression that he wasn't about to give up easily.

"Why aren't you sleeping next door in our bed?' he continued.

"Andre, you can't make me do what I don't want to do. Right now, I want you to leave this room so I can get a good night's sleep. I don't need you to be here with me. I need you to leave this room so I can sleep. Can you please do that?" I repeated.

"No. You need to come next door and sleep in our bed."

"Andre, don't fuck with me. Get out now. Just leave and don't think about waking up the baby because you're not getting your own way. Leave this room."

I sat up in bed to make him realise that I was serious. How dare he continue with his stupid line of questioning? Couldn't he see that I was no longer interested in talking, let alone sleeping in the same bed with him?

"Shantel!" he pleaded.

"No Andre. Go next door and don't wake Leylah up. Get some sleep like I'm trying to do. Goodnight!"

I slid back into the bed, fluffing the pillow before laying on it. I turned my back towards Andre and the door.

"Please, turn off the light and shut the door. Thank you."

I closed my eyes and started to breathe deeply, though it was difficult to meditate while Andre was still in the room, filling it with negative energy.

Andre sat on the bed, for what seemed like an eternity, before getting up, turning off the light and shutting the door behind him. I was free of him, at least for that night. I continued with my meditation to relax me once more. I lay in the bed considering whether I had done the right thing. Yes I had. There was no other way apart from separation. I would cope without him. It was just a matter of time before the finale of 'us.'

I woke up to the delicate sound of harps playing on my mobile phone. So much more suitable than the barking dogs Andre had as his alarm ringtone. I looked around the room and remembered last night's events. I reached for my mobile phone and turned off the melodic harps. It was 7. I needed to ensure that I left to get Leylah to the nursery and to work on time. I wasn't going to rely on Andre to drive us. I got up, went downstairs and made my own coffee before starting the morning's duties. I opened the curtains in the sitting room and looked outside. The sun was rising, but it was still dark. I heard heavy footsteps walking down the stairs.

"Morning." Andre walked towards the kitchen. "Coffee?" he asked.

"Yes, but don't worry, I'll make it." I brushed past him in the kitchen and reached for a large coffee cup. Andre took the instant coffee down from the shelf and passed it to me.

"Thank you." I unscrewed the coffee lid and measured a teaspoon of caffeine.

I didn't offer him one as he never drank coffee in the morning. I decided I needed a sugar boost so scooped a teaspoon of brown sugar into my cup then reached for the kettle. Andre watched me as I manoeuvred around him in our tiny kitchen.

"I'm going to wake Leylah up," I announced and started to walk up the stairs. I heard him pull out the ironing board. He usually ironed his shirts in the evening, but I assumed he was yet again preoccupied on his beloved computer. We got ready that morning as usual. There were hardly any words exchanged between us. This felt like a partnership rather than a relationship between two people who loved each other. While I showered, I made the conscientious decision to reposition my diamond engagement ring. It no longer served a purpose on my left hand. It was now a pretty diamond ring on my right hand. Andre was bound to notice the difference immediately. It was a beautiful ring, but felt awkward on my right hand. I assumed that it wouldn't take too long for me to get used to the feeling of the change, but also the emotional impact it created. Leylah didn't notice, not that she would anyway. Andre did though. When we were in the car on our way to the nursery, he looked at my hand then looked at me, but didn't comment. We dropped Leylah off as usual then made our way to the station. I waited for Andre to get the ticket for the car park then we walked into the train station, in silence. I said goodbye to him. There was no kiss. He didn't deserve it. I just needed to walk away from him and make my way to the office.

I had decided that today was the end. No more sharing a bed. No more cooking, washing and no more support. I couldn't give that man any more than he had already got from me, financially emotionally, physically or mentally. It was time that I started to just look after myself and my daughter. He had ruined friendships, drained me financially, and disrespected me and my parents. The list was endless but I wouldn't allow him to add to it. He wasn't there for me emotionally. He was never my rock. God lived within me and therefore, I was my rock. It's amazing that strength and courage appear when you feel you have nothing left. There was a force within me, convincing me that I could be free. Freedom was now coming. I didn't know what was going to happen next. I only knew there would be considerable changes. He had to know that separation was coming. Why pretend to love him? I wasn't a good liar. My emotions and feelings always came out.

Perhaps he'd already found a replacement for me. Men needed sex more than we did. And selfish men only wanted what they wanted and never considered other people's feelings or emotions. Was this man a sociopath? I considered the description and googled it on my phone to see whether the definition matched Andre: *superficial charm, manipulative and cunning, grandiose sense of self, pathological liar, lack of remorse, shame or guilt, shallow emotions, no capacity for love, need for stimulation, lack of empathy, poor behaviour controls/ impulsive nature, earlier behavioural problems / juvenile delinquency, irresponsible / unreliable, promiscuous, lack of a realistic life plan, criminal or entrepreneurial versatility.*

Damn, I had been in a relationship with a sociopath for all those years and hadn't known! It was doomed before I even knew him. It was inevitable that it would end badly. They are selfish lovers. They are deceitful and cunning. Pathological liars! He would look in my face but his eyes betrayed him. Well, now I had the strength to leave. Damn, I'd even pack his possessions for him. He was dishonest and not to be trusted, but all along, he'd convinced me that I was the untrustworthy one.

Blossom Tree | Sharon Fevrier

I had invested all my money into the house and the car. This was going to work out for me, even if I had to take him to court. I was prepared to do whatever it took to get the freedom that I was promised. The mortgage was high and I would have to speak to my father about the payments if Andre stopped contributing. I was prepared for a fight; I could sense it coming. I paid half the car payments and it was my car that was part exchanged to get the Golf that he was driving. He was a boy when he came into this relationship. I was a woman, growing stronger and adapting every day. I was supposed to be treated like an empress, not a rag doll. I wasn't a trophy or a slave. I was now going to become an independent single parent. Woah, what a title! God would provide me with a good man one day, but I needed that single status.

The day at work flew by and I knew I'd be faced with more drama that evening. Andre needed to know I was back on my wonder drug. There would be no clearer sign to represent the end of our relationship.

On the way home, I prepared Louisa for the anticipated events.

"Hey babe, how are you?" I asked.

"I'm fine. Work was stressful and I can't wait to get out of there. I need a new job," she joked.

"Ok, I hear you babe."

I listened to her for another five minutes, complaining about ineffectual management and work overload. She was desperate for a new job. I had wondered if she needed a career change. I didn't want to burden her with my woes when she was clearly unhappy about her work situation.

"Ok, how are things with you at the moment?" she asked.

"I'm ready to end this relationship. I can't take it anymore. I hate living with him. He's an awful person. I've started taking my wonder drug again."

"Wow, then it really is over," she replied.

"Yes babe. I'm going to let him know I'm back on the pills."

"He doesn't know yet?" she quizzed.

"Not yet."

"Did you discuss it with him before you started taking them?" she asked.

"No. It's my decision. Frankly speaking, I'm not prepared to engage in a conversation with him about the possibility of another child to make me stay even longer in a loveless relationship." I sighed. "I do want another child, but he can't be the father. I don't want two different fathers for my children but I am prepared for that if it happens." I was oozing confidence.

"Shantel, I haven't heard you sound so positive in all the years you've been with Andre. I guess it's time for a change. The thing is Shantel, you changed so much, from the happy jovial person you were. You always used to crack a joke. You used to smile more. He's taken all that away leaving you with a scowl ninety percent of the time. It sounds like you're about to make a positive move to get out of the relationship. You're sounding strong and determined. I love you babe and I will support you with this but you know, when the time is right, you will end the relationship." Louisa was an encouraging voice of wisdom.

"Thanks hun. I'd better go. Will keep you updated," I reassured her.

"Ok, please do. See ya babe."

I ran, hopped, skipped and jumped to get to the nursery on time. I hated rushing but I had no choice. This was my usual manic journey home. I always reached the nursery at literally minutes before six o'clock, or on the dot, with little beads of sweat on my forehead. He didn't have to rush. No, that was always left to me. Fair enough, I worked slightly shorter hours than him, but he never ever made any effort to speak to his employers about flexible working conditions. This lifestyle was no different from that of the average single parent anywhere in the world. I was used to this routine, but I didn't like it. Leylah was getting older and her application for a reception school place was soon to be submitted. We had already seen the priest and had the application signed off for the local Church of England primary school. I was almost ninety-nine per cent sure that she would get a place. It needed to happen. The school was at the top of our road and very convenient. I would have to think about a child-minder and had already received the list from the council. Things were certainly soon to change and the wheels were already in motion. Life had to get easier.

That evening was initially no different from every other evening.

Get home
Cook food
Feed the baby
Eat my food
Bath baby
Dress baby for bed
Andre arrives home

The last element of that sequence was bound to change. I wouldn't have to cook dinner for Andre. I could just eat a big lunch during the day and have a snack in the evening. I could eat sea food and fried fish without the fear that his allergy would turn him into the elephant man. I could just have a bowl of soup. The possibilities were endless. I'd be able to put Leylah to bed and speak on the phone to anyone I wanted to, without the sneaky, creeping spy, listening to my every breath. For dinner, I made a quick chicken stir fry. If he wanted some, he could take some. If he didn't want it, I would use it as my lunch the following day at work. I headed upstairs with Leylah after clearing the kitchen. I put her to bed early as I wanted a peaceful night, but I sensed that the storm was approaching rapidly. Fortunately, she slept quickly so I started to prepare myself for bed. It was only 7:30. As I stripped off my work clothes and headed for the bathroom. I heard the key turn in the front door. I rolled my eyes, realising that he was home, in my space. I picked up my dressing gown from the bedroom and turned on the shower, locking the bathroom door for privacy. We only had one bathroom so if he needed to pee he'd have to go into the garden. I spent twenty minutes under the hot water, washing away the tiring day. I was ready to face another evening with the enemy. I took the time to moisturise my skin with a perfumed lotion.

I could hear him through the door, walking up the stairs. I didn't have time to pick up my camisole but luckily, I had my oversized dressing gown to cover me. He no longer had the privilege of seeing my beautiful temple. My body was my sole property and no one else's. The only hugs and kisses that I was willing to exchange were with my baby girl, definitely not her father. I took a deep breath and unlocked the door. The light was on in our bedroom. I went in and saw him sitting on the bed. He was wearing a white shirt, unbuttoned at the collar and his boxer shorts. He looked up at me as I walked into the room towards the chest of drawers.

"Hello."

"Hiya, how was your day?" he asked.

"Fine." I wondered if he knew that my *feelings inside not expressed.*

"What time did Leylah go down?" he enquired.

"About twenty minutes ago," I replied.

BUT IF YOU WERE A DECENT MAN AND A GOOD FATHER YOU WOULD HAVE BEEN HOME TWENTY MINUTES AGO TO A GOOD WOMAN THAT LOVED YOU AND A CHILD THAT ADORED YOU!

"She was really tired so I put her to bed early."

"Ok. Well, I've got to pop out and see my brother," he said, standing up and pulling on his blue jeans.

"No problem." I replied and took my camisole to the room next door so I could quickly slip it on. I figured that if I left the room there would be no awkward goodbyes.

I was glad he was leaving. That meant no confrontation tonight. I could watch some TV, drink a glass of wine in peace and just sit, without him lurking around or doing whatever he did on the computer next door. Bliss. I went back into our bedroom and threw my dirty clothes into the basket. He was spraying himself with aftershave. I couldn't lie, it smelt good. It was a sweet manly fragrance that would ordinarily have me doing a double take if I smelt it on a man in the street. But in my home, I knew who was wearing it. The scent was wasted on the man. I wondered if I had bought it for him. He pulled on his leather biker jacket and filled his jeans pockets with his keys, his phone and his wallet.

"Have a good night," I said, walking towards the door.

"You too," he replied as I walked down the stairs.

I fetched the bottle of chilled rosé from the fridge and a glass from the cupboard, before entering the living room and closing the door. I heard the front door open and then quickly shut. He'd gone.

Freedom. I took a deep breath and wondered what it could mean to me.

Liberation, salvation, elevation, entitlement
Independence, empowerment
Fluidity, liquidity, hope, peace, release
Eagle, Phoenix, space, choice, fearless, openness
Drums beating to a tune that I can dance to unapologetically
Wings attached to help me glide through the atmosphere
Avoiding the smog that could infect me
Breathing under water as I explore the ocean
Bouncing on a trampoline, with each jump I see more of the colourful world
Smiling to a stranger and receiving a friendly smile back
Accepting kind gestures and genuine compliments
Laughing out loud until the tears of joy run down my cheeks
Being at peace with myself and others
Listening to jazz while sitting on a train
Watching a romantic comedy, with a box of tissues and chocolates on my lap
Walking slowly through the countryside, no footwear, skin to earth
Uniting with loved ones

I looked at the time on my mobile phone. An hour had passed as I was submerged in my thoughts.

That night I slept in the spare room again. I was making the room comfortable and practical. I didn't have a great deal in the master bedroom anyway, just a few items in my bedside drawer. The spare room didn't have a bedside table but I didn't need one. The view of the mature garden was picturesque, though slightly overgrown. The master bedroom had a view of the River Thames but I wasn't prepared to reconsider my sleeping arrangements unless Andre vacated the room.

The summer season was truly over. It was now October. The weather had been relatively dry although the temperature was dropping. I had become frustrated with constantly asking Andre to cut the grass. That Saturday, I pulled on my tracksuit, tied my hair with a scarf and put my old trainers on.

"What are you doing Mummy?" Leylah asked.

"Baby, Mummy is about to cut the grass. It's quite long. This should be the last cut of the year."

I spoke loud enough for Andre to hear me. He was flitting between the sitting room and the dining room, which had an open view of the garden. I was secretly screaming at him inside, begging him to mow the lawn, but he didn't hear me. Maybe he thought I was nagging? Why should he oblige? He didn't have to do anything for me. We were still sleeping in separate bedrooms. He wasn't prepared to save this relationship; if he was, he would try to do the things that I still considered to be a man's job. Was I really meant to do absolutely everything? The only thing he did was drive and that's only because I couldn't. He couldn't even go food shopping by himself.

"Mummy, can I come outside?" Leylah asked.

"Of course you can sweetheart. Just make sure you've got a warm jumper on."

I opened the back door and headed through the garden to the shed. The lawn mower was heavy, but I managed to pull it out. I could see Andre looking at me through the dining room window.

He offered no help. He would rather watch me struggle with the heavy cumbersome mower. Still, I was prepared to try. The lawn mower had a propeller to get it started. It had always been tricky for me to operate. I pulled the cord once, twice, three times. No joy. I tried again and again. Unsuccessful. I was getting tired of yanking the cord. Andre stared at me while Leylah played in the garden. I had to bite the bullet and ask Andre to get the mower started. I wondered if he would at least help me to do that. He didn't have to cut the grass as I had resigned myself to the fact that on this occasion, it was my responsibility.

"Mummy, isn't it working?" Leylah asked.

"Not yet darling," I answered, trying to sound upbeat.

"Andre, can you help me get this lawnmower started?" I shouted toward the house. Surely, he could see me struggling.

"Ok."

He appeared in the hallway and started putting his trainers on. There was no hesitation. I started walking towards the back of the garden, with Andre following behind me, acknowledging Leylah as he walked passed her. Andre pulled once, twice and third time lucky. I thanked him and started mowing the lawn. I put my headphones on to listen to music while I worked. I actually enjoyed it. It gave me a sense of satisfaction, knowing I could alter something to make it aesthetically pleasing. I was listening to Jill Scott. I could sing my heart out and no one would be able to hear me over the noisy engine. In my world, I sounded like Whitney Houston, but just didn't look as glamorous as she did, especially not in my grey tracksuit and floral headscarf. Before long, the waste box on the mower was full. I would have to turn it off and ask Andre to turn it back on once it was emptied. I emptied, I asked, he obliged and I continued. This happened a few times until the garden was finished. Leylah could run up and down on the lawn with no fear of stepping into fox poo. I did it all by myself a job that historically, he would have done. I was proud of my achievement. I had proven to myself that I could do most things around the house, including the gardening. I left the hedge as that wasn't essential to do, and anyway I was tired from pushing around the heavy mower. I put it back in the shed and removed my clothes in the kitchen, put them in the washing machine and ran upstairs naked, hoping that Andre didn't see me. I ran past Leylah, who was sitting in front of the TV watching Nick Junior. I used to feel free about walking around the house naked, but now, I didn't need Andre to be a spectator. I spent the rest of the afternoon doing the mundane household chores while Andre was glued to his computer. I left him to it and concentrated on Leylah and I.

It was now weeks since I had moved into the spare bedroom. There was no reconciliation, just existence. Andre still spent his Friday and Saturday nights at his brother's house, or wherever. I didn't care. Sex with him would have been a chore and he knew it. He didn't ask anymore. The end was close. I was planning it and the freedom I was promised was almost at my fingertips. I was becoming more and more agitated around Andre. We didn't talk anymore but our routine continued as normal. He was becoming frustrated, I was becoming resentful. He was spending more time out of the house. I wished he would just move out. The atmosphere was becoming unbearable. He did nothing in the house to make it work; he just existed.

The walls were still a boring magnolia and white. I'd thrown a few cushions on the sofa to add some colour to the bland living room. Andre added to the clutter in the house. He used the dining room as his office, when I wanted it to be a calming, peaceful environment to sit at the table and eat. The table looked like an admin desk. I was becoming more and more vocal about his lack of participation in his daughter's life. Surely, she was now at an age where he should feel confident enough to take her to the local park and interact with her. In fact, I found myself deliberately picking arguments with him. I had reached rock bottom. There was no way out of this deep blue sea.

Chapter Twenty:
Lights Off

I had grown to detest Andre in the days and weeks since the gardening episode. How could he really leave me to do the gardening by myself? Yes, I felt empowered getting the job done, but I would have been just as happy to see him pull out his finger, leave the computer and cut the grass. Were our roles so undefined? Andre's approach to 'men's work' was to pay someone to do the job. How about taking ownership, saving money and doing it yourself? If I had to pay to get a job done then what was his purpose? What did he do for me apart from drive me to the station in the morning? I needed more; he gave me less. Even when we parked it would be in a disabled bay, saving him money by using my Blue Badge. The venom had built up towards him. I became moodier and less concerned about the dysfunctional harmony that we were trying to exist in.

On this particular morning I asked Andre to make me a coffee while I began to get Leylah ready.

"Andre, can you make me some coffee please?" I requested, flicking on the master bedroom light.

I opened the door to Leylah's room to get her ready. Once she was washed, I brought her back into her bedroom. I took a peep into the master bedroom and saw that Andre was still sleeping. I headed straight over to the stereo and turned the radio on to a dance station. Perfect. I turned the volume up loud enough to wake Andre, but also low enough for him to hear my second request for coffee.

Leylah was ready within ten minutes. She went downstairs to watch TV while I went into the bathroom to shower. Why wasn't he getting ready too? He had gone to bed late because he was either sitting watching TV or at his PC, playing some weird 'shoot-em-up' game. I wouldn't let his issues become mine, but I expected my coffee.

I had to get up and sort out the baby. The least he could have done was make the mother of his child a caffeine fix! I was getting more and more annoyed at him. After finishing in the shower, I hurried to get dressed. I heard Andre step across the hall to the bathroom, slamming the door shut. He was out within two minutes and I was still getting dressed. We literally had five minutes to leave the house. If he was waiting until the very last minute to make me a coffee then there would be no point as I could never drink it piping hot. Today was the day that I wouldn't have my stimulating drink. FINE! I had thrown on some clothes, looked in the mirror and faked a smile. It wasn't genuine, but it would do. I took a deep breath and headed down the stairs. Andre quickly followed behind me.

"Morning," he mumbled.

"Hi." I popped my head around the sitting room door and saw Leylah watching Little Princess on TV. She was fine. Andre was putting his shoes on and walked around the dining room to find his keys and other things that he needed for the day.

"No coffee?" I quizzed.

"I didn't have time," he replied.

"Really?" I questioned.

"Yep. Really!" he responded.

I wished I had practiced deep meditation because, at that moment, I wanted to reach for the largest frying pan and hit him repeatedly with it until he disintegrated into dust. I sighed. I would have to get coffee from the coffee shop near work. I had to provide for myself because he was clearly too busy last night entertaining himself, rather than thinking of ways of reconciliation. I didn't say a word to Andre in the car on the journey to the nursery.

"Silent treatment?" he asked as he parked the car in the nursery car park.

I remained silent. Inside I wanted to scream and shout at him. All I expected him to do was make me a coffee even though I could have made my own. The nursery was only a fifteen-minute walk away. She would have to get used to the walk and the changes that were coming. Surely change was a good thing? I said goodbye to Leylah then he took her into the nursery. I decided to stay in the car. I didn't need to see his sickly-sweet public display of affection. I noticed a letter in the passenger door. It was addressed to Andre. I wondered why he had a hand-written letter in the car. As I looked closer, I noticed that the postage stamp was marked Wandsworth Prison. I decided to slip it into my handbag and read it when I had more time. He probably wouldn't have even noticed it was missing anyway.

Andre was heading back to the car. I felt my chest tighten. If he pushed me with his questioning, I would blow.

He opened the car door and sat down. I stared straight ahead, not looking at him. My peripheral view was not good, but I didn't sense him looking at me. He started to drive to the local train station.

"So, are you not talking to me?" he asked.

"Andre, there's no point. I really have nothing to say anymore." I thought twice. I should tell him exactly how I felt. Forget feeling fine. It was now time to express myself.

"I don't know why I'm with you, or why I waste my time with you. All you had to do this morning was make me a coffee and yet still you found that too difficult to do!" The anger rose with every word I spoke.

"I was tired and slept through the alarm Shantel. What's the problem?" he asked.

"The problem? The problem Andre is *you*. I do so much in this house, for this family and it's clearly too much for you to make me a coffee in the morning. What do you do for me? Have you ever asked yourself that? No. NO YOU HAVE NOT! This isn't just about the coffee. It's about you. I don't love you anymore. You do nothing for me. IT'S OVER. FINITO. FINISHED! I don't want you anymore so you're free to leave. You've tried to change me from day one. You've lied to me and probably cheated. I can't trust a single word you say to me. Just leave me the hell alone!" I yelled.

Andre stopped the car. I realised he had parked in a disabled bay near the train station.

"It's over Andre."

I got out of the car and slammed the passenger door. I started walking down the road in the direction of the station. I was in shock and no doubt he was too. I had a thought. I couldn't allow him to take advantage of the Blue Badge and park for free. My ex-fiancé needed to go find another place to park. I sprinted back to the car as fast as I could. The driver's door was already open and he was standing up. I leant into the car and snatched my badge. There was no way he was going to benefit any further from me or my possessions.

"You're not using this anymore!" I shouted, turned and walked towards the train station. I looked back to see him still in a daze, probably thinking about his next move. He would now be late for work and would need to find somewhere else to park. I didn't care. That was the beginning of my payback for all the hurt and pain he had caused me over the past five years. Five years of his negative, controlling behaviour and making me feel as though I was a bad person. *ENOUGH.*

I entered the Docklands Light Rail station and found a seat. My heart was beating rapidly. The train was due to depart in one minute. He wouldn't have time to follow me onto the train. He still had to park the car, hopefully in a very expensive spot. The doors beeped, then shut and the train started slowly moving through the tunnel. I hated him. I had never hated him as much as I did today. All the pain he had caused me, all the frustration and stress. My concerns about my future left my mind as quickly as the train travelled down the track to the next station. All I could think about was my relationship being over, once and for all. I looked out of the window and stared into the sky. I hadn't noticed how bright the sky was. It was the bluest sky that I had seen in months. There were no clouds. The sun was shining brightly and I felt a warm sense of freedom. I caught a glimpse of the River Thames. It flowed naturally and calmly. I felt the calm after the storm. He had to leave. I closed my eyes and sent my thoughts into the universe.

Thank you for keeping me strong. I need guidance. Andre needs guidance. I need to be free. Please make this happen for me.

I opened my eyes as the DLR pulled into Canning Town Station. It was busy as usual and half the passengers were disembarking at the same time, probably to catch the Jubilee Line. Everyone had their own agenda. I wondered if anyone could read my mind. In the blink of an eye, I was at work. That was the fastest journey ever, or was my mind too pre-occupied with all the dramas in my life? I turned on my computer after greeting the staff in my office. I needed coffee and my head to be clear, not clouded with fatigue. After making my morning potion, I sat down at my desk and took a deep breath, while asking God for inspiration. I pulled Andre's letter out of my bag and slipped on my glasses. The letter was from Andre's former acquaintance Dean. He was accusing Andre of being involved in fraudulent activities. Dean wanted the money back! I was astonished by what I was reading. Dean said that he was sentenced to seven years inside. I jumped when my mobile phone rang. It was Andre. I answered the call and slipped the letter back into my handbag.

"Hi," I said, without saying his name as I didn't need my colleagues knowing who I was speaking to.

"Hi Shantel. I thought I'd let you know that I will be picking up a few things from the house later and I'll stay at my brother's house. I don't want to get in your way so I will be leaving work early to do that," Andre confirmed.

"Good. I'd appreciate that," I responded.

"Ok."

"Goodbye." I hung up.

He finally got the message. I gave thanks to God for working on Andre. That day at work floated by. I occasionally thought back to the morning's events. I was still so angry with him. I wanted him out of my life and today would be the beginning of a new chapter.

That evening, when I got home, I saw that he had taken some of his clothes. His toiletries, shirts, suits and a couple of ties had gone from his wardrobe. Some of his casual clothes had gone too. Not enough had gone for my liking though. Still, it was a start. I had locked all the doors as I came into the house so there was no entering without consent. I felt a little nervous that night, not knowing if Andre would try to call or use his house key to open the door. I stripped the bed in the master bedroom. I vacuumed the house, fed the baby and put her to bed early. I decided to burn some candles, hoping to create a sense of tranquillity and disperse the negative energy. The smell of lavender filled the air. I prayed that the baby would sleep through the night as I lay down on the fresh sheets covering the bed that I had missed so dearly. I was reclaiming what was mine and what I had paid for. He came into this relationship with the shirt on his back. He sure as hell was going to leave with the same shirt. Nothing more, nothing less. I was emotionally exhausted by the drama of the day and ready to close my eyes. I turned off the lamp, took some deep breaths, thanked God for the day and sank into my bed.

"Mummy, where's Daddy?" Leylah asked at breakfast the following morning.

"Your dad is at Uncle Vince's house sweetheart. Keep eating." I said looking at the time.

"When's he coming home?" she enquired.

"I'm not sure darling. Listen, eat quickly. Let's go. Mummy can't be late for work today baby."

I didn't need awkward questions, especially not at 7:30. Over the next few days, there were more questions. I answered them in the same way.

Thursday evening came. While I was preparing Leylah for bed, I heard my mobile phone ring. It was Andre. I hesitated before answering it. Last thing I wanted was for him to think it was alright to pop round, pick up some more things and distract Leylah from her routine. Not tonight.

"Hi Shantel," he greeted nervously.

"Hi," I replied.

"How are you and how is Leylah?"

"Fine," I answered.

"How have you been managing? Is everything ok?"

"Yes, fine. What do you want?" I asked him abruptly.

"Can I speak to Leylah, to say goodnight?"

"Ok."

I handed the mobile phone to her and I went to freshen up in the bathroom. It would be a short conversation as she wasn't a fan of talking on the phone. When I entered her bedroom, she was off the phone and playing with her toys. I put her to bed and went to mine soon after. As I lay there, I wondered whether he would try to make contact again over the weekend. I needed him to come and take the rest of his things from the house to make my sanctuary free of the oppressor. I would deal with Leylah and her feelings as best as I possibly could. It would be tricky, as I felt so much venom towards her father.

Would I even want to stay in this house? I had invested so much money into it, but I never put my mark on it because deep down inside, while I lived with Andre, I knew it would never be a home. Décor, colour schemes, soft furnishing was never high on my list of priorities. The house just had to be functional. He didn't invest any of his cash in the house to make it a home. It was hard enough paying the mortgage and bills. Maybe selling and moving away, back to East London was an option. I would be close to work. But, I needed to relax, have peace and plan my future. However, Andre needed to be clear. I no longer wanted him, whether as a fiancé, a lover or a partner. In fact, he only had to be a father to his child. There wasn't even a guarantee that he'd be able to fulfil that request. In her three years, he had never once taken her out alone. Don't fathers love taking their children to the park and then buy them an ice cream afterwards? He always wanted me to come along, even though I had begged him to give me some time to clean the house and have a moment to myself. Perhaps he thought I would cheat with the Tesco delivery driver. After being with me for five years he still didn't know me, but I knew too much about him. I knew his history. I knew his lies. I knew his pain and his negative feelings towards women. I knew of his fears and insecurities, his doubts and demons. I could never be his saviour, healer or answer to his troubles. His mind was in conflict. He was no longer allowed to poison me or my child with his issues and negativity. He needed to find someone else to charm, sweet talk, lie to, deceive and abuse. Not me though — no more.

It was the first Friday after Andre had left. His computer tormented me each time I walked past the dining room. What was it that entertained him so much? I decided to put Leylah to bed and investigate. Normally I wouldn't have the amount of free time he did in the evenings. I was far too tired most nights. If I had sat on my laptop each evening, then I would no doubt have heard his moans and felt his beady eyes staring over my shoulder. I knew that he had downloaded all my CDs. I recalled him saying that his ex-girlfriend had taken pleasure in disposing of his music when their relationship had ended abruptly. She was a woman scorned and was clearly vengeful for a reason.

Leylah was exhausted after an active day at nursery. Luckily, she went out like a light. That gave me time to sneak around Andre's beloved machinery. I had set myself a glass of wine on the computer table and powered up the hard drive. There was no password to enter the computer as I often used it to play music. Within seconds the desktop appeared. I turned on the Windows magnifier so that I could see clearly. Firstly, I would check my emails and delete all the junk mail that I hadn't signed up for. I clicked Internet Explorer and entered 'hotmail' in the search engine. Surprisingly, it immediately opened to Andre's account. I stared at the page wondering why his email account appeared. Curiosity got the better of me and I clicked on his inbox. I was astonished by what I saw. There was a ridiculous amount of emails sent to him from someone called Shelly-Ann. Who was she? Why were there so many emails? I was baffled. Maybe I shouldn't have been. I started searching through all the emails to and from her.

Monday 10th September. 20:40
From: Andre
To: Shelly-Ann
Shelly, I've been trying to contact you for a while. Please let me know that you're ok.

A while? Who the hell was she?

Wednesday 12th September. 22:53
From: Shelly-Ann
To: Andre
Sorry. I'm fine. I've been busy on this course. Here's the picture I promised you. More than one way to skin a cat! Lol
S xx

I looked at the picture of the happy couple together. I couldn't believe my eyes. I continued reading the messages.

Sunday 23 September. 22:59
From: Andre
To: Shelly-Ann
How are you settling in Japan babe? I've had a busy week at work. If you're around later I'll give you a call. Miss you.

I clicked onto other random messages.

Friday 18th November. 01:36
From: Andre
To: Shelly-Ann
Hi baby, how are you feeling?? Hope you're ok?? Let's Skype.

The rest of his messages seemed to continue along the same lines. There were numerous requests for her to engage in Skype calls. I felt my body temperature rise so I took off my dressing gown and got myself a glass of water from the kitchen. This was unbelievable. He was cyber cheating with a girl in Japan, but clearly, they had been together at some point as the smiling faces in the picture and the intimate personal names they had called each other indicated. I caught the bastard out. Fool. Well, if he preferred spending his time chatting to someone who was on the other side of the world, then so be it. She could have him.

I continued to browse through his inbox. SPYWARE! What the hell was this now? I opened the email. The message was from a company that provided software to download on a computer so that a mobile phone device could be accessed. I was in shock. I froze at the desk, still clutching the mouse. I took a deep breath. After scanning the email, I realised that somehow, he had access to everything on my phone, prior to the upgrade to my new iPhone in September. It was now November. Andre had given me that Samsung phone he was no longer using. I had used it for two years. He had full access to the calls that I had made and received, to my text messages and to what I had downloaded. He even had access to the internet sites that I had visited. I got up from the computer desk in disbelief. He was incredible. I was more shocked by this revelation than I was about Shelly-Ann. Andre had been actively spying on me for two whole years. Who was he? I was totally devoted to him. There was no one else that I had wanted to be with. I would never have cheated on him. I put my heart and soul into the relationship while he was spying on me. I was so thankful that I had upgraded my mobile phone. I took a deep breath and continued with my search. There were emails back and forth from his solicitor. It seemed he was in the process of re-mortgaging his flat to buy a property locally. So, he don't mind re-mortgaging his flat to purchase a new house but he gave me bullshit excuses as to why he couldn't find the deposit when we were arranging the mortgage for this house. He was unreal. Well, fine. I paid the full deposit on this house and I will take it all back if this place sells.

I checked his contacts. There weren't many as predicted, as he really didn't have any friends. I didn't think he trusted himself, let alone other people. I noted his family contacts and considered that I may need to email them all about their sociopathic brother. I had seen enough. In fact, I had seen more than I had bargained for. I decided to see if his Facebook page was also accessible. It was. Again, his list of contacts was sparse. Billy-no-mates! I checked his inbox. Nothing of any relevance there. I wanted to delete all the pictures from his profile I had tagged him in. He can't prance about life as the family man now. He's well and truly a single man who could see whoever he wanted. My daughter and I would be just fine without him. It was time to turn off the computer and digest the information I had found. I turned off the lights to the dining room and to our relationship. I was exhausted from the day and what I'd found. It was time for bed. I needed to sleep and would take time to consider my next move.

Two weeks passed and Andre was still at his brother's house. He had called and asked if I could get a babysitter so we could meet and have a discussion over a coffee. I wasn't enthusiastic, but I had to be clear about our separation; we were at the point of no return. The break from Andre was essential to make me stronger. I was beginning to find Shantel again. My whole being had been stretched unwillingly, stripped, manipulated and converted into someone unrecognisable. My friends and family were incredibly encouraging and praised the new direction I had taken. They saw a sneak preview of the change in me. I was becoming more focused and determined every day. I was not going to be swayed by his efforts because I knew what was behind those eyes. His emails proved that he was not to be trusted.

I arranged for a friend to babysit. Andre picked me up in our car and drove us to Greenwich. He asked me if I wanted to eat. Yes, I wanted to eat something and I also wasn't going to take my purse out of my bag. We went to Café Rouge. If the night was to become difficult I could get a bus home. I always ordered the same thing, my favourite, garlic prawns twice, for my main meal.

"How have you both been?" Andre asked once the waitress had left.

I sipped on my glass of rosé, thinking that the wine was fruity and sweet.

"I'm fine and Leylah is fine."

"So, what about food? How are you doing getting food in the house?" he asked.

"Online delivery. I've had friends asking if we need anything and some have been very helpful."

I wanted him to realise that other people were looking after the family that he had lost. I knew that it would hurt him, but he needed to know I would be fine and, as always, I was taking care of his daughter.

"Ok," he said after gulping his wine down. He sighed. "This is lovely wine."

"Yes, it is."

I had downed two thirds of my glass. Andre topped it up. I think he was trying to get me relaxed and I needed the wine to steady my nerves but also to diffuse my ill feelings towards him. I was prepared for what he had to say because I knew him. I thanked him for the top up.

"I miss you," he confessed.

SKYPE SHELLY-ANN, YOU BASTARD!

I sipped some more of my wine. It wasn't having an immediate effect because I could still hear his slimy words.

"So how is it living at your brother's house? How is he?" I changed the subject so he knew I wasn't interested in talking about reconciling our relationship.

FIND SOMEWHERE PERMANENT AS YOU'RE NOT COMING HOME!

"Yes, it's fine. Vince is well. By the time I get back from work, it's late so I don't get to see a lot of him. I miss you both Shantel. I miss you."

Andre's aura seemed heavy. He looked like a man with the weight of the world on his shoulders.

"Andre, we can't be in a relationship anymore. I don't want you anymore." I shook my head as I said the words.

He needed me to be firm and know that I was serious about the break-up.

YOU MANIPULATING, INSECURE, SELFISH, CHEATING ARSEHOLE!

"But we're a family and we need to make this work for the sake of our family, for the sake of our daughter," he tried to reason.

OH PLEASE!

"Andre, you've never thought about what was best for our family before. Why now? It's too late for that."

I thought back to the spyware emails on his PC and his emails to the girl Japan. He was out most Fridays, probably sleeping with some girls. I had no interest in the sad man sitting in front of me.

"I'll change Shantel. I'll do whatever it takes to make this right. I know I've done so much wrong, and I've hurt you. I've blamed you for things that had nothing to do with you. I am so sorry."

Incredibly, tears welled up in his eyes.

An old Lisa Stansfield song ran through my mind.

'It's too late baby now it's too late
Though we really did try to make it
Something inside has died and I can't hide and I just can't fake
it...'

He quickly wiped away the tears but even at that point I couldn't tell if he was being genuine or disingenuous. He was a born liar and a charmer. I was no longer gullible and I too had cried my tears! I wasn't convinced about his honesty but I was sure about my feelings, my heart and my head. He wasn't the one for me and could never make me happy. There was far too much water under the bridge. He had caused too much damage and I no longer loved him. I would always be wondering what catastrophe would be next. Who else would he piss off? Was there anyone left? Yes, he could interfere with my job. However, that would potentially mess with his finances, so he wouldn't want to do that. My money had always seemed like his money when it came to the house. He was generous in other more superficial ways — flowers when he had done something that required forgiveness, that sort of thing.

"It's too late. I have nothing left. You've pushed and pushed until you've completely pushed me away. I've tried, but I can't see that we could ever get back together. We have both been through a lot and now it's time to move on. I'm going to be focused on our daughter and me. I need to ensure that she has what she needs. I hope that you will do the same."

"Shantel. You know she's my priority. I want us to try again, at least for her sake. Isn't it worth that?" Andre pleaded.

"I can't," I replied and downed my glass of wine.

We finished our meal in silence. Andre requested the bill and we left. He dropped me home and I wished him a good night. There was no kiss on the cheek, no holding of hands, no hug, just goodbye.

That night the lyrics from Prince's 'Purple Rain' continuously ran through my head.

Chapter Twenty-One:
Smooth Chocolate

I t was December and my birthday was coming up, another year older, another year wiser. I was determined to make the festive season special for Leylah. She would miss her father, but I didn't want him around. He was no longer head of this household. He was busy creating his own. I wouldn't stop him from seeing her though; she needed to feel spoilt by him and he needed her love. I encouraged their interaction so did not hesitate to say yes when he asked to help us put up the Christmas tree.

The transition was difficult for all of us. Did I miss Andre? No. But Leylah missed her father even though his living elsewhere hadn't impacted on our daily routine. He only saw her early mornings and late nights anyway. Since our relationship had ended, I'd developed a new lease of life and was embracing a fresh energy. A chance meeting in a local hardware store then gave me the distraction I needed. Apparently, he thought I had looked under challenge in the paint aisle. He had given me constructive advice and his telephone number. It turned out that I had found myself a handsome pastime by the name of Damien. He was a six-foot two, chocolate brown man who turned out to be a temporary fix that made me feel revitalised. He had dramas with the mother of his children. Neither of us wanted a relationship but some good, old-fashioned passionate sex. He knew how to rock my world and make me walk with a spring in my step. It was astonishing what great love-making could do for my spirit, especially after having been deprived for so long. Sex was so much more fun with someone I actually liked and he did all that it took to please me. Though we had only been seeing each other for a few weeks I was comfortable with him, even though I wasn't looking for a long term relationship.

The day Andre was to come and help with the tree, Damien called.

"Hey," he said, with his deep sultry tone.

"Hi babe," I replied, melting in the smoothness of his voice.

"Can I see you tonight?" he asked

"Yes. I'll be free from 9:30. My daughter's dad will be coming round to put her to bed." I was eager to see Damien. "In fact, let's say 10:30. Li-Li will be sleeping by then and her dad would definitely be long gone."

Although putting up the tree could delay Andre's departure, I was becoming excited.

"Cool babe. I'll see you then. Any problems, text me. See you soon" he replied.

That night, Andre spent more time than usual with Leylah. At 9:30, he was still in her bedroom reading her a story. Of all the nights to choose to linger! I wanted to knock on the door to remind him that it was past her bedtime and she still had nursery in the morning. It wasn't him having to struggle to wake her up. I'd struggle waking myself up, especially after my nocturnal activities with the sexy chocolate man. After my shower, I pulled my bedroom door shut so that he wouldn't enter without permission. Damien loved to explore, so I prepared my temple, using a scented moisturiser. I checked my phone. 9:51. I was confident he would leave soon, especially as he must have heard me leaving the bathroom and go into my bedroom. I needed to find a sexy number to wear. I had recently bought some lacy negligees from a store in Westfield, Stratford. Andre had rarely been privy to such treatment. He was accustomed to oversized T-shirts, but chocolate man would experience silky nightwear with lace, tiny ribbons and matching thongs. I chose a black outfit and felt very much like a sex goddess, awaiting her night of adult pleasure. Chocolate man could effortlessly excite me, without even being prompted. He was clearly experienced in his craft and that was all I needed him for.

Leylah's door slowly opened. He had finally finished reading her a story and settling her down. 9:57 on the clock. I started to panic a little. Leylah needed to be in a deep sleep so she wouldn't wake up. I didn't need her father eating into any more of my precious time.

"Is she asleep?" I whispered to him.

"Yes," he replied quietly.

"Can I just come into the bedroom to get a few bits?" he asked.

I wasn't quite expecting that request. He'd really have to move his stuff soon. I didn't care where, just as long as he didn't keep coming into my private space.

"Ok." I opened the bedroom door wider so he could come in without brushing past me.

"You smell nice," he commented as he walked into the room.

"Thanks." I replied and sat on the bed, playing with my mobile phone. I didn't want to engage in a dialogue with him at all. His eyes gazed at the bed.

"New sheets?" he enquired.

Damn this man! Why couldn't he just get his things and leave? I had a very hot date and needed to finish tidying the living room before he arrived.

I nodded. It was obvious they were new sheets. Fresh bedding symbolised a new beginning. I loved the smell and crispness of new sheets, straight out of the packet. I continued fiddling with my phone, while keeping one eye on Andre. I noticed him scanning the room for other changes. There were a few including the bedside lamps, colourful cushions on the bed and scented candles. The room was becoming my boudoir and no longer the crash pad that he had created. There was no need for further conversation. I needed Andre's swift exit and chocolate man's remedy.

"Right, that's it. Thanks." Andre closed the wardrobe door. I stood up as he headed out of the room.

"I need to lock the porch." Andre began to walk down the stairs, but turned to ask me a question while I was standing on the landing.

"Are you seeing someone Shantel?" he asked.

LIKE IT'S GOT ANYTHING TO DO WITH YOU! I was trying my hardest to keep my knowledge regarding his infidelity and spying games under-cover.

"Why?" I asked. I couldn't help but smile. I was an awful liar so I chose to be deliberately evasive.

"Who is he?" Andre asked with a pained smile on his face.

"I don't know what you're talking about," I replied and ushered him down the stairs.

"I'll call Leylah tomorrow, if that's ok with you?" he asked.

"No problem. Goodnight."

"Goodnight," he replied and then walked out of the door.

I immediately locked the porch after him to give the impression that I was shutting down for the night.

The sitting room floor was cluttered with bags, decoration boxes and tinsel. I quickly swept the tinsel off the carpet. Everything else was either hanging or bagged up. I pushed what I could to the side of the room, dimmed the ceiling lights, but left the tree lights on. The hallway mirror showed my pink towelling dressing gown to be unflattering, but I needed it to cover up the sexy nightwear hidden underneath. I ran upstairs to find my satin robe. Enough time had passed and Andre should have been almost at his brother's house or at least on the South Circular. I sent a text to Damien to tell him that the coast was clear and the door would be unlocked for him.

I went back downstairs, unlocked the porch door and poured myself a glass of wine. I sat on the sofa and turned on the TV. Seconds later, I could hear the porch door handle turn. I stood up to greet him at the door. He slipped off his shoes and followed me into the living room. We greeted each other with a kiss on the lips and a warm embrace. His body was sculptured but warm. Chocolate man was tall, strong and his fragrance was enticing. I offered him a glass of wine and asked him to take a seat. As I turned around to give him the glass, I saw that he was still standing, glaring at me with a sly smile.

He took the glass out of my hand and set it down onto the side table. This man had a look of desire. He put his arms around my waist and swooped me towards him. His lips touched mine in a passionate kiss. He loosened the belt of my robe in one quick movement, encouraging the gown to fall to the floor. There I was, in a see-through negligee, being caressed by this beautiful man. This was excitement beyond measure. Damien made me feel alive. He restored my self-esteem and made me feel like a desirable woman again. He pulled off his T-shirt to reveal his smooth, chiselled chest and tight waist. I rubbed my hands over his torso, feeling every groove and muscle. He pulled the straps of my nightwear down to reveal my naked body. He wanted to feel me, skin to skin. He kissed and nibbled on my neck. I moaned at the pleasure of the soft bites and responded in the way he knew I would, going by our previous encounters. His lips lowered to my breasts. He kissed and fondled them until I was ready for his main act. He swept me off my feet and placed me down onto the sofa. His will was my command. I looked at my legs wrapped around his body, noticing the similarities in our skin tones. This man wanted to show me what I had been missing. I allowed him to rock my world that night. I wasn't falling for him. Love was not on my agenda, but he provided me with an escape from my crumbling world. I provided him with the distraction he needed. We laughed, we talked, we sang, we joked and we had more sex. At 3am, I was ready to sleep and he had to leave. I was adamant I wouldn't let Leylah see another man in my bed, especially so soon after her father had left. Damien was my coping mechanism and would remain invisible. I kissed Damien on the lips and told him I wanted to see him again soon.

"Ditto," he replied as he walked out of the porch. "Goodnight sweet cheeks."

"Good night babes," I whispered, locking the porch door, still smiling. I looked up the stairs and realised that in less than five hours, my daughter would wake me up.

Monday morning, while sitting at my desk, Andre called.

"Hiya," I answered, wondering why he was calling me.

"Hi Shantel, how are you?" he asked.

"Good thanks. What's up?" I enquired.

"I've got a removals van and want to pick my things up tonight. My brother Vince will be helping me."

"Why tonight? I'd rather Leylah wasn't at home when you move your things out." I responded quietly, as I was sitting at my desk, surrounded by gossiping colleagues who loved a bit of scandal. I left my office and walked outside for privacy.

"I need to pick them up tonight. I'd rather my things not be in the house when you have men coming around," he stated.

I was speechless. This man was a spy!

"Fine," I replied. "If that's what you want to do, can you at least wait until Leylah is sleeping?"

Our daughter didn't need to witness her father moving out. She would have that memory forever and that was not what I wanted for her. I was still stunned about the fact that he knew I had a man around and that he was using this as an excuse to move his things out. I thought about the spyware software he had downloaded onto my previous mobile phone. Surely he didn't still have access to my phone? He had probably waited outside in the car to see if anyone would visit.

"I'd rather come early as I don't want to be moving my things out too late.

"Fine. Be selfish. Think of yourself. See you later." I ended the call.

I called Louisa.

"Babe, Andre is moving his stuff out tonight."

"It's a Monday night? That's a bit of an odd day to move out. Why doesn't he leave it until the weekend?" she wondered.

"Because he's a frigging arsehole," I retorted, pacing up and down the front of my office building. "He's been spying. He told me that he didn't want his things in the house when I'm entertaining men. Clearly, he knew Damien was with me. He must have been sitting outside in the car last night, waiting to see if someone was coming into the house. And to top it all off, he doesn't care that Leylah will be at home, seeing him moving his things out. He hasn't thought about what this could do to her. I don't want my daughter emotionally scarred." I was vexed.

"Babe, just explain to her that her dad will be collecting a few things. Keep her in the sitting room while he moves his things out," she suggested.

"OK. I'll try to do that, but she'll hear all the commotion and see him carrying his things out. Well, this is his doing, not mine. I just wish he could do it another time but yet again, his needs take precedence. I'll call you once Leylah is sleeping hun." I walked back up the stairs to my office.

"Ok babe. Try not to get too stressed tonight," she said worriedly.

"I won't. Later babes." I hung up.

Monday evening, 7:16. The doorbell rang and they were outside.

"Hello Shantel," Andre said, carrying a roll of black bin liners as he walked into the house, with Vince behind him.

I stepped out of the way so he could walk in without touching me.

"Hello Vince," I greeted. "Helping with the move?" I asked smiling.

"Hello Shantel. Yes I am. How are you?"

"I'm good thanks," I replied.

"Hello Daddy," Leylah said, seeing her father walk up the stairs.

"Hello pumpkin. I thought you'd be asleep by now." Andre walked back down the stairs and gave his daughter a kiss and cuddle. "Ooh I love you pumpkin!"

"I love you too Daddy. Are you moving your things out now?" she asked.

"Yes I am pumpkin. I need my things as I will be staying with Uncle Vince now."

"Ok," she replied. "I'm just watching something on TV Daddy." She turned around and plonked herself back on the sofa where she had been before being disturbed by the visitors.

I had already prepared Leylah for the night's events, explaining that Mummy and Daddy didn't want to argue anymore so he was staying with Uncle Vince. He had to come and get some clean clothes. I had primed her with her favourite thing in the whole wide world to eat, mango, and let her to watch the Disney Channel. I even had salty microwaveable popcorn for her to munch on. She had her blanket and her beloved remote control to keep her entertained. Andre pulled the sitting room door to give her peace and quiet.

His clothes were stuffed into a grey suitcase. I was sure I had bought that suitcase. *Take it.* The rest of his clothes were thrown into the bin liners.

Footwear — into bin liners.

Cosmetics and after shaves. Mainly bought by me. Bin liner.

Boxes of junk in the bottom of his wardrobe. Wrapped in bin liners.

The brothers were up and down the stairs carrying and shifting boxes and bags. They worked quickly together. Why couldn't they work that quickly when I needed a job done in the house? I watched them as they worked to be sure that they didn't take any of my possessions. There seemed to be an endless supply of bin liners. The bedroom was finally clear of his personal items so the brothers descended into the dining room, stripping the connections from his beloved computer. The computer was wrapped in towels and his bed sheets. The ones he came with were the ones he could take. There were the ugly wooden ornaments he had proudly bought in Jamaica. Good riddance. I decided I would help him by taking them off the wall.

"Leave them Shantel," Andre instructed.

"Oh no. It'll be my pleasure for these things to be gone as well," I said sarcastically.

"Shantel, I didn't think you'd be like that," Vince seemed shocked.

"If you don't know, get to know. I'm merely getting rid of these things from my sight. They have to go. I'm sure they will look perfect in their new home," I replied, while unhooking the ornaments and putting them on the floor in the hallway. I came back into the dining room.

"What else can I help you with?" I asked, pretending to wipe the dust from my hands.

"Nothing," Andre replied. "We're pretty much done now. Whatever's left I'll come and collect on the weekend."

"Great," I replied. It was already after 9pm and I needed to get the baby away from the TV and into bed.

"Take care of yourself Shantel," Vince said politely.

"Thanks Vince. You too." Vince walked into the sitting room and said goodnight to his niece then left the house.

Andre then went to say goodnight to his daughter.

"I love you so much pumpkin. Any time you want to talk to me, just pick up the phone and call me, ok?" There was a sadness in his voice. Probably regret that it had ended this way. He would miss his daughter but that was part and parcel of a separation.

"Ok Daddy," she replied, sounding tired.

"I'll call you tomorrow baby. Sleep tight ok. Mummy is going to take you up to bed now. Goodnight pumpkin."

"Goodnight Daddy."

Andre walked out of the house and turned around to look at me.

"Goodbye Shantel."

"Bye." I shut the door.

I immediately locked it and took Leylah upstairs to bed. Within fifteen minutes, she was out. I looked at the carnage left behind after Andre's departure. His wardrobe was still full of rubbish though. His bedside drawer was still full of his coins; that was where he threw his loose change. The money was now mine. The bathroom remained the same. The dining room was no longer an office. That would only take ten minutes to organise. Andre had taken out the sub-woofer in the sitting room. I hated that thing anyway. It sounded awful. He couldn't remove two of the surround speakers, as the wires were trapped under the carpet. Oh well. They would stay. All the furniture and kitchen appliances were mine. I looked around the house again and wondered exactly what he had contributed towards the house. Nothing. Absolutely nothing apart from Leylah's cot and her chest of drawers. The contents of this house were mine. The mortgage was high but I hoped that I could make the house mine too, God willing.

'That night, I organised the house so that Leylah wouldn't see too many changes when she woke up. She would however notice a dramatic difference in the dining room — that would be impossible to mask. Andre spent the majority of his evenings sitting at his precious PC, emailing that woman and doing whatever else he did there, while his family was in bed. He took the PC, but I still had access to his email account as I had guessed his password. The fool! I knew so much about his activities. I really couldn't care less, mainly because I didn't love him anymore. Now he could do whatever he wanted to. I could now start planning the rest of my life without the ball and chain that he had weighed me down with for five years. I sat at the dining table looking at the room with the empty shelves that used to be filled with all of his possessions. The shelves were left in the house by the previous owner. They were old, definitely from the 1970s. The décor in the room was awful. In the morning, I would enquire about getting a decorator to transform it. It had his footprint all over it, but I now had an opportunity to turn the house into my home. I didn't know what the future held and whether I would be able to afford to stay in the house, but while I was there I would try to make it homely. After I had re-organised the house I called my parents in Dominica to update them on the night's events.

"You need to change the locks Shantel," my father instructed.

"How can I do that if he's still paying half the mortgage? It means that he can have access to the house when he wants to. But I will leave the keys in the door so he can't just walk in when he sees fit." I had to reassure my father, knowing that he would tell my mother, and in turn, she would worry.

"I don't like the sound of that Shantel," he replied.

"Well, I have to get on with things and start thinking about putting the house on the market." I was contemplating selling the house that we had never even made a home.

"Well, I think that is the best thing for you to do Sha-Sha. I think you need to get rid of the house and get rid of him. You don't need any ties with him. Do you still have a joint bank account with him?" Dad enquired.

"Yes, I do. It's the account that the bills and mortgage are paid from," I replied, wondering if it was the best time of the day to be having this discussion. I wanted to sleep instead of staying awake worrying.

"Well, you need to close that down. Start to separate your finances from him Shantel. Limit what you have together. All you need to have jointly is your daughter. Everything else needs to be separate. At least you didn't marry him." My father never liked Andre. I totally understood why there was no love lost.

"I'll pass you on to your mother as she wants to speak to you. Ok? I'll speak to you soon," he said with a hurried tone. "I know you probably need to get some sleep now as it's late there. Ok darling, take care."

"Ok Dad, speak to you soon. Goodnight."

"Hello Sha-Sha. How are you darling?" Mum asked.

"I'm fine Mum. Just getting ready to go to bed but I thought I'd give you a quick call to let you know what was happening." I didn't want to have to repeat myself completely but she sounded eager to know the developments.

"So he's moved out! Good. I'm glad. He had to go," she affirmed.

"I'll pack the rest of the things he left and put them in black bags outside the front door. I'll tell him to pick them up on Saturday." I had to have a plan of action.

"Good. Get rid of everything that's his," Mum instructed.

"Don't worry, I will."

I also thought about praying in each room and asking God to remove Andre's spirit from every corner of the house. I would light candles too — the light symbolised new beginnings and a cleansing.

"Ok darling. If you need anything, you just let us know. Ok Sha-Sha?" Mum and Dad were so supportive.

"No problem Mum. I will. I better go to bed now as I'll be up in less than seven hours. I really need some sleep." I was drained. I hoped that the evening hadn't sent my mind into overdrive.

"Ok darling, have a good sleep and we'll speak soon. Love you!" Mum said this in a way that only mothers could, making me feel comforted.

"Goodnight Mum. Love you too. Bye."

That night I splashed some drops of lavender oil onto my pillow so I could get a peaceful night's sleep. And I did.

I spent the next few days bagging up everything he had left behind. Other women might have destroyed his clothes and possessions. Did I really want to do that? My eyes fixed on his beloved leather biker jacket. How tempted I was to slash it across the back, but decided against it. Truthfully, I wanted every scent of him removed. I generally packed at night time when the baby was asleep. I had compiled a soundtrack on my iPod that suited my current state of mind. I played it while I packed.

Track 1: Sunshine Anderson — Heard It All Before
Track 2: Beyoncé — Irreplaceable
Track 3: Kelis — I Hate You So Much Right Now
Track 4: Destiny's Child — Bills
Track 5: Blue Cantrell — Hit 'Em Up Style
Track 6: TLC — No Scrubs
Track 7: Black Eye Peas — Shut Up
Track 8: Beyoncé — If I Was A Boy
Track 9: Jazmine Sullivan — Bust Your Windows

Track 10: Beyoncé — Single Ladies
Track 11: Aretha Franklin — Respect
Track 12: Gloria Gaynor — I Will Survive
Track 13: Toni Braxton — He Wasn't Man Enough For Me
Track 14: Cyndi Lauper — Girls Just Want to Have Fun

It was Saturday evening. I looked at my playlist and realised that Beyoncé had featured quite heavily. She clearly found a niche in the market for women in a situation. I sent Andre a text to inform him that his bags were outside the house and then selected track number 9. I plugged in the headphones to my iPhone and started dancing while continuing to pack his remaining things. How I really wanted to smash the windows of his car, but actually, I had part-exchanged my Vauxhall Corsa for the Golf he was driving and paid half the car bill. The finance was in my name but was not fully paid off. I couldn't destroy anything that had my name on it. He told me the finance couldn't be in his name as he had poor credit. Andre had used me from day one — to decorate his flat, get the car and the house! Worst of all, I had let him, believing in the fairy-tale I was told as a child. Those princess stories should be banned. My happily ever after never actually happened. My daughter needed to know the reality of life and I vowed to guide her as best as I could, so she could grow up to make the best decisions for her and not based on what society thought. I had learnt many lessons from this whole messy experience. I just needed some time to work out what I could do differently in the future.

Track 10 started: *Beyonce — Single Ladies*. Well-timed positive lyrics. I found myself quietly singing along and pretended I was one of her skin-tight-leotard-clad backing dancers. I didn't quite get the moves right, but who cared? I was single, I had taken the ring off and I was free. The bottom of his wardrobe was a mess with flyers, coins, old ties, odd socks, boxer shorts and scraps of paper. I dumped it all in a bin liner. As I carefully examined the scraps of paper for more incriminating evidence, I came across something that looked familiar. It was an extract from an old phone book I had when I first met Andre. I hadn't seen it for years. I remembered it was silver and could fit easily in my handbag. I hadn't needed it anymore as I stored all my contacts' details in my mobile phone. I grabbed a magnifying glass from my bedside table as I couldn't see the names clearly. It was all the Ds. Dillan, Dwayne, Donovan, Darren, Derek. The bastard had details of some of my exes. What was he going to do? Call them and break their bones too? This man was incredible. He was unbelievably insecure and paranoid. Even after all these years he had held onto my past. I wanted to slash that shitty leather biker jacket even more desperately now, but luckily for him I had already packed it away. Besides, it really wasn't in my nature to be so vengeful. I just wanted to get rid and have peace in my heart and in my home. I took the extract of my phone book and placed it on my bedside table. Incidentally, I now had a choice of two bedside tables and thought about how I could change the room round to remove any traces of my oppressor.

Finished. I had packed the last few items and dragged the heavy bags down the stairs to the front porch. Andre had just sent a text saying he was outside. I didn't need to see his now ugly face so the last thing I wanted was him knocking at the door, waking the baby up in the process. I hoped he would be quick about collecting his possessions. He was lucky I had bothered to bag the rest up for him and not paid a visit to the charity shop. Somebody should have got something out of this railroad disaster of a relationship. I decided to stand in the porch to ensure he removed his bags without creating a disturbance. I stood blocking the front door, indirectly suggesting no entry was allowed

"Hi. Thanks for packing the rest of my things." He seemed appreciative.

"No problem," I replied. What I really wanted to say was a little different.

I DON'T NEED YOUR SHIT IN MY HOUSE! OF COURSE I'LL PACK YOUR SHIT BECAUSE I DON'T NEED ANY REMINDERS OF YOU AROUND ME. YOU ARE A DEMONIC LIAR AND A WASTE-MAN! I WANT NOTHING ELSE TO DO WITH YOU.

"Ok. Well I'm just going to load up the car." He grabbed some bags and headed towards the car.

"Ok."

YOU DO THAT, PUNK!

"See ya." I pushed the front door shut, leaving him access to the porch.

I didn't leave the porch light on for him. The neighbours didn't need to witness the fall out of our relationship, though I was certain that curtains were twitching. I looked around the house. I had been through some major, dramatic changes in my life and I was preparing for true independence.

Silently considering
Curiously focusing
Dreaming, believing?
Uncertainty embracing
Panicking, breathing
Story unfolding
Prophecies realising
Point scoring
Battles emerging
Inner strength flourishing
Cocoon smashing
Smile returning
Finances dwindling
Fish surviving
Tree blossoming!

Chapter Twenty-Two:
The Date

The first few weeks without Andre were happy. I explained to Leylah in very simple terms that Mummy and Daddy didn't get on well living together and that we would get along better when we were living in different houses. She seemed to get that. I was now at ease. My soul felt restored. I no longer had to keep looking over my shoulder. I had nothing to hide, but he had a way of making me feel as if I were the guilty party. Well, his emails to the girl in Japan and the photograph of him hugging another woman were evidence of his infidelity. Those emails were a godsend as they gave me the strength I needed to end the relationship.

Knowing that he had cheated added a different dimension to my exit plan, though the thought of him screwing another woman didn't faze me at all. My conscious was clear; at least I knew that I hadn't cheated. I didn't need another man clouding my mind or taking up my time. I needed a break from men, although I was happy to be entertained by Chocolate Man when the mood was right. Andre was still at his brother's house. For whatever reason, he wasn't happy to have Leylah overnight so he would take her for a day over the weekends. That gave me the time I needed to clean the house, do some shopping and have some adult time. I found internet shopping to be a wonderful distraction. I could save my favourite items and do a repeat shop when necessary. The only thing I needed Andre to do was to continue paying his share of the mortgage until we had decided what we were going to do with the house.

I had very mixed feelings about the house. The mortgage was so high and I wasn't sure how I would manage it. That weighed heavily on my mind. I thought back and forth about returning to east London. The idea of packing everything for the move was daunting and literally made me shudder. Still, that was an option that I had to think carefully about. Was I prepared to try and stay in the house and be forever reminded of Andre? In the meantime, I had decided that decorating the dining room would be the beginning of cleansing his negative spirit out of the house and painting away his presence. I needed the room to be transformed from a mish-mash of colours, which I had splashed on in a moment of rage, to elegant adult surroundings for happy dining moments.

One week later, I paid the decorator his fee. It was money well spent, not just for the physical change, but also for the invaluable emotional satisfaction. The room was painted varying shades of creamy coffee and white. The bare wooden floorboards and the mahogany dining table and chairs remained — I had paid for them so they had nothing to do with Andre. Not only was his clutter gone, but the images of him running his cyber affair were erased. It was amazing what could be achieved in a day.

That Saturday Andre had brought Leylah home at 8.30 as arranged. I met him at the porch door and took our sleeping beauty from his arms. He wasn't welcome to come in. I shut the door leaving him outside. I was happy she was asleep meaning I could have a peaceful night. Once she was in bed I returned downstairs to admire the transformed dining room again and dream about how I would accessorise it. I composed a list on my phone.

1. *Curtains with tie backs*
2. *A gothic style light fitting that would complement the fire place*
3. *A curtain pole, black and thin.*
4. *Picture frames*
5. *Paintings*
6. *Table decoration (runner, table mats, coasters)*

The list didn't need to be extensive. I didn't want to over dress the room but just put my stamp on it. Everything else would come eventually. I wanted the room to look stylish and comfortable, just in time for Christmas. That night I searched the internet for the items I needed. The photo frame was red, as was the painting of tulips. The dining table runner was claret, matching the claret red rug that I had purchased for the flat in Clapham.

Christmas was going to be very different this year, and I imagined it to be peaceful and happy. My brother Calvin was coming over and I had also invited my aunt and cousin. Andre's presence would be missed at Christmas, though I didn't want to admit it. I didn't want Christmas to be just Leylah and I. I wanted the house full and busy with family sitting around the table. I wanted everyone to be happy.

They all arrived on Christmas Eve. I allowed Andre to come into the house on Christmas morning to help Leylah open her presents. After that he had to leave. I could tell he didn't feel comfortable as a visitor, especially as he had been used to being the man of the house, the king of his castle. He only stayed for thirty minutes. I was courteous enough to offer him a glass of water, but that was all. I was glad to see the back of him. It was Christmas day and I needed to finish preparing dinner. Andre had lost what he had proclaimed to cherish so dearly — his family. He now had to spend the rest of his Christmas day with his siblings. That was the life he created for himself. For me, it was a family day and I was free of him.

It was January. Andre had clearly missed family life. One weekend, he asked that I meet him with our daughter for lunch. I was reluctant to of course. Although being apart from him had softened my emotions, I still didn't trust him.

"Just lunch Shantel. I thought we could go to Café Rouge. I'll pick you up, we'll have a bite to eat and then I'll drop you both home. I have no other intentions. My treat."

Well, I wasn't going to pay so...!

"It would be nice for Leylah to see us together again, just as her parents, that's all." Andre was persuasive. "I want her to know we're still both here for her and that we can sit down and talk without arguing."

"Ok. What time?" I asked.

"Shall we say 1 o'clock?" he asked.

"Fine, no problem," I replied. "See you then. Bye."

"See you soon. Bye" He ended the call.

I noticed his tone had relaxed after I had accepted his invitation. I hoped he didn't have an ulterior motive. He needed to behave and just concentrate on the fact that we had one thing in common and one thing alone — our precious daughter.

He already had Leylah with him as it was a Saturday morning. I just had to get myself ready which only meant doing my hair and throwing on some clothes. Make-up would have been wasted on him. I thought about the delicious garlic prawns.

Andre arrived promptly. I grabbed my bag, locked the door and walked over to the car. Leylah was sitting in her child seat in the front. I walked around the car and opened the rear passenger side so I would sit behind Leylah, rather than behind Andre as he tended to extend his seat back to accommodate his six-foot two frame.

"Hello." I greeted them both as I sat down.

"Hi Mummy," Leylah replied chirpily.

"Hi." Andre replied.

"How are you Li-Li?" I asked.

"Fine Mummy. We're going to Café Rouge. I'm having the pizza bread Mummy!" She was excited.

"Oh, that's nice darling. I'm looking forward to it too," I responded reassuringly.

My mobile phone rang. I pulled it out of my handbag and saw that it was Louisa.

"Hi babe. You alright?" I asked.

"Yes hun. What are you up to? You sound like you're out?" she enquired.

The radio was playing in the car but I knew Andre was listening intently.

"I'm about to go to Café Rouge in Greenwich with Leylah and Andre. I'm in the car now. I'll give you a call when I get back home."

"Really? Do you feel safe?" she asked with concern.

"Yeah babe. I'll call you when I get home."

"Ok, make sure you call me straight away. We will speak about this." Louisa replied curtly.

"Laters," I said comically, in the manner in which we often said goodbye.

"Laters!" she sang and ended the call.

Within ten minutes, we had parked and were taking the short walk to the restaurant. Leylah held both our hands and we swung her in the air as we used to. She felt heavier this time, though in reality, it had only been a couple of months since we were last together as a family. He had single-handedly destroyed that.

The waiter took us to our table and handed us the menus. Andre chose to sit directly opposite me, whilst Leylah sat beside me. I pulled my glasses out of my handbag and looked at the menu. Andre had ordered me a glass of red wine. He knew me very well. He ordered some drinks for himself and the baby. I put the menu down when the waiter walked away.

"So, how have you been?" Andre asked.

Do you really care?

"I've been well. Everything is ticking along. No problems. How about yourself?" I asked out of courtesy, not curiosity.

"Yeah fine. Work has been really busy. I've been working long hours and it takes longer to get back to Vince's house too. So, early starts and late nights. But I'm coping."

I was feeling cynical; I couldn't help it. But I wanted us to have a comfortable, amicable afternoon with mature conversation centred on our daughter. She was happily colouring in a small booklet given to her by the waiter. Our drinks arrived. We all toasted in the usual manner before sipping our drinks. I took three large sips and placed my glass back down on the table. I would definitely need a refill. Leylah had already drank half of her apple juice.

"Mummy. I need to go toilet," she announced.

I checked my mobile phone was in my bag and quickly sipped some more of my fruity wine. I signalled to Andre that I'd escort her to the bathroom. As I stood waiting for Leylah to finish, I wondered what his real intentions were. So far, so good. He hadn't made any suggestions of reconciliation. Hopefully, he was turning over a new leaf and realising our family was separated and our love had died. When we got back to our table, Andre was placing our order. He knew how to take control when he wanted to. I did like that about him. He didn't feel it necessary to wait for me to order. He then ordered me another glass of wine which was well-timed as my first glass was nearly done.

"I was wondering how you would feel about going away on a caravan holiday?" Andre asked.

Uh oh! I shook my head.

"I don't think so," I replied disappointedly.

"Just a few days, somewhere nice. We can have separate rooms. We could get a caravan that's got three bedrooms." Andre had a plan.

"Sorry, I don't think that will work. I think we should just keep things simple. No complications." I was whispering.

Andre looked deflated.

"Just as friends, for the sake of…," he started, as he pointed towards our daughter.

"I think it's better that we don't have any blurred lines and confuse the matter. Meetings like this, I don't mind. Anything more I'm not sure about."

The waiter soon came with our food and my second large glass of wine. Perfect timing as I didn't want that line of conversation to continue.

"Darling, please put the pencil down and start on your pizza," I instructed, thankful for the distraction.

"Ok Mummy," she chimed, reaching over for the pizza.

I looked over at Andre. He had started eating his lamb and sautéed potatoes. I reflected on what he had asked me. It was all too late. There was far too much water under the bridge. I was happier now. We had only been separated for a short time but I had enjoyed my space, my freedom and my peace. There was nothing like it. I couldn't possibly go back to Andre after what he had put me through. I couldn't see myself being with any man who was controlling, insecure, demanding and disrespectful anymore. I just needed me and my girl to be happy. I wasn't lonely. I was in a zone that I hadn't experienced for what felt like a lifetime. I continued to look after my daughter in the same way I had when he was living with us. I was becoming independent in a way that had become alien to me. I was no longer the Shantel in her twenties with a spring in my step and not a care in the world. I was now a woman in her mid-thirties with one dependant and a visual deficit. I had managed to throw away the shackles and this man was asking me to put the ball and chain back on. *HELL NO!* I had a right to live life and to love life. I was not about to return to an existence of depression, fear and misery. I wanted to blossom through all changes in my life. I had to adapt to a new way of living and Andre was emotionally unsupportive and dismissive of my needs. Instead, he chose to smoulder any fire and passion that we had or could have had with his insecurities and controlling nature. I loved me more than I loved the idea of being with the father of my only child.

We continued to eat and make small talk. Andre paid the bill and drove me back home. I kissed our daughter and told her I'd see her in a few hours. I thanked Andre and went into the house. There was a particular track that I wanted to hear on the Angie Stone 'Mahogany Soul' CD. I kicked off my shoes and pulled it out of the rack. 'Mad Issues'. I put it in the CD player and scanned each track until I could hear the intro. There it was. Perfect! I turned up the volume until the sound filled the house. *Sorry neighbours.* I put the track on repeat and began singing loudly, feeling the effects of two large glasses of red wine. Thank you Andre!

That evening, Andre brought Leylah home, fast asleep. Once again, I put her straight to bed and had an early night myself. As a free woman, I started reconnecting with friends from my past. I had disclosed my journey to a trusted few and the reason for my disappearing act. The Shantel that they had known had been missing for five years and was gone forever. I was happy to be accepted once again for the person I had grown to be. Out of the blue, I received a message on Facebook from a deliciously handsome man, Len, from Bedfordshire. He was always very friendly and polite. I recalled how he used to knock on the door at my parents' home, just to say hi. Or perhaps there were other intentions but nothing ever happened between us. Then, at eighteen, I left Bedford for university and lost contact with him. Len was tall, dark, and handsome, with chiselled features. Real eye candy so I was baffled at why he would be interested in me at that time.

After that initial contact, we rekindled our friendship and arranged to go for a drink one Friday night. My brother had agreed to babysit for me. Len's schedule for the day was busy and couldn't give me a confirmed time to pick me up. It was 9:30pm when he called.

"Hi Shantel, how are you?" he asked politely with his cool, sexy tones.

"I'm fine thanks. Just relaxing now." I chatted as I lay on the sofa, pulling my new leopard print throw over me. It was just one of the many adaptations I had made to transform my house into a home and eradicate my ex's bad aura.

"I've just finished decorating my aunt's place, but I have to drop my cousin off in Leyton and then I'll make my way over to you."

"Wow, ok. That'll take a while. Realistically, you won't be with me until at least 11. I think that's a bit too late for me hun." I sighed. "I had a really early start and wasn't expecting such a late night."

I was looking forward to seeing him but a late night wasn't on my agenda as I was already shattered.

"I could try to get to you within the hour? Is that still too late?" Len asked.

"Well, when will you have time to change your clothes? I don't want to rush you. I just think we should plan it for another time. What do you think?" I really wasn't in the mood to get dressed up and leave the house so late. I really wanted to enjoy my evening and not feel too tired to do so.

I didn't have to work the following day so a lie-in was on the cards. Andre would have pick Leylah up by 8:30 in the morning. I would then have the whole day to shop, clean and relax until the evening.

"Ok. That's alright. I will give you a call a little bit later once I've dropped my cousin off, if that's alright?" Len asked.

"Yes, that'll be fine. Speak later." I replied.

My brother decided to go back to his home seeing as my plans had changed. I locked the door after him and made myself a cup of tea. I had another short conversation with Len and headed to bed. I was tired and reflected on the evening and my conversations with him. I probably wouldn't have been a great companion for him, though he may have thought otherwise. I got ready for bed, put my mobile phone on silent and climbed into the centre of my super king size bed. I stretched every single limb, thanking God for my space, then closed my eyes.

The house phone woke me up. It took me a few seconds to register the sound and that I needed to answer the call. There must have been an emergency.

"Hello?" I answered curiously.

"Shantel, is he with you?"

Chapter Twenty-Three:
Money Talks

"Huh?" I was dazed, but I knew the voice. "Is Len there with you? Is he laying in your bed now? Well, I don't care if he's there. You're fucking him, aren't you? He's there now, isn't he?" Andre was slurring his words.

"How do you know about Len?" I quizzed sleepily. I was baffled.

"Is he there?" Andre shouted.

"Get off my line," I demanded calmly and hung up.

The phone rang again seconds later.

"Don't hang up on me Shantel!" he yelled. "I don't care if he's there or not. I'm driving around. I've had a drink and if anything happens to me, it's your fault." Andre sounded as if he'd drowned his sorrows with a two-litre bottle of rum.

"What are you doing with Len?" he questioned.

"How do you know about Len?" I enquired again, sitting up in bed and feeling completely alert.

"Shantel, I know everything. It doesn't matter how I know. I just know everything!"

"Know this Andre. I want nothing to do with you. Sober up. Leave the car where it is and get to your brother's house another way. You'll regret this in the morning. Don't call me again!" I retorted firmly and hung up.

I switched on my bedside lamp and looked at my mobile phone. There were fourteen missed calls and all of them were from Andre. The house phone rang again. I thought about Leylah waking up and the fact that this crazed caller could be lurking outside the house. I answered the phone again.

"Shantel! Don't hang up!" he demanded, intoxicated and persistent.

"Call me again and I will contact the police. They will do you for harassment. Think about Leylah — you could wake her up. Don't call me again!"

I hung up the phone and disconnected the cable from the socket. I did the same with the phone in the sitting room and prayed that Leylah wouldn't wake up. How dare he think he still has control over me. Me having plans with another man was none of his business. I guess cybersex wasn't satisfying enough for him. I called Andre's brother Vince from my mobile while sitting on the sofa, wondering what game Andre was playing and why he thought he had a right to spy on me.

"Vince, its Shantel. Andre's ex." I didn't know if he still had my phone number.

"Shantel, how are you? It's two in the morning. Everything ok?" he asked, sounding concerned.

"Sorry to bother you at this time but I need your help. Your brother is stalking me and he just called my house phone three times and my mobile fourteen times. He's drunk and driving around. And your brother is spying on me. Let me tell you Vince, if he calls one more time, I will call the police and let them know he is harassing me." I was so angry I was sweating.

"Hold on, hold on. Slow down. What's been happening?" he asked.

'I was sleeping in my bed Vince. He rang the house phone, telling me that he knows I was fucking with Len. Nobody knows anything about Len — he literally just contacted me on Facebook and we hadn't even met yet! I've not even told my best friends! So, how the hell does he know about Len and that I was due to see him this evening. He's spying on me somehow and I don't know how!" I explained.

"I didn't know you were seeing someone called Len," Vince replied.

"Err, I think that's besides the point, don't you? How does your brother know about Len? That's the question Vince. Secondly, he's driving around drunk. He's got a child and if he's locked-up for drinking and driving, his daughter won't be visiting him!" I wanted Vince to speak to his brother.

"Well, Andre wasn't drunk when he left me. We had a couple of drinks but he seemed fine when he was leaving."

"Ok. Can you just please call your brother and let him know that if he calls me again, I will call the police? I'm tired."

I was exhausted having to explain myself to Andre's brother. I believed that Vince was sensible and could influence his little brother's actions, so I tried to remain positive.

"Maybe it's just that he's not over you Shantel, and you two aren't finished yet. He can't handle that you're seeing someone else. There's bound to be some jealousy." Vince was trying to be rational and reason with me, but I wasn't hearing it.

"Vince, I don't want your brother back. I want nothing to do with him, apart from him being active in his child's life. This relationship was over a long time ago and your brother needs to realise that. Stalking and spying on me will never get me back. All it will do is increase the rift between us and create tension. When and who I date is completely my business. Not his, not anyone's business. I have to go now, but please call your brother and tell him not to drink and drive. I'd appreciate if you tell him not to call me again, especially when he's drunk and at this late hour." I was tired of talking and needed to get back to sleep. I definitely didn't appreciate being woken up by Andre and having to deal with his jealous streak at two in the morning.

"Ok Shantel. I'll speak to him. You two need to work it out. It's obvious that you still love him and that he still loves you. You should both stop playing around and just get back together."

"Vince, your opinion is so off target. I will never get back with your brother. If I do that, you will have permission to get me sectioned. Goodnight." He was clearly disillusioned by Andre's version of our troubles so far.

"Shantel, that's cold. Anyway, good night and take care of my niece," Vince replied.

"Will do. Bye." I hung up.

What was it with those two — just as delusional as each other. Andre's problems had become mine. I needed love, not the shackles he bound me with whilst overseeing my every move. He was incapable of real love. I had once loved him, but never again would I have those same feelings. I had broken the chains and been set free, just as God had promised. Why would I choose to go against the strong messages I had already received? No, not for love or money and not for my child. She needed to see Mummy happy and one day, in a positive relationship. She needed to see how two people supported, loved and respected each other. I decided to take a few minutes to meditate, before I went back up to bed. I was still very tired and so it wasn't long before I fell asleep.

I didn't hear from Andre the following morning. He didn't call to say he was picking Leylah up. I knew he was riddled with guilt and undoubtedly, a sore head. His behaviour in the early hours of the morning was irrational. He was a drunken fool who needed to accept that our relationship was over and that I was now a free agent. My priority was to now disassociate myself from the father of my child as quickly as I could.

There was no contact from him until the following Friday evening. He sent a text to confirm that he would be having our daughter the next day. He could no longer call the house phone as I had changed the number. No words were exchanged when he picked her up. I decided I would spend my Saturday morning composing an email to Andre.

To: Andre
From: Shantel
Date: 18 January
Subject: Separation

Dear Andre

It is now time to start thinking about the house and the joint bank accounts. As you are aware, I cannot pay the mortgage by myself and therefore have an expectation that you will continue paying half the mortgage until we are able to reach a final decision.

I would like us to meet as soon as possible to close our joint bank accounts. Can you please give me a date that is convenient for you?

Regards

Shantel

I wasn't expecting an immediate response to my email. He needed to digest what I had requested. This was the end. His actions last Friday night made it clear that we had to separate for good. Later that day, he handed our sleeping daughter to me.

"Sorry," he whispered and walked away.

I put Leylah to bed and returned downstairs to lock all the doors. I was certain he would have received my email and finally realised that there were no more words to be said. I went to bed that night feeling relaxed and wondered what the future would held for me.

Life without Andre over the next few months continued to be an exhilarating experience. The mortgage was transferred to interest only and Andre continued to pay half for a short time. Then he stopped his contributions. I was forced to rent out the spare room to pay the bills. I advertised on the internet for a suitable lodger. It wasn't long before the room was occupied by a young professional called Carlene. We adjusted smoothly to having a new person in the household. Carlene was quiet, friendly and my daughter liked her. Having a lodger enabled me to keep going financially. I still thought about selling the house. I had considered the pros and cons and wrote them down so that I could reflect.

PROS	CONS
• Fresh start, new beginning in my own home	• Distance to Leylah's school may be further
• Lower mortgage payments for a smaller property	• Boxing up all my possessions
• Smaller garden to maintain	• Taking public transport to see properties
• Newer property or newly refurbished	• Super king size bed may be too big for new house
• Would be rid of Andre with no financial connections	• Will have to build new relationships with neighbours in the new area
• No memories of Andre in the new house	• Length of time it would take to get a buyer and sell the house

There were so many uncertainties about remaining in the house. My initial thoughts were just to maintain stability for my daughter. However, I put the house on the market to see whether there was any interest in the property and how much I could raise as a deposit for a new house. I was prepared for a lengthy emotional and mental rollercoaster, but there was some excitement in looking at new homes and visualising a new life.

The estate agent quickly sent viewers to see the house. I'd even received a couple of offers. I started to think long and hard about the implications of moving and the affordability of paying the whole mortgage on my own. I consulted mortgage brokers and investigated the best deals. I became disheartened after I was declined a mortgage by my bank. Perhaps it wasn't meant to be.

Janice, my manager at work, could see I was stressed by something, other than work. She was East London born and bred, now living in the leafy affluent area of Hornchurch. Janice was a banker by trade and still had those assertive and persuasive qualities. She had asked me to accompany her to lunch for a chat. I was comfortable with that, as I liked her as a person. We decided to eat at the noodle bar. It was cheap, cheerful and quick. Our roles were demanding so extended lunch breaks were not often permitted, but she was the boss!

After ordering our food, Janice asked what had been happening in my life recently. Perhaps my face couldn't disguise the truth? She said I had become reserved and distant in the office. I had a lot on my mind and I guess it was visible to those who cared to notice.

"Well, Janice, I'm still blessed." I tried to play my problems down. "I'm tired all the time, but that can't be helped. It's just my health and nothing new."

"Ok, and how is your daughter? How has she coped with the separation?" Janice enquired.

"She's been fine. I haven't had any issues with her. I guess she misses her dad, but she still sees him every weekend. I don't know where he's living, so I won't allow her to stay over at his place. He's apparently moved out of his brother's house and bought somewhere else. He refuses to tell me where he's living."

I still had access to his emails, though it appeared that he had stopped messaging his beloved Shelly-Ann.

"Ok. So is he still contributing towards the mortgage? Have you both separated your finances?" Janice hit the nail on the head.

"Well, I have to find a mortgage somewhere. I'm not sure if I'll be able to afford to stay in the house on my salary. My bank refused me. They're saying that I don't earn enough. Apparently, I have to raise at least £35,000. That's unrealistic and never going to happen. Andre is saying he doesn't want anything from the house and that he wants me to sign an agreement to say that I won't claim any maintenance from him for five years. To be truthful, I just want to be rid of him, whatever it takes." I hoped I wasn't ranting but I thought she would appreciate my frustration.

"Ok. So are you happy to sign the agreement?" she asked as she tucked into her noodle dish.

"Yes I am. If the house is sold then we'd probably battle over money. I think I would be in a better position than he would be in the court room, if it came to that." I realised that I had hardly touched my noodles, while Janice had consumed half of hers.

"Why is that?" she asked.

"I'm our daughter's primary carer; I have a disability and it was my deposit that secured the house. None of this was stipulated in the mortgage agreement but doesn't that carry some weight?"

Perhaps I was just trying to convince myself.

"I tell you what Shantel, I'll come to the bank with you and we will try and get this sorted. We will get you a mortgage," she said with such conviction that I nearly believed her.

"Ok." I replied. It was obvious that she still had her banking skills and, with over twenty years in the trade, pushy was her middle name. We continued to discuss my predicament and issues at work.

The following week we went to the bank for a scheduled appointment with the mortgage adviser.

"Shantel. Please come in. I'm Dylan. We spoke on the phone. Take a seat."

"Hi Dylan. This is my friend Janice." We both sat down.

I explained how much was outstanding on the mortgage and gave him details of my financial position. After a short time calculating some figures, Dylan turned to face me and shook his head uncompromisingly.

"I'm afraid that we cannot lend you that amount as a mortgage. Your salary won't cover it." Dylan continued to use his calculator as if he was still trying to arrange the figures to make them work.

Janice looked at the rates on a leaflet that was sitting on the table.

"Ok," she interjected, as her eyes darted from the rates stated on the leaflet and towards Dylan. "We want that rate." Janice pointed at the leaflet.

"What additional money will Shantel need to raise in order to have that rate?" Janice was not a pushover.

I sat quietly and allowed Janice to negotiate on my behalf. I had said a silent prayer before we entered the bank and found myself repeating my request, as if it were my mantra.

'Dear God. Please be in control and let Janice help me to secure my house.'

"You'll need to raise £10, 000," Dylan explained.

"Can you do that?" Janice asked as she turned towards me.

"Yes, I can." I explained that my flat was being sold back to the council as the estate was being redeveloped. I would be walking away with a small sum of money which would cover the outstanding amount. My only concern was the amount of time it would take for the money to be transferred into my account once the contracts had been exchanged. I would call my father later that evening to be my back-up plan.

Dylan started printing off the essential paperwork for me to sign. He asked for some identification and went to the photocopier.

"Don't worry. It's all in the bag. This is yours and you will have your mortgage!" Janice was beaming a smile in my direction.

"Thank you Janice. I don't know what to say. Thank you for helping me. I really appreciate it."

I was humbled. I held back on the enthusiasm until I knew for definite that the mortgage would be mine. Dylan returned back into his office with my documents and a smile. He explained that the mortgage would need final approval once the checks had been completed by head office.

"What about removing the other name from the mortgage and the deeds?" I asked.

"Your solicitor will be able to arrange that. You and your ex-partner will have to complete some legal forms and they will need to be sent to us, but your solicitor will advise you on that." Dylan looked pleased with himself.

I wanted to secure a future for myself and my daughter. I wanted to be self-sufficient. I was feeling slightly deflated but God had sent me another angel to support and fight for me. If I didn't get the mortgage, I would have to sell and move. There was nothing wrong with a new beginning. I was ready for whatever path my life was about to take. It was in the hands of the Big Man in the sky. Dylan had informed me that I would get my confirmation after the weekend. I vowed to spend my time praying and speaking my requests into the universe. Being patient would no doubt be a challenge.

It was now nearly March. With everything that was going on, I didn't have time to celebrate Leylah's fourth birthday. I wanted her to know that Mummy could still provide, even though her father was no longer living with us. I wanted to prove to myself that I could still achieve without her father. So I planned a belated party. I ordered a cake, sent out the invitations and bought Leylah a new dress. Andre wasn't invited. Why should he be? He wasn't part of my world anymore and he hadn't offered to contribute either. Maybe I was acting selfishly, but he could organise his own party for Leylah with his family. He was clearly more than capable of using a mobile phone and sending emails.

Family and friends were invited to partake in the celebrations. The cake was delivered and the food was ready. There were soft drinks for the children and alcoholic beverages for the adults. I wanted to make the occasion special for Leylah. She deserved a memorable party, especially after the upheaval of her father's departure from the family home. She had been an angel throughout all the changes, and had adapted well to being a daughter of separated parents.

Our guests arrived and, pretty soon, it was a full house. Leylah was so excited about finally celebrating her day. I had given her father permission to attend the party in the end, so that she could spend a little time with him. I had to consider her feelings too. Andre was now an outcast to me, my friends and family, but not my daughter. I really didn't want him around my loved ones, bringing his bad energy. When he eventually arrived, my brothers were still in the house, chatting with one of my oldest friends. They were comfortable conversing and the children were all happily playing. Leylah ran to the door when she heard the doorbell.

"Dad! Daddy!" she screamed.

"Hello pumpkin!" As the door opened wider, he crouched down to her height.

I suggested he come inside the house, as it was still cold outside. Andre saw the remaining guests sitting in the living room. He greeted them with a wave and turned his attention back towards his daughter.

"How was your party pumpkin?" he asked, eyes drifting into the living room again.

"Great Daddy. Let me show you what I've got," Leylah suggested excitedly. She grabbed his hand, pulling him towards the sitting room.

"I'd better take my shoes off Leylah. Your Mum won't like me walking on the carpet with them on."

As Andre was untying the laces on his trainers, Leylah started to bring her gifts out to him in the hallway.

"Wow darling. These are lovely. Aren't you a lucky girl?" he replied enthusiastically, though he remained uncomfortable.

I went into the kitchen and started clearing the leftover food and drink.

"I can't stay for too long pumpkin. Daddy's got to go, but I just wanted to pop in and say happy birthday to you." He started tying his loosened shoelace.

"Aww Daddy, can I stay with you tonight?" she asked.

Her request was unexpected. I stood at the fridge door, waiting for his response. Silence. He had become a selective mute for what seemed like an eternity. I stepped out of the kitchen back into the hallway.

"Sure you can baby. Your dad just needs to tell me where he's living."

I knew I had put Andre on the spot, but it was time he revealed his new address. I wasn't expecting an invitation, but I needed his address to enable our daughter to stay overnight with him. Why should I let her sleep at his house without knowing his address? He knew mine! Perhaps this was also about my power and control over him.

Andre had told me that he was renting a property, but decided not to tell me where. I hadn't pushed him before for an address, but I made it clear I wouldn't be happy with him having our daughter overnight without one. Much as this situation restricted me it was only fair that I knew where my child was staying with her father. I was aware of Andre's plans to buy a new house in Southeast London through his emails that I continued to access. Why couldn't he confirm where he was living and where he took our child every weekend? What was he hiding and why was he so secretive? I was deliberately trying to force his hand and hoped that he wouldn't disappoint me, or his daughter, but I was taking a gamble. I already knew the truth, but for whatever reason he didn't want to share. Surely, he wouldn't break his daughter's heart on her birthday?

"Yay! I'll go pack a bag." Leylah ran up the stairs with excitement.

I looked at Andre. His face betrayed turmoil.

"I'll get you a pen and paper," I offered, walking into the dining room. I returned to find Andre, rubbing his forehead frantically.

"I'm not going to tell you where I'm living Shantel," he replied with a sheepish look.

"Why not? What have you got to hide?" I was becoming frustrated and slightly agitated.

Leylah came down the stairs with a bag bulging with clothes.

"Leylah, I'm sorry darling. Your father says he can't give Mummy his new address. I'm afraid that if I don't get the address then you won't be able to sleep at his tonight."

She immediately ran over to her father.

"Daddy, please give Mummy your address so that I can stay with you!" she begged, with tears already streaming down her face.

Andre went into the dining room and sat on a chair. Leylah fell into his broad chest and cuddled her father.

"Please Daddy! Please!" she wailed

"I can't," he responded hesitantly. "I'm sorry." He held our daughter and looked down at the floor.

"You can, Daddy. Why can't you?" she yelled.

"I just can't Pumpkin."

Leylah was crying hysterically. She was begging her father then she rushed over to me.

"I'll be safe Mummy, I promise. Daddy's house is safe. Isn't it Daddy?" she pleaded with him to agree.

"I'm sure it is baby. Andre, why let Leylah get so upset when all you have to do is write your address down on this piece of paper?" I was angry. My eldest brother came into the dining room. No doubt he could hear all the commotion.

"What's all the noise and crying about?" Ray questioned.

"I won't allow Andre to have Leylah overnight until he gives me his address. For some reason, he's withholding it from me. It's pathetic and now Leylah is upset because she can't stay at his house tonight. Well done for ruining her birthday Andre. You did it again!"

I needed him out of the house and wondered what it would take to calm my daughter down.

"Can't you give Shantel your address? What's the problem Andre?" Ray enquired.

"I just can't do that," he replied uncompromisingly.

"Ok, it's time for you to leave this house. You don't need to be here anymore. This was a good day until you turned up and upset the balance. You're full of lies and deceit. Leave now!" I said firmly.

My frustration was palpable. I was angry beyond belief. How could I have given this man five years of my life?

"This is awful. Leylah go next door so I can talk to your parents," said Ray.

She went next door to the sitting room, still sobbing. At least she would have her family and friends to distract her. The sitting room door shut behind her, clearly done by one of the adults. I turned towards Andre.

"What are you hiding? Is your secret really worth our daughter's distress? I know you've bought a house. It's not a big deal. Just confirm it and you can have Leylah tonight."

I thought about confronting him about his online affair, but then he'd know for sure that I had access to his emails. I couldn't expose my source just yet. I was fuming. I had been calm all day and this man had invaded my home once again and upset a perfect balance. Why did he turn everything upside down? I vowed that it would never happen again.

"I hope this kind of behaviour doesn't happen often, especially in front of Leylah." Ray had never seen us like this before.

"Andre, it's time for you to leave. You're a liar and you're showing your true colours again. You're being purposely secretive. Say goodnight to your distraught daughter and go," I said sharply.

Andre stood up. He walked towards the sitting room.

I walked towards the bottle of rosé sitting on the dining table, picked it up, poured myself a glass, and gulped it down. Ray followed Andre to the sitting room and then to the front door. I checked Leylah. She was occupied with her new toys. I asked God to allow her to have a good sleep and forget about her disappointment. After a couple of minutes, Ray shut the porch door. Andre had left a trail of devastation behind for me to clean up. The glass of wine was a well-deserved sedative.

Ray walked towards the dining room, gesturing for me to follow him. Leylah was happily playing with her cousin. That reminded me that children were so resilient and it was the adults that held on to ill feelings. I walked into the dining room and sat down. Ray was already sitting.

"Leylah won't stay at his house until he confirms the address. He's lied and told me that he was renting a house. If he's renting a house, why the lies? The fact is, he's not renting. He's just bought a property ten minutes away. For some reason, he refuses to tell me the truth!" I sipped more wine and picked at the chocolates and sweets on the dining table.

"How do you know he's bought a property?" Ray enquired.

"I have access to his emails and there was plenty of correspondence between him and his solicitor about the sale of a house. The property is in his name." I was an investigator at work and in my own private life.

"Well, I don't know how you managed to get access to his email account, but things between you need to be less volatile. You need to be civil to each other." Ray was being optimistic but I felt quite the opposite.

Leylah enjoyed the rest of her evening and the guests stayed for another hour, eating, drinking and playing. She was exhausted by the day's events and thankfully, slept as soon as I put her to bed. Once the house was quiet and cleared up, I took some time out, sat in the living room and reflected on the day's events. Perhaps I could have handled Andre and the secrecy about his address a little better. I questioned how well I actually knew that man. He had lies oozing from his pores, while I was completely transparent. I had lived in a fantasy for the first few months of our relationship, but was soon living in the reality of his world. I decided that from that moment onwards I would have limited contact with him. Our communication would be via text messages or emails. I would not allow him to abuse my trust any longer. I didn't deserve his bullshit. He just needed to support his child.

Chapter Twenty-Four:
Magpie Watch

M onday morning, nothing. Monday afternoon passed without a single call from the bank. No letter with good news sitting at home for me, just bills. Tuesday morning, nothing. I was beginning to think the worst, but I held out for a glimmer of hope, praying for some enlightening revelation that would secure my immediate future. It was 4:30pm when my mobile phone rang. The phone number was unrecognisable. I answered, feeling nervous. My heart pounded in my chest and my palms started to sweat.

"Good afternoon. Can I speak to Shantel please?" asked a familiar voice.

It was Dylan from the bank. I moved from my desk and went into an unoccupied office for privacy, away from the sharp ears of colleagues listening in.

"Hi Dylan. How are you?" I asked, moving quickly, shutting the door behind me.

"Fine thanks. I'm sorry it's taken a little longer than I had anticipated to get back to you. I've had the information from head office come through." He hesitated. "They've advised me that your mortgage has been approved. You should be getting the paperwork in the post in the next few days."

"Praise God!" I exclaimed thankfully. I sat down as my legs buckled beneath me.

"You still need to raise the £10,000. You'll receive information about when that will have to be paid. The paperwork will ask you to submit your solicitor's details. How do you feel about that Shantel?" he asked knowingly.

"Ecstatic! I'm so happy." My heart was beating fast and I started feeling a heat rise up inside me. This was my journey to freedom and I was joyously riding the waves.

I knew the universe was working with me. The sale of my flat coincided with the confirmation of the new mortgage. The monthly payments would be less than half of the current mortgage. The next few weeks were spent communicating with the bank, transferring funds, liaising with the council about my flat, evicting my tenant and finalising a contract with Andre. Five years was a long time to wait until I'd received any maintenance from him, but that was the deal. I didn't have the fight in me to take him to court. I had received some constructive advice from the Citizen's Advice Bureau and I knew what that contract was actually worth.

Andre was ambitious. He would become a high-flyer one day, if he didn't piss off his colleagues or management that is. He was a dark character, but his true personality would always come to light. If his position changed, I could go to court and request maintenance. Similarly, if my position changed, health-wise or financially, I could also go to court to request maintenance. I made some minor amendments to the contract.

He had finally admitted that he was living at a nearby address, so I had no issues with our daughter staying overnight with him. He wanted our daughter for one night, every other weekend. Rubbish! I demanded that he had her for two nights. Why should he get off so lightly? That wasn't parenting in my book. If I wanted to go away for the weekend, I could. I wasn't just a mother. I was also a friend, a family member and one day a girlfriend, partner or wife. The contract stipulated that Andre would pay for Leylah's school and casual clothes. I also requested that he pay for all her footwear and her dance and fitness activities. He was not going to get away with being a part-time father. He still had the car, which I didn't need anymore anyway. What was I going to do with a car that I couldn't drive? Besides, he needed to come and pick up his child and take her to his place. I asked him to change his address with his contacts and bank so that I would no longer receive any of his mail. I didn't want him associated with the house in any shape or form. His daughter lived with me and he would not be able to enter the house once the mortgage was completed in my name. I didn't trust him especially after the phone call about Len. I was still baffled about how he knew about him and my plans. Was the house bugged? The sitting room was next on the list for decoration and I hoped that any bugging device would be thrown out with the revamp.

The sale of my flat took almost three months to complete. That inevitably delayed the transfer of the mortgage to my name. Much as the wait was frustrating, I appreciated that it would take time for Andre, his solicitor, my solicitor and whoever else had a part to play in the arrangements to come to an agreement. I had exercised unbelievable patience, whilst regularly chasing the bank for an update. When the deal was finally closed, I didn't celebrate in a grand way. It was a Friday evening and Leylah had gone to her father's house. I ordered a Chinese for one and popped a chilled bottle of Prosecco. That night I fell asleep on the sofa.

Plans were made for the October half-term holiday. I accepted an invitation to visit a friend, Jenny, in Somerset for part of the break. She often went away to her country home to get away from London and be with her extended family. She had two children who attended the same school as my daughter. We both craved adult conversation, knowing the children could entertain themselves. We spent three fun filled days going to the beach, fun fairs, shops and restaurants. We laughed, played, drank, strolled along the shore and ate fish and chips until our hearts were content. My Nikon camera captured every special moments.

We returned home on a Wednesday night. I had unpacked most of our luggage while Leylah was asleep. She would be with her father for the last two days of the half term break. My bag was packed to go to the gym, straight after work. After Andre had picked her up on Thursday morning, I grabbed my bags and headed out of the door for work. The day went quickly and I looked forward to the Brazilian dance class. I had so much fun doing the routines with the other thirty and forty-year-old women. I didn't always recognise them of course. I wondered if they thought I was being rude when I didn't say hello.

I reflected on my social challenges. My disability wasn't obvious. Sometimes I felt helpless though, a complete contrast to the poised, chatty and outgoing person I used to be. From a distance, I simply couldn't tell whether people were looking at me or trying to catch my attention. My close circle of friends understood the predicament I was in. Everyone else had to initiate a conversation with me and if they didn't try, they'd never know.

That evening after my session at the gym, I had arranged to see Damien. He was still my fix for the lonely nights. He kept me happy and was great company. It was a bonus that he didn't snore too. I called him to tell him what time I'd be home.

"Hey D. How are you?" I asked, running for my bus with whatever strength I could muster up after the dance class.

"Hey baby love. Everything cool. Just about to have my shower. What time are you getting home?" he asked in that husky deep voice of his.

"I'll be home in half an hour," I replied, as I sat on the bus. "I'm just making my way home from the gym."

I was feeling warm, though it was a cold night, wrapped up in my long puffa coat. The cold winter's air would never get through my layers.

"Ok babes. I'll be with you by 9. Is that ok?" he asked.

"Sure. See you then. Bye." I looked out of the window into the dark skies.

"Bye baby love."

I was soon off the bus and at my local Indian restaurant to get a takeaway. I opted for a chicken biryani. Within ten minutes, my takeaway was ready. I would have forty minutes to eat and shower before that delicious man arrived on my door step. I needed to prune and pluck a little before he arrived. No make-up was needed as it was bed time and he preferred the natural look. The walk from the Indian restaurant to my home was under five minutes. As I approached my house, I sensed that something was wrong. I looked up to my bedroom window which faced the road. My curtains were drawn. Why? I had left them open. The lights were on. That was strange. The living room curtains downstairs were still open as were the ones in my daughter's bedroom. I rummaged through my handbag to find my keys. The porch door was still locked. Did my lodger come home and borrow something from my room? She had never done that before, and I imagined that she would have asked first rather than just help herself. I opened the porch door and then the front door. My legs were shaking and my palms were moist. I took a deep breath. As I walked through the door, I looked up the stairs. Was someone still there? Who would have turned on the lights and left the porch door locked?

"Hello?" I called.

No response. I turned on both the upstairs and downstairs hallway lights.

"Hello? Anyone there?!" I shouted louder.

Nothing.

I put my bags down at the bottom of the stairs, still holding my keys. I felt my pocket, reassured that my mobile phone was there. I peered through the banister. As I took my first step up the stairs, I noticed that my lodger's bedroom door was open and her possessions were scattered all over the bed and floor. The light was on and her curtains were drawn too. I peered in my daughter's bedroom. It seemed undisturbed. I walked into my bedroom. Everything had been tampered with. I had been burgled. I had been violated. My underwear was strewn across my bed. My private possessions were thrown everywhere. I could barely see my carpet. I froze. What if the culprit was still in the house? My knees turned into jelly. I had to somehow find my way down the stairs and out of my house. I had to get to safety. I flew down the stairs and ran outside. My handbag was still in the hallway. I quickly ran back for it and dashed out again. I took a deep breath and called the emergency services.

"Which service please?" a female voice enquired.

"Police."

I described the scene to the operator. I was advised that the police would be with me shortly.

I called Damien.

"Hey babes. Are you home?" he asked. "How was the gym?"

"D. I've been burgled." I searched my pocket to look for a tissue. No joy. Just my gloves.

"What?" he asked

"Can you come now?" I needed him.

"Sure. Give me 15 minutes," he replied.

"Ok. Bye." I hung up.

I needed to wait somewhere warm until the police arrived. I knocked on my neighbour's door, realising I had walked out of my house without shutting my front door. That was a first. I was always security conscious. Their dog, Freddie, started barking, shortly followed by the sound of the door being opened by Keith.

"Hi Keith. Sorry to disturb you. I've been burgled. Will you come over to the house with me?" I asked, wiping the tears away.

"Yeah sure," he replied, with a shocked look on his face.

He grabbed his jacket and told his wife that he wouldn't be long. Katie had heard me reveal my disturbing news.

"Have you called the police Shantel?" she asked, rushing to her front door.

"Yes," I replied. "I hope they'll be here soon."

Keith and I walked down his front steps and then up mine to my house.

"Are you sure there isn't anyone still in there Shantel?" he asked cautiously.

"I came straight into the house and didn't think that the intruder would still be here. There was no sign of anyone."

There could have been and I would have been in real danger. I didn't think about the risks. I just needed to see what damage had been done. Keith walked towards the kitchen and looked around.

"They've entered through your kitchen window. Look, they've wedged it open," he said, surprised.

"And they left through your back door! They've used the key to get out."

I flicked the lights on in the dining and sitting rooms.

"You shouldn't touch anything," Keith suggested. "The police will want to do finger print checks."

Keith had a point. The intruder could have touched anything in the house and left his grubby little paw prints.

"I just wanted to see whether these rooms have been touched. Everything still looks the same," I confirmed.

I followed Keith upstairs. He had never been in the house before, though his house was next to mine and identical in layout. It was a shame that his first invitation into my home was after an invasion and not a social occasion. It was hardly Pimms and lemonade in the garden. There was no sign of the intruder. I now had to leave my house.

"Maybe we should go," I said, feeling nauseous at the state of my home.

"Come back to ours," he suggested empathetically. "You can wait for the police with us. You don't want to wait here."

We walked back down the stairs. Keith took a left turn back towards the kitchen.

"Yep, it's the kitchen window. They've wedged the window open with something."

I looked at the window, wondering how that would get fixed. I didn't want to sleep alone in an unsecured house.

"Let's go Shantel," he suggested.

I picked up my take-away and left my gym bag on the floor.

"Come in Shantel." Katie welcomed me in with a friendly voice. "Would you like a cup of tea?"

Tea? Really?

"Erm, maybe something a little stronger if you have it." I wanted to numb my fear.

"That's my girl. I've got wine, whisky, brandy..."

"Wine, please," I interrupted.

"Red or white?" she asked.

"Red is great."

I sent Damien a text to tell him to call me when he was outside. Though I had brought my food with me, I wasn't hungry anymore. The shock of my sanctuary being invaded was enough for me to lose my appetite. I didn't want to get stressed about the situation though as I didn't want to compromise my health. I took a deep breath and sipped some more wine. Within minutes, my phone rang. Damien was outside. Keith said that he would get him. Katie encouraged me to eat my food before I returned home and laid a square white plate and a fork in front of me. She was probably right about me eating as food would be the last thing on my mind once I stepped foot into my house. My knight walked into the kitchen. I was so pleased to see him. He kissed me on the cheek and took a seat. I introduced him to Katie, who offered him a glass of wine. He declined and asked me some questions about the break-in. Freddie the dog seemed to take a liking to Damien, but I could see he wasn't impressed or amused at the dog's effort at licking his hand.

"Come Freddie," Keith called beckoning his dog away.

"The place is a mess. It's the bedrooms upstairs. The kitchen window has been broken," I explained, finishing my food. I thanked Katie and Keith for the wine and their compassion. Damien and I went next door. He held my hand tightly and led the way.

The house was now well lit. I unlocked the front door and we stepped inside. Blue lights were flashing through the porch. The police had arrived. Tears started streaming down my face again. Damien wiped the tears away from my cheeks and gave me the biggest bear hug. There was a knock on the door. Damien opened the porch door and invited the officers inside.

"Hello. Are you Shantel?" the female officer asked.

"Yes," I replied, wiping a fresh set of tears away.

"Is it ok if we have a look around?" she asked.

"Sure," I replied miserably, as they started walking around the house. Damien and I followed the officers. Shortly afterwards, another officer arrived to start the forensic examination.

The first two officers walked up the stairs and inspected the carnage left by the intruder.

"Can you work out if anything is missing?" the male officer asked.

"I went away for a few days and left my camera and laptop on the bed. I guess they're gone," I replied.

"What about jewellery?" he asked. Where do you keep your jewellery?"

"My jewellery is kept in a box under the bed."

I stepped over the clothes careful to avoid anything broken on the floor. I looked under the bed and found the jewellery box. It was exactly as it had been the last time I had opened it.

"It's still here!" I exclaimed in amazement.

I glanced at the bed. I could see my blue laptop and camera case hidden under the clothes. I reached for the case. The camera was still inside.

"My laptop and camera are still here!"

I looked at the cash box on the floor; it was wedged open. There were still two passports inside and our birth certificates were still enclosed in an envelope. In the corner of the cash box was a scrunched-up piece of tissue. It was still there. My engagement ring! I couldn't find the original box to store it away, so I kept it wrapped in toilet tissue paper. To the unknowing eye, it looked like used tissue paper. Thank God it was still there.

"My engagement ring is still here. Look!" I said to the officers who watched intently as I unravelled the tissue paper.

"Clever idea," the female officer stated. "No one would have known what was in that. I think I'll try that idea myself."

I continued to search around my bedroom but strangely couldn't find anything missing. Everything was a mess though with clothes all over the floor and bed. My drawers had been pulled out of the wardrobe and turned upside down. But why? Who did this?

"Surely if this was a break-in, then the first thing to take would be the camera. They'd get a tenner for that, wouldn't they? The laptop could have given them fifty quid at least! Why would someone break-in and leave these things? This doesn't make sense." I was baffled by the situation. The forensic officer came upstairs.

"I'm sorry but there were no prints. There was just a partial foot print but not enough for us to get any leads," he confirmed, looking around the crime scene of my bedroom.

"Ok," I replied, thinking that the burglar knew what he was doing. He must have worn gloves. I walked into my lodger's bedroom. Why had her room been turned upside down? I hoped that nothing was taken. That was the last thing I needed.

"Whose things are these?" the male officer asked.

"My lodger's," I replied, thankful her name was registered on the council tax.

The officer took her name down on his note pad.

"I'd better call her now," I said, making my way into the bathroom. The officers talked amongst themselves. It sounded as if they could do nothing more for me. Damien had made his way downstairs and was pulling tools out of the tool box. I could hear him banging away.

"Carlene. I've got some bad news. We've been broken into." I sighed. "We've been burgled."

"What? Oh no!" she replied. "I've got to come home. What have they done? How's my room?"

It sounded like she was out at a party based on the noise in the background.

"Your wardrobe and drawers have been turned out. Your stuff is all over the floor." There was silence. I was waiting for her to speak but she was clearly in shock.

"I'll be home within the hour. See you," she said and hung up.

I went downstairs and headed towards the banging. Damien was outside the house by the kitchen window. He was knocking nails into the woodwork to secure the window shut. I smiled at him through the kitchen window. The officers were finishing their investigation and preparing to leave. It was time to start organising the house and restoring some normality. I definitely didn't want to sleep by myself tonight though.

Damien walked back into the house through the back door.

"Right, you'll need to replace those windows as soon as possible. They're secure for now though."

"Thanks babe. You're a life saver."

He locked the back door and put the keys out of sight.

"You won't be able to open the windows, but it's better to be safe than sorry. Let's go tidy your bedroom," he suggested.

He put the tools away in the cupboard under the stairs and started to make his way towards my bedroom. I wondered if he would stay with me for the night. I was scared the intruder might return. The porch door opened. It was Carlene. I was pleased to see her.

"Hi. Are you ok?" she enquired. Her eyes opened wide as she spotted the officers in the hallway.

"This is Carlene, my lodger," I announced. The officers took notes and had a quick chat with her. Soon afterwards, their investigation was complete. Carlene went to her room to tidy up. I told her to tell me if anything was missing. I would cover the costs. She informed me that her laptop was at work. None of her other possessions had a great deal of financial value. Damien continued to help organise my room. It took over two hours to get the room comfortable enough for me to sleep in.

"Would you like me to stay?" Damien asked as he reassembled the drawer.

I smiled as I started packing my underwear away. "Please." I felt nothing but relief.

We shifted the remaining unsorted items to one side of the room to be dealt with another day. I didn't plan to go into the office the following morning. I wanted my home to be secured and back to normal. I needed it free of the stench of the perpetrator who walked around my house. He would never enter my home again.

I looked in the cash box. The only thing that was missing was a letter; the letter addressed to Andre that I had found in the passenger door of the car. I'm not sure why I held onto it. Maybe I felt it was some kind of insurance. Well, that was gone now, and then it dawned on me that Andre was the perpetrator. If that was the only thing that he took, then so be it. I wanted everything of his gone anyway. I had returned or sold all of his other possessions. With this letter gone, I was finally rid of him. And, he had absolutely no reason to ever enter through my front door again.

I wasn't scared anymore and grateful for the company in my bed. Damien kept me warm and held me close all night. The following day I could concentrate on securing my home, burning my incense and reading Psalms 23 and 91. I slept peacefully that night knowing that a new day was dawning.

One month later.

Freedom had arrived, just as it was promised. I had battled through so many trials and tribulations, but I was sure it was all part of God's plan. I was gracefully walking the journey. I worked full time, proving to myself and others that I was able. Who knew that there would be so much support from the agencies, medical professionals, friends and family? I was going to be okay, and so was my daughter. She continued seeing her father every other weekend, which gave me the freedom to do whatever I wanted. I knew that the road ahead with Andre would be bumpy. I would always have to keep my guard up around him.

I could have confronted Andre about his online affair. I could have confronted him about his need to spy on me and his twisted actions. But I didn't. Even if I had, it wouldn't have made any difference because of his unresolved issues. I was glad to be rid of him. I was glad to be finally free. The lesson I had to learn was not about him but about me. My strength, my resilience, my vision, what I was willing to endure and when I was ready to walk away. I was vulnerable, and he took advantage of my good nature and weakness. Good luck to whoever falls into his spider's web next. Though I am partially sighted, I can see clearly, and it was this clarity that sought no answers from him or desire to understand why, but to accept my lessons and embrace a greater sense of freedom than I had ever known.

My health was good, especially with less stress. I felt energised by the promise of a new life. I was not looking for a relationship. I just enjoyed some occasional company. No commitment, no compromises and no restrictions. I had to recover from the heartache I had endured over these last few years. This would take some time, but I was prepared to work at healing. One day I'd be able to trust again. One day I'd find a new love. I would never again be fooled by charm and a handsome face. Eventually, I would work out what I needed from a future partner. The possibilities of my new life were endless, there was no hurry, so I chose to invest my time and energy in my daughter. She was my priority. I was empowered, successful and happy.

While sipping on my camomile tea
Looking out of the window I could see
The two magpies in the garden
They were free
Just like the birds on my blossom tree
That the carpenter had given me

The End

About the Author

Sharon Fevrier is a mother and first-time author based in South-East London. Having worked in Children's Services within Local Authorities for seventeen years, Sharon currently holds a role in Special Educational Needs and is passionate about helping people progress and find solutions to adverse situations. Her essence is resilience, independence and positivity all of which saw her rise above the challenges that were thrust her way when she developed visual impairment as a consequence of sickle cell disease.

Lightning Source UK Ltd.
Milton Keynes UK
UKHW010641131118
332251UK00009B/349/P